The

BROTHERHOOD

of the

HOLY SHROUD

The
BROTHERHOOD
of the
HOLY SHROUD

JULIA NAVARRO

Translated from the Spanish by

ANDREW HURLEY

JOHN MURRAY

First published in Great Britain in 2007 by John Murray (Publishers)
An Hachette Livre UK company

Paperback edition 2008

6

First published in Spain in 2004 as *La Hermandad de la Sábana Santa* by
Random House Mondadori, S.A.

A CIP catalogue record for this title is available from the British Library

ISBN 978-0-7195-6247-1

Typeset in Monotype Dante 10.75 / 12.75pt by
Palimpsest Book Production Limited, Grangemouth, Stirlingshire

Printed and bound by Clays Ltd, St Ives plc

John Murray policy is to use papers that are natural, renewable and recyclable products and
made from wood grown in sustainable forests. The logging and manufacturing processes
are expected to conform to the environmental regulations of the country of origin.

John Murray (Publishers)
338 Euston Road
London NW1 3BH

www.johnmurray.co.uk

For Fermin and Alex . . . because
sometimes dreams do come true.

ACKNOWLEDGMENTS

My thanks to Fernando Escribano, who revealed the tunnels of Turin to me, and who is always 'on duty' when his friends need him.

I owe a debt of gratitude also to Gian María Nicastro, who has been my guide to the secrets of Turin, his city. He has been my eyes in the city and has generously and swiftly provided me with any information I've asked for.

Carmen Fernández de Blas and David Trías believed in the novel. Thank you.

And thanks, too, to Olga, the friendly voice at Random House Mondadori.

There are other worlds, but they are in this one.
–PAUL ÉLUARD

The
BROTHERHOOD
of the
HOLY SHROUD

1

c. A.D. 30

Abgar, king of Edessa,
to Jesus the good Savior, who appears at Jerusalem,
greetings –

I have been informed concerning you and the
cures you perform without the use of medicines and
herbs.

For it is reported that you cause the blind to see and
the lame to walk, that you cleanse lepers, cast out unclean
spirits and devils, and restore to health those who have
been long diseased, and, further, that you raise up the
dead.

All of which, when I heard, persuaded me of one of
these two: either that you are God Himself descended
from heaven who does these things, or you are the Son of
God.

On this account, therefore, I write to you earnestly, to
beg that you take the trouble of a journey hither and cure
a disease which I am under.

For I hear the Jews ridicule you and intend you mischief.

My city is indeed small, but neat, and large enough for us both.

The king laid down his pen and turned his eyes toward a young man of his own age, waiting motionless and respectful at the far end of the room.

'You are certain, Josar?' The king's gaze was direct and piercing.

'My lord, believe me. . . .' The young man could barely hold himself back as he spoke. He approached the king and stopped near the table at which Abgar had been writing.

'I believe you, Josar, I believe you. You are the most faithful friend I have, and so you have been since we were boys. You have never failed me, Josar, but the wonders that are told of this Jew are so passing strange that I fear your desire to aid me may have confounded your senses.'

'My lord, you must believe me, for only those who believe in the Jew are saved. I have seen a blind man, when Jesus brushed his fingers over the man's dead eyes, recover his sight. I have seen a lame man, whose legs would not move, touch the hem of Jesus' tunic and have seen Jesus gaze sweetly upon him and bid him walk, and to the astonishment of all, the man stood and his legs bore him as your legs, sire, bear you. I have seen a poor woman suffering from leprosy watch the Nazarene as she hid in the shadows of the street, for all men fled her, and Jesus approached her and said to her, "You are cured," and the woman, incredulous, cried, "I am healed, I am healed!" For indeed her face became that of a human once more, and her hands, which before she hid from sight, were whole.

'And I have seen with my own eyes the greatest of all miracles, for when I was following Jesus and his disciples and we came upon a family mourning the death of a relative, Jesus entered the house and commanded the dead man to rise. God must be in the voice of the Nazarene, for I swear to you, my king, that the man opened his eyes, and stood, and wondered at being alive. . . .'

'You are right, Josar, I must believe if I am to be healed. I want to believe in this Jesus of Nazareth, who is truly the Son of God if he can raise the dead. But will he want to heal a king who has been prey to concupiscence?'

'Abgar, Jesus cures not only men's bodies but also their souls. He preaches that with repentance and the desire to lead a life free thenceforth of sin, a man may merit the forgiveness of God. Sinners find solace in the Nazarene, my sire. . . .'

'I do sincerely hope so, Josar, although I cannot forgive myself for my lust for Ania. The woman has brought this plight upon me; she has sickened me in body and in soul.'

'How were you to know, sire, that she was diseased, that the gift sent you by King Tyrus was a stratagem of state? How were you to suspect that she bore the seed of the illness and would contaminate you? Ania was the most beautiful woman we had ever seen. Any man would have lost his reason and given his all to have her.'

'But I am king, Josar, and I should not have lost my reason, however beautiful the dancing girl may have been. . . . Now she weeps over her lost beauty, for the marks of the disease are upon her face, and the whiteness is eating it away. And I, Josar, have a sweat upon me that never leaves me, and my sight grows cloudy, and I fear above all things that the illness will consume my skin and leave me – '

Abgar fell silent at the sound of soft footsteps. A smiling woman, lithe, with black hair and olive skin, entered.

Josar admired her. Yes, he admired the perfection of her features and the happy smile she always wore; beyond that he admired her loyalty to the king and the fact that her lips would never have uttered the slightest reproach against the man stolen from her by Ania, the dancing girl from the Caucasus, the woman who had contaminated her husband the king with the terrible disease.

Abgar would not allow himself to be touched by anyone, since he feared he might pollute all those with whom he came in contact. He appeared less and less frequently in public. But he had not been able to resist the iron will of the queen, who insisted upon caring for him personally and, not just that, who also encouraged him in his soul to believe the story brought by Josar of the wonders performed by the Nazarene.

The king looked at her with sadness in his eyes.

'It is you, my dear. . . . I was talking with Josar about the Nazarene. He will take a letter to him inviting him to come. I have offered to share my kingdom with him.'

'An escort should accompany Josar, to ensure that nothing happens on the journey and to ensure also that he returns safely with the Nazarene.'

'I will take three or four men; that will be enough,' Josar said. 'The Romans have no trust in their subjects and would not look with favor on a group of soldiers entering the town. Nor would Jesus. I hope, my lady, to complete my mission and convince Jesus to return with me. I will take swift horses and will send you and my lord the news when I reach Jerusalem.'

'I shall complete the letter, Josar.'

'And I shall leave at dawn, my lord.'

2

THE FIRE BEGAN TO LICK AT THE PEWS AS SMOKE filled the nave with darkness. Four figures dressed in black hurried toward a lateral chapel. A fifth man, humbly dressed, hovering in a doorway near the high altar, wrung his hands. The high wail of sirens reached a crescendo outside – fire trucks responding to the alarm. In a matter of seconds firefighters would burst into the cathedral, and that meant another failure.

The man rushed down from the altar, motioning his brothers to come to him. One of them kept running toward the chapel, while the others shrank back from the fire that was beginning to surround them. Time had run out. The fire had come out of nowhere and progressed faster than they'd calculated. The man trying so desperately to fulfill their mission was enveloped in flames. He writhed as the fire consumed his clothes, his skin, but somehow he found the strength to pull off the hood that concealed his face. The others tried to reach him, to beat back the flames, but the fire was everywhere, and the cathedral doors began to buckle as the firefighters battered against them. Their brother burned without a scream, without a sound.

5

They retreated then and raced behind their guide to a side door, slipping outside at the same instant the water from the fire hoses poured into the cathedral. They never saw the man hiding among the shadows of one of the pulpits, a silencer-equipped pistol at his side.

Once they were gone, he came down from the pulpit, touched a spring hidden in the wall, and disappeared.

Marco Valoni took a drag off his cigarette, and the smoke mixed in his lungs with the smoke from the fire. He'd come outside for fresh air while the firefighters finished putting out the embers that were still glowing in and around the right side of the high altar.

The piazza was closed off with police blockades, and the carabinieri were holding back the curious and the concerned, all craning their necks to try to see what had happened in the cathedral. At that hour of the evening, Turin was a beehive of people desperate to learn whether the Holy Shroud had been damaged.

Marco had asked the reporters covering the fire to try to keep the crowds calm: The shroud had been unscathed. What he hadn't told them was that someone had died in the flames. He still didn't know who.

Another fire. Fire seemed to plague the old cathedral. But Marco didn't believe in coincidences, and the Turin Cathedral was a place where too many accidents happened: robbery attempts and, within recent memory, three fires. In the first one, which occurred after the Second World War, investigators had found the bodies of two men incinerated by the flames. The autopsy determined that they were both about twenty-five and that, despite the fire, they had been killed by gunshot. And last, a truly gruesome finding: Their tongues had been surgically cut out. But why? And who had shot them? No one had ever been able to find out. The case was still open, but it had gone cold.

Neither the faithful nor the general public knew that the shroud had spent long periods of time outside the cathedral over the last hundred years. Maybe that was why it had been spared the consequences of so many accidents.

A vault in the Banco Nazionale had been the shroud's place of safekeeping. The relic was taken out of it only to be displayed on special occasions, and then only under the strictest security. But despite all the security, the shroud had been exposed to danger – real danger – more than once. It had been moved back to the cathedral only days ago, in preparation for the unveiling of extensive refurbishments.

Marco still remembered the fire of April 12, 1997. How could he forget, since it was the same night – or early morning – he'd been celebrating his retirement with his colleagues in the Art Crimes Department.

He was fifty then, and he'd just been through open-heart surgery. Two heart attacks and a life-or-death operation had finally persuaded him to listen when Giorgio Marchesi, his brother-in-law and cardiologist, advised him to devote himself to the *dolce far niente,* or, at the least, put in for a nice quiet bureaucratic position, one of those jobs where he could spend his time reading the newspaper and taking midmorning breaks for cappuccino in some nearby café.

Paola had insisted that he retire; she sugared the pill by reminding him that he had gone as high in the Art Crimes Department as he could go – he was the director – and that he could honorably end a brilliant career and devote himself to enjoying life. But he had resisted. He'd rather go into some office – any office – every day than to turn into fifty-year-old retired jetsam washed up on some beach somewhere. Even so, he'd resigned his position as director of the Art Crimes Department, and the night before the fire, despite Paola's and Giorgio's protests, he'd gone out to dinner with his friends. By daybreak they were still drinking. These were the same people he'd been working with for fourteen, fifteen hours a day for the last twenty years, tracking down the mafias that trafficked in artworks, unmasking forgeries, and protecting, so far as was humanly possible, Italy's artistic heritage.

The Art Crimes Department was a special agency under both the Ministry of the Interior and the Ministry of Culture. It was a unique collection of police officers mixed with a good number of archaeologists, historians, experts in medieval art, modern art, religious art. . . . He had given it the best years of his life.

It had not been easy to climb the ladder of success. His father had worked in a gas station; his mother was a homemaker. They had just scraped by, and he'd managed to attend the university thanks only to scholarships. But his mother had pleaded with him to find a good, secure job, one with the state, and he had given in to her wishes. A friend of his father's, a policeman who regularly stopped to fill up at the gas station, helped him with the entrance tests for the carabinieri. Marco took them and passed them, but he wasn't cut out to be a cop, so he continued his studies at night, after work, and eventually managed to earn a degree in history. The first thing he did when he got his degree was request a transfer to the Art Crimes Department. He combined his two specialties, history and police work, and little by little, working hard and taking advantage of breaks when they came his way, he rose through the ranks to the top. How he'd enjoyed traveling through Italy, experiencing its treasures firsthand and getting to know other countries, too, as his career progressed!

He had met Paola at the University of Rome. She was studying medieval art; it was love at first sight, and within months they were married. They'd been together for twenty-five years; they had two children and were truly happy together.

Paola taught at the university, and she had never expressed any resentment at how little time he spent at home. Only once had they had a really big fight. It was when he returned from Turin that spring of 1997, after the cathedral fire, and told her he was not retiring after all, but not to worry because he would redefine his job as director. He would embrace bureaucracy. He wasn't going to be traveling anymore or out in the field doing investigations – he was just going to be a bureaucrat. Giorgio, his doctor, told him he was crazy. But the men and women he worked with were delighted.

It was the fire in the cathedral that had changed his mind about staying. He was convinced that it hadn't been accidental, no matter how often he told the press it was.

And now here he was, investigating another fire in the Turin Cathedral. Less than two years ago he'd been called in to investigate another robbery attempt, one of many over the years. The thief had been caught almost by accident. Although it was true he hadn't had any cathedral property on him, it was surely just because he hadn't had time to pull off the job. Artworks and other objects near the shroud's casket were in disarray. A priest passing by just then saw a man running, apparently scared off by the sound of the alarm, which was louder than the cathedral's bells. The priest ran after him, yelling, 'Fermati, ladro!

Fermati!' – 'Stop, thief! Stop!' – and two young men passing by had tackled him and held him until the police arrived. The thief had no tongue; it had been surgically removed. Nor did he have any fingerprints; the tips of his fingers were scarred over from burns. The thief, so far as the investigation was concerned, was a man without a country, without a name, and he was now rotting in the Turin jail. He'd remained obdurate and unresponsive through interrogation after interrogation. They'd never managed to get anything out of him.

No, Marco didn't believe in coincidences. It was no coincidence that all the 'thieves' in the Turin Cathedral had no tongues and had had their fingerprints burned off. Such a pattern would be almost laughable were it not so grotesque.

Down through history, fire had dogged the shroud. Marco had learned that during the time it was in the possession of the House of Savoy, the cloth had survived several blazes. On the night and early morning of December 3 and 4, 1532, fire broke out in the sacristy of Sainte Chapelle, in Chambéry, where the House of Savoy kept the shroud. By the time the four locks guarding the relic could be pried off, the silver reliquary casket that housed it, made to the order of Marguerite of Austria, had melted, scorching the shroud; worse, a drop of melted silver had burned a hole in the relic.

In 1578, the House of Savoy deposited the shroud in the Turin Cathedral, but the incidents had continued. A hundred years after the 1532 fire, another blaze almost reached the resting place of the shroud. Two men were surprised in the chapel, and both, knowing they were caught red-handed, threw themselves into the flames and burned to death without uttering a sound, despite the terrible torment of their passing. Marco wondered whether they had had tongues. He would never know.

Since that time, not a century had passed without a robbery attempt or a fire. Only one of the culprits had been apprehended alive, in recent years, at least – the thief now residing in the city prison.

One of Marco's team interrupted his musings.

'Boss, the cardinal's here; he just got in from Rome and he's really upset by all this. . . . He wants to see you.'

'Upset? I'm not surprised. He's on a bad run – not ten years ago the cathedral almost burned down, two years ago there was a robbery attempt, and now another fire.'

'Yeah, he says he's sorry he let himself be talked into doing the renovations and that it's the last time – this cathedral's been here for hundreds of years, and now, with all the sloppy work and the accidents, it's practically ruined.'

Marco entered the cathedral through a side door bearing a small sign designating the church offices. Two older women who shared a small office looked very busy. Three or four priests paced about, clearly agitated, as agents under Marco's orders moved in and out, examining the walls, taking samples and photographs. A young priest, somewhere in his early thirties, approached Marco and extended his hand. His handshake was firm.

'I'm Padre Yves.'

'Marco Valoni.'

'Yes, I know. If you'll come with me, His Eminence is waiting to see you.'

The priest opened a heavy door that led into a large, luxurious office paneled in dark wood. The paintings on the walls were Renaissance – a Madonna, a Christ, various saints. On the desk was a heavy embossed silver crucifix.

Marco realized it must be at least three hundred years old.

The cardinal's normally friendly face was clouded with concern.

'Have a seat, Signor Valoni, please.'

'Thank you, Your Eminence.'

'Tell me what's happened. Do we know who died?'

'We don't know for certain who the man is or what happened, sir. It appears that there was a short circuit, due to the renovations, and that's what started the fire.'

'Again!'

'Yes, Your Eminence, again. And if you'll allow us, sir, I want to investigate this thoroughly. We'll stay here for a few more days; I want to go over every inch of the cathedral, and my men and I will be talking to everyone who's been in the cathedral over the last few hours and days. I would ask for your full cooperation.'

'Of course, Signor Valoni, of course. We are entirely at your disposal for any questions you may have, as we have been in the past. Investigate whatever and wherever you need. What's happened is a catastrophe, truly – one person is dead, irreplaceable artworks have been burned or ruined beyond repair, and the flames almost reached the Holy Shroud. I don't know what we would all do if it had been destroyed.'

'Your Eminence, the shroud. . . .'

'I know, Signor Valoni, I know what you're going to say – radiocarbon dating has determined that the shroud cannot be the cloth that Our Lord was buried in. But for millions of believers, the shroud is authentic, regardless of what the carbon-fourteen says, and the Church has allowed it to be worshipped. And of course, there *are* those scientists who cannot explain the figure that we take to be Christ's. Furthermore –'

'Excuse me, Your Eminence, I had no intention of calling the religious importance of the shroud into question. It made an unforgettable impression on me the first time I saw it, and it still impresses me today.'

'Ah. Then, what?'

'I wanted to ask you whether anything out of the ordinary had happened in the last few days, the last few months – anything, no matter how insignificant it might seem – that was unusual or that you noticed for some reason.'

'Why, no, honestly nothing. After that last scare two years ago, when they broke in and tried to steal objects from the high altar, it's been very quiet in the cathedral.'

'Think hard, sir.'

'What do you want me to think about? When I'm in Turin I celebrate Mass in the cathedral every morning at eight. Sundays at twelve. I spend some time in Rome; today I was at the Vatican when I received the news of the fire. Pilgrims come from all over the world to see the shroud – two weeks ago, a group of scientists from France, England, and the United States came to perform some tests and –'

'Who were they?'

'Ah! A group of professors, all Catholics, who believe that despite all the studies and the categorical verdict from the radiocarbon dating, the shroud is the true burial cloth of Christ.'

'Did any of them draw your attention in any way?'

'No, not really. I received them in my office in the episcopal palace, and we talked for about an hour. I had had a small lunch prepared. They told me about some of their theories as to why they believed the radiocarbon studies aren't entirely reliable. . . . There was very little else.'

'Did any of these professors seem different in any way from the others? More driven, more aggressive . . . ?'

'Signor Valoni, for many years I have received scientists studying the shroud; the Church has been most open and has given them excellent access. These particular professors were very pleasant, very "nice," shall we say; only one of them, Dr. Bolard, seemed more reserved, less talkative than his colleagues, but I attributed that to the fact that it makes him nervous when we do work on the cathedral.'

'Why is that?'

'What a question, Signor Valoni! Because Professor Bolard has spent years helping us with the conservation of the shroud, and he is afraid – as well he might be, it turns out – that we might be exposing it to unnecessary risks. I have known him for many years; he is a serious, rigorous scientist, a world-renowned scholar, and a good Catholic.'

'How often has he been here?'

'Oh, countless times. As I said, he works with the Church on the conservation of the shroud. He is so much a part of our effort, in fact, that when other scientists come to study it, we often call him in so he can ensure that the shroud won't be exposed to any possible deterioration. We also have files on all the scientists who have visited us, who have studied the shroud, the people from NASA, that Russian – what was his name? I don't remember. . . . Anyway, and all the famous scholars – Barnett, Hynek, Tamburelli, Tite, Gonella – all of them. Oh, and Walter McCrone, the first scientist to insist that the shroud was not the cloth that Christ was buried in; he died just a few months ago, God rest his soul.'

'I'd like to know the dates this Dr. Bolard has been here and to have a list of all the teams of scientists that have done studies on the shroud in recent years, plus the dates they were in Turin. You might include any other noteworthy groups as well.'

'How far back should we go?' the cardinal asked.

'The last twenty years, if possible.'

'My word! Just what are you looking for?'

'I don't know, Your Eminence, I don't know.'

The cardinal gazed at him steadily. 'For years you have insisted that the shroud is somehow connected with all these accidents, that it is the object behind them, but I, my dear Signor Valoni, simply cannot believe that. Who could possibly wish to destroy the shroud? And why? As for the robbery attempts, you know that much of the art in the cathedral is priceless, and there are many unscrupulous men who have no respect even for the house of God.'

'You're right, I'm sure, Your Eminence, but you have to concede that these incidents cannot be random, unrelated events, given the bizarre circumstances – the repeated involvement of these mutilated men. This is a sustained effort of some sort, and it seems to me that only an object of singular renown, such as the shroud, could be at its center.'

'Yes, of course it's disturbing, as you say, and the Church is very, very concerned. In fact, I have gone several times to visit that poor wretch who tried to rob us two years ago. He sits there in front of me and doesn't respond in any way, as though he doesn't understand a word I say.'

Marco sensed that there would be no more concrete information forthcoming from the cardinal, so he gently tried to steer the discussion back to the information he needed.

'So, Your Eminence, will you get that list ready for me? It's just routine, but I have to follow up on it.'

'Yes, certainly, I'll tell my secretary, the young priest who showed you in, to gather the material for you as soon as possible. Padre Yves is very efficient; he's been with me for seven months, since my previous aide passed away, and I must say that his presence is a boon. He's intelligent, discreet, pious, he speaks a number of languages. . . .'

'He's French?'

'Yes, that's right, but his Italian, as you've seen, is perfect; he speaks English, German, Hebrew, Arabic, he reads Aramaic. . . .'

'And who recommended him to you, Your Eminence?'

'My good friend, the aide to the acting Under-Secretary of State for the Vatican, Monsignor Aubry, a remarkable man.'

It struck Marco that most of the men of the Church he'd known were remarkable, especially those who moved through the Vatican. But he remained silent as he gazed at the cardinal – a good man, he thought, wiser and more intelligent than he sometimes let people see and very skilled at diplomacy.

The cardinal picked up the telephone and asked Padre Yves to come in. Almost instantly the young priest appeared at the door.

'Come in, padre, come in. You've met my good friend Signor Valoni. He's asked that we prepare a list of all the scientific delegations and other important groups that have visited the shroud in the last twenty years and when they were here. Will you get to work on that, please? He'd like it right away.'

Padre Yves looked at Marco a moment before asking, 'Forgive me, Signor Valoni, but could you tell me what it is you're looking for?'

'Padre Yves, not even Signor Valoni knows what he's

looking for, but he wants the name of anyone who's had any relationship with the shroud over the past twenty years, and we are going to provide him with that information.'

'Of course, Your Eminence. I'll try to get it to him as soon as possible, although with all this commotion it won't be easy. I'll have to go through the files personally; we have a long way to go in computerizing them.'

'Don't worry, padre,' Valoni replied, 'I can wait a few days, but the sooner you can get me that information the better.'

'Your Eminence, may I ask what the shroud has to do with the fire?'

'Ah! Padre Yves, I have been asking Signor Valoni that same question for years. Every time something like this happens, he insists that the objective is the shroud.'

'My God, the shroud!'

Marco studied Padre Yves. He didn't look like a priest, or at least most of the priests that Marco knew, and living in Rome meant he knew a lot of them. Padre Yves was tall, quite handsome, athletic; more than likely, he played some sport regularly. There was not a trace of that softness that resulted from mixing chastity and good food – a mixture indulged in widely by the priestly population. If Padre Yves weren't wearing his ecclesiastical collar, he'd look like one of those executives who work out in the gym every morning and play squash or tennis every weekend.

'Yes, padre,' the cardinal was saying, 'the shroud. But fortunately the Lord protects it. It has never been severely damaged.'

'I'm just trying to follow up on anything that might shed some light on what's been happening,' Marco assured them, 'and to chase down any loose ends. There have been too many incidents connected with the cathedral. It's time for them to stop. Here's my card and my cell phone number, padre. Let me know when you have that list, and if you think of anything that might help us in the investigation, please call me, anytime.'

'Yes, of course, Signor Valoni. I will,' the young priest assured him.

Marco's cell phone rang as he left the cathedral offices. The coroner's verdict was short and sweet: The deceased was a male around thirty years old, average height, five foot eight, five foot nine, thin. And no, there was no tongue.

'Are you sure?'

'I'm as sure as I can be with a corpse turned to charcoal. The body had no tongue, and it wasn't the result of the fire – it was removed by surgery. Don't ask me when, because given the state of the body it's just too hard to tell.'

'Anything else?'

'I'll send you the whole report. I called as soon as I finished the autopsy.'

'I'll stop by and pick it up, if you don't mind.'

'Come and get it. I'll be here all day.'

Back at Turin's carabinieri headquarters, where the Art Crimes unit maintained a small office, Marco met with one of his senior men.

'Okay, Giuseppe, what do we have so far?'

'In the first place, nothing's missing. They didn't steal anything. Antonino and Sofia have done pretty much a whole inventory – paintings, candelabras, sculptures, everything. It's all there, although some things have varying degrees of smoke or water damage. The flames destroyed the pulpit on the right and the pews, and all that's left of the sixteenth-century statue of the Virgin is ashes. Pietro's been interviewing the guys who were working on the new wiring; the fire apparently started from a short circuit.'

'Another short circuit.'

'Yeah, like the one in '97. He's also talked to the company in charge of the renovation work, and he asked Minerva to get on her computer and find out everything she can about the owners of the business, and also about the workers. Some of them are immigrants, and it'll be tough to get any information on them, but she'll try.'

Giuseppe paused and gazed at his boss. 'And I've asked her to find out whether there's some sect that cuts out its followers' tongues. I know it's probably a stretch – but we've gotta look everywhere, right? And Minerva's a genius with this stuff.' When Marco nodded after a moment, Giuseppe went on.

'Between Pietro and me we've interviewed everybody on staff. There was nobody in the cathedral when the fire started. At three it's always closed, since that's when they are all at lunch.'

'We have the body of one man. Was he working alone?'

'We aren't sure, but we don't think so. It would be tricky for someone working alone to prepare and carry out a major theft in the Turin Cathedral, unless maybe it was a job for hire, a thief somebody paid to come in and grab a specific piece of art.'

'But if he wasn't alone, where are the others?'

Giuseppe didn't answer, and Marco fell silent. He had a bad feeling about this fire, and a hollow pit in his stomach to prove it. Paola had said he was obsessed with the shroud, and maybe she was right: He had always felt that there was much more to the periodic events in Turin than they had been able to uncover – something 'underneath' that connected them all. The bizarre factor of the mutilated men was only the tip of it. He was sure he was missing something, that there was a thread to follow somewhere, and that if he could find it he'd find the solution. He decided to go to the Turin jail and pay a visit to the perp from the last incident. They had been unable to ferret out anything about him; they weren't even sure if the guy was Italian. Two years ago Marco had left him to the carabinieri after weeks of futile interrogation. But the mute was the only lead they had, and like an idiot he'd dropped him.

As he lit another cigarette, he decided to get in touch with John Barry, the cultural attaché to the United States embassy. John was actually CIA, like almost every cultural attaché in foreign embassies around the world. Governments didn't have much imagination for working out covers for their agents. Even so, Barry was a nice guy. He wasn't a field operative; he worked for the CIA's Office of Intelligence Assessment, analyzing and interpreting the intelligence that came in from field agents before it was sent on to Washington. The two men had been friends for years – a friendship forged through work, since many of the pieces of art stolen by the art mafias wound up in the hands of wealthy Americans who – sometimes because they were in love with a particular work, other times out of vanity or to turn a quick buck – had no scruples about purchasing stolen art. It was a dark area of international commerce, where many interests often intersected.

Barry didn't fit the stereotypical image of the American or of the CIA agent. He was fifty-something, like Marco, and he had a doctorate in art history from Harvard. He loved Europe and had married an English archaeologist,

Lisa, a charming and fascinating woman. Not beautiful, Marco had to say, but so full of life that she radiated enthusiasm and charisma. She'd hit it off wonderfully with Paola, so the four of them had dinner together once in a while, and they'd even spent weekends together in Capri.

Yes, he'd call John the minute he got back to Rome. But he'd also call Santiago Jiménez, the Europol representative in Italy, an efficient, very likable Spaniard with whom Marco also had an excellent working relationship. He'd buy them lunch. And maybe, he thought, they could help him in his search, even if he wasn't quite sure what he was looking for.

3

At last, Josar's eyes beheld the walls of Jerusalem. The brightness of the sun at dawn and the light's reflection off the desert sand made the stones of the wall seem to shimmer in a golden haze.

Accompanied by four men, Josar made his way on horseback toward the Damascus Gate, where at this early hour men who lived nearby were beginning to enter the city, and caravans seeking salt made their way out into the desert.

A platoon of Roman soldiers, on foot, was patrolling the perimeter of the walls.

How Josar longed to see Jesus, whose extraordinary figure radiated strength, sweetness, firmness, and deep piety.

He believed in Jesus, believed that he was the Son of God, not simply because of the wonders he had seen him work but also because, when Jesus' eyes fell on him, he could feel something more than human in them. He knew that Jesus could see within him, that not even the smallest and most hidden thought could escape him.

But Jesus did not make Josar feel ashamed of what he was,

because the Nazarene's eyes were filled with understanding and with forgiveness.

Josar loved Abgar, his king, who had always treated him like a brother. He owed the king his estate and fortune. Yet Josar had decided that if Jesus did not accept Abgar's invitation to come to Edessa, he would present himself before his king and ask leave to return to Jerusalem and follow the Nazarene. He was prepared to give up his house, his fortune, his earthly comforts and well-being. He would follow Jesus and try to live according to his teachings. Yes, he had reached that decision.

✝ Josar went to the house of Samuel, a man who for a few coins would care for the horses and allow Josar and his companions to sleep. As soon as they were settled there, he would go out into the streets and try to find Jesus. He would go to the house of Mark, or Luke, for they would be able to tell him where to find him. It would be difficult to convince Jesus to travel to Edessa, but Josar would argue that the journey was short and that, once his king was cured, Jesus could return, should he decide not to remain.

As he left the house of Samuel to find Mark, Josar bought two apples from a poor cripple, and he asked the man about the latest news of the city.

'What would you know, stranger? Every day the sun rises in the east and sets in the west. The Romans – you are not Roman, are you? No, you do not dress like a Roman or speak in their manner. The Romans have raised taxes, to the greater glory of the emperor, and Pilate the governor now fears a rebellion, so he is attempting to win over to his purposes the priests of the temple.'

'What do you know of Jesus, the Nazarene?'

23

'Ah! You want to know about him as well! You are not a spy, then, are you?'

'No, good man, I am not a spy. I am simply a traveler who knows of the wonders that the Nazarene has worked.'

'If you are sick, he can cure you. There are many who say they have been healed by the touch of the Nazarene's fingers.'

'And you do not believe that?'

'I, sir, work from sun to sun, tending my orchard and selling my apples. I have a wife and two daughters to feed. I keep all the laws that a good Jew must keep, and I believe in God. Whether the Nazarene is the Messiah, as people say, I know not – I cannot say he is, and I cannot say he is not. But I will tell you, stranger, that the priests, and the Romans as well, are against him, for Jesus has no fear of their power and he defies them equally. A man cannot stand up against the Romans and the priests and expect any good to come of it. This Jesus will, I think, regret his pride.'

✝ Josar wandered through the city until he came to the house of Mark. There he was told that he could find Jesus beside the southern wall, preaching to a multitude.

Josar soon found him. The Nazarene, dressed in a simple linen robe, was speaking to his followers in a voice that was firm yet wonderfully sweet.

He felt Jesus' eyes upon him. He had seen Josar, he smiled upon him, and he beckoned him to come closer.

Jesus embraced him and bade him to sit there beside him. John, the youngest of the disciples, moved aside so that Josar might sit at the master's left hand.

There they all spent the morning, and when the sun had reached the highest point in the sky, Judas, one of the disciples, brought bread, figs, and water to the crowd. They ate in silence and in peace. Then Jesus stood to leave.

'My lord,' Josar said softly, 'I bring a letter for you from my king, Abgar of Edessa.'

'And what does Abgar want of me, my good Josar?'

'He is ill, my lord, and asks that you help him. I, too, ask it of you, my lord, because he is a good man, truly, and a good king, and his subjects know that he is fair and kind. Edessa is a small city, but Abgar will share it with you.'

Jesus laid his hand on Josar's arm as they walked. And Josar felt privileged to be near the man he truly believed to be the Son of God.

'I will read the letter and answer your king.'

✝ That night Josar broke bread with Jesus and his disciples, who were uneasy at the news of the priests' growing antagonism. A woman, Mary Magdalene, had heard in the market that the priests were urging the Romans to arrest Jesus, whom they accused of being the instigator of certain disturbances, some violent, against Rome's power.

Jesus listened in silence and ate calmly. It appeared that all the matters the others were talking about were already known to him. After they had eaten, he told them that they should forgive those who did them harm or spoke against them, that they should show compassion toward those who wished them ill. The disciples replied that it was not easy to forgive a man who does one harm, to remain passive without returning ill for ill.

Jesus listened, but again he argued that forgiveness was a balm for the soul of the person aggrieved.

At the end of the evening, he sought out Josar with his eyes and beckoned him to come closer. Josar saw that the Nazarene was holding a letter.

'Josar, here is my reply to Abgar.'

'Will you come with me, my lord?'

'No, I will not go with you. I cannot, for I must do my Father's work as I have been bidden. Instead, I will send one of my disciples. But mark me well, Josar – your king will see me in Edessa, and if he has faith he shall be healed.'

'Whom will you send? And how is it possible, my lord, that you shall remain here yet Abgar shall see you in Edessa?'

Jesus smiled and looked calmly but fixedly upon Josar.

'Do you not follow me? Do you not listen to me? You shall go, Josar, and your king shall be healed, and he shall see me in Edessa even when I am no longer in this world.'

Josar believed.

✛ The sun poured in through the small window in the room where Josar sat, composing a letter to Abgar. The innkeeper bustled about, preparing food for Josar's companions.

Josar to Abgar, king of Edessa,
greetings –

My lord, these men bring you the Nazarene's reply. I beg you, sire, to have faith, for Jesus says that you shall be healed. I know that he will work that wonder, but do not ask me how he will do it or when.

I ask license, my king, to remain in Jerusalem, near to Jesus. My heart tells me that I must remain here. I need to hear him, follow him as the most humble of his disciples. All that I have, you have given me, and so, my lord, do as you will with my possessions, my house, my slaves; give them as you see fit to the poor and needy. I shall remain here, and to follow Jesus I will have need of almost

26

nothing. I sense, too, that something is to happen, for the
priests of the temple despise Jesus for calling himself the
Son of God and for living according to the laws of the
Jews, which the priests themselves do not.

I beg of you, my lord, your understanding and your
permission to follow where destiny leads me.

Abgar read Josar's letter and was overcome with despair.
The Jew would not come to Edessa, and Josar was staying
in Jerusalem.

The men who had accompanied Josar had traveled
without rest to bring the king the two missives. He had
read Josar's first, and now he would read Jesus', but from
his heart had passed all hope – he cared little now what the
Nazarene might write to him.

The queen entered the chamber, her eyes filled with
worry.

'I have heard that word has come from Josar.'

'Indeed. The Jew will not come. Josar asks my leave to
remain in Jerusalem. He desires me to portion out his
possessions among the poor. He has become a disciple of
Jesus.'

'Is that man so extraordinary, then, that Josar would
abandon all to follow him? How I would like to know him!'

'You will abandon me too?'

'My lord, you know I will not, but I do believe that Jesus
is a god. What does he say in his letter?'

'I have not yet broken the seal; wait, I will read it to
you.'

Blessings upon you, Abgar, for as much as you have
believed in me whom you have not seen.

For of me it is written: Those who have seen me shall

not believe in me, so that those who have not seen may believe, and be blessed, and live.

As for the favor you ask of me, that I go to you to be by your side – I must bide here and carry out all those things for which I have been sent, so that after I have done I may return to Him who sent me.

But after my ascension, when I have returned to Him, I will send one of my disciples, who will cure your disease and give life to you and all that are with you.

'My king, the Jew will heal you.'

'How can you be sure?'

'You must believe. *We* must believe and have faith and wait.'

'Wait? Do you not see how this disease is eating at me? Every day I feel weaker, and soon I will not be able to show myself even to you. I know that my subjects are whispering and that my enemies await, and that there are even those who whisper to Maanu, our son, that he shall soon be king.'

'Your hour has not yet come, Abgar. I know it.'

4

SITTING AT A DESK AT THE ART CRIMES OFFICE IN the Turin carabinieri station, Sofia Galloni was on the line to Rome with the unit's computer specialist.

'Marco's not here, Minerva. He got up early and went to the cathedral. He said he'd be spending most of the day over there.'

'His cell phone's off – all I get is his voice mail.'

'He's totally wrapped up in the case. You know he's been saying for years that somebody wants to destroy the shroud. Sometimes I even think he's right. With all the cathedrals and churches in Italy, the only one that anything ever seems to happen to is Turin's – there are so many "accidents" that it'd make *anybody* suspicious. And then these guys with their tongues cut out. I mean, it's horrible, right?'

'Giuseppe asked me to do some digging into religious sects, to see if there are any that are into that kind of thing. Marco called me about it too. Tell them I haven't come up with anything yet. The only thing I've been able to find out so far is that the company hired to do the restoration has been operating in Turin for years – over forty – and they've always had plenty of work. Their biggest client is the

Church. Recently they've redone the electrical system in most of the monasteries and convents and churches in the area, and they even remodeled the cardinal's residence. It's a corporation, but one of the stockholders is a pretty big fish – he owns aircraft companies, chemical companies. . . . This restoration business is *peccato minuto* for him.'

'Who is he?'

'I'm sure you've heard of him. Umberto D'Alaqua. He's always in the business pages. A real shark at finance who – get this – also owns a big chunk of that company that installs electrical cables and water pipes, big-bore plumbing stuff. But it doesn't stop there; he's also been a stockholder in other companies that have come and gone, that at one time or another had some relationship to the cathedral in Turin. Remember those other fires before '97 – September of '83, for one, just before the House of Savoy signed the shroud over to the Vatican? That summer the Church had started cleaning the cathedral facade, and the tower was covered with scaffolding. Nobody knows how it happened, but a fire started. D'Alaqua was part owner of that cleaning company. And remember when the pipes broke in the cathedral plaza because of some repaving that was going on, and all the surrounding streets flooded? Well, D'Alaqua had a large percentage of stock in the paving company too.'

'Let's not jump to conclusions,' Sofia said. 'There's nothing strange about a man having stock in several different companies that do work in Turin. There are probably a lot like him.'

'I'm not jumping anywhere,' Minerva protested. 'I'm just laying out the facts. Marco wants to know everything, and in that "everything," D'Alaqua's name has turned up several times. This guy must be very well connected to the cardinal in Turin, which means also to the Vatican. And by the way, he's single. Tell Marco I'll e-mail him everything I've got so far. How long are you guys staying in Turin?'

'No idea. Marco hasn't said. He wants to talk to the cathedral workers and the staff in the episcopal offices himself, and he's also decided to go see the guy from the robbery two years ago. I figure we'll be here three or four more days, but we'll call you.'

Sofia decided to go over to the cathedral to talk to Marco. She wanted to have a look around for herself, to get more of a feel for what was on her boss's mind. She would have asked Pietro, Giuseppe, or Antonino to come along, but they were all absorbed in their own assignments. They'd been working with Marco for years, and he trusted them implicitly.

Pietro and Giuseppe were members of the Italian police force, the carabinieri, incorruptible and like bloodhounds on a case. They, along with Antonino and Sofia, who had doctorates in art, and Minerva, their computer genius, made up the core of Marco's team. There were more, of course, but Marco trusted and relied on the five of them most. Their years together had made them all friends.

Sofia was well aware that she spent more time at work than at home. She'd never married, and she told herself that she hadn't had time – her first priority had been her career, the doctorate, her position with the Art Crimes Department, the travel that came with the job. She'd just turned forty, and she knew – she didn't lie to herself – that her love life was a disaster.

Over the years, perhaps just because of all the time they spent together, she and Pietro had drifted into something more than friendship, falling into a low-key routine of sharing a room when they traveled, spending time together some nights after work. He would go back home with her, they'd have a drink, have dinner, go to bed, and around two or three in the morning he'd quietly get up and leave. But although she and Pietro slept together once in a while, he was never going to leave his wife, nor was Sofia so sure that she wanted him to. It was okay the way it was.

At the office they tried to keep the whole thing under wraps, but Antonino, Giuseppe, and Minerva knew, and Marco had finally taken them aside and brusquely told them that they were old enough to do what they wanted, but he hoped their personal lives wouldn't interfere with their work or with the functioning of the team.

Pietro and she had agreed that whatever happened between them, they had to keep it to themselves; it couldn't be talked about to their colleagues – no airing of clean *or* dirty laundry. So far it had worked, although they'd never really put it to the test. They had very few arguments, and those were only minor, nothing they hadn't been able to fix. They both knew the relationship wasn't going anywhere, so neither of them had any particular expectations.

Marco was deep in thought, sitting only a few yards from the display case that held the shroud. He looked up, startled, when Sofia gently touched his shoulder, then smiled and patted the pew beside him.

'Impressive, isn't it?' he said, as she sat down next to him.

'Yes, it really is – fake, but impressive nonetheless.'

'Fake? I wouldn't be quite so unqualified in my judgment. There's something mysterious in the shroud, something scientists haven't ever been able to explain. NASA determined that the image is three-dimensional. There are scientists who are convinced it's the result of some radiation unknown to science and others who will swear that the prints are blood.'

'Marco, you know as well as I do that radiocarbon dating doesn't lie. Doctor Tite and the laboratories that worked on the tests couldn't possibly allow any errors. The cloth is from the thirteenth or fourteenth century, between 1260 and 1390, and three different labs have said so. The probability of error is something like five percent. And the Church has accepted the carbon-fourteen results.'

'But no one can explain how the image on the cloth was made. And I remind you that the three-dimensional photographs have revealed some words: *INNECE* written around the face three times.'

'Yeah, *to death*.'

'And on the same side, from top to bottom, farther in, there are several letters: *S N AZARE*.'

'Which could be read as *NEAZARENUS*,' Sofia recited. They had been down this road before.

'Above, more letters: *IBER . . .*'

'And some people think that the missing letters spell out *TIBERIUS*.'

'And the coins, the leptons?'

'Blowups of the image show circles over the eyes, and on the right eye especially some people think they see a coin, which was common at the time to keep the dead person's eyes closed.'

'. . . which can be read . . .' Marco prodded.

'There are people who say that by putting the letters together they can read *TIBEPIOY CAICAROC*, Tiberius Caesar, which is the inscription that appears on the coins minted in the time of Pontius Pilate. They were bronze, and in the center was an image of the seer's crook.'

'You're a good historian, dottoressa, which means you take nothing on faith.'

Sofia smiled, then turned serious again.

'Marco, can I ask you a personal question?'

'If you can't, who can?'

'Well, I know you're Catholic – I mean, we all are, we're Italians, for God's sake, and after all those years of catechism and nuns, something has to stick – but do you *believe*? Really believe? Because truly having faith is more than just being "Catholic," and *I* think you have faith, I think you're convinced that the man on the shroud is Christ, so you couldn't care less what the scientists say – you believe.'

'Well, it's complicated. I'm not sure, really, what I believe in and what I don't. It doesn't have much to do with what the Church says, with what they call "faith," and there are some things I just can't square logically. But that piece of linen has something special about it – magical, if you will. It's not just a piece of cloth.'

They fell silent, contemplating the piece of linen with its impressed image of a man who, if not Jesus, had suffered the same torments as Jesus. A man who, according to scholars and the anthropometric studies done by Giovanni Battista Judica-Cordiglia, must have weighed between 175 and 180 pounds, stood between five feet eight and five feet ten inches tall, and whose features corresponded to no particular ethnic group.

In the wake of the fire, the cathedral was closed to the public. It would remain closed for a while, so once again the shroud was to be transferred to a vault in the Banco Nazionale. The decision had been made by Marco, and the cardinal had agreed. The shroud was the cathedral's most precious treasure, one of Christianity's most important relics, and given the circumstances it would be much better protected deep within the vaults of the bank.

Sofia squeezed Marco's arm. She didn't want him to feel alone; she wanted him to know she believed in him. She admired him, almost venerated him, for his integrity and because, behind the unsentimental, tough-guy image he cultivated, she knew there was a sensitive man always ready to listen, a humble man always willing to recognize when others knew more than he, yet a man sure enough of himself never to forgo his authority.

When they argued over the authenticity of a work of art, Marco never imposed his own opinion, he always let the members of his team give theirs, and Sofia knew he deferred especially to hers. A few years back he had started calling her *dottoressa*, in tribute to her academic record: a PhD in the history of art, an undergraduate degree in ancient languages, a degree in Italian philology. She spoke English, French, Spanish, and Greek fluently and had also studied Arabic, which she could read and generally communicate in.

Marco looked at her out of the corner of his eye, comforted by her presence. As much as he respected her academic achievements and relied on her considerable professional expertise, he couldn't help feeling it was a shame that a woman like her hadn't found the right man. She was very attractive – beautiful, really. Blonde, blue-eyed, slender, funny, and intelligent – *extremely* intelligent – although she herself didn't seem aware of how exceptional she was. Paola was always on the lookout for somebody for Sofia, but so far her efforts had all failed; the men were either threatened or overwhelmed by Sofia's intelligence. Marco couldn't understand how a woman like that could maintain a stable relationship with Pietro, who seemed well out of her league, but Paola had told him to stay out of it, that Sofia was obviously comfortable with it.

Pietro had been the last person to come on board the

team. He'd been in the department for ten years. He was a good investigator, meticulous, painstaking, and untrusting by nature – which meant nothing escaped him, however small and seemingly unimportant. He had worked in Homicide for many years but had asked for a transfer – sick, he said, of the blood. Whatever – he'd made a good impression when the guys upstairs sent him in for the interview and opened a position for him on the team in response to Marco's chronic complaints that he was understaffed.

Marco got up, and Sofia followed. They skirted the main altar and entered the sacristy, where they found a priest, one of the young men who worked in the episcopal offices, coming in at another door.

'Ah, Signor Valoni, I was looking for you! The cardinal would like to see you in his office. The armored van will be coming for the shroud in about a half hour. One of your men – Antonino, I think – called to tell us. The cardinal says he won't rest easy until he knows the shroud is safe in the bank, even though one can't take a step without bumping into one of the carabinieri you've sent.'

'Thank you, padre. The shroud will be guarded until it enters the vault, and I will be in the armored van personally to make sure it arrives safely.'

'His Eminence has asked that Padre Yves accompany the shroud to the bank, as the Church's representative and to ensure that everything possible is done for its safety.'

'That's fine, padre, no problem with me.'

The cardinal seemed nervous when Marco and Sofia entered his office.

'Signor Valoni! Come in, come in! And Dottoressa Galloni! Please, have a seat.'

'Your Eminence,' said Marco, 'Dottoressa Galloni and I

will be riding with the shroud to the bank. I understand that Padre Yves will be coming with us.'

'Yes, yes, but that wasn't why I wanted to speak with you. I wanted you to know that the Vatican is very concerned about this matter, this fire. Monsignor Aubry has stressed that the pope himself is troubled, and the monsignor has asked me to keep him informed of all new developments so he can report them directly to the Holy Father. So, Signor Valoni, I must insist that you keep me up-to-date as to how your investigation is proceeding. You may of course count on our absolute discretion.'

'Your Eminence, we don't know anything yet – the only thing we have is a body in the morgue. A man of about thirty, unidentified, without a tongue. We don't know whether he's Italian or Swedish or what. We're working around the clock to develop more leads.'

'Of course, of course . . . I'll give you my private number, in my residence, and my cellular number, so you can get in touch with me twenty-four hours a day should you discover anything of importance. I'd like to know every step you're taking.'

The cardinal wrote out his telephone numbers on a card, which Marco slipped into his shirt pocket. He had no intention of keeping the cardinal informed of the blind alleys his investigation was taking him down, so that the cardinal, in turn, could report to Monsignor Aubry, who could report to the Under-Secretary of State, who could report to the Secretary of State, who could report to God knew who – and then there was the pope.

But he didn't say that to the cardinal. He just nodded.

'When the shroud is safely in the armored vault at the bank, Signor Valoni, I want you and Padre Yves to call me immediately.'

Marco raised a questioning eyebrow. The cardinal was treating him as though he worked for him, not the Art Crimes Department. He decided, though, that he'd let the episcopal impertinence pass. He stood up, and Sofia followed suit.

'If you'll excuse us, Your Eminence; the armored car must be almost here.'

5

THE THREE MEN WERE LYING ON COTS, RESTING, each lost in his own thoughts. They had failed, and they had to leave Turin in the next few days. The city had become dangerous for them.

Their brother had died in the fire, and the autopsy would surely reveal that he had no tongue. None of them did. Trying to go back into the cathedral at this point would be suicide; their contact had told them that the carabinieri were everywhere, interrogating everyone, and that he wouldn't rest easy until they were out of the city.

They would go, but for at least a couple of days, until the carabinieri loosened the noose and the media rushed off to some new catastrophe, they would stay hidden in their underground retreat.

The basement was humid, musty; it smelled of mold and mildew, and there was barely room to walk. Their contact had left them food and water for three or four days. He'd told them that he wouldn't be back until he could be sure the danger had passed. Two days had gone by, and it seemed an eternity.

★   ★   ★

Thousands of miles from that basement, in New York, in a glass and steel tower, in an office completely soundproofed and equipped with state-of-the-art security measures, seven elegantly dressed men were celebrating the failure of the group in Turin with a glass of the finest burgundy.

More than triumph, they felt relief. They had reviewed in detail the information they received. Events had veered perilously close to disaster and they had resolved to take different measures if – when – the need arose again.

The men ranged in age from fifty to seventy. The oldest raised his hand slightly and the others fell silent, expectant.

'My sole remaining concern is what we're being told about this detective, the director of the Art Crimes Department. It appears he's not going to let go of the matter very readily this time and may be looking beyond the immediate incident.'

'We'll double our security measures and be sure that our men continue to blend flawlessly into the background. I've spoken with Paul. He'll try to keep abreast of what this Valoni is doing, but it won't be easy. Anything untoward could expose him to scrutiny. In my opinion, master, we should stay back, keep low, do nothing – just watch.' The speaker was tall, athletic, in his mid-fifties, with graying hair and sculpted features that might have belonged to a Roman emperor.

The man whom he had addressed surveyed the others. 'Anyone else?'

Everyone concurred; for the moment they would simply observe from a distance as Valoni went about his work, and their contact, Paul, would be instructed not to press too hard for information. They went on to set a date for their next meeting and to change the code keys they would use until then.

They were preparing to leave when one of them, his accent French-inflected, asked the question on all their minds:

'Will they try again?'

The master shook his head. 'No, not immediately. There's too much risk. This group will try to get out of Italy, then contact Addaio. Even if they're lucky and make it back to him, it will take time. Addaio will be in no hurry to send a new team.'

'The last time it was two years,' recalled the man with the Roman face.

'And we will still be there waiting for them, as we've always been,' his master replied.

6

Josar followed Jesus wheresoever he went. Jesus' companions had become accustomed to Josar's presence and would often invite him to share a moment of quiet brotherhood with them. It was through these companions that Josar learned that Jesus knew he was to die. He also learned that, despite their counsel that the Nazarene should flee, Jesus insisted that he would remain, to do as his Father had bidden him.

It was difficult to comprehend why the Father would wish the Son to die, but Jesus would speak of it with such serenity that it seemed thus was it indeed meant to be.

Whenever Jesus saw Josar, he would make some gesture of friendship toward him. One day, addressing him, he had said:

'Josar, I must do as I am bidden to do. That is why I have been sent here by my Father. And in just that way, you, Josar, also have a mission you must fulfill. That is why you are here – you shall speak of what I am, of what you have seen, and I shall be near you when I am no longer among you.'

Josar had been puzzled by these words, but he had not

had the courage to ask for explanation or to contradict the master.

In recent days, the rumors had grown more persistent. The priests wanted the Romans to solve the problem of Jesus of Nazareth, while Pilate, the governor, was attempting in turn to incite the Jews to judge the man who was one of them. It was only a matter of time before one or the other acted.

Jesus had gone off into the desert, as he was wont to do. On this occasion he had fasted, preparing himself, he said, to carry out the will of his Father.

One morning Josar was awakened by the owner of the house in which he was lodging.

'The Nazarene has been arrested.'

Josar leapt up from his bed and wiped the sleep from his eyes. Seizing a jug of water from a corner of his chamber, he splashed his face. Then he took up his cloak and hurried to the temple. There he found one of the companions of Jesus standing among the multitude gathered there, listening in fear.

'What has happened, Judas?'

Judas began to weep, and he drew harshly away from Josar, but Josar caught him and held him, his hand upon his shoulder.

'What has happened? Tell me. Why do you flee me?'

Judas, his eyes bathed in tears, tried again to free himself from Josar's grasp, but he could not, and at last he answered him:

'He has been taken. The Romans have taken him away, they are to crucify him, and I . . . .'

Tears coursed down his cheeks, as though he were a child. But Josar, strangely, was unmoved by his grief, and he continued to hold Judas tight so that he might not escape him.

'I . . . Josar, I have betrayed him. I have betrayed the best of men. For thirty pieces of silver I have delivered him up to the Romans.'

Wrathfully, Josar pushed him away and began to run blindly, unsure where to go. At last, in the courtyard before the temple, he came upon a man he had seen from time to time listening to Jesus preach.

'Where is he?' Josar asked, his voice faint.

'The Nazarene? He is to be crucified. Pilate will do as the priests have asked.'

'But what is he accused of?'

'Of blasphemy, they say, for he has called himself the Messiah.'

'But Jesus has never blasphemed, has never spoken of himself as the Messiah. He is the best of men.'

'Take care, my friend, for you are one of those who have followed him, and someone might still denounce you.'

'You followed him as well.'

'Indeed, and that is why I give you this counsel. No man or woman who has followed the Nazarene is safe.'

'Tell me, at least, where I may find him, where he has been taken.'

'They have him. You cannot reach him. He is to die on Friday, before the sun has set.'

✝ On the face of Jesus was the agony of torture. Upon his head they had placed a crown of thorns, and it cut into his flesh. Blood flowed down his face, and his beard was wet with it.

Josar had counted each lash as the Roman soldiers scourged Jesus. One hundred and twenty.

Now, as he bore on his torn back the heavy wooden cross on which he was to be crucified, its weight drove him to his knees on the stones of the road, as it had over and over again along that endless way.

Josar took a step forward to support him, to catch him, but a soldier shoved him back. Jesus looked at him in silent gratitude.

He followed Jesus to the top of the hill where he was to be crucified with two thieves. Tears blinded Josar's eyes when he saw a soldier lay Jesus on the cross and take his right hand by the wrist and nail him to the wood. Then he did the same with the left hand, but the nail did not penetrate the wrist at first, as it had the right. The soldier tried twice more before the nail found the wood.

He nailed the two feet together, with a single nail, left foot crossed over the right.

Time seemed eternal, and Josar prayed to God that Jesus might die soon. He watched him suffer, struggling for breath.

John, the most beloved of the disciples, wept in silence at his master's torment. Nor could Josar contain his tears.

As the spring day gave way to evening, and black storm clouds filled the sky, a soldier stepped forward. He thrust his spear into Jesus' side, and from the wound came forth blood and water.

Jesus had died, and Josar gave thanks to God for that.

By the time Jesus' body was taken down from the cross, there was little time to prepare it as the Jewish laws required. Josar knew that all labors, even the clothing of a body in the death shroud, must be halted at sunset.

And because they were in the time of Passover, the body had to be buried that same day.

Josar, his eyes blurred by tears, watched motionlessly as the body was prepared and Joseph of Arimathea lay Jesus' body upon the fine linen grave cloth.

Josar did not sleep that night, nor did he find rest the day following. The pain in his heart was terrible indeed.

On the third day after the crucifixion of Jesus, Josar made his way to the place where the body had been laid. There he found Mary, the mother of Jesus, and John, and other followers of Jesus, and all were exclaiming that the master's body had disappeared. In the tomb, upon the stone where the body had been laid, was the shroud that Joseph of Arimathea had laid it in, though none of those present dared touch it. Jewish law forbade contact with unclean objects, and a dead man's shroud was unclean.

Josar took it in his hands. He was not a Jew, nor was he bound by the Jews' laws. He held the cloth tight against his breast, and he felt himself filled with peace. He felt the master; embracing that simple piece of cloth was like embracing Jesus himself. At that moment he realized what he was to do. He would return to Edessa and present the shroud of Jesus to his king, Abgar, and the shroud would cure him. Now he understood what the master had said.

He went out of the tomb and breathed the cool air, and then, with the shroud folded under his arm, he sought out the road to the inn. He would leave Jerusalem as soon as he was able.

✝In Edessa, the midday heat drove the inhabitants into their houses until the cool of evening. In the palace, the queen laid moist cloths on the fevered forehead of Abgar, and she calmed him by assuring him that the sickness had not yet begun to eat away his skin.

Ania, the dancing girl, filled with desolation, had been banished to a place outside the city. But Abgar had not wanted her left to her own fate, and so he sent victuals to the cave where she had taken refuge. That morning one of his men, while leaving a sack of grain and a goatskin of fresh water near the cave, had seen her. He told the king that Ania's once beautiful visage was now a hideous, misshapen thing, its flesh dropping away. Abgar would hear no more and had taken refuge in his chambers, where, seized with horror, he was overcome by a fever and delirium.

The queen herself cared for him and would let no one else approach him. Some of the king's enemies had begun to conspire to overthrow him, and the tension increased as the days passed. The worst thing was that no news had come of Josar, who had remained with the Nazarene. Abgar was fearful that Josar had abandoned him, but the queen struggled to keep the king's hope alive, urging him not to allow his faith to falter. Just then, however, her own faith was weak.

'My lady! My lady! Josar is here!'

A slave girl had run into the chamber where Abgar, fanned by the queen, was lying drowsily upon his bed.

'Josar! Where?'

The queen rushed out of the king's chamber and ran quickly through the palace, to the astonishment of the palace soldiers and courtiers, until she found Josar. The faithful friend, still covered by the dust of the road, stretched out his hands to her.

'Josar, have you brought him? Where is the Nazarene?'

'My lady, the king shall be healed.'

'But where is he, Josar? Tell me where the Jew is.'

The queen's voice betrayed the desperation she had so long contained.

'Take me to Abgar, my lady.'

Josar's voice was firm and resolute, and all who looked upon the scene were struck by his strength. Without a word more, the queen turned and led him to the chamber in which the king lay.

The king's eyes were fixed on the door, and when he saw Josar he breathed deep with relief.

'You have returned, my dear friend.'

'Yes, my lord, and now you will be healed.'

At the door of the chamber, the king's guard stood in the way of curious courtiers pushing forward to witness the reunion of the king and his best friend.

Josar helped Abgar sit up and he laid in his hands the cloth, which the king held tightly to his breast, though he knew not what it was.

'This is Jesus, and if you believe, you shall be healed. He told me that you would be made whole again, and he has sent me to you with this shroud.'

The firmness of Josar's words, his deep conviction, gave hope to Abgar, who held the cloth yet more tightly against his body.

'I do believe,' said the king.

And his heart was true. And then the miracle happened. Color returned to the king's face, and the traces of the disease faded. Abgar felt the strength returning to his blood and a sense of peace invading his spirit.

The queen wept silently, overcome by the miracle, while the soldiers and courtiers knew not how to explain the king's sudden recovery.

'Abgar, Jesus has healed you, as he promised. This is the shroud in which his body was laid, for you must know, my lord, that Pilate, with the complicity of the Jewish priests, ordered that Jesus be tortured and crucified. But be not of heavy heart, for he has returned to his Father, and from his place on high he shall help us and help all mankind until the end of time.'

News of the miracle of the king's healing spread quickly through the city and throughout the surrounding countryside. Abgar asked Josar to speak of Jesus, to continue the teachings of the Nazarene. He and the queen and all their subjects, he pledged, would take the religion of Jesus, and he ordered that the temples to the old gods be pulled down and that Josar preach to him and his people and make them followers of the Christ.

'What shall we do with the shroud, Josar?' Abgar asked his friend one day.

'My king, you must find a safe place for it. Jesus sent it to you that it might heal you, and we must preserve it from all harm. Many of your subjects have asked me to let them touch the cloth, and I tell you, it has worked yet further miracles.'

'I shall have a temple built, Josar.'

'Yes, my lord.'

Each day, as the sun rose in the east, Josar rose and began to write. His intention was to leave a written testament of the wonders done by Jesus, both those he had witnessed and those recounted to him by the companions of the master while he had lived in Jerusalem. That done, Josar would go to the palace and speak with Abgar, the queen, and many others of what he had learned of the teachings of the Nazarene.

He would see the wonder in their faces when he preached that one should not hate one's neighbors or wish one's enemies ill. Jesus had taught his followers to turn the other cheek.

Josar was supported in his desire to plant the seed of the teachings of Jesus not just by the king but also by the queen. And in a short time, Edessa was a Christian city, and Josar sent epistles to some of the companions of Jesus, those who, like him, took the good news to other towns and peoples.

When Josar had completed his history of the Nazarene, Abgar ordered his scribes to make copies, so that men might never forget the life and teachings of the extraordinary Jew who, even after his death, had healed a king.

7

AS HE PARKED HIS CAR OUTSIDE THE JAIL, MARCO thought he was probably wasting his time. Two years earlier, he hadn't been able to get anything out of the tongueless man, or 'the mute,' as he always called him. He'd brought in a doctor, a specialist, who examined the man and assured Marco that his hearing was perfect, that there was no physical reason he couldn't hear. Yet the mute had remained so tightly locked within himself that it was hard to know whether he could really hear or, if he could, whether he had any understanding of what was being said to him. It was more than likely that the same thing would happen now, but Marco felt compelled to see him nevertheless.

The warden was not in, but he'd left orders that Marco was to be allowed to do whatever he asked. What he asked was to be left alone with the prisoner.

'No problem,' said the head jailer. 'He's a real quiet guy. He never makes any trouble – in fact, he's kind of mystical, you know? He'd rather be in the chapel than out in the yard with the others. He hasn't got much time left on his sentence; they let him off easy, three years. So another year and he's on the street. If he'd had a lawyer he could've asked for early out on good behavior, but he didn't. No lawyer, no visitors, nothing . . . .'

'Does he understand when people talk to him?'

'Huh! Now, *that's* a mystery! Sometimes you think so, sometimes not. Depends.'

'That clears that up.'

'It's that the guy's strange, you know? I mean, I'd never take him for a thief; he sure doesn't act like one. He spends all his time looking straight ahead or sitting in the chapel.'

'Does he ever read or write? He's never put in a request for books, a newspaper, anything?'

'No, never. He never watches television – he's not even interested in the World Cup. He's never gotten mail, and he doesn't write to anybody.'

When the mute entered the interview room where Marco was waiting for him, his eyes showed no surprise – just indifference. He remained standing near the door, his eyes lowered slightly, his posture expectant but unfearing.

Marco gestured for him to sit down, but the man remained on his feet.

'I don't know whether you understand me or not, but I suspect you do.'

The mute raised his eyes off the floor slightly, in a gesture that would be imperceptible to anyone not a professional in human behavior – but Marco was a professional.

'Your friends have broken into the cathedral again. This time they set a fire. Fortunately, the shroud was unharmed.'

The man betrayed not the slightest reaction. His features remained unmoving, seemingly without any effort on his part. Yet Marco had the impression that his probes, his flailings in the dark, were hitting something. Perhaps, after two years in prison, the mute was more vulnerable than when he'd been arrested.

'I suppose it makes a man desperate, being in here. I won't waste your time, because I don't want to waste mine either. You had a year left, and I say "had" because we've reopened your case in the course of our investigation of this fire in the cathedral a few days ago. A man was burned to death – a man without a tongue, like you. So you may have a long wait in jail while we proceed, tie up all the loose ends – two, three, four years, it's hard to say. Which brings me to why I'm here. If you let me know who you are and who your friends are, we might be able to reach an agreement. I'd try to convince the authorities to let you out early, and if you're afraid of your friends, you could go into our witness protection program. That means a new identity, and *that* means that your friends could never find you. Think about it. It could take me a week or it could take me ten years to close this case, but as long as it's open, you'll be sitting in this prison, rotting.'

Marco proffered a card with his phone numbers.

'If you want to get in touch with me, show this card to the guards; they'll call me.'

Nothing. Marco left the card on the table.

'It's your life, not mine.'

As he left the interview room he avoided the temptation to look back. He'd played the role of the tough cop and one of two things had happened – either he'd wasted a little time or, against the odds, he'd managed to plant the seed of doubt in the man's mind and he just might react.

When the mute returned to his cell, he fell onto his cot and stared up at the ceiling. He knew security cameras covered every inch of the chamber, so he had to remain impassive.

A year – he had thought he would be free again in a year. Now this man had told him it might be *ten* years. It could be a bluff, but it could also be the truth.

Since he deliberately shunned the television and other sources of news in the prison, he knew almost nothing of what was happening in the outside world. Addaio had told them that if they were captured they were to isolate themselves, serve out their sentence, and find a way back home.

Now Addaio had sent another team. He'd tried again. A fire, a brother dead, and the police once more searching for clues.

In prison he had had time to think, and the conclusion was obvious: There was a traitor among them. It was not possible otherwise that every time they planned an action something went wrong and somebody wound up in prison or dead.

Yes, there was a traitor among them, and there'd been one in the past as well. He was certain of that. He had to go back and make Addaio see that, convince him to investigate, find the person responsible for so many failures and for his own misery, the years in jail.

But he had to wait, whatever that meant to him personally. If this man had offered him a deal, it was because he had nowhere else to turn. It was a bluff, and he couldn't fall for it. His strength came from his resolute silence, the strict isolation he imposed on himself, the vows he had made. He had been well trained for this. But how terribly he had suffered during these two years without a book, without news from the outside world, without communicating, even by signs, with the other prisoners.

He had convinced the guards that he was a poor

inoffensive mental case, remorseful at having tried to steal from the cathedral, which was why he sat in the chapel and prayed. That's what he'd heard them say when they talked about him. He knew they felt sorry for him. Now he must go on playing his role and hope that they trusted him and would talk in front of him. They did that all the time, because for them, he was just part of the furniture.

He had deliberately left the man's card on the table in the interview room. He had not even touched it. Now he had to wait – wait for another year to pass.

'He left the card right where you put it – didn't even touch it.' The warden had called Marco to report the status of his prisoner, as promised.

'And have you noticed anything unusual these past few days?'

'Nothing. He's the same as always. He goes to the chapel when he's out of his cell, and when he's in his cell he's staring at the ceiling. The cameras record him twenty-four hours a day. If he did anything unusual I'd call you.'

'Thanks.'

Marco hung up. He thought he'd struck a nerve, but he was wrong. The investigation was going nowhere.

Minerva would be arriving any minute. He'd asked her to come to Turin because he wanted the entire team on hand. Maybe if they all sat down together they'd be able to see something.

They'd stay on in Turin for two or three more days, but then they had to go back to Rome; they couldn't devote themselves exclusively to this case – that wouldn't fly with the department, much less the ministries. And the worst thing that could happen would be somebody starting to think he was obsessed. The guys upstairs were already restive – the shroud was unharmed, no damage done, nothing taken from the cathedral. There was the body of one of the perps, of course, but nobody had figured out who he was, and nobody seemed to care much either.

Sofia and Pietro walked into the office. Giuseppe had gone to the airport to pick up Minerva, and Antonino, always punctual, had been there for some time, reading files.

Sofia raised a hand in greeting.

'How're things, boss?'

'Great. The warden assures me the mute hasn't taken the bait – it's like I was never there.'

'That sounds like the way he's acted since the beginning,' said Pietro.

'Yeah, I guess so.'

A peal of laughter and the clacking of high heels announced the arrival of Minerva. She and Giuseppe came in, laughing.

The atmosphere brightened with Minerva's arrival, as it always did. She was happily married to a software engineer who, like her, was an authentic computer genius, and she seemed to be in a perpetual good mood.

After the usual round of greetings, the meeting got under way.

'Okay,' said Marco, 'let's go over what we've got. And when we're done I want each and every one of you to give me your opinion. Pietro, you start.'

'First, the fire. The company that's doing the work in the cathedral is named COCSA. I've interrogated everyone who's working on the electrical system – nobody knows anything, and I think they're telling the truth. Most of them are Italian, although there are a couple of immigrants: two Turks and three Albanians. Their papers are all in order, including work permits.

'According to them, they get to the cathedral every morning at eight-thirty, as the first Mass is ending. As soon as the worshippers leave, the doors are closed and there are no more services until six in the evening, when the workers go home. They take a break for lunch, from one-thirty to four. At four sharp they're back, and they get off at six.

'Although the electrical system is not all that old, they're removing it to install better lighting in some of the chapels. They're also repairing some of the walls – humidity has caused chunks of stucco to come loose and drop off. They figure that they'd have been done in two or three more weeks.

'None of them remembers anything unusual happening the day of the fire. In the area where the fire broke out, there were three men working: one of the Turks – a guy named Tariq – and two Italians. They say they can't understand how the short circuit happened. All three of them swear they left the wiring in order when they went to lunch at a little tavern near the cathedral. They have no idea how it happened.'

'But it did happen,' said Sofia.

Pietro glared at her and went on:

'The workers are happy with the company; they say the pay is good and the bosses treat them well. They told me that Padre Yves oversees the work in the cathedral, that he's a nice guy but he doesn't miss a thing, and that he's very clear about how he wants the work done. They see the cardinal when he officiates at the eight o'clock Mass and a couple of times when he's reviewed the work with Padre Yves.'

Marco lit a cigarette, despite Minerva's reproachful look.

'But,' Pietro went on, 'the experts' report is conclusive.

Apparently some cables that were hanging above the altar in the Virgin Chapel touched and caused a short circuit; that's where the fire started. An accident? Oversight? Neglect? Hard to say. The workers swear they left the cables apart, in perfect condition, but we have to ask ourselves whether that's true or just self-justification. I interviewed Padre Yves. He assured me the workers have always seemed very professional, but he's convinced that somebody fucked up. Not a direct quotation, by the way.'

'Who was in the cathedral at the time of the fire?' asked Marco.

'Apparently,' Pietro answered, 'just the porter, an older guy, about sixty-five. People are in the offices until two, when they go to lunch. They come back around four-thirty. The fire started around three, so the porter was the only one there. He was in shock. When I interrogated him he broke down crying; he was scared, you could tell. His name is Francesco Turgut – an Italian citizen, father Turkish, mother Italian. Born and raised in Turin. His father worked at Fiat, and his mother was the daughter of the porter in the cathedral and helped him clean it. The Church maintains a house for the porter that actually shares a wall with the cathedral, and when Turgut's mother and father married, they moved in with the mother's parents, into the porter's residence. Francesco was born there; the cathedral is his home, and he says he feels guilty for not having been able to prevent the fire.'

'Did he hear anything?' Minerva asked.

'No, he was watching TV and was half asleep. He gets up early to open the cathedral and the office annex. He says he jumped up when somebody rang the buzzer at the door. A man passing by in the piazza alerted him to the smoke. He ran in and discovered the fire and immediately set off the alarm and called the firemen. Since then he's been beside himself – all he does is cry. He says he walked through the cathedral before closing it up, and nobody was there. Part of his work is precisely that – seeing that nobody remains inside. He swears that when he turned off the lights, the cathedral was empty.'

'So what do you think?' Marco asked him. 'Was it set intentionally, or do you think it was caused by neglect or some sort of accident?'

Pietro hesitated. 'If we hadn't found the body, I'd say it was an accident. But we've got the body of a man we don't know anything about, except that he's missing a tongue, just like the other guy. What was he doing there?'

'Plus,' Pietro went on, 'somebody, in fact, broke in. The side door to the offices was forced. You can get from there to the cathedral. There are marks on the doorjamb. Whoever it was knew how to get in and how to get inside the cathedral. Since he did it without attracting the porter's attention, we assume he did it pretty quietly and when he knew there'd be nobody there.'

'We're sure,' Giuseppe put in, 'that the thief, or thieves, knew somebody who works in the cathedral or has some relationship to it. Somebody who told them that that day, at that hour, there wouldn't be anybody around.'

'Why are we sure of that?' Minerva asked.

'Because in this fire,' Giuseppe said, 'as in the purported robbery attempt two years ago, as in the fire in '97, as in all the other "accidents," the thieves knew there was no one inside. There's just one entrance besides the main entrance that's open to the public – the entrance to the offices. The others are permanently boarded over. And it's always been that side door that's been forced. The door is reinforced, but that's no problem for professionals. We think there were other men with our dead guy and they got away. Raiding a cathedral is not something one man does alone. According to the records, all these incidents have taken place when work is being done on the church. Whoever these guys are, they seem to take advantage of repairs to get people in there when no one else is around, maybe short-circuit some wiring or flood the place or otherwise create chaos. But this time, like all the times before, they didn't take anything. Which is why we keep asking ourselves – what were they looking for?'

'The shroud,' said Marco. 'But why? To destroy it? To steal it? I don't know. I wonder whether forcing the door isn't a red herring, something they do to throw us off. It's too obvious . . . I don't know. . . . Minerva, what've you got?'

'I can tell you that one of the controlling shareholders of the company in charge of the work, COCSA, is Umberto D'Alaqua. I've mentioned this to Sofia and sent you some of it by e-mail. This is a solid company that works for the Church, not just in Turin but all over Italy. D'Alaqua is a man the Vatican knows well and thinks highly of. He works with them as a consultant on some of the Vatican's big – and I mean big – investments, and he's made the Church large loans for operations where the Vatican wants to keep its presence quiet. He is trusted at the highest levels and he's also taken part in delicate diplomatic missions for the Church. His businesses range from construction to steel, including oil exploration, etc., etc. He owns a big block of COCSA.

'And he's an interesting man. Single, attractive, fifty-seven years old, serious. Never makes any show of the money or power he has. He's never seen at jet-set parties, never been known to have a girlfriend.'

'Gay?' Sofia asked.

'No, apparently not, but boy, does he walk the straight and narrow. It's as though he's taken a vow of chastity, although he doesn't belong to Opus Dei or any other lay order that would indicate a particularly religious bent. His hobby is archaeology – he's financed excavations in Israel, Egypt, and Turkey, and he himself has actually worked at the digs in Israel for a couple of seasons.'

'It doesn't sound like Signor D'Alaqua jumps out as a prime suspect,' Sofia commented wryly.

'No, but he's quite a figure,' Minerva insisted. 'As is Professor Bolard. These guys are heavyweights. See, boss, this professor is a renowned French chemist, one of the most famous investigators associated with the shroud. He's been studying it for over thirty-five years, doing tests on it, probing every aspect imaginable. Every three or four months he comes to Turin; he's one of the main scientists the Church has entrusted with the conservation of the shroud. They don't take a step without consulting him.'

'Right,' added Giuseppe. 'Before moving the shroud to the bank, Padre Yves spoke with Bolard, who gave very precise instructions as to how the transfer was to be done. Years ago a small room was constructed for it, literally inside the bank vault, and it was built to the specifications of Bolard and other scholars.'

'Okay, well, so Bolard,' Minerva continued, 'is the owner of a big chemical company. He's single and rich as Croesus, just like D'Alaqua, and has never been known to have a romance either.'

'So . . . do D'Alaqua and Bolard know each other?' Marco asked.

'Not that I've found, although I'm still working on that. Of course, there'd be nothing strange if they did – Bolard also has a passion for the ancient world, and they're both involved with the Vatican. They travel in the same circles.'

'What have you found out about our Padre Yves?' Marco asked her.

'Quite a guy, this priest of ours. *Very* sharp cookie. He's French, his family belongs to the old aristocracy, lots of influence in high places. His father, no longer with us, was a diplomat and one of the bigwigs in the Foreign Ministry under de Gaulle. Yves's older brother is a delegate to the French National Assembly, not to mention that he's held several posts in the Chirac administration. His sister is a justice of the French Supreme Court, and he himself has had a meteoric career in the Church. The person who's most directly helped that career is Monsignor Aubry, the assistant to the Vatican Under-Secretary of State, but Cardinal Paul Visier, keeper of the Vatican finances, also looks with favor on our Yves – he was Yves's older brother's roommate at university. So he's gotten one promotion after another, done his time in the diplomatic service. He's held posts at the nunciatures in Brussels, Bonn, Mexico City, and Panama. He was placed as secretary to the cardinal here at Turin specifically on the recommendation of Monsignor Aubry, and it's rumored that he'll soon be made auxiliary bishop in the diocese. There's nothing special in his biography except for the fact that he's totally devoted to the priesthood, with an influential family that supports his clerical career. His academic record is not so shabby either. In addition to theology, he's studied philosophy, he has a degree in ancient languages – the dead ones, Latin, Aramaic, and so on – and he speaks a number of living languages fluently.

'The only peculiar thing about him – for a priest, anyway – is that he likes martial arts. Apparently as a child he was kind of a ninety-seven-pound weakling, so to keep him from being hammered on all the time, his father decided he needed to learn karate. He took to it, and besides having his black belt with who knows how many notches or whatever in it, he's also a master at tae kwon do, kickboxing, and aikido. The martial arts seem to be his only indulgence, but considering the other predilections one runs across in the Vatican, this one is nothing. Oh, and despite how good-looking he is – I'm judging by the photographs – he's never been known to stray from his vows of chastity, with girls *or* boys. Nothing, absolutely celibate.'

'What else have we got?' Marco asked without aiming the question at anyone in particular.

'We've got squat, boss,' Giuseppe said. 'We're still at square one. No leads and, what's worse, no motive. We'll look into the door being forced if you think it could be a plant to throw us off, but then where the hell do they get in and out? We've gone over the cathedral with a fine-tooth comb, and I can promise you there are no secret doors or passages. The cardinal laughed when we asked him about that possibility. He assured us that the cathedral has nothing like that. And I think he's right – we've looked at the maps of the tunnels that run under big parts of the city, and in that area there aren't any. In fact, Turin makes a lot of money taking tourists into the tunnels and giving them the history of its hero, Pietro Micca, and there's no hint of anything under the cathedral.'

'The motive is the shroud,' Marco insisted. 'They're looking for the shroud. I'm still not sure whether they want to steal it or destroy it, but the objective is the shroud, that I'm sure of. Okay, any suggestions?'

There followed an uneasy silence. Sofia looked over at

Pietro, but Pietro, head down, was busying himself lighting a cigarette, so she decided to just dive in.

'Marco, I'd turn the mute loose.'

Everyone stared at her.

Sofia plunged on. 'I mean, if you're right, Marco, and this is an organized, long-term effort to go after the shroud, then it's clear that this mutilation is part of their MO – they send tongueless men in to do the job, so if they're caught, like this guy in the Turin jail, they can keep silent, cut themselves off, not be tempted to communicate. And not only tongueless, right? Their fingerprints are burned off, so there's no way to discover who they are, where they come from. And in my opinion, Marco, threatening this guy is not going to get you anywhere. He let somebody cut out his tongue and burn off his fingerprints – do you think *you* scare him? So there's no way he's going to look at your card and say, "Hmm, maybe I'll just have a chat with this cop." He'll serve out his time – a year is all he's got left.

'We can do one of two things: wait a year, or try to convince the big boys upstairs to approve a new line of investigation – turn the guy loose, and once he's on the street put a tail on him. He'll have to go somewhere, get in touch with somebody.

'It's a thread that might lead us through this knot, get us into the conspiracy – our own Trojan horse. If you decide to go that route, though, there're a lot of preparations that have to be made first. We can't turn him loose right away; we'd have to wait I'd say at least a couple of months and even then do a lot of acting so he doesn't suspect why we've let him go.'

'God, we've been idiots,' Marco said after a long moment. Then he slammed his fist down on the table. 'How could we have been so stupid! Us, the carabinieri, everybody. We had the solution right in front of us, and we've spent the last two years with our heads up our asses.'

Marco's next words dispelled any final doubts Sofia had about her thinking.

'Sofia, you're dead right. It's what we should have done from the beginning. I'll talk to the ministers and explain it to them – we need to get them to talk to the judges, the prosecutor, whoever, but get them to let him out, and from there we start an operation to follow him, every step he takes. No one can argue seriously anymore that this is random. And I'll make sure that no one wants to be on the wrong side of securing the shroud for good. It's time – well past time – to get to the bottom of what's been going on. And end it.'

'Boss,' Pietro interrupted, 'we shouldn't rush into this. Let's think first about how to sell the mute guy the idea that we're turning him loose. Two months, as Sofia suggests, doesn't seem like enough time, considering that you just talked to him and told him he was going to rot in jail. If we turn him loose now, he'll know it's a trap and he won't move.'

Minerva shifted uncomfortably in her chair, while Giuseppe looked distracted and Antonino stared into space. They knew that Marco expected to hear from each of them.

'Antonino, why haven't you said anything?' Marco asked the team's other art historian.

'Honestly, boss, I think Sofia's plan is brilliant. I think we ought to do it, but I agree with Pietro that we can't turn the guy loose too soon; I'm almost inclined to let him serve out the year he's got left.'

'And meanwhile what? Sit back and wait for the next group to try something?' Marco almost shouted.

'The shroud,' Antonino replied, 'is in its own vault at the bank, and it can stay there for the next year. It won't be the first time it's spent that long without being exhibited to the public.'

'He's right,' Minerva broke in, 'and you know it. I mean, I agree that it's hard to have to sit and wait, but if we don't, we could lose the only lead we've got.'

'Giuseppe?'

'I hate to wait, boss,' the cop answered. 'But I think we have to.'

'I don't want to wait,' Marco said emphatically. 'Not a year.'

'Well, it's the most sensible thing to do,' Giuseppe argued.

'I'd do more.'

All eyes turned back to Sofia. Marco raised his eyebrows and extended his hands, inviting her to go on.

'In my opinion we need to go back to the workers and interrogate them again, until we're absolutely certain that the short circuit was really an accident. We also need to investigate COCSA, which means interviewing D'Alaqua too. Behind that impressive facade there could be something we've missed.'

Pietro glared at her. He was the one who'd interrogated the workers, and he'd done so exhaustively. He had a file on every one of them, the Italians as well as the immigrants, and he'd found nothing on them in either the police computers, the files of Europol, or the background checks he'd done. They were clean.

'You think we need to have another go at them because they're foreigners?' he snapped.

Sofia rounded on him. 'You know that's not it, and I resent the implication, Pietro. I said exactly what I think; I

66

think we should go back and investigate them all again, Italians and foreigners both, and if you pushed me I'd say the cardinal too.'

'We'll all go over what we've done so far, and we won't close off any line of investigation,' Marco interjected, to cut off their escalating debate.

Pietro squirmed angrily in his seat. 'What is this, we're going to make everybody a suspect?'

Marco didn't like his tone. 'We're going to continue our investigation,' he repeated. 'But I'm going back to Rome now. I want to talk to the ministers; we need to get their green light on the Trojan horse plan. I'll try to come up with some way to turn the mute loose sooner rather than later, without him suspecting that something's up. I want two or three of you to stay here for a few more days. The others will go back with me, but I want it clear that everyone is still on the case. Work it into whatever you've already got on deck. Okay, then – who's staying?'

'I will,' said Sofia.

'Me too,' said Giuseppe and Antonino simultaneously.

'I think,' remarked Minerva, 'that I'll be more useful with my computers back in Rome.'

'All right. Minerva and Pietro will go with me. I think there's a plane at three.'

Sofia and Pietro sat in silence. Marco had left to stop by the office of the chief of the Turin carabinieri before he went to the airport, while Minerva, Giuseppe, and Antonino had decided to go down to the bar on the corner for coffee, to give the couple some privacy. Everyone had noticed the tension between them. She busied herself with papers, while he stared out the window.

'Are you angry?' Sofia finally asked.

'No. You don't have to tell me everything you're thinking.'

'Come on, Pietro, I know when you're upset.'

'I don't feel like arguing about it. You came up with a half-baked plan that I could have helped you with if you had talked to me about it. But you talked Marco into it, so that's a gold star for you. And now we'll all work to make sure your Trojan horse works. Don't brood about it, or we'll wind up in a stupid fight that won't get us anywhere except pissed.'

'Is your problem with the plan that it came from me? Or do you really see weak spots?'

'It's a mistake to turn the mute guy loose. He'll figure out that something's not right and he won't lead us anywhere. We'll probably wind up losing him. As for investigating the workers again, go right ahead. Let me know if you find anything.'

Sofia didn't bother to respond. She was glad he was going back to Rome. If he stayed, they'd wind up *really* fighting, and neither of them needed that, especially right now. Not to mention that the work would suffer, and although the shroud wasn't an obsession with her like it was with Marco, she was challenged and intrigued by the case and looked forward to solving it. And she had a feeling that the Trojan horse might just lead to that solution.

Yes, the best thing was for Pietro to go back to Rome; a few days would pass and everything would go back to normal. They'd kiss and make up. . . .

8

THE MAN RAISED THE TRAPDOOR AND TURNED
the beam of his flashlight into the darkness of the
subterranean chamber. Three haggard faces stared up at
him. He clambered down the rough-hewn ladder,
suppressing a slight shudder. He was eager for the
unspeaking ones to be on their way, but he also knew that
any rash move could land them all in prison and, worse,
add to the shame of yet another failure, guaranteeing
Addaio's eternal contempt – even, perhaps, his order for
their excommunication.

'The investigators from Rome have left. Today they had
their last meeting with the cardinal, and their chief, Valoni,
has had a long meeting with Padre Yves. I am hearing that
the carabinieri have concluded that our dead comrade was
working alone and have pretty much wrapped up their
efforts. So I think that it is safe for you to begin to make
the journey home. As Addaio instructed, each of you will
follow a different escape route.'

The oldest of the unspeaking ones, a man in his mid-
thirties who appeared to be their leader, nodded as he
wrote a note on a piece of paper.

Are you sure there is no danger?

'As sure as I can be. Do you need anything?'

The man wrote again. *We need baths, shaving equipment. We can't leave here like this. Bring us more water, a tub to wash ourselves in. And what about the trucks?*

'You leave first. Between midnight and one tonight, I will come down to get you, and I will take you through the tunnel to the cemetery. From there, you will make your way to the Merci di Vanchiglia station, on the other side of the piazza. A truck will be waiting there, but it will wait no more than five minutes.' He handed the man a piece of paper with a number written on it. 'This is the license-plate number. It will take you to Genoa. There you will embark as a sailor on the *Stella di Mare*, and in a week you will be home.'

The leader nodded again. Through all this, his two comrades had sat expectantly. They were younger, hardly into their twenties, one tall, broad-shouldered, muscular, with black hair cut in a short military style, the other shorter, lanker, and not as muscled, with brown hair and a face twisted with tension.

Their contact then turned to the black-haired young man.

'Your truck will come to pick you up tomorrow between one and two in the morning. You and I, again, will follow the tunnel to the cemetery. When you come out on the street, turn to the left, toward the river; the truck will be waiting for you. You will cross the border into Switzerland and from there make your way to Germany. Someone will be waiting for you in Berlin; you know the address of those who will see that you get home.'

The last of the three was looking fixedly at their emissary, who suddenly was frightened by the rage he saw in the young man's eyes.

'You will be the last to leave. You must remain here for two more days. The truck will pick you up at one or two, as before, and you will be taken directly home. I will have more details when I come for you. Good luck to you all. I'll be back with the things you need.'

The leader grabbed his arm and signed that he had another question, which he wrote out quickly on the piece of paper.

'Mendib?' the go-between responded. 'He is in prison, as you know. He behaved like a madman; he would not wait for his brothers to arrive but went into the cathedral alone and reached the chapel. I do not know what he did there, but he must have tripped the alarm. He was caught as he was running from the cathedral. There is no more to tell. I have orders from Addaio not to take any risks, so I cannot help him. None of us can.

'Now, follow instructions and you'll all be fine – there should not be any problems. No one knows about this cellar or about this tunnel. Take care to keep it that way. There are dozens of these tunnels crisscrossing under the city, but not all are known. It would be a disaster if they ever find this one – the beginning of the end for all of us and our sacred mission.'

When they were alone again, the leader of the three motioned his companions to him. In only a few hours the next stage of their long journey would begin. They would either reach their homes or be detained – or killed. Fortune had not totally frowned on them so far; they were alive, after all. And yet the way home was mined with peril. They prayed that God would hear their prayers and allow them to reach Addaio.

Their tears mixed as they embraced one another.

9

'Josar! Josar!'

A young man ran into the chamber in which Josar was sleeping. Light was just appearing on the horizon.

It was difficult for Josar to open his eyes, but when he did so they met the tall, thin figure of Izaz, his nephew, a bright and promising boy.

Izaz was learning to be a scribe. Josar was teaching him, and so they spent much time together. The boy was also taking lessons from the philosopher Marcius, from whom he was learning Greek, Latin, mathematics, rhetoric, and philosophy.

'A caravan is arriving, and a merchant has sent a message to the palace asking for you. He says that among the travelers is a man called Thaddeus, a friend of Jesus, and he is bringing you news of Thomas.'

Josar smiled with happiness as he rose from the bed, and he questioned Izaz as he hurried to make his ablutions.

'Are you certain that Thaddeus has arrived in Edessa? You have not confused the message?'

'The queen has sent me to find you; it was she who told me what to say to you.'

'Oh, Izaz! I cannot believe that such happiness is possible. Thaddeus was one of the followers of Jesus. And Thomas . . . Thomas was one of those the Savior trusted most, one of the closest disciples of the twelve. Thaddeus will bring news of Jerusalem, of Peter, of John. . . .'

Josar dressed himself quickly, so that he might come soon to the place where the caravans rested after their long journeys. He would take Izaz with him so that his young nephew might meet the disciple.

They rushed out of the modest house in which Josar lived. Since his return from Jerusalem, Josar had sold his belongings, his comfortable house and all its furnishings, and given the money to the poor of the city. He had found shelter in this small and humble dwelling, which contained all that he owned and needed: a bed, a table, stools, and parchments – dozens of rolls of parchment that he was reading and others that he used for his own writings.

Josar and Izaz hurried through the streets of Edessa until they came to the outskirts of the city, where they found the place of the caravans. At that early hour of the morning, merchants were preparing their goods for their entry into the city, while a swarm of slaves rushed about, feeding and watering the animals, tightening the ropes on bales of merchandise, blowing on the cooking fires.

'Josar!'

The deep voice of the leader of the king's guard stopped Josar in his tracks. He turned to find Marvuz with a group of soldiers.

'The king has sent me to escort you to the palace with this Thaddeus who has come from Jerusalem.'

'Thank you, Marvuz. Wait here while I find him, and we will go with you to the palace.'

'I have asked, and the tent belonging to the merchant he accompanies is that large one there, the one as gray as a storm. I was on my way to it.'

'Wait, Marvuz, wait, let me greet my friend alone.'

The guard gestured to his men, and they stood back while Josar made his way to the merchant's tent. Izaz followed two steps behind him, knowing the emotion his uncle felt at once more meeting this disciple of the Savior. Josar had spoken to him of these men many times – John, the master's favorite; Peter, whom Jesus trusted though he had been denied by him; Mark and Luke; Matthew and Thomas; and so many others, whose names Izaz hardly remembered.

Josar was trembling as he approached the entrance of the tent, from which at that moment emerged a tall man with open, amiable features, dressed as the rich merchants of Jerusalem were wont to dress.

'You are Josar?'

'I am.'

'Enter. Thaddeus is awaiting you.'

Josar entered the tent and there, sitting on a cushion on the ground, was Thaddeus, writing on a parchment. The eyes of the two men met and both smiled broadly, happy to find each other again. Thaddeus stood up and embraced Josar.

'My friend, I am glad to see you,' he said.

'I never imagined that I would see you again. I am filled with joy – how often I remember you all! Thinking of you makes me feel close to the master.'

'He loved you, Josar, and trusted in you. He knew that your heart was filled with goodness and that you would spread his word wheresoever you might go, wheresoever you might be.'

'And so I have, Thaddeus, so I have, though always fearing that I am not able to speak as I should the master's words.'

Just then the merchant entered.

'Thaddeus, I shall leave you here with your friend, so that you two may talk. My servants will bring you dates and cheese and cool water and will not trouble you save you need them. I must go now to the city, where my goods await me. I shall return this evening.'

'Josar,' said Thaddeus, 'this good merchant is called Joshua, and I have traveled from Jerusalem under his protection. He would often go to hear the teachings of Jesus, yet he hid himself in fear that the master would send him away. But Jesus, who sees all men, told him one day to come closer, and his words were a balm to Joshua's spirit, for his wife had recently died. He is a good friend who has helped us greatly. His caravans take news from one of us to another, and he helps us spread the master's word on every journey.'

'Welcome, Joshua,' Josar replied. 'Here you are among friends, and you must tell me if there is any way we might help you.'

'Thank you, good friend, but I need nothing, though I am grateful for your offer. I know that you followed the master, and Thaddeus and Thomas hold you in great esteem. I will return from the city at evening. Enjoy your reunion; you must have much to talk about.'

As Joshua left them, a man as black as night set out plates with dates and other fruits and a jug of water. As silently as he had entered, he departed.

Izaz contemplated the scene in silence. He dared not

draw attention to his presence. His uncle seemed to have forgotten about him, but Thaddeus smiled at him and motioned him to come closer.

'And this young man?'

'My nephew, Izaz. I am teaching him my former calling as a scribe, and one day he may hold my old position in the palace. He is a good boy, a follower of Jesus' teachings.'

As Josar spoke, Marvuz entered the tent.

'Josar, forgive me for interrupting, but Abgar has sent a servant from the palace for news of you and this man who has arrived from Jerusalem.'

'You are right, Marvuz, my joy at seeing my friend again has made me forget that the king expects word from us. He will wish to meet you and honor you, Thaddeus, because Abgar has abandoned the pagan practices and believes in one God, the Father of our Savior. And the queen and court also profess faith in Jesus. We have built a temple, a small one, without adornments, where we meet to ask God's mercy and speak of the teachings of Jesus. I have written down everything I remember of what I heard, but now that you are here with us, you will be able to speak to us of the teachings of our Lord and explain better than I what Jesus was like and how he died to save us.'

'Let us go, then, and see the king,' Thaddeus said, 'and on the way you shall tell me the news. Merchants brought word to Jerusalem that Abgar had been healed of his disease after touching the shroud of Jesus. You must tell me of that miracle done by our Savior and how the faith has taken root in this city.'

✝Abgar was impatient. The queen tried to calm him. Why were Josar and Thaddeus taking so long? The sun was high above Edessa, and they still had not arrived. The king was eager to hear the disciple of Jesus, eager to deepen his knowledge of the Savior. He would ask Thaddeus to stay in Edessa forever, or at least for many years, so that every citizen might hear from his lips other stories of Jesus, in addition to those that Josar had recounted. It was sometimes difficult for Abgar, king of that prosperous city, to understand some of the things that the master had said, but his faith in the man who even after death had healed him led him to accept them all.

He knew that many men and women in the city were displeased by his decision to put aside the gods the people of Edessa had worshipped since the beginning of days and to put in their place a god with no image, who had sent His son to earth to be crucified – a son who, despite the torments he knew awaited him, had preached forgiveness of one's enemies, who preached that it would be easier for a camel to pass through the eye of a needle than for a rich man to enter the kingdom of heaven, while the poor might enter freely. Many of Abgar's subjects continued to worship the ancestral gods in their houses and went up into the mountains, into caves, to make libations to statues of the moon god, Syn, and other gods.

He, Abgar, allowed them to do this; he knew that he could not impose a god upon his people, and that, as Josar said, time would convince the unbelieving that there was but one God.

Indeed, it was not that his subjects did not believe in the divinity of Jesus; it was that they believed him to be another of many gods. In this way, they did accept him, though without renouncing the gods of their fathers.

✝As they walked toward the palace, Josar told Thaddeus how he had felt the need to take the grave cloth of Jesus, even knowing that none of those at the tomb would dare to touch it. Thaddeus nodded at his friend's explanation. He had not realized that the shroud was missing; indeed, he had forgotten about that piece of cloth until news reached him that a miracle had occurred – King Abgar had been returned to health. It had surprised and amazed him, although all the followers were accustomed to the miracles that Jesus wrought.

Thaddeus then explained to his friend the reason for his visit:

'Thomas always remembers you with warmth and affection and recalls your pleading with the master that he journey to Edessa to heal your king. He remembers, too, that the master promised to send one of his own. Thus, after learning that the shroud had healed Abgar and that you were spreading the teachings of our Savior, he asked me to come here to serve you as I might and to help you. I shall remain as long as you need me, and I shall help you preach the words of Jesus to these good people. But someday I shall have to depart, for there are many cities and many men and women who must be taught the true words of our Lord.'

'Do you wish to see the shroud?' Josar asked.

Thaddeus hesitated. He was a Jew, and the law was the law – it was the law of the Savior as well. Still, that piece of cloth brought to the tomb by Joseph of Arimathea so that the body of Jesus might be laid to rest in it seemed impregnated with the powers that Jesus once had. Thaddeus was not sure what to say or do. He hardly knew what to think.

Josar saw the dilemma of his friend, and he squeezed his arm in friendship.

'Be not troubled, Thaddeus. I know the law of the Jews,

and I respect it. But for us, the citizens of this ancient city, a grave cloth is not an impure object that must not be touched. You need not touch it, or even look upon it, but simply know that Abgar ordered a fine ark to hold the shroud be made by Edessa's most skilled artisan and that it is in a safe place, guarded by the most trusted members of the king's personal guard. The shroud works miracles – it healed Abgar and it has healed many more who have come to it with faith. You should know that the blood and sweat of our Savior produced an image of his face and body in the cloth. I tell you, my friend, that as I look upon the shroud I see our master and suffer the very torments that the Romans inflicted upon him.'

'I shall ask you to show me this grave cloth someday, Josar, but I must first seek within my heart to know when it shall be.'

✝They arrived at the palace, where Abgar received them warmly. The queen, at his side, was unable to hide the joy she felt on meeting a friend of Jesus.

'Welcome to you, friend of Jesus and our own,' the king greeted Thaddeus. 'You may remain in our city as long as you desire, where you shall be our guest and want for nothing. We ask only that you speak to us of the Savior, that you remember his words and deeds, and I, with your permission, shall bid my scribes to listen carefully to your words and write them down so that the men and women of my city and other cities may know the life and teachings of our Lord.'

Thaddeus accepted the king's invitation to remain in Edessa, and during all that day and part of the night, with Josar always close by, he recounted to the king and his court the miracles done by Jesus. When it came time to rest, he accepted only a small room with a bed in a house near that of Josar, and he refused, as Josar had upon his return from Jerusalem, to have any slave to aid him.

And as the days and weeks passed, he spoke with the king so that Josar might be his scribe and write down all the things he remembered of the life and words of Jesus.

10

NEW YORK WAS FLOODED WITH SPRINGTIME sunlight – it was one of those perfect days that came so rarely. The old man tore his eyes from the morning splendor pouring through the windows as he turned to answer the ringing telephone. The communications system in the office was configured for absolute security.

'Yes,' he said firmly into the receiver.

'Number one is moving.'

'No problems?'

'They're still using the same contacts as before and the same routes, and it all looks clear for them. The police haven't turned up.'

'What about number two?'

'He leaves tonight. Number three, tomorrow; he'll be moved directly, in a truck carrying screws and bolts. He's the one who's most on edge.'

'I'll speak with our people in Urfa today. We have to know how Addaio is reacting and what he's going to do.'

'They might be better off if they never made it back there.'

'Let things run their course. We need to know what

Addaio does and what he decides. Anything new on his man in the cathedral?'

'His nerves are gone, at least for the moment. But neither the cardinal nor the police suspect him; they're taking him for a good man upset over what happened.'

'We have to keep an eye on him.'

'Of course. Our people there are on it.'

'What about our brother?'

'They've been investigating him. Who he is, what his tastes run to, how he got to where he is today. They've been checking up on me and the others too. The cop, Valoni, is sharp, and he has a good team around him.'

'We must be very careful.'

'We will be.'

'Next week in Boston.'

'I'll be there.'

The members of the Art Crimes team who'd remained in Turin reconvened the morning after the others returned to Rome.

'Where do we start, dottoressa?'

'Okay, Giuseppe, I think we ought to go talk to the workers again and see if they stick to what they told Pietro. Let's keep digging – where they live, who they live with, what their neighbors think about them, whether there's anything unusual in their lives. . . .'

'That'll take time,' Antonino pointed out.

'Yes, which is why Marco asked the chief of the carabinieri here to lend us a couple of men. They know the city better than we do, and they'll know if something we're told is off. Giuseppe can take that angle, and you and I will go back to the cathedral, talk to the employees again, the porter, Padre Yves. . . .'

'Right,' Giuseppe said, 'but another round of questions might make them nervous, tip them off that we're really pushing this.'

'If one of them gets nervous, it'll tip *us* off. I also think we need to interview D'Alaqua.'

'He's a big fish. Maybe too big for questioning at this point. If we step on his toes, Rome could come down on us,' Antonino warned her.

'I know, Antonino, but we've got to try. I'm curious about him.'

'Watch out, dottoressa, don't let that curiosity of yours get us in hot water!' Giuseppe ribbed her.

They split up the work. Antonino would reinterview the cathedral employees, Giuseppe would talk to the electricians, and Sofia would probe further into D'Alaqua and his interests and work on getting an appointment with him. They would try to finish up in a week, and then they could decide what to do next, assuming they turned up a lead.

Sofia convinced Marco to pull some strings to make sure D'Alaqua talked to her.

Marco had grumbled a bit, but he agreed that the man had to be interviewed. So the director of the Art Crimes Department made a direct request to the Minister of Culture, who told Marco he must be crazy if he thought he was going to let him stick his nose into a company like COCSA and investigate a man like D'Alaqua. In the end, though, Marco convinced the minister that it was essential to speak to the man and that Dottoressa Galloni, a cultured and extremely well-educated investigator, would proceed with infinite discretion.

The minister made an appointment for Sofia with

Umberto D'Alaqua for the next day at ten. When Marco told her, she laughed delightedly.

'Boss, you're amazing! I know what this must have cost you.'

'Then you know not to screw this up or we'll both be pushing files around in the archives division. Please, Sofia, take it slow and easy, all right? D'Alaqua is not just a big deal here but all over the world – he has investments across Europe, the US, the Near East, Asia. . . . You have to handle this guy with kid gloves.'

'I'm with Minerva. I've got a hunch about him.'

'I hope your hunches don't backfire.'

'Trust me.'

'If I didn't, you wouldn't be going.'

Umberto D'Alaqua's secretary looked more like a top executive than a secretary, no matter how important his employer was. He was a discreetly elegant middle-aged gentleman who introduced himself to Sofia as Bruno Moretti and asked if she'd like coffee while she waited for Signor D'Alaqua to end another meeting.

When she demurred, Moretti excused himself and left her alone. The room in which she found herself was breathtaking. On its walls hung a Canaletto, a Modigliani, a Braque, and a small Picasso.

Absorbed in the Modigliani, Sofia was startled by a voice behind her.

'Good morning, Dottoressa Galloni.'

She turned to find herself facing the most attractive man she had ever encountered, studying her with severe yet curious eyes. She felt herself blush, as though she had been caught doing something wrong.

Umberto D'Alaqua was tall and elegantly dressed,

probably in his mid-fifties. He radiated self-assurance and strength.

'Good morning. I'm sorry, I was looking at the Modigliani. It's stunning.'

D'Alaqua merely smiled slightly. 'We'll be more comfortable in my office, Dottoressa Galloni.'

Sofia nodded and followed him to a nearby suite of rooms. D'Alaqua's office was comfortable, furnished with contemporary furniture that highlighted the magnificent works of art covering the walls: several da Vinci drawings, a *quattrocento* Madonna, a Christ by El Greco, a Picasso harlequin, a Miró. . . . On a small table in a corner across from the large desk, the simplicity of a crucifix carved from olive wood drew her attention.

D'Alaqua gestured her toward the couch, and he seated himself in an armchair beside her.

'Well, Dottoressa Galloni, how may I help you?'

Sofia hit him without preamble. 'Signor D'Alaqua, we suspect that the fire in the cathedral was not an accident. In fact, we believe that none of the unfortunate events that have occurred in the Turin Cathedral have been accidents.'

Nothing in D'Alaqua's expression betrayed the slightest sign of concern, or even surprise. He looked at her calmly, apparently waiting for her to go on, as though nothing he was hearing had anything to do with him.

'Did you know the men who were working in the cathedral? And do you feel you can fully trust them?'

'Dottoressa Galloni, COCSA is one of many corporations I own or on whose board of directors I sit. You can understand that I don't personally know all the employees of those corporations. In this as in any other business, there is a human-resources office, which I'm sure

85

will have provided you with all the information you need on the men working in the cathedral. But if you require more, I'll be glad to ask the head of that department to put everything you need at your disposal.'

He picked up the telephone and asked to be put through to the head of personnel.

'Signor Lazotti, I'd appreciate your meeting with Dottoressa Galloni of the Art Crimes Department. She needs more information on the men working in the cathedral. My secretary will bring her to your office in a few minutes. . . . Yes, thank you.' He put down the receiver and looked at her calmly; clearly he considered the interview over. She'd blown it.

'Do you think what I've told you is utterly absurd, Signor D'Alaqua?' Sofia pressed.

'Dottoressa Galloni, you and your team are the professionals, and you do your job. I have no opinion at all with respect to your suspicions or your line of investigation. Is there anything else I can help you with?'

Sofia raised her chin slightly and smiled. 'We may have more questions for you as our inquiry proceeds, Signor D'Alaqua. We just wanted to advise you of our thinking and that therefore we're going to be doing a thorough investigation of your personnel.'

'Signor Lazotti will give you all the help you need, I'm sure.'

D'Alaqua wasn't going to say another word. Sofia stood up and extended her hand.

'Thank you for your cooperation.'

'A pleasure to meet you, Dottoressa Galloni.'

Sofia was furious with herself but managed to chat amiably with Moretti, D'Alaqua's secretary, as he walked her to Mario Lazotti's office.

Lazotti greeted her with a smile. 'Tell me, Dottoressa Galloni, what is it you need?'

'I need all the information you have on the men who were working in the cathedral, including all the personal details you have.'

'I gave all that information to one of your colleagues in the Art Crimes Department and to the police, but I'll be happy to give you a copy of the entire file as well. I've already asked my secretary to prepare it for you. As for personal information, I'm afraid we won't be of much help there; COCSA is a large corporation, and it's difficult to get to know each and every employee. The supervisor at the cathedral might be your best source in that regard.'

A young woman came in with a large file folder, which Lazotti handed to Sofia.

Sofia thanked him and settled more comfortably into the chair he had offered her. 'Signor Lazotti, have you had many accidents like the one in the Turin Cathedral?'

'What do you mean?'

'COCSA is a company that does a lot of work for the Church. You've made repairs and done maintenance work on almost every cathedral in Italy.'

'Italy and most of Europe. And accidents, unfortunately, happen, even though we closely comply with all security and safety regulations and take strict measures of our own.'

'Could you give me a list of all the accidents COCSA has had in the course of its work on cathedrals?'

'I'll look into it and do everything I can. It won't be easy. In every job there are problems, incidents of one sort or another – cuts, bruises, falls, broken arms, that sort of thing – and I'm not sure we keep a record of all of them. Normally, the chief engineer or supervisor files a report at the time, though, so . . . . How far back would you want me to go?'

'Let's say the last fifty years.'

Lazotti allowed himself an incredulous look, but he never lost his air of cool efficiency.

'I'll do what I can,' he repeated. 'Where do you want the information sent?'

'Here's my card, and here's my cell phone number. Call me, and if I'm in Turin I'll come by and pick it up. If not, you can send it to my office in Rome.'

'I hope you'll excuse my asking, Dottoressa Galloni, but what is it you're looking for?'

Sofia measured him with a quick look, then decided to tell him the truth.

'I'm looking for whoever it is that creates "accidents" in the Turin Cathedral.'

'Sorry?' Lazotti seemed genuinely puzzled.

'We don't think these events are accidents. We're looking for the person or persons behind them.'

'You're joking! But of course you're not. But who would want to damage the cathedral? You suspect our employees?'

'That's what we want to find out – who and why.'

'But are you sure? On what evidence? You're directly accusing COCSA's employees of involvement in this?'

'It's not an accusation, but it's something we need to investigate.'

'All right. Of course. You can count on us to cooperate fully.'

'I *am* counting on you, Signor Lazotti.'

Sofia left the glass-and-steel building, mulling whether she'd chosen the right strategy in revealing her suspicions to COCSA's head of human resources as well as to

D'Alaqua. At that very moment D'Alaqua might be calling the minister to complain. Or he might not be doing anything – either because he gave their suspicions no importance, or because he did.

She needed to call Marco immediately. If D'Alaqua was talking to the minister, she had to prepare her boss for what was coming.

She had also come to a decision about Pietro. She was going to break it off. Their relationship suddenly struck her as disgusting.

11

I zaz's quill filled parchment after parchment with the
stories that Thaddeus told.

Abgar and the queen had praised the scrolls he had so
carefully produced, and he dreamed that someday he, too,
might become a royal scribe. Thaddeus called for him
often, to dictate to him the memories of the Nazarene that
were so dear to him, and the young man knew by heart
the adventures that Thaddeus and Jesus had shared.

Thaddeus would close his eyes and seem to submerge
himself in a dream as he told the stories – what Jesus was
like, the things he said, the things he did.

Josar had also written his own remembrances and had
had them copied down, and one copy of each account was
kept in the royal archives. They would do the same with
the stories told by Thaddeus. Thus had Abgar ordered, for
the king dreamed that Edessa might leave to its children
the true story of Jesus.

Time had passed, and Thaddeus had remained. The
queen and Abgar had asked him to stay, to help them be
good Christians, to help Josar spread the teachings of Jesus,

and to make Edessa a place of refuge for all those who believed in him.

Izaz was glad that Thaddeus had not left the city. His uncle was comforted that there was another person in Edessa who had known the Nazarene, and Josar sought the counsel of Thaddeus with respect to what he should say to the citizens of the city who came to his house to learn of the Savior and to pray.

Every day Thaddeus went with Josar to the first temple that the queen had had raised to Jesus. There he spoke to and prayed with groups of men and women who came to seek consolation for their tribulations, came in hopes that their prayers might reach that Jesus who had saved Abgar from his cruel disease. He also sat with the faithful who congregated in a new temple built by the great Marcius, the royal architect.

Thaddeus had asked Marcius to make the new temple as simple as the old one, which was little more than a house with a great atrium in which the word of Jesus might be preached. He told Marcius how Jesus had cast the moneylenders out of the temple in Jerusalem and how the spirit of Jesus could live only in a place of simplicity and peace.

✝ 'I, Maanu, prince of Edessa, son of Abgar, implore thee, Syn, god of gods, to aid me in destroying the impious men who confound our people and incite them to abandon thee and betray the gods of our fathers.'

On a rocky promontory a few leagues from Edessa, the altar to Syn was illuminated only by the flickering torches inserted into the walls of the cave that served as the god's temple. The relief portrait of Syn was carved into the stone wall with such art that it looked almost real, as though the gods were with them.

Maanu breathed deeply of the incense and aromatic herbs that intoxicated the senses and helped him communicate with the powerful moon god. At his side was his faithful Marvuz, the leader of the king's guard, who would become Maanu's principal counselor when Abgar died and who also worshipped Syn and the other ancient deities, as did other Edessians faithful to the traditions of the ages.

Syn seemed to hear Maanu's prayer, for he burst forth from the clouds of incense and illuminated the sanctuary.

Sultanept, the high priest of the cult, told Maanu that this was a sign, the manner by which the god showed men that he was among them.

Along with five others priests, Sultanept lived in hiding in Sumurtar, sheltered by the tunnels and subterranean chambers in which they served the gods – the sun, the moon, and the planets, alpha and omega of all things.

Maanu had promised Sultanept to restore him to the power and wealth that Abgar had taken from him when he set aside the religion of their fathers.

'My prince, we should go,' Marvuz murmured. 'The king may call for you, and we left the palace many hours ago.'

'He will not call me, Marvuz; he will think I am drinking with my friends in some tavern or off fornicating with a dancing girl. My father hardly cares for me, so downcast is he that I will not accept the worship of his Jesus. The queen is to blame for it. She has convinced him to betray our gods and has made that Nazarene their only god.

'But I assure you, Marvuz, that the city shall turn its eyes once more to Syn and destroy the temples that the queen has built to honor the Nazarene. The moment Abgar goes to his eternal rest, we will kill the queen and put an end to the life of Josar and his friend Thaddeus.'

Marvuz trembled. He bore no affection for the queen; he considered her a hard woman, the true ruler of Edessa since Abgar had first fallen ill, despite the king's recovery of his health. And the queen distrusted Marvuz. He could feel her icy gaze upon him, following his every move, for she knew that he was a friend of Maanu. But even so, could he kill her? For he was certain that Maanu would ask him to do it.

He would have no problem killing Josar and Thaddeus. He would run them through with his sword. He was weary of their sermons, their words filled with rebuke because he fornicated with any woman who would go with him and because, in honor of Syn, he drank without moderation on nights of the full moon until he lost his senses, for he, Marvuz, still worshipped the gods of his fathers, the gods of his city. He did not accept the imposition of this effeminate and virtuous god that Josar and Thaddeus never ceased speaking of.

12

THE SUN WAS RISING ON THE BOSPHORUS AS THE *Stella di Mare* cut through the waves near Istanbul and her crew rushed about in preparation for docking.

The captain watched the dark-skinned young man silently swabbing the deck. In Genoa, one of his men had gotten sick and could not make the voyage, and his executive officer had brought him this fellow. The XO had assured him that, although the new man was mute, he was an experienced sailor recommended by one of the regulars at the Green Falcon, the tavern on the docks they all frequented when they were in port. At the time, given their imminent sailing, the captain hadn't noticed that the man's hands were soft, with not a single callus – the hands of a man who had never done a seaman's work. But the mute followed every order he was given during the crossing, and his eyes showed no emotion, no matter what job he was given.

The XO had said that the man would depart the ship in Istanbul, but all he'd done was shrug his shoulders when the captain asked him why.

The captain was Genovese. He'd been a sailor for forty

years, and he'd docked in a thousand ports and known every kind of person. But this young man was a strange one, with failure etched on his face and resignation in his every gesture, as though he knew he'd come to the end. But the end of what?

Istanbul was more beautiful to him than ever. He breathed deep as his eyes scanned the port. He knew that someone would be coming for him, perhaps the same man who had hidden him when he arrived from Urfa. He yearned to return to his own town, embrace his father, feel the arms of his wife about him again, hear the happy laughter of his daughter.

He feared his meeting with Addaio, feared the pastor's disappointment. But at this moment failure, his own failure, meant very little to him, for he was alive and almost home. It was more than his brother had been able to do two years earlier. They had heard nothing, nothing from him since that black evening when he'd been arrested like a common thief. Their contact in Turin had told him that Mendib was still in prison but should be free in a year.

He got off the boat without saying good-bye to anyone. The night before, the captain had paid him the wages they'd agreed upon and asked him if he didn't want to stay on with the crew. With signs, he had refused.

He left the dock area and began to walk, not knowing exactly where to go. If the man from Istanbul didn't appear, he would find some way to get to Urfa on his own. He had the money he'd earned as a sailor.

He heard quick footsteps behind him, and when he turned he saw the man who'd given him shelter a few months earlier.

'I've been following you for a while, watching, to be

sure no one else was on your tail. You'll be sleeping tonight at my house; they'll come for you early tomorrow morning. It's best you not leave the house until then.'

The mute nodded. He'd have liked to walk around Istanbul, wander through the narrow streets of the bazaar, find perfume for his wife, a gift for his daughter, but he wouldn't do that. Any further complication would anger Addaio even more.

A soft rapping on the woven-rush door of the house woke Josar from a troubled sleep.

Dawn had not yet broken over Edessa, but the soldier at the door brought him orders directly from the queen. At dusk, Josar and Thaddeus were to come to the palace. The guard was unable to mask his uneasiness, and his message delivered, he was clearly glad to be away.

✝ On his knees, his eyes closed, Josar prayed that God might give him balm for the disquiet that filled his soul.

Izaz arrived a few hours later, at almost the same time as Thaddeus. Josar's nephew had grown into a robust, intelligent young man. He brought news of the rumors that were circulating wildly in the palace. Abgar's strength was ebbing; he was failing almost before one's eyes. The physicians spoke in hushed voices, and rumor had it they had told the queen that there was little hope the king would emerge from what appeared to be death's last assault upon his life.

Knowing that he was dying, Abgar had asked the queen to call his closest friends and advisers to his bedside so he might impart the instructions to be followed after his death. That was why the queen had called Josar, then. To Izaz's surprise, he, too, had been called to the side of the king.

When they arrived at the palace they were escorted quickly into the presence of the king, who was lying on his couch, his pallor dramatically worse than in recent days. The queen, who was cooling Abgar's brow with a cloth moistened with rose water, sighed with relief when she saw them enter.

Two other men entered the king's chamber: Marcius, the royal architect, and Senin, the wealthiest merchant in Edessa and a blood relative of Abgar, to whom he maintained absolute allegiance.

The queen motioned them all toward the king's couch as she sent the servants away and ordered the guards to close the doors and allow no one else to enter.

'My friends, I wanted to take my earthly leave of you and instruct you in my last wishes.'

Abgar's voice was weak. The king was dying and he knew it, and the respect and love the men bore him prevented them from speaking words of false hope. Thus they stood in silence at his bedside, to hear what he wished to say to them.

'My spies have told me that when I die, my son, Maanu, will unleash cruel persecution against all the Christians of the city and that some of you have been marked for death. Thaddeus, Josar, and you, Izaz, must leave Edessa before I die. You will not be safe here afterward. Maanu will not dare murder Marcius or Senin, even though he knows they are Christians, because they are of the noble families of Edessa, who would take vengeance against him.

'He will burn the temples to Jesus and destroy the

houses of those of my subjects most faithful to the worship of the Christ. Many men, women, and children will be murdered as he terrorizes our Christian brothers and sisters and attempts to force them to return to the worship of the old gods.

'I fear for the shroud of Jesus; I fear that the grave cloth will be destroyed. Maanu has sworn to burn it in the marketplace before all the citizens of Edessa, and on the day of my death he will do just that. You, my friends, must save it.'

The five men listened in silence to the king's words. Josar looked at the queen, and for the first time he realized that the beauty that had always graced her was now fading and that the stray hairs one could see among the folds of her veil were silver. His lady had aged, although the brightness of her eyes was unchanged and her presence was as majestic as always. What would happen to her? He was certain that Maanu, her son, hated her.

Abgar sensed Josar's concern. He knew of his friend's undying devotion to the queen.

'Josar, I have asked the queen to leave the city as well. There is still time, but she will not listen.'

'My lady,' said Josar, 'your life is in more danger than ours.'

'I am the queen of Edessa, Josar, and a queen does not flee. If I must die I will do so here with my people, those who believe in the Christ as I do. I will not abandon those who have placed their trust in us, the friends I have prayed with. I will remain beside Abgar; I could not bear to abandon him to his fate in this palace. So long as the king lives, Maanu will not dare act against me.'

Abgar sat up on his couch, clutching the queen's arm. Over the last few days he and she had talked for hours, through the nights and until sunrise, devising the plan that the king was now about to explain to his most beloved friends.

'My last command to you, my friends, is that you save the shroud of Jesus. Upon me it worked the miracle of life, enabling me to live to this old age that is now upon me. The sacred cloth belongs not to me but to all Christians, and it is for them that you must save it – and yet I ask that it not leave Edessa but that the city preserve it for all time. Jesus sent it here, and here it shall remain. The last loyal members of my guard maintain it in the first temple we built to him. Thaddeus, Josar, you will retrieve the shroud and deliver it over to Marcius. You, Marcius, will find a hiding place for it, to save it from the wrath of Maanu. Senin, I ask that you organize the flight of Thaddeus, Josar, and young Izaz. My son will not dare attack your caravans. I place my faithful subjects under your protection.'

'Where would you have me hide the shroud, Abgar?' asked Marcius.

'That is for you to determine, my good friend. Neither the queen nor I must know, though you must choose one person to share the secret and put that person, too, under the protection of Senin. I feel my life ebbing away. I know not how many days remain to me, but I hope I may be given enough to allow you to carry out those things I have asked of you.'

Then, as dusk deepened into night, knowing it might be the last time, the king took his leave of them.

✝ The sun was just rising as Marcius reached the western wall. Workers were already there, awaiting his instructions. As the king's architect, Marcius was charged not only with constructing the buildings that gave glory to Edessa but also with overseeing all the public works in the city, such as this construction at the western wall, which was being broadened so that a grand ornamental gateway might be made in it.

He was surprised to see Marvuz, on horseback, speaking with Jeremin, the overseer of the work.

'Greetings, Marcius.'

'What brings the head of the king's guards to the wall? Has Abgar sent for me?'

'I am sent by Maanu, who soon enough will be king.'

'He will be king if God wills it.'

The loud laugh that came from Marvuz echoed in the silence of the dawn.

'He will be king, Marcius, he will be king, and you know that, for you were with Abgar last evening. You saw that his death is upon him.'

'What is it you want here? Speak quickly, for I have work to do.'

'Maanu wishes to know what orders Abgar has given. He knows that not only you but also Senin, Thaddeus, Josar, and even Izaz the scribe were at the king's bedside well into the night. The prince wishes you to know that if you vow loyalty to him, no harm will befall you; if you do not, he cannot be responsible for the fate you encounter.'

'You come here to threaten me? Has the prince so little respect for himself that he would stoop to threats of violence? I am too old to fear anything men might do to me, Marvuz. Maanu can only take my life, and it has already run its course. Now go, and let me work.'

'Will you tell me what Abgar has told you?'

Marcius turned on his heel without replying and began to inspect the mortar that one of the workers was removing.

'You will be sorry for this, Marcius, you will be sorry!'

shouted Marvuz as he swung his mount about and galloped off to the palace.

For the next few hours Marcius seemed absorbed in his work. The overseer watched him out of the corner of his eye; Marvuz had paid him well to spy on the royal architect. He regretted that he was forced to betray the old man, who had always been kind to him, but Marcius's time had passed, and Marvuz had assured the overseer that Maanu would repay his services most generously.

The sun stood at its zenith when Marcius told the overseer that it was time for a break. Sweat poured from the bodies of the workers, and even the overseer was weary from the labors and ready to sit and rest awhile.

Two young servants from the house of Marcius came just then with two baskets. The overseer saw that they brought fruit and water, which the architect began to share among the workers.

For an hour they all rested, although Marcius, as so many times before, remained absorbed in the study of his plans. Indeed, he was so dedicated to his work that at one point he broke off his examination of the plans to climb up a ladder and mount a high scaffolding, examining the wall to ensure that it was being built firm and solid. The overseer closed his eyes, weary with the heat and the labors, while the workmen barely had the strength to talk.

It was not until the sun was sinking in the west that Marcius allowed the workmen to cease their labors. He wished them all a good evening and, accompanied by his servants, made his way home.

There was little for the overseer to report on Marcius's activities, but he repaired to the tavern at the sign of the cloverleaf, to meet there with Marvuz.

★　　★　　★

✝ Marcius, childless and widowed, for his wife had died years ago, loved his two servants as though they were his own sons. They were Christians, as he was, and he knew that they would not betray him.

The night before, Marcius had made a promise to Thaddeus and Josar before leaving the palace of Abgar: When he had determined where to hide the shroud of Jesus, he would send them word. Josar would devise a plan to deliver the shroud to Marcius without arousing Maanu's suspicions, since they knew, as Abgar had warned them, that Maanu would send spies to watch them. They also decided that Marcius would tell Izaz alone where the shroud was hidden, and this meant that the moment Izaz received the information, it was imperative that he go to Senin and flee the city. Thaddeus had made arrangements for him to journey to Sidon, where there was a small but prosperous community of Christians. Timaeus, the spiritual leader of the community, had been sent there by Peter to preach. Izaz would find refuge with Timaeus, who would safeguard the secret of the shroud's location.

Despite Abgar's plea that they save their lives, Thaddeus and Josar had made the decision to remain in Edessa. They would share the fate of their Christian brothers and sisters. Neither of them wished to leave the shroud behind, though they would never know where Marcius had hidden it.

They met in the temple that evening with many other Christians of the city. They prayed together for Abgar, asking God's mercy for their king.

That morning, Josar had carefully rolled up the grave cloth and hidden it in the bottom of a basket, as Marcius had counseled him. Before the sun had risen to its zenith, Josar went to the market, the basket over his arm, and wandered among the merchants' stalls, conversing with the tradesmen. At the hour they had agreed upon, he spied one of Marcius's servants buying fruit from an old man; Josar went up to the youth, who was carrying a basket like Josar's, and greeted him warmly. Then, stealthily and with great care, they exchanged baskets. No one noticed the exchange, and Maanu's spies saw nothing suspicious in the fact that Josar was greeting one of his fellow Christians.

Nor was the overseer suspicious when Marcius, high on a scaffolding, picked up an apple from the fruit basket he had carried with him and bit into it distractedly from time to time as he went along the wall, testing its firmness, tapping to find dangerous hollow spaces among the fired bricks. Marcius had always enjoyed masonry and even today liked to lay bricks – what did it matter to the overseer if he spent his strength in the noonday sun when all about him were drowsy with the heat and the buzzing of the flies?

✝ Marcius refreshed himself with the cool water that one of his servants had brought to his bedchamber. Resting from the heat of the day, the royal architect removed his dusty tunic and put on a clean one. He sensed that the days of his life were numbered. The moment Abgar died, Maanu would attempt to learn where the shroud was hidden so that he might destroy it. He would torture anyone he believed might know where it was hidden, and Marcius was among the friends of the king whom Maanu would suspect of sharing the secret. That was why he had come to a decision, about which he would tell Thaddeus and Josar that very night – a decision he would carry out the instant he learned Izaz was safe.

Accompanied by his two young servants, he made his

way to the temple, where he knew his comrades would be praying. When he arrived, he took a place at a little distance from the others, where the community of the faithful would not see him. Though they were all Christians and loyal to one another, Maanu's money was plentiful, and it might persuade one of them to betray him.

Izaz glimpsed the architect standing in the shadows. Taking advantage of the moment when Thaddeus and Josar asked him to help distribute the bread and wine among the worshippers, he approached Marcius, who gave him a small, tightly rolled scroll of parchment, which Izaz tucked into the folds of his tunic. Then he signaled to a huge man who appeared to be awaiting a sign and slipped quietly out of the temple. Outside, followed by the enormous man, Izaz hurried toward the place of the caravans.

Senin's caravan had been readied for its departure from Edessa. Harran, the man charged by Senin with leading the caravan to Sidon, was waiting impatiently. He showed Izaz and the colossus, who was called Obodas, the place reserved for them and gave the order to depart.

Izaz did not unroll the parchment until the sun was well up in the sky the following morning. He read the two lines whereon the architect had written in clear characters the hiding place of the Holy Shroud. He then tore the parchment into tiny pieces and slowly scattered the pieces across the desert as they marched on.

Obodas watched over him attentively, keeping his eye ever alert to their surroundings. He had orders from Senin to protect the young man's life with his own if need be.

Three nights later, Harran and Obodas thought they were far enough from Edessa to take a brief respite from their journey and send a messenger to the house of Senin.

It would take him three days to arrive, and by then Izaz would be safe.

✝ Abgar was dying. The queen sent for Thaddeus and Josar, to tell them that within hours, perhaps minutes, the king's life would be at its end. He no longer recognized even her.

It had been ten days since Abgar called his friends into that same room to speak to them; they had conversed together until the blackest darkness of the night. Now the king was nearly lifeless; he did not open his eyes, and only a faint haze on the mirror held beneath his nose indicated that he was still alive.

Maanu, impatiently awaiting the king's death, had not set foot outside the palace. The queen would not allow him to enter the royal chambers, but that was of no importance. He would learn of his father's death, because he had promised a young slave girl her freedom if she told him everything that took place in Abgar's chamber.

The queen knew she was being spied upon, so when Josar and Thaddeus arrived she sent all the servants out of the chamber, and the friends conversed in whispers. She smiled with relief when she learned that the shroud was safe. She promised to inform them immediately when Abgar died; she would send the scribe Ticius, who was a Christian and a loyal servant. The three old friends made their farewells with emotion, for they knew that they would never see one another again in this life, and the queen asked Thaddeus and Josar to pray that God might give her strength to face the death that her son surely intended for her.

Josar, his eyes filled with tears, could not bear to say good-bye to the queen. She was no longer the beautiful woman of many years ago, but her eyes were bright with intelligence and energy, and her regal bearing remained unbowed. Conscious of the devotion the old scribe Josar bore her, she squeezed his hand and embraced him, so that he might feel that she knew how much he had loved her and to show that she loved him as the most loyal of her friends.

✠ For three days more, Abgar lay dying. On the third day, the palace was dark, and the night outside black, and only the queen was watching over him. He opened his eyes and smiled at her in gratitude, his gaze filled with tenderness and love. Then he expired, at peace with himself and God. The queen clutched her husband's hand. Then she softly closed his eyes and kissed his lips.

She allowed herself only a few moments to pray, asking that God take Abgar into His keeping. Then, stealthily, she slipped through the dark corridors of the palace until she came to a nearby apartment where for some days now the royal scribe Ticius had been staying.

He was asleep, but he awoke when he felt the queen's hand upon his shoulder. Neither spoke a word. Then, under the cover of night and darkness, the queen returned to the royal bedchamber, while Ticius crept carefully out of the palace and made his way to the house of Josar.

The sun had not yet risen when Josar, filled with desolation, heard from Ticius the news of the king's death. He, too, had only moments for prayer. He had to send a message to Marcius, as the royal architect had bidden. Their plan depended on it. And he had to advise Thaddeus, for the life of them both, he was certain, had come to an end.

14

'ALL RIGHT, MARCO, SPIT IT OUT – WHAT'S ON your mind?'

Santiago Jiménez's direct question took Marco by surprise.

'Is it that obvious?'

'Jesus, aren't we supposed to be detectives?'

Paola smiled. Marco had asked her to invite John Barry, the US cultural attaché, and Santiago Jiménez, Europol's representative in Rome, to dinner at their house. John had come with his wife, Lisa. Santiago was single, so his companion was always a surprise – and never the same girl twice. This time he'd come with his sister Ana, a vivacious young woman, a journalist who was in Rome covering a summit of the heads of state of the European Union. Now, after several convivial courses, they were all relaxing around the table with dessert and coffee.

'All right, then, you know that there's been another accident at the cathedral in Turin,' Marco began. He took his time, summing up the case for them, outlining in general the relevant history and the fantastic similarities among the incidents, thoughtfully responding to their comments and questions.

'The history of the shroud is interesting – the way it's appeared and disappeared over the centuries, the dangers it's been exposed to – but it's hard to imagine someone would be so determined to destroy it or steal it,' Lisa mused as the conversation began to wind down, her interest as an archaeologist sparked. 'It's been in the cathedral at Turin since the House of Savoy deposited it there. As I recall, the story is that the cardinal of Milan, Carlos Borromeo, promised to walk from Milan to Chambèry, where the shroud was at the time, to pray that the plague that lay on his city be lifted. The Savoys, who owned the shroud, were moved by his piety and decided to move it halfway, to Turin, to keep the cardinal from having to walk so far. And it's still there today. So think about it – obviously, if there've been so many accidents in the cathedral, and you don't believe they're unrelated, and you've got to admit that it can't have been the same individual who set the fire two weeks ago *and* over a hundred years ago, then –'

'Lisa, slow down,' John scolded her. 'Let Marco finish.'

'Yes, but what I can't figure out is what's behind it – I can't see any motive. It may just be some fanatic who wants to destroy the shroud.'

'A fanatic could have caused the accidents over the last ten, fifteen, twenty years, but a hundred years ago?' Ana took up the argument. 'It's a great story, though. I'd love to write it.'

'Ana! You're not here as a reporter!' Her brother glared at her across the table.

'It's okay, Santiago, it's okay. I'm sure we can count on Ana to keep this off the record and strictly confidential. Right, Ana?' Marco smiled at the journalist, but his meaning was clear. 'And, John, Lisa's gone to the heart of it. I'm asking you and Santiago to help me think about this, to find some plausible explanation for this mystery. I don't know whether my people and I are too close to this thing – I'd appreciate some outside eyes. I've prepared a report that details all the unexplained events that have happened in the cathedral or in relation to the shroud over the last hundred years. I know I'm presuming on our friendship and that you're both up to your ears in work, but it would be a great favor to me if you'd read it and let me know what you think.'

'I'll be glad to give you a hand,' the Spaniard said warmly. 'Plus, you know you're welcome to take a look at the Europol files on the shroud anytime you want.'

'Thanks, Santiago.'

'Of course I'll take a look, too, Marco, and give you my honest opinion. You know you can count on my help in anything you need, officially and unofficially,' promised John.

'I'd like to read it, too, if I could,' Santiago's sister interjected.

'Ana, you're not a cop, you don't have anything to do with this. Marco can't give you an official, confidential report.'

'I'm sorry, Ana – ' Marco began.

'Your loss, chief,' Ana interrupted. 'Let me give you a reporter's tip, though. My intuition tells me that if there *is* something, you've got to go at whatever it is from the history angle, not the police angle. But it's your case.'

As they walked to his car, Ana gave Santiago a playful hug. 'You know, big brother, I think I'll stick around a few days longer.'

'Ana, Marco is a friend of mine. Besides, I'd be in deep

shit professionally if anybody found out that my sister was publishing stories on police cases that she could know about only through me. It would ruin my career – it's that simple. I don't care how great the story is.'

'Oh, come on, don't be so melodramatic. I won't write a line, I promise.'

'You won't? You'll keep this all totally off the record?'

'I promise I will, take it easy. I respect my sources when they tell me something off the record – I wouldn't last long if I didn't.'

'I don't know why you decided to be a goddamn reporter!'

'Yeah, right, being a cop is a real step up!'

'Come on, I'll buy you a drink at the new "in" place, so you can tell your friends all about it when you get back to Barcelona.'

'All right, but I'm not taking it as a bribe, and I hope you'll let me in on what's in that report. I honestly think I could help, and I promise I'd do it without saying anything to anybody or writing a word of it. It's just that I love this kind of story. You know I do. There's something fascinating here. I can feel it.'

'Ana, I can't let you mess around in an investigation that belongs to the Art Crimes Department, not to me – I'd be in deep trouble, I told you.'

'But nobody would ever find out, I swear. Trust me. I'm sick of writing about politics, and sniffing out government scandals. I know I've been lucky and done well, but I still haven't come across the big story, and this could be it.'

'How can this be your big story if you're not going to say or write a word?'

'Look, I'll make you a deal. You let me investigate on my own, without saying anything to anybody. I'll tell you what I find out – if, that is, I find out anything. If in the end I come across a lead, or whatever, that helps Marco close the case, then I'll expect permission to let me tell the story, or at least part of it. But nothing before the case is closed.'

'No way.'

'Why not?'

'Which part don't you get? This thing doesn't belong to me, and I won't – can't – make deals, with you or anybody. Jesus, why did I ever take you to Marco's house with me?'

'Take it easy, Santiago. I love you and I'd never do anything to hurt you. I love what I do, but you come first. I never put my job before people, ever. Much less in your case.'

'I want to trust you, Ana, I do. I don't have a choice. But you're leaving tomorrow, back to Spain. You're out of here.'

15

ZAFARIN LET HIS EYES WANDER OVER THE HEAVILY trafficked highway. The truck driver taking him to Urfa seemed to be as mute as he was – he'd hardly spoken a word to him since they left Istanbul.

That morning at the house where he had been hidden overnight, Zafarin had recognized him as an Urfa man, one whom Addaio trusted.

He wished for news of Addaio, of his family, of his town, but the man just drove, in stubborn silence. During their journey he spoke only two or three times, to ask Zafarin if he was hungry or needed to go to the bathroom.

He looked tired after so many hours behind the wheel, so Zafarin made a gesture indicating that he could drive, but the truck driver refused.

'It is not far now, and I do not want problems. Addaio would not forgive me if I failed him. We have had enough failure recently.'

Zafarin clenched his teeth. A brother had died, he himself had risked his life, and this stupid man was rebuking him for having failed. What did he know of the danger he and his comrades had faced! Of the sacrifices they had made!

There were more and more cars and trucks on the road as they went on. The E-24 was one of Turkey's busiest highways, since it led into Iraq and the Iraqi oil fields. There were also many military trucks and cars patrolling the Syrian-Turkish border, watching especially for the Kurdish militias that operated in the area.

In less than an hour he would be home, and that was the only thing that mattered.

'Zafarin! Zafarin!'

His mother's voice, choked with emotion, was like the music of heaven. There she was, small and lean, her hair covered by a hijab, the ever-present head scarf worn by Near Eastern women. Despite her small stature, Zafarin's mother ruled the family – his father, his brothers and sisters, him, and of course his wife, Ayat, and his daughter. None of them dared go against her wishes.

Ayat's eyes were filled with tears. She had begged him not to go, not to accept the mission. Not to allow himself to be mutilated forever. But how could he refuse an order by Addaio and the most sacred calling of their community, a calling his brother had answered before him? His family's shame would have been unbearable.

He got down out of the truck and in a second felt Ayat's arms around his neck, while his mother also grappled to embrace him. His daughter, frightened, began to cry.

His father looked on with emotion, waiting for the women to stop pulling and pushing him with their shows of affection. At last the two men could embrace, and Zafarin, feeling the strength of his peasant father's arms around him, was overcome and began to weep, to weep as he had as a young boy in his father's arms, bearing the marks of some fight he'd had on the street or at school. His father had always given him that sense of security, the security that he could count on him, that whatever happened, he would be there to protect him. Zafarin knew he would need all his father's strength when they stood before Addaio.

16

THE LAWN AND GARDEN OF THE GEORGIAN-style mansion were awash with light. A breeze off the bay cooled the exclusive Boston neighborhood, as local police and Secret Service agents competed to guarantee the security of the guests at the dinner party. The President of the United States and his wife were among those invited, as were the Secretaries of Treasury and Defense, a number of influential senators and representatives from across the political spectrum, the CEOs of various American and European multinationals, a dozen or so bankers, and a sprinkling of doctors, scientists, white-shoe lawyers, and stars from the academic world.

The occasion for the gathering was Mary Stuart's fiftieth birthday, which her husband, James, had wanted to celebrate with all their friends. The truth was, thought Mary, there were more acquaintances than friends present that evening. She would never hurt James by telling him that she would have preferred that he surprise her with a trip to Italy, with no fixed itinerary, no social engagements. Just the two of them, wandering through Tuscany, as they had done on their honeymoon thirty years ago. But that would never have occurred to James. They were, in fact, traveling to Rome the week after next, but that was primarily for business, with a few days of tightly scheduled social and cultural engagements shoehorned in.

A tall man skillfully maneuvered his way toward her through the crowd. She smiled with genuine pleasure. 'Umberto!'

'Mary, my love, happy birthday.'

'I'm so glad to see you and honored that you came!'

'I'm the one who's honored to be invited. Here, something for you. I hope you like it.'

He held out a small box wrapped in shiny white paper.

'Oh, Umberto, you shouldn't have. . . . May I open it?'

'Of course. You must open it immediately,' he said, smiling.

Mary was transfixed by the figure that nestled within the tissue paper inside the box.

'It's a figure from the second century B.C. A lady as beautiful and charming as you.'

'Umberto, it's beautiful. Thank you, thank you so much. I'm overwhelmed.' Mary felt an arm slip around her waist as her husband joined them, and she held up the box for him to see. The two men shook hands warmly.

'What incredible surprise have you brought my wife this time, Umberto? Oh, how wonderful! But not fair – now my humble offering pales into insignificance!'

'James, stop this second. You know I adore these. He gave me this ring and these earrings, Umberto. They're the most perfect pearls I've ever seen.'

'They're the most perfect pearls there are, my dear. All right, go put this glorious lady somewhere safe while I get Umberto a drink.'

Steel-fabricating plants, pharmaceutical laboratories,

technology interests, and a vast range of other businesses made James Stuart, at sixty-two, one of the wealthiest and most influential men in the world. He and D'Alaqua continued to chat as they moved together back into the throng.

Ten minutes later, James Stuart had left Umberto D'Alaqua with the President and other guests while he himself went from group to group, making sure conversations, drinks, and hors d'oeuvres all continued to flow smoothly.

As the evening progressed and glittering groups drifted together and swirled apart, no one paid much attention to the seven men talking together off to one side, changing the subject whenever someone else approached, to the crisis in Iraq, the latest summit at Davos, any of the multitude of other issues that naturally would be of concern to such men. For the moment, though, they were undisturbed.

'Marco Valoni has asked the Minister of Culture to let the prisoner in Turin out of jail,' said one of the men in impeccable English, despite the fact that his native language was Italian. 'And the Minister of Culture has taken the matter to the Minister of the Interior, who has agreed to the idea. The idea came from one of Valoni's colleagues, Dottoressa Galloni, an art history expert, who finally came to the obvious conclusion that only he can lead them to anything worthwhile. She's also convinced Valoni that they should investigate COCSA, from top to bottom.'

'That's unfortunate. Is there any way to have her removed from the case?' a tall, thin man, the oldest among them, asked.

'We could always exert pressure. Or COCSA could protest to the Vatican and let the Church press the Italian government to keep hands off. Or we could act directly through the Minister of Finance, who is surely none too happy that one of the country's most important corporations is being dragged into this and put under a microscope, all because of a fire that had no major consequences. We've arranged to replace the damaged artworks with pieces of equal or greater significance. But in my opinion we should hold off on doing anything about the dottoressa just yet.'

The older man's eyes were fixed on the speaker. He had made his points impassively, but there was a subtle quality in his tone of voice that sharpened his senior's attention. He decided to press harder, to see the reaction.

'We could also make her simply disappear. We can't afford a talented investigator on this case digging too deep.'

Another in the group spoke up, his accent French-inflected.

'No, that seems unnecessary. An overreaction. We shouldn't do anything for the moment. Let her proceed. We can always head her off later or get rid of her one way or the other.'

'I agree,' seconded the Italian. 'It would be a mistake to move too fast or to interfere with her work – or her. That would just inflame Valoni and confirm that there *is* something more to be found, and that would mean that he and the rest of his team would never give up on the case, even if they were ordered to. Dottoressa Galloni *is* somewhat of a risk; she's intelligent, perhaps exceptionally so. But we have to run that risk. Let's not forget that we have a major advantage – we know exactly what they're doing and thinking.'

'Our informer is safe? No suspicions?'

'About one of the people that Valoni trusts the most? Certainly not.'

'Very well. What else do we have?' the older man asked, scanning the group.

A man who looked like an English aristocrat spoke next.

'Zafarin arrived in Urfa two days ago. I don't have any news yet about Addaio's reaction. Another of the group, Rasit, has arrived in Istanbul, and the third one, Dermisat, is supposed to arrive today.'

'Good, then they're all safe. Now the problem is Addaio's, not ours. We need to consider how to deal with the one in the Turin jail, though.'

'Something could happen to him before he gets out of prison. That would be the safest thing,' the Englishman suggested. 'If he gets out he'll lead them to Addaio.'

'It would be the most prudent thing, I agree,' said a second Frenchman.

'Could we do it?' the older man asked.

'Of course. We have connections inside the jail. But we'd have to arrange it carefully. If anything happens to his prize, Valoni will never accept the official report.'

'He can rage and turn blue, but he'll have to accept it. Without that angle, his case is finished, at least for the moment,' the older man retorted. 'But let's continue to observe. I don't want to give them anything else to grab hold of just now.'

'What about the shroud?' asked another of the men.

'It's still in the bank. When the repair work in the cathedral is completed, it will be returned to the chapel for exhibit. The cardinal wants to celebrate a thanksgiving Mass in honor of the shroud's being saved once again.'

'Gentlemen . . . hatching a deal over here, are we? Cornering the aluminum market?'

'No, Mr. President, but that's not a bad idea!'

They all laughed as the President of the United States, accompanied by James Stuart, joined them. The remainder of their discussion would have to wait.

'Mary, that man over there, who is he?' Lisa Barry had flown in for her sister's birthday the night before, along with Mary and James's daughter, Gina, who was staying with Lisa and John in Rome.

'One of our best friends, Umberto D'Alaqua. Don't you remember him?'

'Oh, yes, now that you mention his name I do. He's as impressive as ever, isn't he? *Nice*-looking.'

'Forget it. He's a confirmed bachelor. It's a shame, because he's not just gorgeous, he's an incredibly lovely man. Thoughtful and kind each time we see him.'

'I heard something about him not long ago . . . what was it . . . .' Lisa began.

Then it came to her. The report on the fire in the Turin Cathedral that Marco had sent John talked about a corporation, COCSA, and its owner, D'Alaqua. Umberto D'Alaqua. She stopped in mid-sentence. She couldn't say anything to Mary about that. John would never forgive her.

'He gave me a ceramic figure from the second century B.C. It's stunning – I'll show you later,' Mary promised. She linked her arm in Lisa's. 'Let me take you over.'

The two sisters approached D'Alaqua.

'Umberto, you remember my sister, Lisa.'

'Of course I do. So nice to see you.'

'It was so long ago, when Mary last visited. . . .'

'Yes, Mary – you don't come to Italy as often as you

should. Lisa, I think I remember that you live in Rome. Is that right?'

'Yes, it feels like home now. I'm not sure I could live anywhere else.'

'Gina is in Rome with Lisa, Umberto, working on her doctorate at the university. And she'll be joining Lisa's group at the excavation in Herculaneum.'

'Ah! Now I remember – you're an archaeologist!' D'Alaqua's enthusiasm was obvious.

Mary answered for her. 'Yes, and Gina has inherited her aunt's passion for digging in the sand.'

'I can't imagine a more exciting job than studying the past.' Lisa smiled. 'And Umberto, I think I remember that you're no stranger to archaeology.'

'Absolutely. I try to escape to work a dig myself at least once or twice a year.'

'Umberto's foundation finances excavations,' Mary added.

As they launched into an animated conversation about their mutual fascination with the past, James came up and, to Lisa's dismay, took D'Alaqua off to another group. She could have talked to him all night. John wouldn't believe her when she told him she'd been chatting with this man who'd turned up in Marco Valoni's report. Even Marco would be surprised. She laughed to herself, thinking what a good idea it had been to accept James's invitation to surprise her sister on her birthday. She'd have to put a dinner party together for the Stuarts when they came to Rome, she thought. She'd mention it to her niece; the two of them would make a list of people to invite. Lisa had several names in mind already.

17

The young servant wept in fear and horror. Marcius's face and chin were spattered with blood. The other servant had run to Josar's house to tell him of the tragedy in the residence of the royal architect.

'Then we heard a terrible cry, a shriek, and when we entered the chamber we saw Marcius with a sharp dagger in one hand, with which he had cut out his own tongue. He has fallen senseless to the ground, and we know not what to do. He had told us that something would take place tonight and ordered that we not be frightened, no matter what we might see. But my God, he has cut out his own tongue! Why? Why?!'

Josar and Thaddeus were not surprised at the servant's story. They tried to calm the boy as they made their way with him to the house of Marcius, and there they found their friend still unconscious, the bedclothes stained crimson with blood, while his servant cowered in a corner, weeping and praying and waving his arms in fear and terror.

'Calm yourself!' Josar ordered the other youth. 'The physician will be here at once, and he will help him. But tonight, my friends, you must be strong. You must not be daunted either by fear or compassion, for if you are, the life of Marcius could be in grave danger.'

The young servants began to grow calmer. When the physician arrived, he sent everyone out of the chamber and remained there alone with his assistant. They were long in coming out.

'He is resting quietly. For a few days, I want him to remain undisturbed; these drops, mixed in the water you give him to drink, will make him sleep and ease the pain until the wound has healed.'

'We wish to ask you a favor,' Thaddeus said to the physician. 'We, too, wish to cut out our tongues.'

The physician, a Christian like them, looked at them in distress.

'Our Lord would not look kindly upon these mutilations.'

'We must do this,' Josar explained, 'for it is only in this way that Maanu will be unable to make us speak. He will torture us to learn where the shroud that was the grave cloth of Jesus has been hidden. We do not know, but we might say something that would endanger those who do. We do not wish to flee the city; we must remain here with our brothers and sisters, because surely all Christians will suffer the wrath of Maanu.'

'Please,' Thaddeus pleaded, 'help us. We are not as brave as Marcius, who cut out his tongue with his own knife.'

'What you ask me is contrary to the laws of God. My duty is to help heal; I cannot mutilate any man.'

'Then we shall do it ourselves,' said Josar.

The resolute tone of Josar's voice convinced the physician.

They went first to the house of Thaddeus, and there the healer mixed the contents of a small vial with water. When Thaddeus had fallen into a deep slumber, the physician asked Josar to leave the chamber and go to his own house. He would follow him there soon.

Josar impatiently awaited the arrival of the physician, who after a short time entered with a gesture of contrition.

'Lie on the bed and drink this,' he told Josar. 'It will make you sleep. When you awake you will have no tongue. May God forgive me.'

'He has already forgiven you, my friend.'

✝ The queen had made her ablutions and carefully arranged her hair and tunic. The news of the death of Abgar had reached the farthest corner of the palace, and she expected her son, Maanu, to appear at the door of the royal chambers at any moment.

The servants, with the aid of the physicians, had prepared Abgar's body for viewing by the citizens of Edessa. The king had asked that prayers be said for the repose of his soul before his body was placed in the royal mausoleum.

The queen did not know whether Maanu would allow her to bury Abgar in accordance with the laws of Jesus, but she was prepared to fight that last battle for the man she loved.

During the hours that she sat alone with the body of Abgar, the queen looked deep within her heart for the reason her son might hate her so. And she found the answer; indeed, she had always known it, though until that morning she had never faced it. She had not been a good mother. No, she had not. Her love for Abgar excluded all others; she had not allowed anything or anyone, even her

125

children, to keep her from the side of the king. In addition to Maanu, she had brought four other children into the world: three daughters and a son, who died soon after he was born. Her daughters had held little interest for her; they were quiet children who were soon married off in order to strengthen alliances with other kingdoms. She had hardly felt it when they were gone, so intense was her love for the king.

That devotion was also why she had suffered in silence the pain of Abgar's love for Ania, the dancing girl who had infected him with her fatal illness. The queen let not a word of reproach pass her lips, so that nothing might cloud her relationship with the king.

During her life she had had no time for Maanu, so all-absorbing was her love for Abgar. And now she was going to die, because she was certain that Maanu would not allow her to live. She was sorry for the manner in which she had failed her son, for not having been a true mother to him. How selfish she had been! Would Jesus forgive her?

The powerful voice of Maanu reached the royal chamber before the prince himself did.

'I want to see my father!'

'He is dead.'

Maanu glared at her defiantly.

'Then I am the king of Edessa.'

'You are, and all shall recognize you as such.'

'Marvuz! Take the queen away!'

'No, my son, not yet. My life is in your hands, but first we must bury Abgar like the king he was. Allow me to carry out his last instructions, which the royal scribe will confirm for you.'

Ticius approached warily, bearing a roll of parchment.

'My king, Abgar dictated to me his last wishes.'

Marvuz whispered something in Maanu's ear. Maanu looked all around the chamber, and he saw that the head of the royal guard was right: In addition to the servants, the apartment was filled with scribes, physicians, guards, and courtiers, all watching expectantly. He could not allow himself to be guided by hatred, at least not obviously, or he would frighten those who would be his subjects. Far from gaining their cooperation and consent, he would find they conspired against him. He realized that the queen had won yet again. He wanted to kill her on the spot, and with his own hands, but he had to wait, had to agree to bury his father with all the pomp and respect accorded a king.

'Read, Ticius,' he ordered.

Slowly, and with trembling voice, the scribe read Abgar's last instructions. Maanu, flushed with rage, swallowed hard.

Abgar had instructed that a Christian religious rite be celebrated over him, and that his entire court pray for his soul. At this ritual, Maanu was to be present and accompanied by the queen. For three days and three nights his body was to lie in that first temple that he had ordered Josar to build. After three days, a procession led by Maanu and the queen was to accompany his body to the royal mausoleum.

Ticius cleared his throat and looked first at the queen and then at Maanu. From the folds of his sleeve he produced a second scroll.

'If I may, my lord, I shall also read what Abgar has asked that you do as king.'

A murmur of surprise ran through the chamber. Maanu gritted his teeth, certain that his father, even in death, had laid a trap for him.

The scribe began to read:

I, Abgar, king of Edessa, order my son, Maanu, now
become king, to respect the Christian citizens of this city
and to allow them to continue their worship of the Lord
Jesus. I hold him responsible, likewise, for the safety of his
mother, the queen, whose life is dear to me. The queen
may choose her place of residence. She shall be treated
with the respect and deference due her rank and shall
want for nothing.

You, my son, shall be the guarantor of all these things
I order. Should you not carry out my final orders, God
shall punish you, and you shall not find peace in life or in
the death thereafter.

All eyes fell upon the new king. Maanu shook with impotent rage, and it was Marvuz who took charge of the situation.

'We shall bid farewell to Abgar as he has desired. Now let each of us return to our duties.'

Slowly, all those who had been in the royal chambers began to file out into the corridor. The queen, pale and quiet, awaited her son's decision on her fate.

Maanu waited until the chamber was empty, and then he addressed his mother: 'You will not leave this room until I call for you. You will speak to no one inside or outside the palace. Two servants will remain with you. We will bury my father as he has requested. And you, Marvuz, shall see that my orders are followed.'

Maanu strode quickly from the chamber. The head of the royal guard turned to the queen.

'My lady, it will be best that you obey the orders of the king.'

'I shall, Marvuz.'

The queen's eyes met his with such intensity that the

head of the guard lowered his eyes in shame; then, bowing quickly, he left her alone.

The instructions Maanu then imparted to Marvuz were clear: He would bury Abgar as the old king had desired, and an instant after the royal mausoleum was sealed, the royal guard would arrest the leaders of the Christians, the hated Josar and Thaddeus. They would destroy all the temples in which the Christians met to pray. Maanu had also personally charged Marvuz with finding and bringing to the palace the sacred shroud of Jesus.

The queen was not allowed to leave her chamber until the third day after the death of Abgar. The king's body lay until that time on a richly ornamented bier placed in the center of the first temple that Abgar had ordered built in honor of Jesus.

The royal guard watched over the body of the man who had been their king, and the citizens of Edessa filed by to pay homage to the man who for so many decades had secured peace and prosperity for their city.

'My lady, are you ready?'

Marvuz had come for the queen; he was to accompany her to the temple. There, with Maanu, she would lead the procession to the mausoleum where Abgar would rest for all eternity.

The queen had put on her finest tunic and richest veil, and she had adorned herself with the best of her jewels. She looked majestic despite the lines of age and the signs of suffering on her face. By the time they reached the small Christian temple, it was filled with people. The entire court and the principal elders of Edessa were there. The queen looked about for Marcius, and for Josar and Thaddeus, whom Maanu had summoned, but did not see them. She felt uneasy. Where were her friends?

Maanu, wearing Abgar's crown, was in obvious high temper at the open defiance of his orders and his guard's inability to secure the shroud of Jesus, which was no longer in the place where for so many years it had been kept.

A young disciple of Thaddeus began the ceremony of farewell with a prayer. As the funeral procession was about to depart for the mausoleum, Marvuz was able to approach King Maanu.

'My lord, we have searched the houses of the leaders of the Christians, but we have not found the shroud. Nor is there any sign of Thaddeus and Josar.'

Then the head of the royal guard fell silent. There, before him, pushing their way through the crowd, came Thaddeus and Josar, pale as death. The queen opened her arms and, fighting back tears, took each of them by the hand. Josar looked at her tenderly but spoke not a word. Thaddeus, too, was silent.

Maanu gave the order for the procession to begin. He would settle accounts with the Christians later.

A silent multitude accompanied the body to the mausoleum. There, before the entrance could be sealed, the queen requested a few moments to pray.

When the tomb was finally sealed with its stone door, Maanu made a gesture to Marvuz, and Marvuz signaled the guard, who rushed forward to arrest Josar and Thaddeus, in the full sight of all those present. A murmur of terror ran through the multitude as the people realized that Maanu would not obey the will of Abgar, that he was determined to persecute the Christians.

Some tried to flee, whispering that they would leave Edessa that very night.

But there was no time even to try. At that instant the

royal guard was destroying their houses, and many believers were slain on the spot.

Horror was on the face of the queen as Marvuz dragged her away, back to the palace. She saw Thaddeus and Josar seized. Neither man offered any resistance or uttered the slightest sound.

✝ Edessa trembled with fear and anguish. All about the city, men and women howled in pain and desolation. The smell of fire rose to the top of the hill on which the palace stood, while Maanu, in the throne room, drank wine and observed with smug satisfaction the terror on the faces of his courtiers.

Maanu had ordered the queen to remain standing. Nearby, Josar and Thaddeus, their hands tied behind their backs and their tunics tattered by the lashes dealt them by the royal guard, still had not spoken a word.

'Ten lashes more! I will have them beg me to end their torment.'

The guards furiously lashed the old men, but to the wonderment of the court and the wrath of the king, they uttered not a sound.

The queen cried out when Thaddeus fainted, while tears flowed down the face of Josar, whose back was covered in flayed skin and blood. Then he, too, sank senseless to the floor.

'Enough! Stop this!' she demanded.

'How dare you give orders!' Maanu shouted.

'You are a coward – torturing two old men is not worthy of a king!'

With the back of his hand Maanu slapped his mother. The queen staggered and fell to the floor. Cries of horror rose from the throats of the courtiers.

'They will die here, before you all, if they do not tell me where they have hidden the shroud, and their accomplices will die as well – all of them! No matter who they may be!'

Two guards entered with Marcius, the royal architect, followed by his frightened young servants.

'Has he told you where the shroud is?' Maanu snapped at the guards.

'No, my king.'

'Then whip him until he talks!'

'We can whip him, my lord, but he will not speak. His servants have told us that he has done a terrible thing: Several days ago he cut out his tongue.'

The queen looked at Marcius, and then she looked at the unconscious bodies of Thaddeus and Josar. She realized what they had done. In order to keep the secret of the Holy Shroud, they had made this terrible sacrifice so that they would not falter under the torture they would surely suffer.

She began to weep in grief for her friends, knowing that her son would make them pay dearly for this affront to his will and power.

Maanu's entire body trembled with rage, and his face was red with wrath. Marvuz approached him, fearing what he would do next.

'My lord, we will find someone who knows where the shroud has been hidden. We will search everywhere in Edessa, and we will find it –'

The king was not listening. Turning to his mother, he pulled her up from the ground and shook her as he screamed at her: 'Tell me where it is! Tell me, or I will cut out *your* tongue!'

The queen sobbed, her body racked by convulsions. Some of the nobles of the court stepped forward to intervene, seized with shame by their own cowardice, for they had stood by as Maanu struck his mother. If Abgar had seen such an action, he would have had him killed!

'My lord, release her!' begged one.

'My king, calm yourself; do not strike your own mother!' another pleaded.

'You are the king and should show mercy!' counseled a third.

Marvuz seized the king's arm as he was about to strike his mother again.

'My lord!'

Maanu dropped his arm and leaned on Marvuz, exhausted. His mother and the two miserable old men had defeated him. His wrath was spent.

His hands tied, Marcius contemplated the scene. He prayed to God to be merciful, to take pity on them all. He thought about Jesus' agony on the cross, the torture inflicted on him by the Romans, yet how he had forgiven them. Marcius sought deep within himself to forgive Maanu, but he felt only hatred for the arrogant new king.

The head of the royal guard ordered the queen taken to her chambers. He then drew the king to a chair and set a goblet of wine before him. Maanu drank greedily.

'They must die,' he said, in almost a whisper.

'Yes,' Marvuz replied. 'And they shall.' He made a sign to the soldiers, and they dragged Thaddeus and Josar out of the room.

The king raised his head and glared at Marcius.

'All you Christian dogs shall die. Your houses, your estates, everything you possess, I shall distribute among those who are loyal to me. You, Marcius, have betrayed me doubly. You are one of the great leaders of Edessa, yet you have sold your heart to these Christians who have so bewitched you that you have defiled and mutilated yourself. But I will find the shroud, Marcius, and I will destroy it. That, I swear to you.'

At a sign from Marvuz, a soldier took the architect away.

'The king will rest now,' Marvuz announced to the courtiers, motioning them out of the room. 'It has been a long and trying day.'

When the two men were alone, Maanu embraced his accomplice and broke into tears. His mother had embittered the taste of vengeance.

'I want my mother to die.'

'She will die, my lord, but in good time. You must wait. First we will search for the shroud and gather and kill the Christians, all of them. Then the queen's turn will come.'

Cries of agony and horror and the roaring, crackling sound of fire from the city below echoed in every corner of the palace throughout the long hours of the night.

18

ANA JIMÉNEZ COULDN'T STOP THINKING ABOUT the fire in the Turin Cathedral. She spoke to her brother every week, and each time she called she asked about Marco's investigation. Santiago invariably fumed at her and refused to indulge her curiosity. He sounded close to hanging up on her as they spoke now.

'You know you're obsessed, but it doesn't matter. Ana, for God's sake, forget about it, will you?'

'But I can help you, Santiago. I know it.'

'I keep telling you it's not my case. It belongs to the Art Crimes Department. Marco wanted my opinion and I gave it to him. So did John. That's it. The end.'

'Jesus, Santiago, give me a break. Give me one little peek at the file – I know how to chase down a story. I can see things that cops don't even look for.'

'Ah, yes – you reporters are God's gift to investigations and can do our job ten times better than we can.'

'Don't be so damn touchy. You know I'm not saying that.'

'What I know is that you're not going to start poking around in Marco's investigation.'

135

'At least tell me what *you* think.'

'I think things are usually simpler than they appear to be.'

'That's not an answer.'

'Well, it's all you're going to get.' And with that he hung up.

Ana slammed the phone down on her end, too, just to make herself feel better. She looked at the pile of papers lying on her desk, alongside more than a dozen books, all on the Shroud of Turin. She had been reading about the shroud for days. Esoteric treatises, religious books, histories . . . .She *knew* the key lay somewhere in the object's long history. Marco Valoni had said as much: There had been nothing remarkable about the Turin Cathedral until the shroud was installed there. The incidents weren't new – and therefore neither was the motive for them. She was sure of it.

The hell with Santiago. She made a decision: Once she'd gone as deep as she could into the history of the shroud and traced it back as far as was possible, she'd put in for some vacation time and go to Turin. It was a city she'd never particularly liked; she'd never have chosen it as a holiday destination, but that's where the story was – a story she was more determined than ever to write.

Marco had called the meeting for immediately after lunch. It hadn't been easy to convince the necessary ministers, but he had at last been given full clearance to mount the Trojan horse operation his way, with no interference and with additional resources at his command. They were authorized to turn the mute loose and trail him to Timbuktu if he took them there. Now he wanted to brief the team on the details.

Sofia was the last to arrive. Marco couldn't put his finger on it, but he had found her different somehow on her return to Rome from Turin. As stunning as always, but changed in some subtle way.

'Okay, the plan is simple,' he began. 'You all know that every month the parole board makes the rounds to all the various prisons and jails. On the board there's a judge and a state attorney, psychologists and social workers, and the warden of each installation. They visit all the prisoners, especially those who are approaching the end of their sentences, have demonstrated good behavior, and may have earned some consideration for early out. Tomorrow I'll be in Turin to meet with the board members. I'm going to ask them to mount a little charade.'

Everyone listened attentively as he continued.

'I want them to help us gauge the mute's reactions if possible and to also start acclimatizing him to the idea of release. When they're in Turin next, they'll visit him and talk about him among themselves, the way they always have, thinking he doesn't understand them. Only this time I'll ask the social worker and the psychologist to let it drop that they don't see much sense in keeping him behind bars any longer – his behavior has been exemplary, he poses no threat to society, and, according to the law, he's eligible for parole. The warden will make some objection, and they'll leave. We'll have variations on that played out over the next couple of months, until they finally let him loose.'

'Will they cooperate?' Pietro asked.

'The ministers are relaying instructions to the relevant department heads. I don't think anyone will object; when it comes right down to it, they're not turning loose some murderer or terrorist, just a nickel-and-dime thief.'

'It's a good plan,' Minerva said.

'Absolutely,' seconded Giuseppe.

'I've got more. Sofia, you'll like this. Lisa, John Barry's wife, called me. Lisa's sister is a woman named Mary Stuart – who just happens to be married to James Stuart. And James Stuart, in case you didn't know, is one of the wealthiest men in the world. Friend of the President of the United States and heads of state of half the countries in the world – the rich countries, that is – chairmen and CEOs of major international corporations, and most of the bankers on the planet. The Stuarts' daughter, Gina, is an archaeologist, like Lisa, and is spending some time in Rome, in her aunt's house; she's also working on the financing for the excavation at Herculaneum. So here's the deal: Mary and James Stuart are coming to Rome in two weeks. Lisa is going to throw a dinner party for them, with a lot of their prominent Italian friends in attendance. And among those friends is *your* friend Umberto D'Alaqua.' Marco nodded at Sofia. 'Paola and I are going, and I'm hoping that John and Mary will kindly let me take you, too, Dottoressa Galloni.'

Sofia's face lit up, her pleasure obvious. 'That's one way to get us closer to this guy,' she said wryly. 'Probably the only way.'

After the meeting, she and Marco chatted for a few minutes.

'I remember Lisa, of course,' she said to him. 'I wouldn't have thought that a woman like her would have a sister married to a business mogul.'

'It's not really that much of a stretch. Their father was a medieval-history professor at Oxford, and they both followed pretty much in his footsteps. Mary studied medieval history just like him; Lisa went into archaeology. Lisa got a fellowship to do her PhD in Italy, and while they remained close, Mary's life took another direction. She went to work at Sotheby's as an expert in medieval art and began to mix with a more rarefied set of people, among them her future husband, James Stuart. They met, fell in love, and got married, and while they lead very different lives than Lisa and John, they apparently are genuinely happy, from what Lisa has to say. Mary prefers high society; Lisa worked hard to make a name for herself in academia. Her sister supports her, as she does her daughter, Gina, by underwriting excavations from time to time.'

'Well, we're lucky that you're friends with John.'

'Yes, they're both really wonderful people. John is the only American I know with zero interest in making tons of money, and they both really love it here. He resists being transferred anywhere else, and I imagine the Stuarts' influence can't hurt with the embassy.'

'You think they'll let you take me to the party?'

'I'm going to ask. D'Alaqua made an impression on you, didn't he?'

'I have to say he did, Marco. Of course, he's one of those larger-than-life personalities that any woman could fall in love with.'

'Which is not, I hope, your case.'

'No? Why not?'

'Sofia, for heaven's sake, you can't get mixed up with somebody we're investigating, and you shouldn't get mixed up with *this* guy at all – rich, never married, clearly not looking for the woman of his life. . . .'

'Marco, please. I hope you know my feet are planted firmly on the ground, and there's not a thing – or man – in the world that could change that. Nor is D'Alaqua exactly in my league, for that matter. So not to worry.'

'I'm going to ask you a personal question. If it makes

you uncomfortable, you can tell me to screw myself. What's going on with Pietro?'

'You don't have to go screw yourself, boss. I'll tell you the truth: It's over. It was going nowhere.'

'How does he feel about it?'

'We're having dinner tonight, to talk. But he's not stupid – he knows. I think he feels the same way, honestly.'

'I'm glad.'

'Glad? How come?'

'Because Pietro's not the right one for you. He's a nice guy, with a great wife who'll be immensely happy to get her husband back. And you, Sofia, one of these days ought to get out of here and start a new career, with other people, other ways of looking at the world. Frankly, the Art Crimes Department is small potatoes for you.'

'Marco! Don't say that! Are you trying to tell me something? Don't you know how happy I am here? I don't want to leave; I don't want to change a thing!'

'You know I'm right. But put it on a back burner if it's too much to think about right now. I'm happy to have you as long as you want to stay.'

'Your house?' Pietro asked Sofia as they left work later that day.

'No, let's go to a restaurant.'

Pietro took her to a small tavern in Trastevere, the same place they'd gone the first time, when their relationship began. It had been a long while since they'd been back. They ordered dinner and talked about small things, putting off the moment when they had to face each other.

Finally, over coffee, Sofia put her hand on his. 'Pietro –'

'It's okay. I know what you're going to tell me, and I agree.'

'You know?'

'Anyone would. In some things you're an open book.'

'Pietro, I care about you, but I'm not in love with you, and I don't want a commitment. I'd like us to be friends and to work together the way we have so far, with no awkwardness or hard feelings.'

'Sofia, I love you. Only an idiot wouldn't be in love with you, but I'm well aware that we're from different sides of the tracks –'

Sofia, uncomfortable, made a gesture to stop him. 'Don't say that. That's ridiculous.'

'I'm a cop. I look like a cop and I act like a cop. You're a university girl, a woman with class, whether you're in jeans or Armani. I've been lucky to be with you, but I've always known that someday you'd be out the door, and that day has come. D'Alaqua?'

'Where did *that* come from? He couldn't have been less interested. No, Pietro, this isn't about someone else. It's just that we took what was between us as far as it could go. We've come to an end. You love your wife, and I understand that. She's a great person, and beautiful to boot. You'll never divorce her; you couldn't bear to live without your kids.'

'Sofia, if you'd given me an ultimatum I would have left her.'

They sat in silence. Sofia struggled to hold back tears. She'd made up her mind to break it off with him and not let herself be swayed by any emotion that put off the decision she should have made months ago. 'I think it's best for us both,' she finally said. 'Can we be friends?'

'I don't know,' he answered after a moment.

'Why not?'

'Because I don't know. I honestly don't know how I'll

141

feel when I see you and can't be with you, or when you come in one day and announce there's another man in your life. It's easy to say we'll be friends, but I don't want to lie to you – I don't know if I'll be able to. And if I can't, I'll leave before I start hating you.'

Sofia was moved by Pietro's candor. His eyes were filled with tears. She had never dreamed that he cared so much. Or maybe it was just injured pride. Marco was so right – it was deadly to mix work and private life. But what was done was done. Now they had to get past it.

'No, I'll go,' she told him. 'I just want to see our work on the shroud through to the end. Then I'll ask for a transfer, or a leave.'

'No, that wouldn't be fair. I know that you'll be able to treat me as a friend, just one of the guys. I'm the problem, not you – I know myself. I'll ask for the transfer.'

'No, Pietro. You like Art Crimes, it's been a move up for you, and you're not going to lose it because of me. Marco says I should be looking for something new, and the truth is, I feel like taking on other things – teaching at the university, doing archaeology, maybe even opening an art gallery. I feel like one phase of my life is ending and another one is beginning to open up. Marco has seen that, and he's been encouraging me to find something else – and deep down I know he's right. I just want to ask you one favor: Do everything you can to stick it out for a few more months, until we wrap up this investigation. Please, let's make these months as good as they can be.'

19

I zaz and Obodas devoured the cheese and figs that
Timaeus had set before them. They were weary from
the long days of travel, which had been shadowed by the
constant fear of capture by the soldiers of Maanu.

But now they were here, in Sidon, at the house of
Timaeus. Harran, the leader of the caravan, had promised
them he would send a messenger to Senin in Edessa, to
report that their journey had ended safely.

Timaeus's gaze was penetrating, despite his advanced
years. He had greeted them warmly and insisted that they
rest before they recounted the incidents of their journey,
knowing they were weary in body and soul. He had been
expecting them for months, ever since he had received a
letter from Thaddeus telling him of his concern over
Abgar's health and explaining the difficult situation the
Christians would face when the king died, despite the
queen's support for them. The queen herself had sent
messages as well.

He had arranged that Izaz and Obodas would stay with
him in his home, sharing a small room, the only one he
had besides his own. His was a modest residence, in

keeping with a follower of the true teachings of the Christ.

As they ate, Timaeus told his guests about Sidon's small community of Christians. The group met every evening at dusk to pray and share the news; there was always some traveler who brought word of Jerusalem, or a family member who sent letters from Rome.

Izaz listened to the old fellow attentively, and when he and Obodas had finished their meal, he asked to speak with Timaeus alone.

Obodas frowned. Senin's instructions had been clear: He was not to let Josar's nephew out of his sight, and he was to defend him with his own life.

Old Timaeus, seeing the cloud of uncertainty in the giant's eyes, spoke to him soothingly. 'Be not troubled, Obodas. We have spies always watching, and we will know if Maanu's men should reach Sidon. Rest while I speak with Izaz. We will be just outside, and you will be able to see us from the window of the room you are to sleep in.'

Obodas dared not contradict the old man, but when he reached his chamber he sat beside the little window, where he could observe Izaz every moment. He watched as the young man spoke softly with Timaeus. His words were lost on the soft morning breeze, but Obodas could see a multitude of emotions cross the old man's face. Amazement, grief, concern – these and other emotions came as he listened to Izaz's story.

When Izaz finished speaking, Timaeus embraced him warmly and blessed him with the sign of the cross, in memory of Jesus. Then they came back into the house, where Izaz and Obodas would rest until that evening, when they would join the small community of Christians in Sidon, their new home. They knew that they would never be able to return to the land of their forebears.

When the two had drifted off to sleep, Timaeus entered the small temple next to the house. There, he knelt and prayed to Jesus, asking the Lord to help him know what to do with the secret that Izaz had confided to him and for which Josar, Thaddeus, Marcius, and other Christians had by now almost certainly been martyred.

Only he and Izaz now knew where the shroud of Jesus was hidden. Timaeus trembled to think that a secret of such magnitude lay with them alone. At some moment he in turn would confide the secret to another man, because he was old and would soon die. Izaz was young, but what would happen when he, too, became an old man? Maanu, of course, might well die before them, so that Christians could return to Edessa, but what if he did not? They must ensure that the secret of the place where Marcius had hidden the shroud was preserved until it could be reclaimed. Neither he nor Izaz could carry the secret to the tomb.

Hours passed without Timaeus's noticing. There, on his knees praying, Izaz and Obodas found him at sunset. By that point, the old man had made a decision.

Timaeus rose to his feet slowly. His knees were stiff and painful. He smiled at his guests and asked them to accompany him to the house of his grandson, which was just across a small garden from his own home.

'John! John!' the old man called outside a whitewashed house shaded from the sun by a grapevine. A young woman with a child in her arms emerged. 'He has not yet returned, Grandfather. He will not be long; he always returns for the hour of prayer.'

'This is Alaida, my grandson's wife. And this is her daughter, Myriam.'

Alaida invited the strangers inside. 'Come in. There is cool water with honey.'

'No, my daughter, not now; our brothers and sisters will be arriving to pray to our Lord. I wanted only for you and John to meet these two young men, who will live with me now.'

The three men made their way to the community's temple, where there was already a group of families talking amicably among themselves – country people and small artisans who had converted to faith in Jesus. Timaeus introduced them, one by one, to Izaz and Obodas and then asked the two young men to recount their flight from Edessa.

Timidly at first, Izaz began to relate the news of Edessa and to reply to the questions asked him by members of the community. When he finished speaking, Timaeus invited the group to pray to Jesus to help their brothers and sisters in Edessa. And so they all prayed and sang and shared among themselves the bread and wine that Alaida had brought.

John's skin was dark olive and his beard was black, as black as his hair; he was neither tall nor short. He had arrived late, in the company of Harran and several men from the caravan, bearing heavy sacks. Timaeus instructed them to bring them to his house.

'My lord Senin,' Harran said to them there, 'wishes to present you with these gifts, which will aid you in your support of Izaz, Josar's nephew, and his guardian, Obodas. He also bids me give you this bag of gold, which will be useful to you in times of hardship.'

Izaz looked on in astonishment at the presentation of so many things. Senin was very, very generous; before Izaz had left Edessa Senin had given him, too, a bag of gold, enough to live comfortably for the rest of his life.

'Thank you, Harran, my good friend,' Timaeus said, his

voice filled with emotion as he grasped the caravan leader's hands. 'I pray that you return to find Senin as you left him and that the wrath of Maanu has not fallen upon him. Tell your lord that these presents, like those you brought me from the queen several months ago, shall be dedicated to help the poor, as Jesus taught us, and to secure the well-being of our small community. Since you will not be leaving Sidon to return to Edessa for several more days, I will have time to write Senin myself.'

✝ Nightmares plagued Izaz's sleep. In his dream, he saw faces consumed by fire, a field running with blood. When he awoke, just at dawn, he was covered with sweat, the sweat of fear.

He stepped outside the house to the water basin next to the garden, and he found Timaeus there, cutting back a lemon tree. Timaeus bade him go for a walk with him, down to the seaside, to enjoy the coolness of the morning.

'Will Obodas not be alarmed when he awakes?'

'I will ask John to watch, so that when your guardian awakes he can tell him where we have gone.'

After he had given the instructions to his grandson, who had already risen and was preparing to work in the garden he shared with his grandfather, Timaeus led Izaz down to the water.

The Mare Nostrum, as the Romans called it, was angry that morning. Waves beat against the pebbles of the shoreline and washed the sand from the beach. It was the first time Izaz had seen that immensity of water, which seemed to him a miracle, and he watched its turmoil in awe. There, on the shore of that ancient sea, Timaeus told Josar's nephew of the plan he had devised.

'Izaz, it is God's will that you and I be repositories of a

great secret – the place where the shroud of His Son, who has performed so many miracles, is hidden. The place to which Marcius entrusted it should remain a secret with us for as long as needed, never to be revealed before Edessa is once again Christian and we are certain that the shroud is in no danger. You and I may never see that day, so when I die you must choose a man to keep the secret and transmit it in his turn to another, and so on until no cloud darkens the presence of Christians in Edessa. If Senin survives, he will send us word from time to time of all that is happening in the kingdom. But in any case, I shall keep the promise I made to Thaddeus, your uncle Josar, and the queen when they sent me missives explaining what the future would hold when Abgar died. They bade me, come what might, to see that the seeds planted by the Christ not die in Edessa and that, should the worst come to pass, after some years to send Christians once more to the city.'

'But that would be to send them to their deaths.'

'Those who go will do so without revealing their beliefs. They will take up residence in the kingdom, work there, and try to seek out any Christians who still remain, in order to rebuild the community, in secret. They will seek not to provoke Maanu's wrath or unleash a persecution, but rather act in such a way that the seeds of Jesus' teachings may take root and grow again among the people there. That was the Lord's wish when he sent Josar with the shroud to Abgar. Jesus sanctified that land with his presence and his miracles, and we must obey the wishes of our Lord in this matter, regardless of the price we and those who follow us must pay or how long it might take.

'We will wait for Harran to return with a caravan, and then we will be able to decide what to do and when. But whatever happens, or has happened, the shroud of Jesus must never leave Edessa, and we must do all in our power to ensure that belief in Jesus never falters in the city. We will dedicate our lives to fulfilling these promises, made in the name of those who have sacrificed all for our faith.'

20

ZAFARIN TREMBLED. ONLY THE PRESENCE OF HIS father kept him from turning and fleeing. His mother was holding his arm, and his wife, Ayat, with their little daughter, walked at his side without a word – they were as frightened as he was. A thin, frail-looking little man, modestly dressed, had opened the door and greeted them quietly.

Now he led the women into another room. 'Wait here,' he told them, closing the door behind him as he turned back to Zafarin and his father. He led them through the foyer to the threshold of a richly carved double door, opened it, and ushered them inside. Shelves lined the walls of the room, overflowing with books and other objects that were impossible to discern in the flickering candlelight. Heavy curtains over the windows blocked every ray of sun, maintaining the effect of a perpetual twilight in which the shadows seemed alive.

The man at the head of the immense, elaborately carved wooden table should have been dwarfed by the enormous chair in which he sat, but it only made his imposing figure more intimidating. There was not a hair on his head, but the wrinkles around his eyes and mouth left no doubt as to his age, which was also apparent in his bony, large-knuckled hands, which were clasped before him on the table, veins seeming to pulse through almost transparent skin.

Along each side of the table were four high-backed chairs. Sitting in them were eight men, dressed in severe black. Their eyes remained lowered as Zafarin and his father entered the room.

'You failed.'

Addaio's voice echoed through the oppressive chamber. Zafarin lowered his head, unable to hide the shame and terror that lay deep within his soul. His father took a step forward and fearlessly met the pastor's eyes.

'I have given you two sons. Both Zafarin and his brother Mendib before him have been selfless and brave; they have sacrificed for you; each has given his body, his voice, his future. Mendib languishes in a foreign prison. They will not speak until the Day of Judgment, when God raises them from the dead again. Our family does not deserve your recriminations. For centuries, the best of us have dedicated our lives to Jesus Christ and to this community. We are human, Addaio, only human, and we fail. Zafarin is intelligent, and you know it. You yourself insisted that he, like Mendib, go to the university. My son believes that there is a traitor among us, someone who has access to your plans even as you are plotting them out and knows each move we intend to make before we even begin.

'The failure is here, Addaio, inside, and you must find the traitor who lives among us. Betrayal has lived in our community down through time. That is the only way to explain the fact that so far every attempt to rescue what is ours has failed.'

Addaio listened without moving a muscle, but his eyes filled with fury.

Zafarin's father stepped forward, up to the table, and placed a sheaf of more than fifty pages, covered front and back with handwriting, on its polished surface.

'This is the report my son has prepared on what happened. His suspicions are there too.'

Addaio ignored the papers. He stood up and began to pace silently back and forth. Then he rounded on Zafarin, looming over the younger man as though he were about to strike him.

'Do you know what this failure means? Months, perhaps years before we can try again! The police are investigating, they've begun to connect your failure to your brother's and all the others and they are determined this time to get to the bottom of it. Some of our men may be arrested. If they talk, what then?'

'But these others know nothing of the truth . . . why they were sent – ' Zafarin's father interrupted.

'Quiet! What do you know? Our people in Italy, in Germany, in other countries, know what they need to know, and if they fall into the hands of the police, they'll be made to talk, which means the trail may lead to us. Then what do we do? Do we all cut out our tongues so that we will be unable to betray our Lord?'

'Whatever happens, it shall be the will of God,' Zafarin's father said.

'No! It will not be the will of God at all! It will be the result of the failure and stupidity of people who cannot fulfill His will! It will be my fault for not being able to choose better people to do what Jesus asks of us, people worthy of his sacred mission.'

The door opened, and two more young men were shown in, accompanied like Zafarin by their fathers.

Rasit, the second man who had been with Zafarin in Turin, and Dermisat, the third, embraced him, as Addaio looked on in contempt. Zafarin had not known that his companions had arrived in Urfa. Addaio had imposed a vow of silence on families and friends so that the three would not learn of one another's presence in the city.

The fathers of Rasit and Dermisat spoke on behalf of their sons, pleading for understanding and clemency.

Addaio seemed not to be listening; he seemed distracted, lost in his own frustration and despair. Silence prevailed in the chamber for a time. Then the pastor raised his head, his eyes cold.

'The three of you will pay for your failure, which is a sin against our Lord.'

'Are the sacrifices our sons have already made not enough for you? They have allowed themselves to be mutilated, and one has died. What further punishment would you have them suffer?' Rasit's father burst out.

'You dare defy me?' asked Addaio ominously.

'No. God forbid! You know that our faith in our Lord is unswerving and that we obey you in all things. I ask only compassion for our sons, who have given so much for us, for our mission,' the father replied.

Dermisat's father, more contrite, distanced himself from the others. 'You are our pastor,' he said, 'and your word is law. Do what you will with them, for you represent our Lord on earth.'

All six of the men fell to their knees then and, heads

bowed, began to pray. All they could do was await Addaio's judgment.

None of the eight men who surrounded Addaio had yet spoken. At a sign from him, they filed out of the room. Addaio followed without another glance at the kneeling men.

'Well?' asked Addaio, when they had gathered in an adjoining room. 'Is there a traitor among us?'

The group's continued silence enraged him. 'You have nothing to say? Nothing, after all that has happened?'

'Addaio, you are our pastor, our Lord's chosen one; we look to you for guidance in this,' ventured one of them at last.

'You eight were the only people who knew the entire plan. You eight know who our contacts are. Who is the traitor?'

The men looked at one another nervously, unsure whether Addaio was, in fact, accusing them. They were, after him, the highest leaders of the community. Their families could be traced back to the earliest history of their people, and they and their forebears had always been faithful to Jesus, faithful to their city, faithful to their vow.

'If there is a traitor, he shall die.'

Each of the eight knew Addaio was capable of killing anyone who betrayed the cause. Their pastor was a good man who lived modestly and who fasted for forty days each year in memory of Jesus' fasting in the desert. He helped all those who came to him in need, whether of work, money, or mediation in a family dispute. His word was law to all his followers, but even more, it was counsel in difficult times. He was a respected man in Urfa, where the non-Christians took him to be a lawyer and recognized and respected him as such. But all of them had seen the terrible forces that simmered just beneath his devout surface.

Like the members of the council, Addaio had lived a clandestine life since childhood, praying in the shadows, where neighbors and friends would not see him, because he was the repository of a secret that would define their lives as it had defined the lives of their fathers and their fathers' fathers.

They knew he would have preferred not to have been called upon to be their pastor, that he had longed to live a life free of the all-consuming responsibility required by his role. But when he was chosen, he accepted the sacred honor and sacrifice and swore what others before him had sworn, that he would do the will of Jesus and dedicate his time on earth to the well-being of the community and the restoration of the Holy Shroud to its ordained place among them.

Another of the council members cleared his throat. Gray hair covered his head like a mantle; his lined face was wise and venerable.

'Speak, Talat,' Addaio commanded.

'We must not let suspicions destroy the trust we have in one another. I do not believe there is a traitor among us. We are facing powerful and intelligent forces; that is what keeps us from recovering what has belonged to us since the beginning. We must go back to work and formulate a new plan, and if we fail, we must try yet again. The Lord will decide when we are worthy of succeeding in our mission.'

Talat fell silent then, waiting for the others to speak.

'Show compassion to the three chosen ones,' another, Bakkalbasi, pleaded. 'Have they not suffered enough?'

'Compassion? Do you think, Bakkalbasi, that we will

survive by our compassion? That has not helped us in the past.'

Addaio clenched his hands together in frustration. His voice was tormented. 'Sometimes I think you made a mistake when you chose me to be your pastor – I am not the man that Jesus needs for these times and circumstances. I fast, I do penitence, and I pray to God to give me strength, to enlighten me, and to show me the path, but Jesus does not answer my prayers, or send me a sign. . . .'

Then the pastor seemed to gather himself. He looked at each of them in turn as he spoke. 'But so long as I am your pastor, I will make decisions and act as my conscience directs me, and with one clear objective: bringing back to our community what Jesus gave it and seeking the welfare of us all. Above all other things, I will see to our safety. God does not want us dead; He wants us alive. He does not need more martyrs.'

'What will you do with them?' Talat asked of the three who awaited their fate.

'For a while I will command them to live in isolation, in prayer and fasting, here, where I can observe them. If and when I think they have been sufficiently chastised, I will send them back to their families. Too much is at stake. We cannot treat failure lightly. They must pay a penance for it. Meanwhile, you, Bakkalbasi, will devote your fine analytical mind to reviewing our operations as a whole.'

'To what end, Addaio?'

'I want you to consider carefully – very carefully – whether there is room among us for betrayal, and where it might be, and why.'

'Then you believe that Zafarin and his father may be right?'

'We must not resist the evidence. If there is a traitor, we will find him.'

Each of the men knew what would follow.

When they returned to the council room, they found the young men and their fathers still on their knees in prayer. The pastor and the elders resumed their seats.

'Stand up,' ordered Addaio.

Dermisat was quietly weeping, Rasit's eyes were angry, and Zafarin seemed to have grown serene.

'You will do penance for failing in your mission with retreat from the world and prayer and fasting for forty days and forty nights. You will remain here, with me. You will work in the gardens while you still have strength. When the forty days have passed, I will tell you what more awaits you.'

Zafarin gave his father a worried look. The father read his son's eyes and spoke for him.

'Will you allow them to say good-bye to their families?'

'No. The expiation has begun.'

Addaio rang a silver bell that was on the table. Seconds later, the little man entered.

'Guner, take them to the rooms that open on the gardens. Find clothes for them and give them water and fruit juices. That is all they will have to eat or drink while they remain with us. I want you to explain the customs of the house and our hours for waking and working and sleeping. Now, you three, leave us.'

The men embraced their fathers briefly, not daring to linger. When they had followed Guner out of the room, Addaio spoke again, as he and the members of the council rose from their chairs.

'Go back to your families. You will have word of your sons in forty days.'

The fathers filed by Addaio, bowing and kissing his hand and inclining their heads in respect before the elders of the community, who stood as motionless as statues.

When they were alone again, Addaio led the others down a gloomy hallway to a small door, which he unlocked with a key hanging at his belt. It was a chapel, which they would not leave until nightfall.

That night, Addaio did not sleep. Though his knees were raw from long hours of prayer, he felt the need to mortify himself. God knew how much Addaio loved Him, but love alone could not persuade God to forgive Addaio for his anger – the anger he had never been able to cast out of his heart. Satan would be delighted, he knew, if that mortal sin cost him his eternal soul.

By the time Guner quietly entered Addaio's room again, the dawn had given way to morning. The faithful servant had brought coffee and a pitcher of cool water. He helped Addaio to his feet and then over to the only chair in the austere room.

'Thank you, Guner. How are the young ones?'

'They are at work in the garden, eyes red and swollen from their miserable night. Their spirits were broken before they arrived.'

'You are not pleased with this punishment, are you, Guner?'

'I obey, sir. I am your servant.'

'No! You are not! You are my only friend, and you know that, you help me to –'

'I serve you, Addaio, and I serve you well, as I've done since my tenth birthday, when my mother put me into your service. She considered it an honor that her son be chosen to serve you. Her last wish was that I always take care of you.'

'Your mother was a saint.'

'She was a simple woman who accepted the teaching of her fathers without question.'

'Do you, Guner, doubt our faith?'

'Addaio, I believe in God and our Lord Jesus Christ. But it is hard for me to see the virtue in this fever that has possessed the pastors of our community for centuries, the acts of madness that they have committed or ordered to be committed in God's name. God is worshipped with the heart.'

'You dare to question the foundations of our community? You dare to say that the holy pastors that went before me erred? Do you think it is easy to keep the commandments of our forebears?'

Guner lowered his head. He knew that Addaio needed him and loved him like a brother, for he alone had a place in Addaio's private life. After so many years at the pastor's side, Guner knew that only with him was Addaio truly himself, an angry man consumed by the responsibility of leading the community and carrying out its ancient mission, a man who trusted no one and exercised his authority over all. Over all except him, Guner, who washed his clothes, brushed his suits, kept his quarters spotless. The only man who saw him with sleep in his eyes or covered with sweat after a night of fever. The only man who knew his frustrations and depressions and his efforts to appear before his flock clad in an aura of majesty and infallibility, so that he might calm their souls and lead them on the treacherous path they had chosen.

Guner would never abandon Addaio. He, too, had made a vow of chastity and obedience, and his family – his parents while they lived and now his brothers and sisters and their children – enjoyed the financial comfort that

Addaio granted them and the status they enjoyed within the community.

He had served Addaio for forty years, and he had come to know him as well as he knew himself. That was why he feared him, despite the trust that had long been between them.

'Do you think there is a traitor among us?' Addaio asked him now.

'There may be.'

'Do you suspect anyone in particular?'

'No.'

'And if you did, you'd tell me, wouldn't you?'

'No, I would not, not unless I was sure. I would not want someone condemned solely on suspicion.'

Addaio looked at Guner fixedly. He envied Guner's goodness, his equanimity, and it struck him not for the first time that his servant would be a better pastor than he was – those who had chosen him had made a mistake; his lineage had weighed too heavily on them. They had chosen him because of the absurd yet age-old habit of showering the descendants of great men with honors and privileges, even when they were unworthy.

Guner's had been a humble family of country people whose forebears, like Addaio's own, had followed their faith in secret.

What if he resigned? What if he called the council together and recommended that they choose Guner as their pastor? No, he thought, they would never do it, they would think he had gone mad. And in fact, he felt that he *was* going mad in this impossible role, struggling constantly against his own nature, trying to tame his sinful wrath, speaking the certainties that the faithful demanded, and protecting the secrets of the community above all else.

He remembered every detail of the terrible day his father, racked with emotion, had accompanied him to this house in which the former pastor Addaio had then lived, and left him there.

His father, a prominent man in Urfa and a clandestine militant of the True Faith, had told Addaio from the time he was a child that if he behaved himself, if he lived well and purely, one day he might succeed the older Addaio. Addaio had always resisted the idea, assuring his parents that it was the last thing he wanted. The wonder and color of the world filled him with joy: running through gardens filled with fruits and vegetables, swimming in the river, exchanging looks and winks with the teenage girls in whom life was beginning to awaken, as it was in him.

He had especially liked the daughter of one of their neighbors, sweet Rania, a girl with almond eyes and long dark hair. He dreamed of her in the darkness of his room.

But his father had different plans for him. Barely out of adolescence, he was ordered to go to live in the house of old Addaio and to make his vows in preparation for the mission for which, people said, God had chosen him. The community had decided for him that he would be Addaio.

His only friend in those painful years was Guner, who never betrayed him when he escaped to go and hide near Rania's house, hoping to see her even from a distance.

Like him, Guner was a prisoner of the wishes of his parents, whom he honored with his obedience. The poor country people had found for their son, and thus for their entire family, a better destiny than working in the fields from sunup to sundown. Addaio's mother and father, believing the boy worthy, had honored him and his whole family when they accepted his service on behalf of their chosen son.

And so the two men had submitted to the will of their parents, and of their community, and of all those who had come before them, and had ceased forever to be themselves.

21

John found Obodas digging in the garden, absorbed in his labor.

'Where is Timaeus?"

'With Izaz. They are talking. You know that Timaeus is teaching him so that someday he may be a good leader of the community.'

Obodas wiped the sweat from his brow with the back of his arm and followed John into the house.

'I bring news,' John began, as Timaeus and Izaz greeted him. 'Harran has arrived with a caravan.'

'Harran! Excellent! Where is he?' asked Izaz, jumping to his feet.

'Wait, Izaz. The caravan does not belong to Senin, though Harran is traveling with it.' John stopped, his face twisted with emotion.

'What is it? Speak, John, for God's sake!'

'Yes, I must tell you, though it is hard. . . . Harran is blind. When he returned to Edessa, Maanu ordered the guardsmen to tear out his eyes. His master, Senin, has been murdered and his body thrown to the carrion-eaters in the desert.

'Harran swore that he knew nothing about you, that he had left you in Tyre, on the docks, and that by now you should be in Greece, but that enraged Maanu even more.'

Izaz began to weep. It was for his sake that these good men had suffered. Timaeus put his arm around him to comfort him.

'We must go to him and bring him here. We will help him. He will stay with us if he wishes.'

'I begged him to come with me, but he refused. He wanted you to know of his blindness before he came. He insists that he will not burden you with his keeping.'

Izaz, accompanied by Obodas and John, hurried to the place of the caravans. One of the guides told them where they might find Harran and what had happened.

'The leader of the caravan is a relative of Harran. That is why he consented to bring him here. Harran has no one in Edessa: His wife and children have been murdered, and his master, Senin, was tortured and killed in the plaza before all those who wished to witness the spectacle of his suffering. Maanu has cruelly punished all the friends of Abgar.'

'But Harran was not a friend of Abgar.'

'Senin was, and Senin refused to reveal the hiding place of the shroud of Jesus with which Abgar was healed. Maanu destroyed Senin's house, burned all his possessions, and built a huge pyre on which he sacrificed his livestock. He tortured and tormented his servants – some had their arms cut off, others, their legs, and Harran had his eyes gouged out, the eyes that had guided Senin's caravans across the desert. Harran should be glad to be alive.'

They found Harran sitting on the ground outside one of the tents, and Izaz pulled him up and embraced him.

'Harran, my good friend!'

'Izaz? Is it you?'

'Yes, Harran, yes – I have come for you. You must come with me. We will care for you, and you will want for nothing.'

Timaeus greeted Harran warmly. He asked John to take Harran into his house while another room was built onto the little house he shared with Izaz and Obodas.

Harran was comforted to know that he would have a place among friends and that he would not have to wander about the city, begging for alms. His voice quivering, he told them that Maanu had ordered all the Christians' houses burned, even the nobles who had professed their faith in Jesus. He had shown no mercy, even to women and children and the aged. The blood of innocents had stained the snowy marble of the city's streets, which even now reeked with the smell of death.

Obodas, his voice breaking, asked about his family, his father and mother, who were servants of Senin and, like him, Christians.

'They are dead. I am sorry, Obodas.'

Tears bathed the giant's face, and the words of Timaeus and Izaz were no comfort to him.

At last Izaz asked the question he had feared to ask, of the fates of Thaddeus and his uncle Josar.

'Josar was murdered in the plaza, like Senin. Maanu wanted the death of nobles to serve as a warning to the people, so that they might know that he would show Christians no mercy, no matter their estate. Josar made no sound. Maanu went to witness his torture personally and forced the queen to witness it as well. The queen entreated him – she fell to her knees and begged for your uncle's life, but the king simply smiled to see her suffer. I know naught of Thaddeus. I fear it was the same.'

Izaz struggled to contain his tears. They all had reason to be overwhelmed by sorrow and despair. They had all been sinned against and had lost those who were precious to them. He felt a knot in his stomach turning slowly to a burning desire for vengeance.

Old Timaeus observed the struggle taking place in the young man's heart – the same struggle occurring in the heart of Obodas.

'Vengeance is not the answer,' he murmured to them. 'I know that you both would be comforted if Maanu was punished, if you could see him die a long and agonizing death. I assure you that he will be punished, because he will have to account to God for the terrible things he has done.'

'Do you not say, Timaeus, that God is infinite mercy?' Obodas threw at him, weeping.

'But infinite justice as well.'

'And the queen – does she still live?' Izaz asked Harran, fearing the reply.

'After the death of your uncle, no one saw her again. Some servants in the palace say that she died of grief and that Maanu had her body taken into the desert and thrown to the carrion-eaters there. Others say that the king had her killed. No one has seen her. I am sorry, Izaz . . . sorry to bear such grievous news.'

'My friend, the messenger is not to blame for the news he brings,' Timaeus said. 'Let us pray together and ask God to help us bear our pain at the loss of our loved ones and to take the anger from our hearts.'

22

THE NIGHT WAS FILLED WITH THE FRAGRANCE
of flowers. Rome sparkled at the feet of John and Lisa
Barry's guests, who were chatting with one another in
small groups on the broad terrace that overlooked the city.

Lisa was nervous. John had blown up when, on his
return from Washington, she told him that she'd decided
to give a party for Mary and James and that she'd invited
Marco and Paola. He knew exactly what she was doing and
had accused her of disloyalty to her sister.

'Are you going to tell Mary what's going on? No, of
course not, because you can't – you absolutely cannot.
Marco is our friend, and I'm willing to help him in any way
I can, but that doesn't mean involving my family, much less
letting you fool around in his investigation. You're my wife,
Lisa, and I have no secrets from you, but that's it. Don't
stick your nose in my work – I don't mess with yours. I
can't believe you'd use your own sister this way – and for
what? What the hell do you care about a fire in a
cathedral?'

It was the first serious argument they'd had in years,
and she had to admit John was right. She'd gotten carried

away and acted frivolously, and now she was filled with guilt.

Mary had had no objections to the guest list Lisa sent her by e-mail. Nor had her niece, Gina, objected when she saw the name Marco Valoni and his wife, Paola. She knew they were good friends of her aunt and uncle. She'd met them two or three times; they were very nice, and both of them were interesting to talk to. She had, however, asked who this Dottoressa Galloni was that was coming with the Valonis. Her aunt explained that she was a scholar who worked in the Art Crimes Department and a close friend of Marco and Paola. That had been enough for Gina.

Waiters passed among the guests with trays of drinks and hors d'oeuvres. 'I feel kind of out of place,' Marco whispered to Paola and Sofia when they arrived. The crowd was impressive, even considering the circles in which the Stuarts moved. The guests included two government ministers, a cardinal, several high-ranking diplomats, among them the US ambassador to Italy, and a number of important businessmen, not to mention the half dozen professors that were friends of Lisa's and the handful of archaeologists Gina had invited.

'Yeah, me too,' replied Paola, 'but we're here, and there's no turning back now.'

Sofia scanned the party for Umberto D'Alaqua. She saw him across the terrace, talking to a beautiful, sophisticated-looking blond woman who resembled Lisa slightly. They were laughing, clearly comfortable in each other's company.

'Hey, there! Welcome! Paola, you look wonderful. And you, I imagine, are Dottoressa Galloni. A pleasure to meet you.' John knew his discomfort would not be lost on

Marco. He'd been on edge about this ever since he'd found out about Lisa's little game and had subtly tried to encourage Marco to decline the invitation – gently, with not a false note, but he'd tried nevertheless. Marco, for his part, asked himself why.

Lisa came over, smiling. Like John, she seemed tense. Marco wondered if he was getting paranoid. But no, Lisa's smile was just a bit stiff, and John's eyes, usually so warm, seemed uneasy. Gina also came to greet them, and then her aunt began to take them around to introduce them to the other guests.

John took note of Sofia's effect on the men. Most were eyeing her surreptitiously, or not so surreptitiously, even the cardinal. Dressed in a white Armani tunic, her blond hair long and loose, with no jewelry but diamond studs in her ears and a Cartier tank watch, she was unquestionably the most beautiful woman there that night. In short order she was taking an enthusiastic part in the conversation among a group of ambassadors, a minister, businessmen, and bankers.

They were analyzing the war in Iraq, and the minister turned and asked her opinion.

'I'm sorry, but I've been against it from the start,' Sofia said. 'In my opinion, Saddam Hussein was not a threat to anyone except his own people.'

Hers was the only dissenting opinion, so it added a definite spark to the conversation. She piled one argument on another against the war, gave a succinct lecture on the history of the region, and soon had her interlocutors viewing her with well-merited respect.

Meanwhile, Marco and Paola were conversing with two of Gina's archaeologist friends, who felt as out of place as they did.

Sofia kept her eye on the blond woman conversing so animatedly with D'Alaqua. When she saw John approach her friends, she seized the moment to excuse herself and join them.

'Thank you so much for inviting me, Signor Barry.'

'We're delighted you could come with Marco and Paola. . . .'

The blond woman turned with a smile and waved.

Barry returned the greeting. 'My sister-in-law. Mary Stuart,' he explained.

'She looks so much like Lisa,' Marco said. 'Would you introduce us?'

Sofia lowered her head. She knew that Marco was making his move. Just then, Lisa came over.

'Darling,' Barry said, 'Marco wants to meet Mary and James.'

'Oh, of course!'

Lisa escorted them over to where her sister and her husband were conversing with D'Alaqua and three other couples. Sofia's eyes were fixed on D'Alaqua, but he hardly seemed to notice. Perhaps he didn't even remember her.

'Mary, I'd like you to meet two of our best friends, Marco and Paola Valoni, and Dottoressa Sofia Galloni, who works with Marco.'

The blond woman gave them a big smile. 'A pleasure,' she said, then courteously included them in the group and introduced them to the others. D'Alaqua politely nodded and smiled indifferently.

Mary turned to her sister. 'Are they archaeologists too?'

'No, Marco is director of the Art Crimes Department, Paola teaches art history at the university, and Sofia, as I said, works with Marco.'

'Art Crimes Department? What's that?'

Marco spoke up. 'We're a special office devoted to investigating crimes involving precious objects and Italy's cultural heritage – art thefts, forgeries, smuggling. . . .'

'Oh! How interesting!' Mary responded politely. 'We were just talking about that painting auctioned recently in New York – a Christ by El Greco. I'm trying to get Umberto to admit that he's the person who bought it.'

'Unfortunately not, as I've told Mary,' D'Alaqua said, with a slight smile. Then he turned to Sofia, his tone perfectly natural and polite, but distant.

'How is your investigation going, Dottoressa Galloni?'

Mary and the rest of the group looked at him, puzzled.

'You two know each other?' Mary asked.

'Yes, I met Dottoressa Galloni in Turin a few weeks ago. You've all heard of the fire in the cathedral, I'm sure. The Art Crimes Department was – perhaps still is, Dottoressa Galloni? – investigating it.'

'And what do you have to do with it?' Mary asked.

'Well, it was COCSA that was doing the repair work in the cathedral. Dottoressa Galloni was looking into certain suspicions she and her colleagues had about the incident.'

Marco was struck by D'Alaqua's extraordinary self-possession. He projected absolute innocence without ever acknowledging in the slightest that it might be in question.

'Tell me, Dottoressa Galloni, what was suspicious?' asked one of the women in the group, a princess who appeared in all the society and fashion magazines. 'I thought it was a simple accident.'

Sofia gave D'Alaqua a wounded look. With one brief comment he'd made her feel awkward, clumsy, as though she'd crashed the party. Paola and Marco looked uncomfortable too.

'When an accident takes place in a site where there are

cultural treasures of this magnitude – like the cathedral, in this case – it's our responsibility to consider all the possibilities,' Sofia responded.

'And have you reached any conclusions?' the princess asked.

Sofia looked at Marco, who cleared his throat to indicate that he'd take it from here.

'Our job is more routine than it might appear, principéssa. Italy has an extraordinary inventory of art of all kinds, as you know, and our job is to preserve it.'

'Yes, but –'

Lisa interrupted the princess, calling on a waiter to serve another round of drinks, and most of the group began to drift toward the buffet. John took advantage of the break to take Marco gently by the elbow and lead him to another cluster of guests; Paola followed. But Sofia stood firmly where she was, never taking her eyes off D'Alaqua.

'Sofia,' said Lisa, trying to move her away, 'I want you to meet Professor Rosso. He's head of the excavations at Herculaneum.'

'What is your specialty, Dottoressa Galloni?' asked Mary.

'I have a PhD in the history of art, and I did my undergraduate work in Italian philology and dead languages – Aramaic, Latin, that sort of thing. I speak English, French, Spanish, Greek, and pretty good Arabic.'

She had spoken with pride, but she realized too late that she'd sounded ridiculous, pedantic, trying to impress these people who could not have cared less who she was or what she knew. She was furious at herself and at being put under their microscope, observed like some exotic specimen by these beautiful women and powerful men.

Lisa tried again. 'Coming, Sofia?'

'Lisa, let us have Dottoressa Galloni a little while longer. This is very interesting.'

D'Alaqua's words took Sofia by surprise. Lisa turned away, resigned, but drew Mary along with her. Suddenly Sofia and D'Alaqua found themselves alone.

'You seem uncomfortable, Dottoressa Galloni. Is anything wrong?'

'I am uncomfortable, and I expect you know why.'

'Ah, well, you shouldn't be upset with Mary, in any event, for her genuine interest in your work. She is an extraordinary woman, really – intelligent and sensitive, and her question was absolutely innocent, believe me.'

'I suppose so.'

'The truth is, you and your friends have come to the party to see *me*, isn't that right, Dottoressa Galloni?'

Sofia felt herself flushing. Once again he had scored a direct hit.

'My boss is a friend of John Barry's, and I . . . I . . . .'

'And you left my office with nothing, so you and he decided to arrange a coincidence – what a surprise, meeting here like this! Too obvious, Dottoressa Galloni.'

Sofia's face burned. She wasn't prepared for this duel, for the frankness of this man, who was so sure of his own superiority and who looked at her with amusement.

'It isn't easy to meet with you.'

'No, it isn't, so now that we're here, go ahead and ask whatever you'd like.'

'I told you: We suspect that the supposed accident in the cathedral was no accident and that only some of the men who work for you could have set the fire, but why?'

'You know I have no answer for that question. But you

have a theory, so tell me what it is and I'll see if I can help you.'

At the other end of the terrace, Marco was observing them with amazement, as were the Barrys. At last, John couldn't contain his irritation at the situation any longer and sent Lisa to liberate D'Alaqua.

'Sofia, forgive me, but Umberto has so many friends here who want to talk to him, and you're monopolizing him, my dear. James is looking for you, Umberto.'

Sofia felt like a fool.

'Lisa, it's I who is monopolizing Dottoressa Galloni. You'll let us finish our talk, won't you? It's been a long time since I've have such a fascinating conversation.'

'Oh, of course, I . . . well, if you need anything . . . .'

'It's a gorgeous evening, the party is lovely, and you and John are wonderful hosts. I'm so happy you've invited me to share this with Mary and James. Thank you, Lisa.'

Lisa beat a quick retreat back to her husband and whispered something in his ear.

'Thank you,' said Sofia.

'Please, Dottoressa Galloni, don't underestimate yourself!'

'I never have.'

'I think you may have tonight.'

'It was stupid for us to come.'

'It was obvious, I'll admit. And our hosts' discomfort confirms that they engineered this little "encounter." I'd be surprised if Mary and James knew about it, though.'

'They don't – or didn't. I'm sure they're wondering why Lisa invited us, though, because we're totally out of place. I'm sorry; it was a mistake.'

'You still haven't answered my question.'

'Your question?'

'Yes. I'd like to know your theory of the crime – or alleged crime.'

'We believe that someone wants the shroud – whether to steal it or destroy it, we don't know. But we're sure the fire was related to the shroud – and so were all those other so-called "accidents" in the cathedral in the past.'

'That's an interesting theory. Now tell me who you suspect, who you think might want to steal or destroy the shroud, and – especially – why.'

'That's what we're looking at now.'

'And you have no clues that bear out your suspicions, am I right?'

'That's right.'

'Dottoressa Galloni, do you think I want to steal or destroy the shroud?'

D'Alaqua's words were spoken with a hint of mockery that amplified Sofia's sense of ridiculousness.

'I won't say we suspect you directly, but it's possible that some employee of yours might be involved.'

'My human-resources man at COCSA, Signor Lazotti – I gave strict orders that he cooperate with you fully. Has he?'

'Yes, we have no complaint there. He's been very efficient and very generous with his time, and he sent us a long report on all the information I requested.'

'Then allow me to ask you one more question, Dottoressa Galloni – what did you and your boss expect from this "chance encounter" with me this evening?'

Sofia lowered her head and took a sip of champagne. She had no answer to that, at least no legitimate answer. You couldn't give a man like D'Alaqua excuses like 'Marco had a hunch.' For the second time, she felt she'd failed some subtle test.

She shrugged lightly and smiled. 'We thought we'd just

come and see what happened, Signor D'Alaqua.'

'Shall we have something to eat?'

Startled by his abrupt change in course, Sofia looked at him. Had she heard right? But then Umberto D'Alaqua took her gently by the elbow and led her to the long buffet table. James Stuart, accompanied by the Minister of Finance, strolled over to them.

'Umberto, Horacio and I were having a little argument over the effect that the Asian flu is going to have on the European markets this year. . . .'

Sofia listened as D'Alaqua outlined his interpretation of the Asian economic crisis, stunned by his mastery of the subject. She soon found herself drawn into the debate with the Minister of Finance and contesting some of Stuart's points, while D'Alaqua listened with interest. When their little group broke up, she and D'Alaqua seated themselves at a table with other guests, where he continued to be attentive and charming. Sofia could see that he was at ease and enjoying himself, and she felt herself relaxing too.

'Your friend is delightful.' Mary Stuart's cheery voice brought Marco back to reality as he watched his dazzling colleague across the terrace. Or was it Paola's surreptitious nudge in his ribs?

'Yes, she is,' Paola replied. 'Intelligent, accomplished, and charming.'

'And lovely,' Mary added. 'I've never seen Umberto so interested in a woman. She must be exceptional if Umberto is so taken with her. He looks so happy, so relaxed with her.'

'He's single, isn't he?' Paola asked.

'Yes, but we've never understood why. He's got it all – intelligence, looks, education, culture, money – and he's a wonderful person into the bargain. I don't know why you don't see more of him, John, and you, too, Lisa.'

'Mary, dear, we don't actually travel in Umberto's circles. Nor yours – even if you are my favorite sister.'

'Oh, Lisa, don't be silly.'

'I'm not being silly, sweetheart. In my daily life, I don't run across ministers or bankers or multinational business-men. There's no reason for me to. Or for John to.'

'Well, you should see more of Umberto. He loves archaeology. He's financed several digs, and I'm sure you two have a great deal in common,' Mary insisted.

It was almost one o'clock when Paola reminded Marco that she had to get up early the next day. Her first class was at eight. Marco asked her to tell Sofia they needed to go.

'Sofia, we're leaving,' Paola said, leaning over the dottoressa's chair. 'Do you want us to drop you off?'

'Thanks, Paola, I'd appreciate it.'

D'Alaqua rose as Sofia did, kissed her hand in farewell, and promptly extended the same courtesy to Paola. He smiled, but his eyes had turned distant again. From time to time, as they had talked, Sofia thought she glimpsed something else there. But she read him perfectly now.

As Lisa and John accompanied them to the door, Sofia glanced one last time at the terrace. Umberto D'Alaqua was conversing animatedly with a group of guests.

They were barely in the car before Marco's curiosity got the better of him.

'So spill it, dottoressa; tell me what the great man said.'

'Nothing.'

'Nothing?'

'Well, Marco, he *did* say it was more than obvious that we'd come to the party to see *him*. He made me feel like an absolute fool, caught flat out in a lie. And he asked straight out – dripping with sarcasm, of course – whether we thought that he was the one after the shroud.'

'That's it?'

'The rest of the night we talked about Asian flu, oil prices, art, and literature.'

'Well, you two certainly seem to have hit it off,' Paola said.

'I suppose we did, in a way, but that's it.'

'He might not think so,' Paola insisted.

'You two planning on seeing more of each other?' Marco asked.

'No, I don't think that's going to happen. He was charming, as I said, but that's it.'

'And that hurts.'

'I guess if I was to be perfectly honest about my emotions I'd say it does, but I'm a big girl. I'll get over it.'

'Which means it hurts,' said Marco, grinning.

'You make a nice couple.' Paola wouldn't give up.

'It's nice of you to say so, Paola, but I'm not kidding myself. A man like Umberto D'Alaqua isn't interested in a woman like me. We have nothing in common.'

'You have a *lot* in common,' Marco insisted. 'Mary told us he loves art and archaeology, even finances excavations, sometimes goes on digs himself. And you, in case you didn't know, are also intelligent, educated, cultured, and gorgeous – right, Paola?'

'Well, of course. Mary even made a point of telling me that she'd never seen D'Alaqua as interested in a woman as he was in you tonight.'

'All right, you two, let's drop it. The bottom line is that he told me in no uncertain terms that we'd crashed the party. Let's hope he doesn't lodge a protest with some government minister or president somewhere.'

*   *   *

It was raining steadily, but a crackling fire enhanced the comfortable masculine luxury of the room, a library. Several paintings by Dutch masters revealed the sober taste of its owner. Settled on rich leather couches, the six men were deep in conversation.

They stood as the door opened and their elderly chief entered. One by one they stepped forward to embrace him. He motioned to them to resume their seats. 'I'm sorry to be late, but it's hard to get anywhere in London at this hour. I couldn't get out of my bridge game with the duke and his friends and our brothers.'

A soft tinkling sound at the door announced the butler, who entered to remove the tea service and offer the men drinks. When they were once again alone, the elderly man was the first to speak.

'All right, then, let's have a review.'

'Addaio has confined Zafarin, Rasit, and Dermisat to his estate outside Urfa. The penitence he's imposed on them is to last forty days, but my contact assures me that Addaio will not let it go at that, that he's preparing something further for them. As for sending a new team, he hasn't decided about that yet, but sooner or later he *will* send one. He's concerned about Mendib, the prisoner in jail in Turin. Apparently he's had a dream, one he can't shake, that Mendib will bring ruin to the community. Since then, he hardly eats, and he's not himself. My contact fears for his health and for what he might decide to do.'

The man who had spoken was middle-aged, with a thick beard and skin tanned dark brown. He was well dressed, straight-backed, and spoke in an impeccable upper-crust accent. His bearing and presence were those of a retired military officer, accustomed to discipline and order.

The elderly man gestured to another of the men to speak.

'The Art Crimes Department knows a lot, but it doesn't know what it knows.'

They all looked at him with concern and curiosity as he went on.

'They're pursuing their theory that all these "accidents" that have happened in the Turin Cathedral over the years aren't accidents at all.' He paused and looked around the room at his fellows. 'They're convinced the events are tied to the shroud, that someone wants to steal or destroy it. But they can't figure out the motive. And they're still investigating COCSA, thinking they'll find their link there. As I reported earlier, their Trojan horse operation is under way, and Mendib will be set free from the Turin jail in a couple of months.'

'The time has come to act,' said the elderly man, a slight accent surfacing to reveal that English was not his native language.

'Mendib has to be taken care of,' he went on. 'And as for the Art Crimes Department, it's time to pressure our friends to stop this Valoni. He and his people are moving in dangerous directions.'

'Addaio may have reached the same conclusion, that the safety of the community requires Mendib's elimination,' said the military gentleman. 'Maybe we should wait to see what Addaio decides before we do anything ourselves. I'd prefer not to have his death on our conscience if we can avoid it.'

'There's no reason for Mendib to die. All we have to do is make sure he reaches Urfa,' said one of the other men.

'That's dicey,' said another. 'Once he's on the street, the Art Crimes Department will put a tail on him. They're not amateurs; they'll have a first-rate operation, and we could wind up in the position that to save his life we'll have to sacrifice many others – we're talking about dead cops and carabinieri. It looks like this last episode is going to burden our conscience however it plays out.'

'Ah, yes. Our conscience!' exclaimed the elderly man. 'All too often we put it aside, telling ourselves there's no other way. Ours is a history in which death has always played a part. As has sacrifice, faith, mercy. We are human, only human, and we act in accordance with what we believe to be best. We make mistakes, we sin, we act correctly. May God have mercy on all of us.'

For a moment no one spoke. The other men lowered their eyes, sorrow shadowing their faces. Finally, their master raised his eyes and sat up in his chair. 'All right, then – I'll tell you what I believe we must do, and then I'll hear your opinions.'

Night had descended by the time the meeting ended. The rain was still falling all across the city.

23

A.D. 542–544

'Eulalius, a young man is here asking to speak with you.
He comes from Alexandria.'

The bishop finished his prayers and got to his feet with
difficulty, assisted by the priest who had interrupted him.

'Tell me, Ephron, why is this visitor from Alexandria so
important that you disturb my prayers?'

The priest was expecting the question, although
Eulalius knew well that Ephron would summon him only
on a matter of importance.

'He is a strange young man. My brother sent him.'

'Abib? And what news does this strange young man
bring?'

'I cannot say. He says he will speak only to you. He is
weary; for weeks he has been on the road, journeying here.'

Eulalius and Ephron left the small church and made
their way to a nearby house, where the bishop greeted the
dark-skinned young man, whose exhaustion was evident
in his eyes and parched lips.

'I come to speak to Eulalius, bishop of Edessa,' the traveler said, as he drank the water Ephron offered him.

'I am Eulalius. Who are you?'

'Praise God! Eulalius, I am about to tell you an extraordinary thing, which will fill you with amazement. Can we not speak in private?'

Ephron looked at Eulalius, who nodded. The priest withdrew, leaving the two alone.

'You still have not told me your name,' the bishop said, turning back to his visitor.

'John. I am called John.'

'Be seated, then, John, and rest while you tell me this extraordinary thing.'

'Extraordinary it is, sir. And it will be hard for you to believe me, but I trust in the help of God that I may convince you of what I have come to say.'

'So – out with it.'

'It is a long story. I have told you that I am called John, as was my father, and my father's father, and his grandfather and great-grandfather. I have traced my family to the fifty-seventh year of our era, when Timaeus, the leader of the first Christian community, lived in Sidon, now Alexandria. Timaeus was a friend of two disciples of our Lord Jesus Christ, Thaddeus and Josar, who lived here in Edessa. Timaeus's grandson was called John.'

Eulalius listened intently, waiting for the young man to come to the heart of his tale.

'You must know that in this city there was a community of Christians under the protection of King Abgar. On Abgar's death, Maanu, the king's son, inherited the throne and persecuted the Christians of the city. He stripped them of their goods and possessions and subjected many of them to the pains of martyrdom for clinging to their faith in Jesus.'

'I know the history of this city,' Eulalius said impatiently.

'Then you know that Abgar, afflicted with leprosy, was cured by Jesus. Josar brought to Edessa the shroud in which the body of our Lord had been buried. When the shroud was placed upon the skin of the sick king, a miracle occurred. On the shroud there is something extraordinary: the image of our Lord and the signs of his martyrdom. As long as Abgar was alive, the shroud was an object of veneration in the city, for upon it was the face of the Christ.'

'Tell me, young man, why has Abib sent you?'

'Forgive me, Eulalius, I know that I am trying your patience, but I beg you to hear me out. I myself chose to come to you and merely asked Abib to vouch for me. When Abgar sensed that he was dying, he charged his friends Thaddeus and Josar and the royal architect Marcius to protect the shroud above all else. Marcius was charged with hiding it, and not even Thaddeus and Josar, the two disciples of Jesus, ever learned where this hiding place was. Marcius cut out his tongue so that no matter what tortures Maanu inflicted upon him, he could never tell. And suffer tortures he did, Eulalius, as you must know, for they were the same tortures as the most prominent Christians of Edessa were made to suffer. But one man did know where Marcius had hidden the shroud with its image of Jesus.'

Eulalius's eyes gleamed with surprise, and a shiver ran down his spine. He had heard tales of this wondrous shroud, which had vanished so long ago. The story John told was a fantastic one, yet he did not seem to be a madman.

'Marcius told Izaz, the nephew of Josar, where he had hidden the shroud. Izaz fled the city before Maanu could have him killed, and he reached Sidon, where Timaeus and his grandson, John, lived. Those were my forebears.'

'He fled with the shroud?'

'No, he fled with the secret of its hiding place. Timaeus and Izaz swore that they would obey the last commands of Abgar and the disciples of Jesus: The shroud would never leave Edessa. It belonged to this city, but it was to remain hidden until they could be sure it was in no danger. They agreed that if before they died, the Christians of this city were still being persecuted, they would confide the secret to another man, and that man in turn was sworn not to reveal the secret unless he was sure that the shroud was in no danger, and so on until Christians were able to live in the city in peace. Before he died, Izaz told the secret to John, the grandson of Timaeus, and the secret passed from one John to another. Down through the generations, one man of my family has been the repository of the secret of the grave cloth in which the body of Jesus was buried.'

'Great God! Are you sure of this? Is it not a fable? If it is, you deserve a severe chastisement, young man, for one does not take the name of God in vain. Tell me, where is it? Do you have it?'

John, weary, seemed not even to hear Eulalius, and he doggedly went on with his story.

'A few days ago, my father died. On his deathbed he told me the secret of the sacred shroud. It was he who told me the story of Thaddeus and Josar, and he told me also that Izaz, before he died, drew a map of Edessa so that the first John might know where to look. I have the map, and it shows the place where the royal architect, Marcius, hid the shroud of our Lord Jesus.'

The young man fell silent. His feverish eyes showed the

effort under which his body and spirit had labored since he had learned the secret.

'Tell me, why has your family not wished to reveal the secret of the hiding place until now?'

'My father told me that he had kept the secret so long in fear that the shroud might fall into the wrong hands and be destroyed. None of my forebears dared reveal what they knew; each left that responsibility to his successor.'

John's eyes gleamed with tears. He was overcome by the rigors of his journey and the shattering events that had transformed his life in the preceding weeks. Grief at his father's death gnawed at his entrails, and he was in anguish over being the sole repository of a secret that would shake Christianity to its foundations.

'You have the map?' Eulalius asked.

'Yes,' the young man answered.

'Give it to me,' commanded the old bishop.

'No, I cannot. I must go with you to the place where the shroud is hidden, and we must tell no one the secret.'

'But, my son, what is it you fear?'

'The shroud works miracles, sir, but many Christians died in the struggle over its possession. We must be certain that it is in no danger, and I fear I have arrived in Edessa at a bad time. My caravan met with travelers who told us that the city may soon again be under siege. For generations the men of my family have been the silent guardians of the shroud of the Christ; I must not be the one to make a grievous error and now put the shroud in danger.'

The bishop nodded. The distraught young man clearly needed to rest and to pray. He would ask God to enlighten him as to what to do.

'My son, if what you say is true and the shroud of our Lord is somewhere in this city, I shall not be the man to put it in danger. You shall rest in my house, and when you have recovered from your journey we will talk, and between us we will decide what's best.'

'You will tell no one what I have told you?'

'No one, my son, I promise you.'

Eulalius's stern demeanor and the firmness of his response reassured John. He prayed to God that he had not made a mistake. When his dying father had told him the story, he warned him that the fate of the shroud that bore the image of Jesus lay in his hands, and he made him swear he would never reveal the secret unless he was certain the time had come for Christians to recover the shroud once more.

But he, John, had felt an overwhelming urgency to set out on his journey to Edessa. In Alexandria he had been told of the existence of Eulalius, and of his goodness, and he believed that the moment had come to give Christians back what his family, guardians of a wondrous secret, had protected for them.

But he may have acted too swiftly, he thought now, assailed by doubt. Recovering the shroud at a time when Edessa was about to face a new war would be a bold step. John feared he might have misjudged.

John was a physician, as his father had been. The older man had imparted all his own knowledge to his son, who had also studied with the finest teachers of the city. The most prominent men of Alexandria came to his house to seek out his knowledge and his skills. His life had been a happy one until the death of his father, whom he loved and respected above all men, even more than his lithe, sweet wife, Myriam, with her beautiful face and deep black eyes.

Eulalius accompanied John to a small room in which there was a bed and a rough wooden table.

'I will send something to eat and more water, so that you may refresh yourself after your journey. Rest as long as you wish.'

Then the old bishop, deep in thought, made his way again to the church. There, kneeling before the cross, he hid his face between his hands and asked God to show him what to do, should the young traveler's story be true.

In one corner, mantled by shadow, Ephron watched his bishop with concern. He had never seen Eulalius troubled or overwhelmed by responsibility. He decided to seek out a caravan going to Alexandria so that he could send a letter to his brother Abib asking for information about the strange young man who seemed to have laid such a burden upon the bishop.

The moon's wan light was on the city by the time the bishop made his way home from the church. He was weary; he had hoped to hear the voice of God but had found only silence. Neither his reason nor his heart had given him the slightest enlightenment. He found Ephron waiting at the door, his noble features creased with worry.

'You must be tired. It is late,' the bishop said quietly to the priest.

'I was waiting for you. Can I help you in any way?'

'I'd like you to send someone to Alexandria to ask Abib to tell us more about John.'

'I have already written a letter to my brother, but it will be difficult for it to reach him. In the place of caravans they told me that the last caravan departed two days ago for Egypt and that another one will not be leaving for some time. The traders and merchants are worried. They think war with the Persians is inevitable, so a number of caravans left the city earlier than planned. Eulalius, let me ask you what this young man has told you to trouble you so.'

'I cannot tell you yet. I pray God I may do so soon, for it will bring comfort to my heart. Shared burdens weigh less upon one, but I have given my word to John that I will keep his secret.'

The priest lowered his eyes; he felt a twinge of pain. Eulalius had always confided in him; together they had shared the tribulations and dangers that had sometimes beset the community.

The bishop, conscious of Ephron's emotions, was tempted to reveal to him the secret brought by John, but in the end he remained silent.

The two men, each burdened in his own way, bade each other good night.

✝ 'Why are you enemies of the Persians?'

'We are not their enemies; it is they who, greedy for what is not theirs, wish to possess our city.'

John was conversing with a young man of more or less his own age in the service of Eulalius.

Kalman was preparing to be a priest. He was the grandson of an old friend of Eulalius, and the bishop had taken him under his protection. He had become John's best source of information, explaining the details of the city's politics, the vicissitudes its people faced in these dark days, the palace intrigues.

Kalman's father was the king's overseer, and his grandfather had been the royal archivist; he himself had considered the idea of following in his grandfather's footsteps, but his sponsorship by Eulalius had marked him, and he dreamed now of being a priest, perhaps one day a bishop.

Ephron slipped quietly into the room where John and Kalman were talking, unnoticed by the two young men. For a few seconds he listened to their animated conversation, but then, coughing softly, he made them aware of his presence.

'Eulalius would like to speak with you,' he said, addressing John. 'He is in the room where he works, waiting for you.'

John thanked Ephron and made his way to the bishop's chambers. Ephron was a good man, and a dedicated priest, but John felt his distrust and was not comfortable in his presence.

'I have bad news, my son,' the bishop said when John had seated himself. Eulalius looked weary and his voice was filled with concern. 'I fear that soon we may be besieged by the Persians. If that comes to pass, you will not be able to leave the city, and your life, like all our lives, will be in great danger. You have been in Edessa a month, and I know that you are still unsure whether to reveal to me the place where the shroud of our Lord is hidden. But I fear for your life, John, and I fear for the shroud that bears the visage of our Lord. If what you have told me is true, you must save the shroud and leave the city as soon as possible. We cannot run the risk of the city being destroyed and the true face of Jesus being lost forever.'

Eulalius saw uncertainty flood John's face. He wished it were not necessary to command such a drastic step, but he saw no other choice, given the peril they faced. Since the day the young man arrived, the bishop had found no calm in sleep, fearing day and night for the fate of the grave cloth that John spoke of. Sometimes he doubted its very existence, but at other times, the limpid eyes of the young man led him to believe in it with his whole heart.

John rose to his feet. 'No! I cannot leave here! I cannot take away the shroud in which the body of our Lord was buried! It must remain in Edessa!'

'Calm yourself, John; I have decided what is best. You have a wife in Alexandria; you must not remain here any longer. We know not what will become of the kingdom. You are the keeper of an important secret, and you must continue to be so. I will not ask you to tell me where the shroud is but only how I can help you recover it, so that you may save it.'

'Eulalius, I must stay here, I know I must stay here. I cannot leave now, much less expose the shroud to the dangers of the journey. My father made me swear to obey the command of Abgar, Josar, and the apostle Thaddeus. I cannot take the shroud from Edessa, for I have sworn not to.'

'John, you must obey *me*,' the bishop corrected him.

'I cannot; I must not. I will stay and deliver myself over to the will of God.'

'Tell me, what is the will of God?'

John felt the grave, weary voice of the bishop like a hammer beating at his heart. He stared at Eulalius and suddenly understood how troubled the old man had been made by his arrival and the fantastic story of the shroud.

Eulalius had been patient and generous with him, but now he was commanding him to leave Edessa. The bishop's decision forced John to face the truth. He knew that his father had not lied to him, but what if his father had been lied to? What if at sometime during the long centuries since the birth of our Lord, someone had seized the shroud for himself or destroyed it? What if the entire story was a fable?

The old bishop saw a storm of emotions cross John's

face, and he felt deep compassion for the young man's anguish.

'Edessa has survived sieges, wars, starvations, fires, floods. . . . It will survive the Persians, but you, my son, must act according to the dictates of reason, and for your good and for the good of the secret your family has kept for so many decades, you must save yourself. Make arrangements now for your departure, John, for in three days you will leave the city. A group of merchants has mounted a caravan; it is your last chance to save yourself.'

'And if I tell you where the shroud is?'

'I will help you save it.'

John's mind was in turmoil as he left the bishop's study, and his eyes were filled with tears. He went out into the street, where the coolness of morning had not yet been dispelled by the burning sun of June, and he wandered aimlessly. For the first time, he fully understood that the citizens of Edessa were preparing for the siege that they knew was upon their city.

Laborers were working tirelessly to reinforce the walls, and soldiers bustled throughout the city, their faces stern, their brows furrowed. In their stalls, merchants displayed few goods, and on the faces of all he met he saw fear.

John realized how self-centered he had been in not heeding what was happening all around him, and for the first time since he had arrived, he felt homesick for Myriam, his young wife. He had not even written to tell her he was well. Eulalius was right: Either he left Edessa immediately or he faced the same fate as its citizens. A shiver of fear and foreboding ran through him, for he felt that his fate might well be death.

He did not know how many hours he spent wandering through the city, but when he returned to the house of

Eulalius, he suddenly became aware of the thirst that had been with him all day and the hunger that gnawed at him. He found Eulalius with Ephron and Kalman, speaking with two circumspect nobles sent from the palace.

'Come in, John. Hannan and Maruta bring us sad news,' the bishop said. 'The siege is upon us. Edessa will not surrender to the Persians. Today, two wagons have arrived at the city's gates. Inside were the heads of a group of soldiers who had gone out to gauge the strength of the forces under Khusro. We are at war.'

The two nobles, Hannan and Maruta, looked at the young Alexandrian without much interest, and then they continued to report to the bishop on the situation.

Confounded and stunned, John listened to the men talk. He realized that even if he wished to, leaving the city would not be easy. The situation was worse than Eulalius had thought: There would be no more caravans. No one wished to run the certain risk of losing his life upon the road.

John lived through the next few days as though in the midst of a nightmare. From the walls of Edessa one could clearly see the Persian soldiers around their campfires. The attacks sometimes lasted the entire day.

Men kept their families inside the walls of their houses, while the soldiers met the constant attacks. There was still no shortage of foodstuffs or water because the king had stored up wheat and dried and salted meat, as well as brought many animals into the city, so that his soldiers might nourish themselves and remain strong.

✝ 'Are you asleep, John?'

'No, Kalman, I seem not to have slept in days. The whistling of the arrows and the thunder of the battering rams against the walls have invaded my head, and I cannot sleep.'

'They say the city will soon fall. We cannot resist much longer.' Months had passed, almost two years, as Edessa fought on.

'I know, Kalman, I know. I am weary with binding the wounds of the soldiers and attending women and children who die in my arms in convulsions or with the plague. My hands are callused from digging graves in the earth to bury their bodies. In the end, Khusro's soldiers will show no mercy to anyone. How is Eulalius? I have not been able to see him. . . . I am sorry.'

'No, he wishes you to help those who most need it. He is very frail from this prolonged fast and the pain that grips his bones. His belly is swollen, but he never complains.'

John sighed. He seemed never to rest, running from one place to another on the wall, treating the mortal wounds of the soldiers to whom he could no longer give relief because he had no more plants with which to prepare his unguents and potions.

Day and night desperate women came to his door, pleading with him to save their children, and he would spill tears of impotence, for there was nothing he could do for them. They were starving and exhausted, and their lives simply slipped away.

How his life had changed since he left Alexandria. When he dozed off from exhaustion he dreamed of the clean smell of the ocean, the soft hands of Myriam, the hot food his old serving woman prepared for them, his house surrounded by orange trees. During the first months of the siege he had cursed his fate and reproached himself for having come to Edessa in search of a dream, but he no longer did that. He had no strength for that now, and the dream remained buried, perhaps out of reach forever.

John shook off his torpor and rose to his feet. 'I will go to see Eulalius,' he told the priest.

'It will do him good to see you.'

Accompanied by Kalman, he made his way to the room where the bishop lay in bed praying.

'Eulalius . . .'

'Welcome, John. Sit here beside me.'

The physician was pained by the changed aspect of the old bishop. He had shrunk, and the outline of his bones was visible through his almost transparent skin. His pallor presaged death.

The sight of the dying man moved John deeply. He, who had arrived almost arrogantly in Edessa, proud to show Christianity the visage of the Lord, had not had the courage to complete his undertaking. He had thought rarely of the shroud through the long months of the siege, and now, seeing the approach of death upon the face of Eulalius, he knew that death would not be long in coming for him as well.

'Kalman, leave me alone with Eulalius, please.'

Weakly, the bishop made a sign to the priest to leave them. Kalman worried as he left the room, for he knew that neither of the men was well. In John, it was clear that grief had left its mark; in Eulalius, it was the flesh that was yielding.

John looked into the eyes of the bishop and, taking him by the hand, sat beside him.

'Forgive me, Eulalius, I have done nothing but ill since I came here, and the worst of my sins has been to not confide in you. I have sinned by pride in not sharing with you the secret of the place where the shroud is hidden. I will tell you now, and you shall decide what we must do.

May God forgive me if what I am about to say betrays doubt, but if upon the shroud the visage of our Lord is truly impressed, then he will save us, as he saved Abgar from sure death.'

Eulalius listened with amazement to John's revelation of the secret. For more than four hundred years the shroud of Jesus had lain behind the bricks of a niche cut out of the wall above the west gate of the city. It was the only place that had withstood the battering of the Persian army.

The old man struggled to sit up and, weeping, he embraced the Alexandrian.

'Praise God! I feel a great joy in my heart. You must go at once to the wall and rescue the shroud. Ephron and Kalman will help you, but you must go now. I feel that Jesus may still have mercy upon us and work a miracle.'

'Eulalius, I cannot present myself before the soldiers who are risking their lives guarding the western gate and tell them that I am seeking a niche hidden in the wall. They will think I am mad, or that I am hiding a treasure. . . . No, I cannot go there.'

'You shall go, John.'

Suddenly Eulalius's voice was firm and strong again. So firm, indeed, that John lowered his head, knowing that this time he would obey.

'Let me, then, Eulalius, say that you have sent me.'

'It *is* I who have sent you! Before you arrived, in my dream I heard the voice of Jesus' mother telling me that Edessa would be saved. And so it shall be, God willing.'

Outside, they could hear the cries and shouts of the soldiers mixed with the crying of the few infants who were still alive. Eulalius sent for Kalman and Ephron.

'I have had a dream. You must go with John to the western gate and –'

'But, Eulalius,' Ephron exclaimed, 'the soldiers will not let us pass.'

'You will go, and you will obey John's orders. Edessa can be saved.'

✝ The captain, enraged, ordered the two priests and their companion to leave the area.

'The gate is about to give way, and you want us to go and look for a hidden niche – you are mad! I don't care if the bishop sent you! Begone!'

John stepped forward and told the captain that with or without his help they would climb the wall above the western gate and dig.

Arrows fell all around them, but before the astonished eyes of the soldiers, they remained untouched. Calling upon their last reserves of strength, the soldiers redoubled their efforts to defend that part of the wall, as the three men dug frantically.

'There is something here!' Kalman cried.

Minutes later, John held in his hands a basket darkened by time. He opened it and gently touched the folded cloth.

Without waiting for Kalman or Ephron, he clambered down and began to run toward Eulalius's house.

His father had told him the truth: He and all his fathers before him had been the guardians of the secret of the shroud in which Joseph of Arimathea had laid the body of Jesus.

The bishop trembled with emotion when John entered his chamber. The young man took the shroud from under his tunic and held it out to the bishop, who rose from his bed and went down on his knees in wonder at the face of a man perfectly impressed upon the cloth.

24

SURROUNDED BY BOOKS, SOFIA WAS SO ABSORBED in her reading that she didn't realize Marco had come into the office. She had been there for hours already, taking advantage of the early-morning quiet before their day officially began.

'Whatever it is must be fascinating,' he said, 'because you haven't even noticed that I'm here.'

'Oh, sorry, Marco,' Sofia replied, jumping a bit.

'What are you reading?'

'The history of the shroud.'

'But you already know it by heart. Christ, every Italian knows it.'

'That's true. But I wanted to dig a little deeper. There might be something in here to give us a lead.'

'Something in the history of the shroud?'

'Let's call it speculative research. No stone unturned.'

'Interesting. Have you found anything?'

'Not yet. I'm just reading, hoping for the light to come on.' Sofia smiled and tapped her forehead.

'How far along are you?'

'The sixth century, when a bishop in Edessa named

Eulalius had a dream in which a woman revealed to him where the shroud was. You know that during all that time, the shroud was lost, no one knew where it was. In fact, there was no knowledge that it even existed. But Evagrius –'

'Evagrius? Who's Evagrius?' Minerva dropped her things on a nearby desk and joined them.

'Evagrius Ponticus. According to Evagrius in his *Historia Ecclesiasticus*, in 544 Edessa had been besieged by the army of the Persian king Khusro, but the city somehow fought back against the Persians and won – all, supposedly, thanks to the Mandylion, which the city bore in procession along the battlements and –'

'But who the hell is Evagrius and what the hell is the Mandylion?' Minerva insisted.

'If you'd let me finish,' Sofia said with barely concealed impatience, 'you might find out.'

'Sorry.' Minerva raised her hands and cringed.

Marco smiled. 'Sofia,' he explained, 'is going over the history of the shroud, and we were talking about its appearance in Edessa in 544, when the city was under siege by the Persians. The Edessans were desperate, about to surrender or be overrun. No matter how many fire-tipped arrows they shot at the Persians, the siege engines wouldn't catch fire.'

'So what happened?' Minerva asked.

'Well, according to Evagrius,' Sofia continued, raising her eyebrows at Marco and giving him a nod in acknowledgment, 'Eulalius, bishop of Edessa, had a dream in which a woman revealed to him where the shroud was hidden. They went to look for it, and they found it at the western gate of the city, in a niche hollowed out in the wall. The discovery restored the city's faith, and the shroud was carried in procession along the battlements on top of the walls, while the defenders continued to shoot their fiery arrows at the Persian siege machines. But this time the engines *did* catch fire, and the Persians wound up abandoning their siege.'

'Nice story, but is it true?' Minerva asked.

'Think about it, Minerva. There are any number of things that for long periods were regarded by historians as legends passed down through the ages but that have turned out to be accounts of events that actually happened. The best examples are Troy, Mycenae, Knossos . . . cities that for hundreds of years were believed to belong to the world of myth but whose historical existence was finally demonstrated by Schliemann, Evans, and other archaeologists,' Sofia replied.

'But whatever else happened, the bishop must have *known* the shroud was there, right? No matter how credulous you want to be, you can't believe that business about the dream, can you?'

'Well, that's the story that's come down to us,' Marco answered, 'but you're probably right. Eulalius had to know where the shroud was hidden, or maybe he had it put there so that he could pull it out at the right moment and say a miracle had occurred. Who knows the truth of what happened fifteen hundred years ago? As for your question about the Mandylion, it's thought to be a small cloth that was draped over Christ at death, which bore the image of his face. Many consider it to be the shroud but folded to show only the face, not the full body.'

Just then Pietro, Giuseppe, and Antonino came in, arguing heatedly about soccer.

Marco called everyone together to update them on the release of the mute in Turin.

Pietro looked at Sofia out of the corner of his eye. The

two had been avoiding each other as much as possible, and although they tried to maintain a professional, civil relationship, they were clearly uncomfortable together. It was obvious that Pietro was still in love with Sofia and that she was beginning to shun him. Marco and the others did their best to keep them apart.

'All right, then,' Marco began. 'The parole board will be back at the Turin jail in a few days. When they come to the mute's cell, the warden, the social worker, and the prison psychologist will be asked for their current assessment of him. All three will agree that he's a petty thief who presents no danger to himself or society and has been in long enough.'

'Too easy,' Pietro broke in.

'No, it won't look that way,' Marco explained. 'They'll go through the motions. The social worker will propose that he be sent to a special center, a psychiatric unit, for evaluation on whether he's capable of living on his own. We'll see whether he gets nervous over the idea of being locked up in a psychiatric hospital or stays cool. The next step will be silence. We'll let him stew for a while and have the guards observe his reactions. If all goes well, a month later the board will go back to the jail again, make their final decision, and two weeks later he'll be freed. Sofia, I want you to go to Turin with Giuseppe and start putting the team there together. Tell me what we're going to need.

'And don't forget dinner tonight,' he reminded them as he finished. It was his birthday and Paola was having a small party at their house.

'So you're going to turn the guy loose. That's some fucking risk.' Marco and Santiago Jiménez sipped Campari sodas Paola had just brought over as they talked.

'Yeah, but he's the only lead we've got. Either he leads us somewhere or this case will be open for the rest of our lives.'

Since the table wasn't large enough to seat everyone, Paola had prepared a buffet and, with the help of their daughters, was now going about refilling glasses and plates and seeing after the twenty-odd guests. Along with members of Marco's department and other friends, John and Lisa Barry were coming.

'Sofia and Giuseppe will start setting things up in Turin next week.'

'My sister Ana is going to Turin too. I've got to tell you – ever since you had us to dinner, she's been obsessed with this thing. She just sent me a long e-mail about the shroud's history – that's where she thinks the key is.' Santiago kept going, in spite of Marco's annoyed expression. 'Anyway, I wanted to let you know. She's sworn she won't publish a word of what we talked about, but she's decided to investigate on her own, in Turin. She's good, you know – smart, tough, and pushy, like all good reporters, I suppose – and she's got great instincts. I hope her investigation won't cause you any problems, but if you hear there's a reporter poking around where she shouldn't be and making trouble for you, let me know. I'm sorry, Marco – this is what comes of dealing with the press, even if it's family.'

'Could I see the e-mail?' Marco asked.

'Ana's?'

'Yeah. Sofia's been going over the history of the shroud too. They're thinking along the same lines, and I have to say I don't think it's a bad idea.'

'No kidding! Sure, I'll send it to you, but it's all very speculative. I doubt there's anything you can use.'

'I'll pass it on to Sofia, although I really don't like getting a reporter involved in this or anything else. Sooner or later they fuck everything up, and to get a scoop they're capable of –'

'No, no, Marco, I'm being straight with you. Ana is as honest as the day is long, I swear, and she's my sister, she loves me – she'd never do anything that would hurt me. She knows I can't have problems with the authorities here, much less someone I've introduced her to.'

'She'll tell you if she finds something?'

'Yup. She wanted to make a deal with you – send you everything she's sure she's going to find out, in exchange for which you'll give her what you know. Obviously, I told her she was dreaming if she thought she could make a deal with you or anybody associated with you, but I know her, and if she finds something out she's going to need to corroborate it, so she'll call me and try to get me to tell you –'

'So we've picked up a volunteer – an Art Crimes intern, you might say! All right, Santiago, no sweat. I'll tell Giuseppe and Sofia to keep their eyes open for her when they get to Turin.'

'What are we keeping our eyes open for?'

'Sofia!' Marco turned to the historian as she joined them. 'Santiago was telling me about his sister Ana – I don't know whether you've met her. . . .'

'I think so, a couple of years ago. Wasn't she with you at that party for Turcio's retirement?' she asked Santiago.

'Uh-huh, you're right. Ana was in Rome then and went with me. She comes to see me a lot – I'm the oldest, and her only brother. Our father died when she was just a little girl, and we've always been very close.'

Sofia nodded. 'I remember we talked for a while about

press–police relations. She said sometimes there was a marriage of convenience between the two, but that it always wound up in divorce court. I liked her – she's smart.'

'I'm glad you liked her, because you're probably going to run into her in Turin, going after the story of the shroud,' Marco told her.

Sofia raised her eyebrows in surprise, and Santiago hurried to fill her in.

'You know what Santiago just told me, though, Sofia?' Marco said when he had finished. 'Ana's been poking around in the history of the shroud too. She thinks that's where we'll find our answers.'

'Yes, I've thought the same thing, I told you.'

'That's what I told Santiago. He's going to forward us an e-mail that Ana sent him about it. She may wind up running rings around us!'

'So why don't we talk to her?' Sofia asked.

'Let's stick with our own team for now,' Marco answered thoughtfully.

'It wouldn't be the first time, and you know it, that police have worked with a reporter during a case.'

'I know, but I want to keep a low profile – and keep the story within a controlled circle – as long as we can. If Ana finds something we can use, then we'll rethink it.'

25

GUNER FINISHED BRUSHING OFF ADDAIO'S BLACK
suit and hung it in the closet in the dressing room. On his
way back to the bedroom he straightened the papers
Addaio had left on the desk and put a couple of books back
on the shelves.

Addaio had worked late. The sweetish scent of
Turkish tobacco permeated the austere room. Guner
threw the windows open and stood for a few seconds
looking out at the garden. He did not hear the quiet
footsteps behind him or see the troubled expression on
his master's face.

'What are you thinking about, Guner?'

Guner turned around, trying not to let any emotion
show through his impassive facade.

'Nothing, really. It is such a lovely day – it makes one
feel like getting out.'

'Why don't you spend a few days with your family? You
can go as soon as I've left.'

'You're leaving?'

'Yes. I'm going to Germany and Italy – I want to visit
our people. I need to know why we're making mistakes

and where the betrayal lies. My inquiries here have gone nowhere.'

'You shouldn't go, Addaio. It will be dangerous.'

'I can't have all of them come here; *that* would be dangerous.'

'Have them meet you in Istanbul. The city is full of tourists all year long – no one will notice them there.'

'But not all of them would be able to come. It's easier for me to go to them than for them to come to me. At any rate, it's decided. I'm leaving tomorrow.'

'What will you tell people here?'

'That I'm tired and am taking a little vacation, to visit friends in Germany and Italy.'

'How long will you be gone?'

'A week, ten days, no longer than that – so take advantage of it and have a rest for yourself. It will do you good to be rid of me for a while. You've seemed tense recently, angry with me. Why is that?'

'All right, Addaio. I'll tell you the truth. Perhaps you'll consider it while you are away. I have suffered, deep inside, about this for months, maybe years.' The servant paused and looked at the pastor, then took a deep breath and continued. 'It seems to me that we have come to betray all we have vowed to uphold. My heart breaks for those boys you sacrifice. The world has changed, but you are adamant that everything must go on the same. You cannot go on presiding over these barbaric mutilations and sending young men to their death, and –'

His master cut him off before he could go further. 'We have survived for two thousand years because of the sacrifice and silence of those who came before us, sacrifices against which ours pale in comparison. Yes, I demand great sacrifices – I, too, have sacrificed my life, a life that has *never* belonged to me, as your life does not belong to you. Dying for our cause is an honor; sacrificing one's voice is as well. I do not cut their tongues out; they voluntarily offer that sacrifice because they know that it is essential to our cause. By doing that thing, they protect us all and protect themselves.'

'Why do we not come out into the light?'

'Are you mad, Guner? Do you actually think that we would survive if we revealed ourselves? You know the power of those who oppose us and the danger we represent to them. Our histories are linked and they have eradicated all, *all* through the centuries who have tried to follow those links to their origin. We ourselves have found only half-truths and lies, despite all our efforts. What's wrong with you, what demon has possessed your mind?'

'Sometimes I think that the demon has possessed *you*. You have become hard and cruel. You feel pity for no one, nothing. Is that in service to your vows, Addaio? Or is it someone who all your life you did not want to be?'

They stood in silence, staring at each other. Guner realized that he had said more than he should have, and Addaio surprised himself by accepting, without a word, Guner's reproaches. Their lives were irremediably intertwined, and neither of them was happy.

Was Guner capable of betraying him? Addaio rejected the thought – no, he was not. He trusted Guner; in fact, he entrusted his life to him. 'Pack my bags for tomorrow,' he finally ordered.

Without replying, Guner turned and busied himself closing the windows. His jaw ached as he clenched his teeth. He breathed deep when he heard the quiet sound of the door closing behind the pastor.

He noticed a piece of paper on the floor, beside Addaio's bed, and he stooped to pick it up. It was a letter written in Turkish, unsigned. The person who wrote it was informing Addaio that the parole board in Turin was studying the possibility of freeing Mendib, and he asked for instructions, especially what to do if Mendib was released.

Guner asked himself why Addaio hadn't put away a letter as important as this. Had he wanted Guner to find it? Was he testing Guner – did he think he was the traitor?

Carrying the letter, he strode to Addaio's office, knocked softly at the door, and waited for the pastor to give him permission to enter.

'Addaio, this letter was on the floor next to your bed,' he said without preamble when he again faced his master.

The pastor looked at him impassively and put out his hand for it.

'I read it. I imagine you intentionally dropped it so I *would* find it and read it – a trap to see whether I'm the traitor. I'm not. I have told myself a thousand times that I should leave; I've thought a thousand times about telling the world who we are and what we do. But I haven't, and I won't, in memory of my mother, and so that my family can go on living with its head held high and my nieces and nephews can enjoy a better, happier life than mine has been. For their sake, and because I do not know what would become of me, I don't reveal our existence. I'm a man, a poor man, too old to start a new life. I am a coward, like you – both of us became cowards when we accepted this life.'

Addaio looked at him in silence, trying to see in Guner's expression some thought, some emotion, the trace of *something* that would tell him that his only friend still felt some affection for him.

'Now I know why you're leaving tomorrow,' the little servant continued. 'You're worried, you're afraid of what might happen to Mendib. Have you told his father?'

'Since you are so certain that you will never betray me, I will tell you that I'm worried that they will set Mendib free. If you've read the letter, then you know that our contact in the jail saw the head of the Art Crimes Department visit Mendib, and tells us that it seems clear that the warden is planning something. We can take no risks.'

'What are you going to do?'

'Whatever may be necessary to ensure the survival of our community.'

'Even have Mendib murdered?'

'Is it you or I who has reached that conclusion?'

'I know you, and I know what you're capable of.'

'Guner, you are the only friend I have ever had. I have never hidden anything from you; you know all the secrets of our community. But I realize now that you feel no affection for me whatever, and never have.'

'You are wrong, Addaio, you are wrong. You were always good to me, from the first day I arrived at your house, when I was ten. You knew how it grieved me to leave my parents, and you did everything in your power to help me see them. I shall never forget how you would go to my family's house with me and let me spend the evening while you wandered through the countryside, taking your time so that your presence would not be a burden to us. I can never fault you for your behavior toward me. But your behavior toward the world, toward our community, the terrible pain you cause – *that* I cannot countenance.'

Guner left the office and made his way toward the chapel. There, kneeling, he allowed his tears to wet his cheeks as he sought in the cross lying on the altar an answer to the questions that tormented him.

26

A.D. 944

Edessa was in flames. The cries of its people rose above the crash of burning timbers and the sounds of battle as the emperor's army began to engulf the city.

Why had God abandoned them?

The old bishop rose unsteadily to his feet as the towering commander of the emir's forces entered the chapel, his battle-weary face creased with regret. The Muslim defenders of the city had fought fiercely on the Christians' behalf, dying by the hundreds to preserve for Edessa the Mandylion of the great prophet Jesus, may Allah protect him.

But now there was no choice. The Mandylion must be surrendered. A great cry rose from the throng of Christians filling the church as the bishop moved forward to the altar and removed the precious cloth from the simple casket in which it had rested.

Then, with the elders of his community clustered around him, he made his way with halting steps to the waiting soldier and gave the carefully folded cloth over to him. They fell to their knees as the shroud of Jesus was taken from them, to begin its long journey from its ordained place in Edessa into the hands of the Emperor of Byzantium. They had broken their oath, the oath their forebears had died to uphold.

These men – descendants of the scribe Timeaus, the giant Obodas, Izaz the nephew of Josar, John the Alexandrine, and so many Christians who had sacrificed their lives for the Holy Shroud – would recover it, and if they did not, then their own children, and their children's children after them, if need be, would not rest until that mission had been accomplished.

They swore this before God, before the imposing wooden cross that hung above the altar, before the painting of the Blessed Mother, before the Sacred Scriptures.

27

'YOU'RE GETTING A LITTLE NEUROTIC ABOUT this, boss,' Giuseppe complained as Marco brought up the subject of the Turin tunnels yet again. 'We've studied the maps, and there's no tunnel that goes to the cathedral. Period.'

'Listen, Giuseppe, these guys are going in and out through something other than the front door. The ground under Turin is like Swiss cheese. It's full of tunnels, and they're not all on the maps.'

Sofia thought Marco was right. The cathedral intruders seemed to appear and disappear as though by magic, and without a trace.

Her boss had decided at the last moment that he'd go to Turin with them. The Minister of Culture had persuaded the Ministry of Defense to issue Marco a permit to explore the tunnels, including those closed to the public. On the army maps of Turin's subsurface infrastructure, there was no tunnel that led to the cathedral, but Marco figured the maps were wrong. With the help of a commander in the engineering section and fortifications specialists from the Pietro Micca regiment, he was going to explore the tunnels that were closed. He had signed a waiver exempting the army and the city government from all responsibility if he got himself killed or injured, and the minister had told him in no uncertain terms that he was not to endanger the lives of the men who accompanied him.

'Giuseppe,' Sofia broke in, 'we simply don't know what's under Turin. If we were to dig, God knows what we'd find. Some of the tunnels that run underneath the city have never been explored in modern times; others seem to go nowhere. The truth is, one of them *might* lead to the cathedral. It would be logical, after all – the city has been under siege how many times? And the cathedral has dozens of irreplaceable objects that the citizens would want to safeguard if the city was assaulted or conquered by an enemy.'

Giuseppe fell silent. He knew when to give up.

They had checked into the Hotel Alexandra, near the historic old center of the city. The next day they would start working. Marco would go through the city's tunnels, Sofia had asked for an appointment with the cardinal, and Giuseppe was meeting with the city carabinieri to decide how many officers they'd need for the tail on the mute. But at the moment, at Marco's invitation, they were enjoying dinner at Al Ghibellin Fuggiasco, a classic, comfortable Turin restaurant known for its world-class seafood.

The second course had just been served when they were surprised by Padre Yves. The priest approached their table with a smile and shook everyone's hand warmly, as though he was delighted to see them.

'I didn't know you were coming to Turin too, Signor Valoni. The cardinal did tell me that Dottoressa Galloni would be visiting us – I believe you have an appointment with His Eminence tomorrow, dottoressa?'

'Yes, that's right,' Sofia answered.

'And how is your investigation going? Well, I hope?' Marco nodded but said nothing as Padre Yves went on. 'The work on the cathedral is finished, and the shroud is on view for the faithful once again. We have strengthened our security measures, and COCSA has installed a state-of-the-art fire control system. I don't think there'll be any further catastrophes now.'

'I hope you're right, padre,' said Marco.

'Yes, actually I do too. Well, I'll leave you. *Buon appetito.*'

They watched him sit down at a nearby table, where a dark-haired young woman was waiting for him. Marco laughed.

'Know who that is with our good Padre Yves?'

'A good-looking girl, obviously – you gotta wonder about those priests,' said Giuseppe in surprise.

'It's Ana Jiménez, Santiago's sister. Now it's my turn to go over and say hello!'

Marco crossed the floor, making his way over to them. Ana gave him a big smile and asked if he could spare a few minutes to speak with her when he had some time. She'd arrived in Turin four days ago.

Marco was noncommittal; he told her he'd be delighted to have coffee if he had time but he wasn't going to be in Turin very long. When he asked what hotel he might call to find her, Ana told him the Hotel Alexandra.

'What a coincidence. We're staying there too.'

'My brother recommended it, and it's perfect for a few days.'

'Well, then, I'm sure we'll find a minute to talk.'

'She's staying at the Alexandra,' he said when he rejoined Sofia and Giuseppe.

'No kidding! What a coincidence!'

'It's no coincidence. Santiago recommended it to her – I might have known. That's going to make it harder to avoid her.'

'I'm not sure I want to avoid a good-looking thing like that!' Giuseppe said, laughing.

'Well, you will, and for two reasons: first, because she's a reporter and she's determined to find out what we're doing on the cathedral case, and second, because she's Santiago's sister and I don't want complications, all right?'

'All right, boss, it was just a joke.'

'Ana Jiménez is a determined, intelligent woman – I'd take her seriously if I were you.'

'The e-mail she sent her brother is full of interesting ideas. I wouldn't mind talking to her,' Sofia interjected.

'I won't say no, Sofia, but we need to be careful with what we tell her.'

'I wonder what she's doing with Padre Yves,' Sofia mused.

'She's smart,' Marco answered. 'As I said – we'll have to be careful.'

The elderly man hung up the telephone and let his eyes wander to the scene outside the window for a few seconds. The English countryside glowed emerald-green in the warm sunshine.

His companions waited expectantly for him to speak.

'He'll be released within the month. The parole board has formally taken up the parole request.'

'That's why Addaio has gone to Germany and, according to our informant, will be crossing into Italy. Mendib has become his biggest immediate problem,' said the Italian.

'Do you suppose he'll kill him?' the gentleman with the French accent asked.

'Addaio can't let the police follow Mendib home or lead them to any of their other contacts. Because even if Mendib doesn't approach them, he could reveal their presence without intending to. Addaio has realized that it's a trap, and he's come to prevent the obvious outcome,' replied the former military man.

'Where will they eliminate him?' the Frenchman wanted to know.

'In the jail, of course,' said the Italian. 'It's the safest place. There will be a small scandal but nothing more.'

'So what do you gentlemen propose?' the elderly man asked.

'It will be best for everyone if Addaio solves our problem,' said the Italian.

'What arrangements have you made if Mendib manages to leave the prison alive?' asked the old man.

'Our brothers will try to prevent the police from following him,' replied the Italian.

'It is not enough that our brothers *try;* they cannot fail.' The leader's voice was as stern as thunder.

'They will succeed,' the Italian replied. 'I hope within the next few hours to learn all the details of the operation.'

'All right, we have come to the central issue in this matter – there can be only one conclusion: We must divert the carabinieri from Mendib, or . . .'

The elderly man did not finish his sentence. The others nodded, almost in unison; they knew that with respect to Mendib, their interests coincided with Addaio's. They could not allow the mute to become a Trojan horse and bring the community under scrutiny.

A light knock at the door, preceding a liveried servant's entrance into the room, served to bring the early-morning meeting to an end.

'The guests have begun to dress for the hunt, sir. They will be coming down soon.'

'Very well.'

One by one, the seven men, dressed for the day's hunt, left the library and entered a warm dining room, where breakfast awaited them. A few minutes later, an elderly aristocrat accompanied by his wife entered the room.

'Heavens, I thought we were the early birds, but you see, Charles, that our friends have risen even earlier than we have.'

'Early birds indeed, out to get the worm. No doubt taking advantage of the morning to talk business,' huffed the husband.

The French gentleman assured them that they wanted nothing more than to get started. More guests continued to drift into the dining room, until at last there were thirty people standing or milling about. There was a good deal of animated conversation.

The elderly man looked at them resignedly. He hated hunting, as did his colleague-brethren, but he could not stand off from such a very English diversion. The members of the royal family adored this sport, and they had asked him, as on so many occasions in the past, to organize an event on his splendid estate. And there they were.

Sofia had spent most of the morning with the cardinal. She hadn't seen Padre Yves; another priest had showed her into His Eminence's office.

The prelate was happy with the finished repair work and remodeling. He had special praise for Umberto D'Alaqua, who had personally interceded to increase the number of workers on the job, at no additional cost to the cathedral, and to ensure that the work was completed sooner than estimated.

Under the supervision of Dr. Bolard, the shroud had been returned to the Guarini Chapel, to its silver display-case. But neither Sofia nor Marco had called the cardinal to update him on the progress of their investigation, and he subtly let her know he was not pleased. Sofia apologized, and she managed to win her way back into his good graces by giving him a broad, undetailed outline of where they were with their work. On Marco's instruction, she gently urged him to take even greater safety precautions than usual now that the shroud was back in the cathedral and she advised him of Marco's search for possible entry points from the tunnels beneath the city.

'You say that Signor Valoni is looking for an under-ground tunnel that leads to the cathedral? But that's absurd. Your team asked Padre Yves to review our archives, and I believe he sent you a detailed report on the history of the cathedral. Nowhere does it indicate that there is a tunnel or secret passage.'

'But that doesn't mean there isn't one.'

'Or that there is. Don't believe all the fantastic stories written about cathedrals.'

'Your Eminence, I'm a historian. I don't generally deal in fantastic stories.'

'I know, I know, dottoressa; I apologize. I admire and respect the work you and your team do. It was not my intention to offend you, I assure you.'

'I'm sure of that, Your Eminence, but I want to assure you, too, that history is not just what's written down. We don't know everything that happened in the past, much less the intentions of the people who lived in it.'

*   *   *

When Sofia returned to the hotel she ran into Ana Jiménez in the lobby. She had the feeling the reporter had been waiting for her.

'Dottoressa Galloni . . . .'

'How are you?'

'Fine, thank you. Do you remember me?'

'Of course. You're our friend Santiago Jiménez's sister.'

'Do you know what I'm doing in Turin?'

'Investigating the fires in the cathedral.'

'I know your boss isn't too happy about that.'

'That's only natural, don't you think? You wouldn't like it much if the police started meddling in your work.'

'No, I wouldn't, and I'd try my best to give them the slip. But this is different. I know I may seem naive, but I really believe I can help you, and I want you to know you can trust me. My brother is everything to me – I'd never do anything to get him in trouble, or even give him a headache, for that matter. It's true that I'd like to write a story on this – I'm dying to cover it. But I won't. I swear to you I won't write a line until you and your team have closed the investigation, until the case has been solved.'

'Ana, this isn't about trusting you or not. You have to understand that the department can't let you into its investigative team "just because" – because you're honest and trustworthy and have an interest in the case. Surely you understand that?' Sofia responded.

'But we can work in parallel. I can tell you what I'm finding out, and you do the same with me.'

'Ana, this is an official investigation.'

'I know, I know. . . .'

Sofia was struck by the urgency in the young woman's expression. 'Why is this so important to you?' she asked.

'I don't know if I can explain. The truth is, I never cared about the shroud at all or paid any attention to any of the things that happened in the cathedral. But my brother took me to dinner at your boss's house under the impression it was just another dinner – a few friends over, that sort of thing – and it turned out that Signor Valoni wanted Santiago and another man, John Barry, to give him their opinion of the fire. They talked all night, speculating, you know, and I was hooked. There's so much there – layers and layers of history, intrigue –'

'What have you found out?' Sofia interrupted her.

'Shall we get some coffee?'

Sofia hesitated, then said, 'Sure,' instantly regretting her decision when Ana beamed with relief.

She liked this young woman, even thought she could trust her, but Marco was right – why should they? What was the point?

'All right, tell me what you've found out so far,' Sofia said when they'd found a table.

'I've read several versions of the history of the shroud – it's fascinating.'

'Yes, it is.'

'In my opinion, someone wants the shroud, just as Signor Valoni speculated that first night. The fires are a smoke screen, if you'll excuse the expression, to throw the police off. Or maybe there's some other factor linking the incursions with accidents. Either way, the objective is to steal the shroud. But we need to look in the past. It's not just a question of *stealing* the shroud – someone wants to get it *back*,' Ana half whispered intensely. 'Someone with some tie to the past, the shroud's past.'

'And how have you reached that conclusion?'

The reporter shook her head and shrugged. 'I don't

know. It's just a feeling I have when I think about the long road it's traveled, the hands it's passed through, the passion it has always inspired. I have a hundred theories, each one crazier than the last, but –'

'Yes, I read your e-mail.'

'So what do you think?'

'I think you've got a great imagination, no doubt about that, and maybe you're even right.'

Ana abruptly changed course. 'I think Padre Yves knows more than he's saying about the shroud.'

'Why do you say that?'

'Because he's too perfect, too correct, too innocent, and too transparent – it makes me think he's hiding something. And handsome – I mean, he's really hot, you know? Don't you think so?'

'He's a very attractive man, he certainly is. How did you meet him?'

'I called the bishop's office, explained that I was a journalist and wanted to write a story about the shroud. There's an older lady there, a former reporter, who's in charge of press relations. We met for two hours, and she basically repeated what the tourist brochures say about the shroud, although she also gave me a history lesson on the House of Savoy.

'I left knowing no more than I'd come with. She wasn't exactly the right person to expect a lead from. So I called again and asked to speak to the cardinal; they asked me who I was and what I wanted, and I explained I was a journalist investigating the fires and other accidents that had happened in the cathedral. They sent me back to the nice press lady, who this time was a bit huffy with me. I pressed her to get me an appointment with the cardinal. No go. Finally I played my last card –

I told her they were hiding something and that I was going to publish what I suspected, plus certain things I'd found out.

'So then Padre Yves called me. He told me he's the cardinal's secretary and that the cardinal couldn't see me but that he'd asked Yves to "put himself at my disposal," which I took to be a good thing. So we met, and we talked for a long time. He seemed pretty straightforward when he told me what had happened this last time, and he went with me to visit the cathedral – then we went for coffee. We agreed to talk again. When I called for an appointment yesterday, he told me he was going to be busy all day but said if I didn't mind we could have dinner. And that's it.'

'He's a very odd priest,' allowed Sofia, thinking out loud.

'I imagine when he says Mass the cathedral is full to the rafters, eh?' laughed Ana. 'If he weren't a priest, I'd. . . .'

Sofia was surprised at how uninhibited Ana Jiménez was. She'd never have told a stranger that she found a young priest sexy. But younger women were that way. Ana couldn't be more than twenty-five, and she belonged to a generation that was used to screwing when they felt like it, without hypocrisy or complications, although the fact that Padre Yves was a priest did seem to slow her down a bit, at least for the moment.

'You know, Ana, I find Padre Yves intriguing, too, but we've looked into him and there's just nothing that would indicate there's anything but what meets the eye. Sometimes people are like that – clean, transparent. So, what are you planning to do next?'

'If you could cut me some slack, we could share information. . . .'

'No, I can't.'

'No one would find out.'

'Don't misread me, Ana. I don't do anything behind anyone's back, much less the people I trust, the people I work with. I like you, but I've got my work and you've got yours. If Marco should decide at some point that we should let you into the loop, then I'll be delighted to share information with you, and if he doesn't, then honestly, it's all the same to me.'

'If someone wants to steal or destroy the shroud, the public has a right to know that.'

'I'm sure you're right. But you're the one making those claims. We're investigating the cause or causes of the fires. When we've concluded our investigation we'll send our report to our superiors, and they will make it public if they believe what we've found is of public interest.'

'I'm not asking you to betray your boss.'

'Ana, I understand what you're asking me, and the answer is no. I'm sorry.'

Ana bit her lip in disappointment and got up from the table without finishing her cappuccino.

'Well, what're you gonna do?' She shrugged, then smiled. 'Anyway, if I discover something, is it all right if I call you?'

'Sure, call whenever you like.'

The young woman smiled again and strode purposefully from the hotel café. Sofia wondered where she was headed. Her cell phone rang, and when she heard the voice of Padre Yves she almost laughed out loud.

'We were just talking about you,' she said.

'Who?'

'Ana Jiménez and I.'

'Oh! The reporter. She's charming, and very sharp, eh? She's investigating the fires in the cathedral, just like you, it seems. She told me that your boss, Marco, is a friend of her brother, Spain's representative to Europol in Italy.'

'That's right. Santiago Jiménez is a friend of Marco and all of us. He's a good person and a total professional.'

'Yes, yes, so it appears. But the reason for my call, Dottoressa Galloni, is that the cardinal asked me to phone you. He'd like to invite you and Signor Valoni to a reception.'

'A reception?'

'Yes, for a committee of Catholic scientists that comes to Turin periodically to examine the shroud. They make sure it's maintained in good condition. Dr. Bolard is their chairman. Whenever they come, the cardinal has a reception for them – not too many people, thirty or forty at the most – and he'd like you to come. Signor Valoni had mentioned that he'd like to meet these scientists, and now the opportunity has presented itself.'

'And I'm invited too?'

'Yes, of course, dottoressa, His Eminence expressly asked that you be invited. Day after tomorrow, at the cardinal's residence, at seven. We are also expecting a number of businessmen who work with us in maintaining the cathedral, the mayor, representatives of the regional government, and perhaps Monsignor Aubry, aide to the interim Vatican Under-Secretary of State, and His Eminence Cardinal Visier, in charge of Vatican finance.'

'All right, padre. Thank you very much for the invitation.'

'Our pleasure, Dottoressa Galloni.'

Marco was in a foul mood. He'd spent most of the day in the tunnels under Turin. The archaeological logs showed that some of them had been made in the first centuries A.D. Many of them dated back to the sixteenth century, others to the eighteenth, and there were even some that Mussolini had widened along certain stretches. Going through them was hard, treacherous work. There was a whole other Turin under the ground – in fact, several Turins: the old territory of the city-state conquered by Rome; the Turin besieged by Hannibal; the Turin invaded by the Lombards; and then finally the city that came under the rule of the House of Savoy. It was a place in which history and fantasy intermingled constantly, at every footstep.

Comandante Colombaria had been patient and helpful – to a point. That point came when Marco tried to persuade him to venture down a tunnel in bad condition or to tear down part of a wall to see whether there was a passage hidden behind it that led in some other direction.

'My orders are to guide you through the tunnels, Signor Valoni, and I won't endanger your life or my men's unnecessarily by going down tunnels that aren't on the maps or that could collapse. And I'm not authorized to break through the walls. I'm sorry,' the comandante said stiffly.

But the one who was sorry was Marco, who by the end of the day had the feeling he'd made the trip through the underground tunnels of Turin for nothing.

Giuseppe tried to provide some perspective, without much success. 'Oh, come on, get over it, Marco. Comandante Colombaria was right. He was just following orders. It would've been crazy to start hammering away at the walls like coal miners, for God's sake.'

Sofia's attempt didn't fare much better. 'Marco, what you want to do is only possible if the Ministry of Culture, working with the Turin Archaeological Council, puts a team of archaeologists and technicians at your disposal to excavate more tunnels. But you can't expect to just walk in and hammer away wherever you have a hunch there might be a hidden tunnel. I mean, it's not going to happen. You're not being logical.'

'If we don't try we'll never know whether there's something there or not,' he fumed.

'So talk to the minister and –'

'One of these days the minister is going to tell me where to stuff my hunches. He's getting a little tired of me *and* the shroud case.'

'Well, I've got some news that might cheer you up,' Sofia ventured. 'The cardinal has invited us to a reception day after tomorrow.'

'A reception? And who's "us"?'

'Us is you and me. Padre Yves called me. That committee of scientists in charge of keeping the shroud in good shape is in Turin, and the cardinal always has a reception for them. Every important figure in the city associated with the cathedral will be there. Apparently you showed some interest in meeting these scientists, so he's invited you.'

'I'm really not in the mood for parties. I'd rather talk to them under other circumstances – like, I don't know, in the cathedral, while they're examining the shroud. We never got anywhere running down the names and organizations on the lists the cardinal supplied. But this is what there is, eh? So we'll go. I'll send my suit out to be ironed. And you, Giuseppe, what've you got?'

'The chief here hasn't got enough men – or any men, really – for the team we need. He said he'd do what he can when the time comes. I spoke to Europol like you told me, and they should be able to help us out with two or three men. So you'll have to talk to Rome for the others.'

'I don't want men from Rome. I'd rather keep it within the team. Which of ours can come?'

'The department is snowed under, boss,' Giuseppe said. 'There's just nobody available, unless somebody stops what they're doing, if they can, and you bring them in when the operation gets going.'

'That's what I'd rather do. I'd feel better with our own people on the tail. We'll take what the carabinieri here can give us, and then the rest of us will play cop for a while.'

'I thought that's what we were,' Giuseppe said sarcastically.

'You and I are, but Sofia's not, or Antonino, or Minerva.'

'You mean *they're* going to tail the guy?'

'We're all going to do whatever it takes, is that clear?'

'Clear as a bell, chief, clear as a bell. So, if that's it, I'm supposed to have dinner with a friend of mine in the carabinieri, a good guy who's willing to help us out. He'll be here in like half an hour. Maybe you guys could have a drink with us before we leave?'

'Sure, count me in,' said Sofia.

'All right,' said Marco, 'I'll go up and shower and be back down. What're your plans, dottoressa?'

'I don't have any – if you want, you and I can have dinner around here.'

'Great. Maybe that'll improve my mood.'

28

SOFIA HADN'T BROUGHT ANYTHING SUITABLE
for a reception, so she looked in the shops on Via Roma
until she came to Armani, where, in addition to a black silk
dress for herself, she bought a tie for Marco.

'You'll be the prettiest girl there,' Giuseppe told her, as
she and Marco left for the cardinal's residence.

'Definitely,' Marco seconded.

'I'm going to start a fan club with you two,' Sofia said,
laughing.

Padre Yves greeted them at the door. His collar and
priestly wardrobe were nowhere in evidence. Instead, he
wore a midnight blue suit and an Armani tie exactly like
the one Sofia had given Marco.

'Dottoressa . . . Signor Valoni . . . come in, come in. His
Eminence will be so glad to see you.'

Marco looked at Padre Yves's tie out of the corner of
his eye, and Padre Yves gave him a slight smile.

'You have excellent taste in ties, Signor Valoni.'

'The good taste is Dottoressa Galloni's. It was a gift
from her.'

'That's what I thought!' laughed the priest.

They made their way over to the cardinal, and he introduced them to Monsignor Aubry, a tall, lean Frenchman with an elegant bearing and a kindly manner. He was somewhere around fifty, and he looked like what he was – a seasoned and skillful diplomat. And he was keenly interested in the course of the investigation into the shroud, as he wasted no time in letting Marco and Sofia know.

They had been chatting for several minutes with the monsignor when they noticed that all eyes had turned to two new guests arriving.

His Eminence Cardinal Visier and Umberto D'Alaqua had just come in. The cardinal and Monsignor Aubry excused themselves and went over to greet them.

Sofia could feel her pulse beginning to race, despite herself. She had told herself that she wouldn't be seeing D'Alaqua again. Would he be coolly courteous or ignore her entirely?

'Sofia, you're red as a beet,' Marco whispered.

'Me? I'm just surprised.'

'There was every possibility that D'Alaqua would be here.'

'It hadn't occurred to me. I just never thought.'

'He's one of the Church's benefactors, a "man of trust," as they call these people. Some of the Vatican's finances pass discreetly through his hands. And remember that, according to Minerva's report, he's the one who pays for the scientific committee that's here tonight. But take it easy, you look spectacular – if D'Alaqua likes women, there's no way he won't be falling at your feet.'

They were interrupted by Padre Yves, who had the mayor and two elderly gentlemen in tow.

'I want you to meet Sofia Galloni and Marco Valoni,

who is the head of the Art Crimes Department,' he said to his charges. 'The mayor, Dr. Bolard, and Dottore Castiglia . . . .'

They began an animated conversation on the shroud, although Sofia's mind was elsewhere and she heard only half of it.

She jumped when Umberto D'Alaqua stepped before her. He was accompanied by Cardinal Visier.

After the usual round of greetings, D'Alaqua took Sofia by the arm and, to everyone's surprise, drew her away from the group.

'How is your investigation getting on?'

'I can't say that we've made much progress, frankly. It's a question of time.'

'I didn't expect to see you here.'

'The cardinal invited us; he knew we wanted to meet the members of the committee, and I hope we can spend some time with them before they go.'

'So you've come to Turin for this reception. . . .'

'No, not exactly.'

'In any case, I'm glad to see you. How long will you be here?'

'I'm not certain yet –'

'Sofia!' A shrill male voice interrupted the moment. Sofia smiled wanly when she saw an old professor of hers from the university approaching – her medieval art professor, a famous scholar with a number of books to his credit, a star in European academic circles.

'My best student! I'm so, so glad to see you! What are you doing these days?'

'Professore Bonomi! I'm glad to see you.'

'Umberto, I didn't know you knew Sofia. Although I'm not surprised: She's one of the most outstanding specialists in art in Italy. It's a shame she didn't want to stay in academia. I offered to make her my assistant, but my pleas fell on deaf ears, I fear.'

'Please, professore!'

'No, I tell you, I never had a student as intelligent and capable as you, Sofia.'

'Yes,' D'Alaqua interrupted, 'I know that Dottoressa Galloni is quite competent.'

'Competent, no – brilliant, Umberto, and with a wonderfully speculative mind. Forgive my indiscretion, but what are you doing here, Sofia?'

'I work for the Art Crimes Department,' Sofia said uncomfortably, 'and I'm just in Turin for a few days.'

'Ah! The Art Crimes Department. I somehow hadn't seen you working as an investigator.'

'My work is more scientific. I don't really do investigative work per se.'

'Come, Sofia, I'll introduce you to some colleagues I'd like you to meet.'

D'Alaqua took her arm and held her in place, preventing Professor Bonomi from taking her away.

'Wait, Guido. I was about to introduce the dottoressa to His Eminence.'

'Oh, well, uh. . . . Are you coming to the Pavarotti concert tomorrow night, Umberto? And the dinner I'm giving for Cardinal Visier?'

'Yes, of course.'

'Why don't you bring Sofia? I'd love you to come, my dear, if you have no other plans.'

'Well, I –'

'I'd be delighted to accompany Dottoressa Galloni if she has no other plans. Now, if you'll excuse us, the cardinal is waiting. . . . We'll talk later, Guido.'

D'Alaqua led Sofia back to the group standing with Cardinal Visier. The cardinal looked Sofia over with curiosity, as though evaluating her; he seemed amiable but as cold as ice. He did appear to have a close relationship with D'Alaqua; they treated each other familiarly, as though they were joined by some subtle thread.

For a while they talked about art, then politics, and then about the shroud.

It was a little past nine when the guests began to disperse. D'Alaqua was preparing to leave with Aubry and the two cardinals, plus Dr. Bolard and two other scientists, but first he sought out Sofia, who at that moment was with Marco and her former professor.

'Good night, dottoressa, Guido, Signor Valoni. . . .'

'Where are you having dinner, Umberto?' asked Bonomi.

'At the residence of His Eminence the cardinal of Turin.'

'Ah. Well, I hope to see you tomorrow night with Sofia.'

Sofia could feel herself blushing.

'Yes, of course. I'll be in touch, Dottoressa Galloni. Good night.'

Sofia and Marco said their good-byes to the cardinal and Padre Yves. The cardinal confirmed that they had set a meeting with Dr. Bolard and then suggested that Yves take Sofia and Marco to dinner. And despite the protestations of the two, they all left together for La Vecchia Lanterna, one of the best restaurants in the city.

It was after midnight when Padre Yves dropped Sofia and Marco at the door of their hotel. It had been a convivial evening. They had talked about all sorts of things and dined splendidly, as was only to be expected at a restaurant as celebrated as La Vecchia Lanterna.

'This social life is killing me!' Marco laughed as he and Sofia walked toward the hotel bar for a nightcap and a postmortem on the evening.

'But we had a good time.'

'You're a princess, so you were in your element. I'm a cop, and I was working.'

'Marco, you're a lot more than a cop. You've got a degree in history, and you've taught all of us more about art than we ever learned at the university.'

'Oh, come on. . . . Now – what can you tell me about D'Alaqua?'

'I don't know *what* to tell you. Padre Yves and he are a lot alike, I think: They're both intelligent, correct, "nice," good-looking, and totally inaccessible.'

'It didn't look to me like D'Alaqua was so inaccessible to *you;* besides, he's not a priest.'

'No, he's not, but there's something about him that makes him seem like he's . . . like he's not of this world, if you know what I mean, as though he were kind of floating above all of us mortals down here. . . . I don't know, it's a strange feeling, I can't quite explain it.'

'He seemed to hang on your every word.'

'But no more than on anybody else's. I'd like to think he was interested in me, but he's not, Marco, and I'm not going to delude myself. I'm old enough to know when a man's interested in me.'

'What did he say to you?'

'The short time we were alone, he asked me about the investigation. I avoided telling him what we were doing here, except that you wanted to meet the committee that deals with the shroud.'

'What did you think about Bolard?'

'It's odd, but he's the same kind of man as D'Alaqua

and Padre Yves. Now we know that they know one another – I guess *that* was predictable, huh?'

'You know what? I've thought the same thing – there's something really striking and unusual about them. I'm not sure exactly what it is. It's got me a little spooked. I'm used to studying people – it's part of my nature – but there's something different going on here. These men are incredibly imposing, almost otherworldly, as you say. Maybe it's their physical presence, their elegance, their self-assurance. They're accustomed to giving orders. Our talkative Professore Bonomi told me that Bolard is entirely dedicated to science, which is why he's never married.'

'Why do you think he's so devoted to the shroud, when carbon-fourteen dates it only from the Middle Ages?'

'I don't know. But when he talked about it tonight there was no doubt he considers it his life's work. We'll see how my meeting with him goes tomorrow. I want you to come. What's happening with dinner at Bonomi's?'

'He insisted that D'Alaqua take me to the opera and then to his house, to the dinner he's giving for Cardinal Visier. D'Alaqua had no choice but to agree. But I don't know whether I should go.'

'Oh, you're definitely going. And you're going to keep your eyes and ears open. It's a mission, and you accept; all those respectable, powerful men have skeletons in their closets, and one of them may know something about our case.'

'Marco, please! It's absurd to think that those men have anything in the world to do with any of this –'

'No, it's not absurd, dottoressa. Now it's the cop talking to you. I don't trust the high and mighty. To get where they've gotten they've had to wade through a lot of shit and step on a lot of toes. You'll recall, too, that every time we dismantle some team of art thieves we find the receiver of the artwork is some eccentric millionaire who just has to have objects that belong to all of humanity in his own private gallery.

'You're a princess, like I said, but they're sharks, and they consume everything that stands in their way. Don't forget that tomorrow night. All their perfect manners, their refined conversation, the luxury they live in – facade, pure facade. I trust them less than the thieves and pickpockets in Trastevere, believe me.'

29

THE BRIDE WAS RADIANT AS SHE RECEIVED congratulations from her countless relatives. The ballroom was filled to overflowing. It was the perfect cover, thought Addaio.

He had traveled with Bakkalbasi, one of the eight secret bishops of the community, officially a prosperous merchant in Urfa. The wedding of the bishop's niece had allowed the pastor to meet with most of the members of the community in Berlin.

With the seven leaders of the community in Germany and the seven in Italy, he stepped into a discreet alcove off the enormous ballroom, where they all lit up long cigars. One of Bakkalbasi's nephews kept watch near them so that no one would approach unexpectedly.

He patiently listened to the men's reports, the details of the life of the community in those barbarian lands. Then one of the Italian leaders broached the subject uppermost in Addaio's mind.

'This month Mendib will be set free. The warden has spoken several times by telephone with the head of the Art Crimes Department. They're putting on a charade of sorts, to allay any suspicions Mendib might have. The social worker and the psychologist have protested, but it is clear the plan is moving forward.'

'Who is your contact inside the jail?' Addaio asked.

'My sister-in-law. She works there as a cleaning woman. She has cleaned the administrative offices and other areas of the jail for years, and she says they are all so accustomed to her being there that they pay her no attention. When the warden comes in in the morning he just motions to her to keep working even when he is involved in sensitive phone conversations or is meeting with one or another official. They trust her. She is more than sixty years old, and no one ever suspects a gray-haired old lady with a mop and pail.'

'Can we find out the exact day that Mendib will be released?'

'Yes, of course,' the man replied.

'How?' Addaio persisted.

'The release orders come in to the warden's office by fax. My sister-in-law is there before the warden arrives, and she already has orders to go through whatever may be there to see whether Mendib's early-release order has come in. If it does, she will telephone me immediately. I bought her a cell phone specifically for that call.'

'Who else do we have inside the jail?'

'Two brothers serving a sentence for murder. One of them worked as a chauffeur for a high-ranking official in the Turin regional government; the other had a vegetable stand. One night, at a discotheque, they got into a fight with some men who were saying things to their girlfriends. Our men took umbrage, you might say, and one of the other men died of a stab wound. They are good men and true to our cause.'

'May God forgive them! Do they truly belong to our community?'

'No, no, but one of their relatives does. He has talked to them and asked them if they could . . . you know, if they could. . . .'

The man shuffled uncomfortably under Addaio's fixed gaze.

'And what did they say?'

'It depends on the money. If we give their family a million euros they will do it.'

'How can we get word to them?'

'Someone from their family will visit them and tell them whether we have the money and when they should . . . proceed . . . with what you have ordered.'

'You shall have the money. But we must prepare ourselves for the possibility that Mendib may leave the jail alive.'

A young man with a thick mustache and an elegant manner spoke up.

'Pastor, should that come to pass, he would try to make contact with us through the usual channels.'

'Review them.'

'He would go to Parco Mario Carrara, in the northern part of the city, at nine o'clock and walk around in the southern area of the park, near the Corso Appio Claudio. Every day at that hour, my cousin Arslan passes by as he takes his daughters to school. For years, members of the community who are in trouble have gone there if they are certain they aren't being followed. When they see Arslan pass by, they drop a piece of paper saying where they can be found a few hours later. When the teams you send arrive in Turin, we give them these instructions.

'Arslan then contacts me, tells me where the meeting is

to be held, and we organize a team to find out whether our men are being followed; if they are, we do not approach them, but we do follow them and get in touch if we can.

'If contact is not possible, the brother or brothers know that something is wrong, and they try for another meeting. This time they must go to a greengrocer's on the Via dell'Accademia Albertina, in the center of the city, and buy apples; when they pay, they give the grocer a piece of paper with the place for the next meeting. The greengrocer is a member of our community, and will contact us.

'The third meeting place –'

'I hope there will be no need for a third meeting place,' Addaio interrupted. 'If Mendib leaves the jail alive, he must not survive the first meeting. Is that clear? We run a great risk in this. The carabinieri will surely follow him, and they are experts at their job. We must find a team that is able to do what must be done and disappear without being caught. It will not be easy, and it is most regrettable, but we cannot give him a chance to contact one of us. Is that understood?'

The men nodded gravely. One of them, the oldest of all, spoke.

'I am Mendib's father's uncle.'

'I am sorry.'

'I know that you do this to save us, but is there no possibility of getting him out of Turin?'

'How? They will have a team following him wherever he goes. They will photograph and tape-record everyone who goes near him or whom he approaches, and then they will investigate those people. We would fall like a house of cards. Even if he manages to elude them for a time, he is now known to them, marked. They will post his photograph with police across Europe. I feel the same pain you do, but I cannot allow him to reach us. Against all odds, we have maintained our vows for two thousand years. Many of our forefathers have given their lives, their tongues, their possessions, their families in this cause. We cannot betray them or betray ourselves. I am sorry.'

'Very well, pastor. I understand and accept your judgment. Will you allow me to do it if the boy leaves prison alive?'

'You? You are an honorable man, an elder of our community. How can you do it? You are his great-uncle.'

'I have no one. My wife and two daughters died three years ago in a car accident. I planned to return to Urfa to spend my last days with what remains of my family. I will soon turn eighty, I have lived as long as God has wished me to live, and He will forgive me if it is I who takes Mendib's life and then my own. It is the most sensible way to do this.'

'You will take your own life?'

'Yes, pastor, I will. When Mendib goes to the Parco Carrara, I will be waiting for him. I am his great-uncle; he will suspect nothing. I will embrace him, and in that embrace my blade will take his life. Then I will stab that same blade into my heart.'

No one in the group uttered a word. They looked at the old man in respectful – awed – silence.

'I am not sure this is a good idea,' Addaio finally replied. 'This is not something we – I – can expect you to do. And they would have your body. They will discover who you are.'

'No, they will not be able to find that out. I will pull out all my teeth and burn off my fingerprints. For the police, I will be a man of no identity.'

'Will you truly be able to do this?'

'I am weary of life. I will make the same sacrifice so

many of our brothers have. Let this be my last act of service – the most painful – so that the community may survive. Will God forgive me?'

'God understands why you do this.'

'Then if Mendib leaves the prison, send for me and prepare me for death.'

'If you betray us, the rest of your family in Urfa will suffer for it.'

'Do not offend my honor or my name with threats. Do not forget who I am, who my ancestors were.'

Addaio lowered his head in a sign of acceptance, and the old man left their circle to be alone with his thoughts.

The pastor broke the silence that Mendib's great-uncle left in his wake. 'What is the status of Francesco Turgut, the porter at the Turin Cathedral?'

He was answered by a short, muscular man with the look of a stevedore, who worked as a janitor in the Egyptian Museum.

'Turgut is frightened. The people from the Art Crimes Department have interrogated him several times, and he believes that the cardinal's secretary, a Padre Yves, considers him suspicious.'

'What do we know about this priest Yves?'

'He is French, he has influence in the Vatican, and soon he will be made auxiliary bishop of Turin.'

'Might he be one of *them*?'

'He might be. He has all the characteristics. He is not a typical priest. He belongs to a family of aristocrats, he speaks several languages, has an excellent education, excels at sports . . . and he is celibate, totally celibate. You know that they never break that rule. He is a protégé of Cardinal Visier and Monsignor Aubry.'

'Who we are sure belong to their order,' Addaio said flatly.

'Yes, there is no doubt of that. They have been very skillful in infiltrating the Vatican and reaching the highest ranks of the Curia. I would not be surprised if someday one of them became pope. That, truly, would be a mockery of fate.'

'Turgut has a nephew in Urfa – Ismet, a good boy. I'll have him go live with his uncle,' the pastor mused.

'The cardinal is kind; I imagine he will allow Francesco to take in his nephew.'

'Ismet is quick-witted; his father has asked me to look after him. I will give him the mission of establishing himself in Turin and preparing to relieve Turgut when the time comes. To do that, he will have to marry an Italian girl, so he can remain in the cathedral as porter in place of his uncle. In addition, he will keep an eye on this Padre Yves and try to find out more about him.'

'Is our tunnel still undiscovered?'

'It is. Two days ago the head of the Art Crimes Department inspected the underground tunnels; there were soldiers with him. When he came out, the frustration on his face told it all. They found nothing.'

The men continued to talk and drink raki until late that night, when the bride and groom took leave of their families. Addaio, who did not drink, had not even tasted the liquor. Accompanied by Bakkalbasi and three men, he left the hotel where the wedding party had taken place and made his way to a safe house that belonged to one of the members of the community.

The next day he would return to Urfa. He had planned to go to Turin himself, but that would put the community at ultimate risk. He had given very precise instructions; everyone knew what they were to do.

He spent the rest of the night praying, seeking God in repeated exhortations, but he knew, as he always knew, that God was not listening – God had never been near to him, or given him any sign. Yet he, Addaio, miserable Addaio, had destroyed his life and the lives of so many others in His name. What if God didn't exist? What if it was all a lie? Sometimes he had let himself be tempted by the devil and allowed himself to think that his community was kept alive by a myth, by dusty dreams, and that none of what they had told the children was true.

But there was no turning back. His life had been chosen for him: to serve the community and lead it and, above all, to secure for it the shroud of Jesus Christ. He knew that *they* would try once again to prevent that – they had been doing so for centuries. The community had fought back as it could, tracking its adversaries and their plunder through the centuries, tracing their activities in pursuit of a common goal. The knowledge they had gathered led down tantalizing avenues, to mysteries and answers Addaio sensed lay just beyond his grasp. But there was no mystery about his overarching purpose on this earth. Someday the community would recover the sacred cloth that had been bequeathed to it, and it would be he, Addaio, who at long last achieved that impossible goal.

30

UMBERTO D'ALAQUA HAD SENT A CAR TO PICK Sofia up at the hotel, and at the door of the opera house the assistant manager of the theater had been waiting to escort her to her host.

That touch was impressive, but she felt the full impact of D'Alaqua's stature when she entered his box. The other guests were members of the city's – and the country's – rich and powerful elite: Cardinal Visier, Dr. Bolard, two eminent bankers, a member of the Agnelli family and his wife, and Mayor Torriani and his wife.

D'Alaqua stood up and welcomed her warmly, with a squeeze of her hands. He seated her next to the mayor and his wife and Dr. Bolard. He himself was seated next to Cardinal Visier, who had greeted her with a cool smile.

She felt the men looking at her out of the corners of their eyes – all except the cardinal, Bolard, and D'Alaqua. She'd taken pains to look not just good but stunning. That afternoon she had gone to the hairdresser's and returned to Armani, this time to buy an elegant red tunic-and-pants outfit. It was a color the designer didn't often use, but it was spectacular, Marco and Giuseppe had assured her. The tunic had a low neckline, and the mayor couldn't seem to keep his eyes off it.

Marco was surprised that D'Alaqua had sent a car to pick Sofia up rather than coming personally, but Sofia understood the message. D'Alaqua had no personal interest in her; she was simply his guest to the opera. The man put unbreachable barriers between them, and though he did so subtly, he left no room for doubt.

At the intermission, they repaired to D'Alaqua's private salon for champagne and canapés.

'Are you enjoying the opera, dottoressa?'

Cardinal Visier was looking her over as he asked her the clichéd question.

'Yes, Your Eminence. Pavarotti has been wonderful tonight.'

'He has indeed, although *La Bohème* is not his best opera.'

Guido Bonomi entered the salon and effusively greeted D'Alaqua's guests.

'Sofia! You look absolutely gorgeous! I have a whole list of friends dying to meet you, and not a few wives jealous because their husbands' opera glasses have been on you more than on Pavarotti! You're one of those women who make other women *very* nervous, my dear!'

Sofia blushed. She was losing patience with Bonomi's inappropriate effusions and looked at him furiously. The professor read the message in her blue eyes and changed course abruptly.

'Well, then, I'll be expecting you all for dinner. Your Eminence, dottoressa, mayor. . . .'

D'Alaqua had seen Sofia's discomfort and stepped to her side.

'Guido's like that; he always has been. An excellent

246

man, an eminent medievalist, but personally a bit . . . shall we say . . . exuberant? Don't be upset.'

'I'm not upset with him, I'm upset with myself. I have to ask what I'm doing here; I don't belong. If you don't mind, when the performance is over I'll go back to the hotel.'

'No, don't go, dottoressa. Stay, and forgive your old professor, who can't seem to find the proper way to express his admiration for you. But he *is* sincere in that.'

'I'm sorry, but I really should go. There's no reason at all for me to go to dinner at Bonomi's house; I was a student of his, that's all. I shouldn't even have let myself be invited to the opera on account of him. To take a place in your box, among your guests, your friends . . . really, I apologize for the trouble I've caused you.'

'You've caused me no trouble at all, I assure you.'

The bell announced the end of the intermission, and Sofia reluctantly allowed D'Alaqua to guide her back to his box.

As the next act unfolded Sofia noticed that D'Alaqua was discreetly watching her. She felt like fleeing on the spot, but she was damned if she'd behave like a silly girl. She'd stick it out to the end, then she'd say her good-byes and never cross his path again. He had nothing to do with the shroud – it was absurd, and she intended to tell Marco that once and for all.

When the performance was over, the audience gave Pavarotti his usual standing ovation. Sofia took advantage of the moment to say good evening to the mayor, his wife, the Agnellis, and the bankers. Finally, she approached Cardinal Visier.

'Good night, Your Eminence.'

'You're leaving?'

'Yes.'

Visier, surprised, tried to catch D'Alaqua's eye, but he was conversing animatedly with Bolard.

'Dottoressa, I'd be very disappointed if you did not come with us to dinner,' the cardinal told Sofia.

'Oh, Your Eminence, I'm sure you understand better than anyone how uncomfortable I am. I really must go. I don't want to be any trouble.'

'Well, if there is no way to convince you . . . but I do hope to see you again. Your view of modern archaeological methods intrigued me – your ideas are so innovative, really. I studied archaeology before devoting myself entirely to the Church, you know.'

D'Alaqua interrupted them.

'The cars are waiting. . . .'

'Dottoressa Galloni is not coming with us,' Visier told him.

'I'm so sorry, I'd hoped you would, but if you'd rather not, the car will take you to your hotel.'

'Thank you, but I'd prefer to walk – the hotel is not far.'

'Forgive me, dottoressa,' the cardinal interrupted, 'but I don't think you should walk alone. Turin is a complicated city; my mind would be easier if you would let the car take you.'

Sofia gave in so they wouldn't think her entirely ungracious.

'All right, thank you.'

'Don't thank me,' the cardinal murmured. 'You are a formidable person, of great merit – you mustn't allow others to affect you so. Although I imagine that your beauty has been more of an inconvenience for you than an advantage, precisely because you have never traded on it.'

The cardinal's unexpected words were comforting. D'Alaqua accompanied her to the car.

'I'm glad you came, Dottoressa Galloni.'

'Thank you.'

'Will you be staying in Turin for a few more days?'

'Yes, perhaps for as long as two weeks.'

'I'll ring you, and if you have time I'd like us to have lunch together.'

Sofia stammered a soft 'All right' as D'Alaqua closed the car door and gave the driver instructions to take her to her hotel.

As the rest of the party departed, Cardinal Visier confronted Sofia's old teacher.

'Professore Bonomi, you have offended Dottoressa Galloni and offended all of us who were with her. Your contribution to the Church is undeniable, and we are grateful for all you've done as our principal expert in sacred medieval art, but that does not give you the right to behave like a lout.'

D'Alaqua watched, floored.

'Paul, I didn't think Dottoressa Galloni had made such an impression on you,' he commented a few moments later when they were alone.

The cardinal shook his head. 'I think Bonomi behaved terribly – he acted like an old lecher, and he offended her unnecessarily. Sometimes I ask myself how Bonomi's artistic talents can be so unrelated to the rest of the man's life. Galloni seems to me a good, serious person – intelligent, well educated, refined – a woman I could fall in love with were I not a cardinal. If we . . . if we weren't who we are.'

'I'm surprised at your candor.'

'Oh, please, Umberto, you know as well as I do that

celibacy is a hard, hard option – as hard as it is necessary. I have kept my vow, God knows I have, but that doesn't mean that if I see an intelligent, beautiful woman I don't appreciate her. I'd be a hypocrite if I denied it. We have eyes, we can see, and just as we admire a statue by Bernini, or are moved by the marbles of Phidias, or tremble at the hardness of the granite of an Etruscan tomb, we recognize the value of the people around us. Let's not offend each other's intelligence by pretending we don't see the beauty and worth of Dottoressa Galloni. I hope you'll do something to make it up to her.'

'Yes, I'm going to call her and ask her to lunch. I can't do any more than that.'

'No. We can't do any more than that.'

'Wow! You look terrific! Been to a party?' Ana Jiménez was just entering the hotel as Sofia got out of the car.

'Been to a nightmare. What about you? How are things going?'

'All right, I guess. This is harder than I thought, but I'm not giving up.'

'Good for you.'

'Had dinner yet?'

'No, but I'm going to call Marco's room; if he hasn't eaten yet I'll see if he wants to come down to the dining room.'

'Mind if I join you?'

'*I* don't. Don't know about Marco – hold on a minute and I'll let you know.'

Sofia came back from the front desk holding a message.

'He's gone out to dinner with Giuseppe. They're at the Turin carabinieri comandante's house.'

'So let's you and I eat. It's on me.'

'No, I'll treat.'

They ordered dinner and a bottle of Barolo and measured each other.

'Sofia, there's one episode in the history of the shroud that seems very confused.'

'Just one? I'd say they all are. Its appearance in Edessa, its disappearance in Constantinople. . . .'

'I read that in Edessa there was a very well established and influential Christian community, and it was so fierce that the emir of Edessa battled the Byzantine army rather than be forced to turn over the shroud.'

'Yes, that's right,' Sofia confirmed. 'In 944 the Byzantines stole the shroud in a battle with the Muslims, who at that time ruled Edessa. The emperor of Byzantium, Romanus Lecapenus, wanted the Mandylion, which is what the Greeks called it, because he thought if he had it he'd have God's protection and be invincible. He sent an army under his best general and offered a deal to the emir of Edessa: If the emir turned over the shroud, the army would withdraw without doing the city any harm, he would pay generously for the Mandylion, and he would free two hundred Muslim captives.

'But the Christian community in Edessa refused to turn over the Mandylion to the emir, and since the emir, even though he was a Muslim, feared that the shroud had magical powers, he decided to fight. The Byzantines won, and the Mandylion was taken to Byzantium in August of the year 944. The Byzantine liturgy celebrates the day. The Vatican archives contain the text of Pope Gregory's homily on August 16 when he received the cloth.

'The emperor sent it for safekeeping to the Church of St. Mary of Blachernae in Constantinople, where every

Friday it was worshipped by the faithful,' she continued. 'From there it disappeared and it wasn't seen again until it appeared in France in the fourteenth century.'

'And that's what I've been trying to figure out. Did the Templars take it?' Ana asked. 'Some authors say that it was the Knights Templar that stole the shroud from the Byzantines.'

'It's hard to say. The Templars are blamed for everything – they're pictured as these supermen who could do anything. They may have taken the Mandylion, or they may not have. The Crusaders sowed death and destruction – and *confusion* – wherever they went. Or it may be that Balduino de Courtenay, who became emperor of Constantinople, pawned it, and after that it was lost.'

'He could pawn the shroud?'

'It's one of many theories. He didn't have enough money to maintain his empire, so he went begging to the kings and princes of Europe and wound up selling off all sorts of religious relics brought back by the Crusaders from the Holy Land – in fact, his uncle Louis IX of France bought a number of them. It's also possible that the Templars, the most powerful bankers of the time, who were also constantly trying to recover sacred relics, paid Balduino for the shroud. But there's no document to support that.'

'Well, I think the Templars took it.' Ana's eyes were defiant.

'Why?' Sofia didn't understand this leap of reasoning, which turned out not to be reasoning at all.

'I don't know, just hints in what I've read. You yourself pointed to that possibility. They took it to France, where it finally reappeared.'

The two women continued talking for quite a while,

Ana speculating about the Templars, Sofia reeling off facts.

Marco and Giuseppe bumped into them on the way to the elevators.

'What are *you* doing here?' asked Giuseppe in surprise.

'We had dinner together and had a great time, right, Ana?'

Marco greeted the reporter warmly but he asked only Sofia and Giuseppe to have one last drink with him in the hotel bar.

'What happened, what are you doing home so early?' he asked when they sat down.

'Oh, Bonomi pissed me off. He fell all over me and made us both look like fools. I felt really uncomfortable, and when the opera was over I came back here. I mean, honestly, Marco, I don't want to be where I don't belong – I was totally out of place there, and it was embarrassing.'

'What about D'Alaqua?'

'He was a total gentleman, and surprisingly enough, Cardinal Visier was too. Let's leave them alone, shall we?'

'We'll see. I don't intend to close off any line of this investigation, no matter how far-fetched it may seem. This time I'm running down every possibility.'

Sofia knew he meant what he said.

Sitting on the side of the bed – the rest was covered with paper, notes, and books – Ana Jiménez turned over in her mind the conversation she'd had with Sofia.

What, she wondered, had Romanus Lecapenus, the emperor who stole the shroud from Edessa, been like? She pictured him as cruel, superstitious, power-mad.

Really, the history of the shroud had not been a happy one: wars, fires, thefts . . . and all for the thrill of possession and out of the conviction, rooted deep in the heart of men, that there are objects that are magical.

She was not Catholic, at least not a practicing Catholic. She'd been baptized like almost everyone else in Spain, but she couldn't remember ever having been back to Mass since her first communion.

She pushed the papers aside. She was sleepy, and as always before going to sleep, she picked up a book by Cavafy and looked absentmindedly for one of her favorite poems:

> Voices, loved and idealized,
> of those who have died, or of those
> lost for us like the dead.
>
> Sometimes they speak to us in dreams;
> sometimes deep in thought the mind hears
>   them.
>
> And with their sound for a moment return
> sounds from our life's first poetry —
> like music at night, distant, fading away.

She fell asleep thinking about the battle fought by the Byzantine army against the emir of Edessa. She heard the voices of the soldiers, the crackling of the burning wood, the crying of children who held tight to their mothers' hands as they frantically sought refuge. She saw a venerable old man surrounded by other old men, and a throng of the devout, on their knees, praying for a miracle that didn't happen.

Then the old man approached a small, simple wooden casket, took out a carefully folded piece of cloth, and gave it to a massive Muslim soldier who could hardly contain his emotion at taking these people's most venerated treasure.

The general leading the Byzantine army received the Mandylion from an Edessan nobleman and, victorious, rode swiftly off toward Constantinople.

Smoke obscured the walls of the city's houses, and the Byzantine soldiers who were swarming through the streets looting the city carried off their booty in large mule-drawn wagons.

Later, in the stone church that still, somehow, remained standing, beside the cross, surrounded by priests and the most faithful of the Christians, the bishop of Edessa swore – and they swore with him – that the Mandylion would one day be recovered, though it cost them their lives to do it.

Ana moaned in her sleep. She sat up with tears streaming down her face, racked with anguish.

She went to the minibar for water and opened the window to let in some cool air.

Cavafy's poem seemed to have come true, and the voices of the dead had stormed her sleep. So real had the dream been that she felt that what she had seen and heard as she slept had actually happened. She was sure that the events had unfolded just that way.

After a shower she felt better. She wasn't hungry, so she stayed awhile in her room looking through the books she'd bought for information on Balduino de Courtenay, the emperor gone begging. There was little to be found, so she went online, even though she didn't always trust what she discovered on the Internet. She was looking for information on the Templars, too, and to her surprise she came across a page supposedly posted by the Order of Knights Templar itself – an order that no longer existed. It was well known that it had been eradicated by the king of France in the fourteenth century. She called the head of IT at her newspaper and explained what she needed.

A half hour later the IT man called her back. The website server was in London – and the site was perfectly registered, perfectly legitimate.

31

c. A.D. 1250

'My lord, a messenger has just arrived from your uncle.'

The emperor of Byzantium stirred at the sound of his servant's voice and then sat up slowly, blinking sleepily. As he came fully awake and realized Louis's long-awaited response was at last at hand, Balduino leapt out of bed and ordered his manservant to send the messenger in.

'You should dress, my lord,' murmured Balduino's chief adviser, who had also entered the chamber. 'You are the emperor, and the envoy is a nobleman from the court of France.'

'Pascal, if you did not remind me, I would happily forget that I am emperor. Help me, then. Is there an ermine cape I've not yet sold or pawned?'

Pascal de Molesmes, himself a noble sent by the king of France to serve the king's disgraced nephew, remained silent.

Indeed, however, there was no ermine cape. Not long

ago the emperor of Byzantium had even ordered the lead stripped from the roof tiles of his palace in order to sell it off to the Venetians, who were making enormous profits off Balduino's financial straits.

By the time the emperor was seated in the throne room, his courtiers were whispering nervously as they awaited the news from the French king.

Robert de Dijon touched his knee to the floor and bowed his head before the emperor. Balduino gestured for him to rise.

'So, my lord, what news bring you from my uncle?'

'His Majesty the king is in fierce battle in the Holy Land, attempting to liberate the sepulcher of our Lord. I bring you the good news of the conquest of Damietta. The king advances and shall conquer the lands of the Nile on his way to Jerusalem. Thus at present he cannot aid you as he would wish, for the cost of his expedition far exceeds the Crown's annual levies. He recommends that you have patience and faith in the Lord. Soon you will be called to his side as the faithful and most beloved nephew that you are, and he will aid you then in overcoming the tribulations that you now suffer.'

Balduino's eyes filled with tears at the devastating message. A harsh look from Pascal de Molesmes steadied him.

'I have also brought you a letter from His Majesty.'

Dijon took from his belt a document bearing the seal of the king and held it out to the emperor, who took it limply and passed it to de Molesmes. Balduino then extended his hand to the noble messenger, who bowed once more and kissed the emperor's ring.

'Shall there be a reply to His Majesty's letter?'

'You are returning to the Holy Land?'

'First I am to journey to the court of Blanca de Castilla; I am taking her a letter from her son, my good King Louis. One of the knights who accompanies me is burning to return to the king's side to battle the infidels, and he shall bear whatever message Your Majesty might wish to send your uncle.'

Balduino nodded and stood up. He left the throne room without looking back.

'What am I to do now, Pascal?' he cried to de Molesmes when they were alone.

'What you have done on other occasions, my lord.'

'Go to the courts of my relatives, who seem unable to grasp how vital it is that Constantinople be saved for Christianity? I do not ask these things for myself! We are the last Christian bastion between them and the Muslims – but the Venetians are an avaricious people, who are forging an alliance with the Ottomans behind my back; all the Genovese care about is the profits from their trade; and my cousins in Flanders complain of not having enough resources to help me. Lies! Am I to prostrate myself again before those princelings, beg them to help me preserve the empire? Do you think God will forgive me for pawning the crown of thorns worn by His crucified son?

'I have no money to pay the soldiers, or the people of the castle, or my nobles. I have nothing, nothing. From the moment I became emperor at twenty-one, I have dreamed of restoring the empire's splendor, recovering the lands it has lost, and what have I done? Nothing! Since the Crusaders divided the empire and sacked Constantinople, I have barely been able to maintain the kingdom, and good Pope Innocent is deaf to my pleas.'

'Calm yourself, my lord. Your uncle will not abandon you.'

'Did you not hear the message?'

'Yes, and in it he tells you that he will send for you when he defeats the Saracens.'

The majestic chair in which the emperor was seated had been stripped of its gold leaf some time ago. Balduino stroked his beard reflectively, his left foot beating a nervous staccato on the tiles.

'My lord, you must read the king's letter.'

De Molesmes handed Balduino the sealed scroll Dijon had presented.

'Ah! Yes, my uncle no doubt recommends that I be a good Christian and not lose faith in our Lord.'

Breaking the king's scarlet seal, the emperor scanned the missive, a look of growing astonishment suffusing his face.

'My God! My uncle does not know what he is asking for!'

'The king makes a demand of you, my lord?'

'Louis assures me that despite the difficulties he is experiencing with the cost of the Crusade, he is willing to advance me a certain amount of gold if I deliver the Mandylion to him. He dreams of showing it to his mother, the most Christian lady Doña Blanca. He bids me sell him the relic or allow him to hold it for a number of years. He says that he has met a man who assures him that the Mandylion has miraculous qualities, that it has already healed a king of Edessa of leprosy, and that the man who possesses it shall never suffer. He says that if I agree to his request, I can negotiate the details with the Comte de Dijon.'

'And what will you do?'

'What a question, Pascal! You know that the Mandylion is not mine to give. Even if I wanted to deliver it over to my uncle, I could not. It belongs to the Church.'

'My lord, the Mandylion is all that remains to bargain with. If you could convince the bishop to give it into your keeping –'

'Impossible! He will never do that.'

'Have you asked?'

'He guards it most zealously. The shroud miraculously survived the Crusaders' sacking of the city. It was entrusted to the bishop by his predecessor, and he swore to protect it with his life.'

'You are the emperor.'

'And he is the bishop.'

'He is your subject. If he fails to obey, there are measures you can take. He would not wish to lose his ears or his nose.'

'My God, Pascal!'

'You will lose the empire. The cloth is sacred; the man who possesses it has nothing to fear. Try.'

The emperor wrung his hands. He feared a confrontation with the bishop. What could he tell him that would convince him to turn over the Mandylion?

'Very well, speak with the bishop,' he said at last. 'Tell him you go in my name.'

'I will, my lord, but he will not treat with me about this. You must speak with him yourself.'

Balduino took a sip of pomegranate-colored wine, and then with a wave of his hand he shooed de Molesmes from the room. He needed to think.

✝ The knight walked along the beach, his mind and spirit lulled by the washing of the waves against the pebbles on the shore. His horse stood by patiently, untethered, like the faithful friend it had been in so many battles.

The evening light illuminated the Bosphorus, and

Bartolome dos Capelos felt in the beauty of the moment the breath of God.

His horse whinnied and pricked up its ears, and Bartolome turned to see a figure on horseback approaching through the dust of the road. He put his hand on his sword, a gesture more instinctive than defensive, and waited to see whether the man riding toward him was the person he was expecting.

The rider clambered awkwardly from his horse and strode swiftly along the shoreline to where the Portuguese knight stood waiting.

'You are late,' said dos Capelos.

'I was attending the emperor until he dined. It was only then that I could slip out of the palace.'

'Very well. What is it you have to tell me, and why here?'

The olive-skinned man was short and stocky. His rat's eyes weighed the Templar knight. He had to tread carefully with this one.

'Sire, the emperor is going to ask the bishop to turn the Mandylion over to him.'

Bartolome dos Capelos didn't move a muscle, as though the information meant nothing to him.

'And how did you come to know this?'

'I overheard the emperor talking with de Molesmes.'

'What would the emperor do with the Mandylion?'

'It is the last valuable relic remaining to him; he will pawn it. You know that the empire has no money. He will sell it to his uncle, the king of France.'

'And what more have you heard?' the knight asked.

'Nothing, sire.'

'Very well. Here. Now begone.'

Dos Capelos put a few coins into the outstretched palm

of the man, who rode off congratulating himself on his good fortune. The knight had paid him well for the information.

For several years he had been spying in the palace for the Templars. He knew that the knights of the red cross had other spies in the palace, but he did not know who they were. The Templars were the only ones in the impoverished empire who had good hard coin and there were many, even noblemen, who lent them their services.

The Portuguese knight had shown no emotion when he'd told him that the emperor was planning to sell or pawn the Mandylion. It might be, he thought, that the Templars already had the news from another of their spies. But no matter. It was not his problem. He patted the gold in his pouch.

✞ Bartolome dos Capelos rode to the chapter house the Templars kept in Constantinople, a walled castle near the sea, where more than fifty knights lived with their servants and the grooms for their horses.

He made his way to the chapter hall, where at that hour his brothers would be praying. André de Saint-Rémy, their superior, made a sign to him to join the prayers. It was not until an hour after his arrival that Saint-Rémy sent for him. By then, the superior was in his study.

'Have a seat, my brother. Tell me what the emperor's cupbearer has told you.'

'He confirms the information from the captain of the royal guard: The emperor wishes to pawn the Mandylion.'

'The shroud of Christ. . . .'

'He has already pawned the crown of thorns.'

'There are so many false relics. . . . But the Mandylion is not false. On that cloth is the blood of Christ, the true visage of the Savior. I await permission from the Grand Master, Guillaume de Sonnac, to purchase it. Weeks ago I sent a message explaining that the Mandylion is now the only true relic that remains in Constantinople, and the most precious. We must get hold of it, to protect it.'

'But what if the Grand Master's reply does not come in time?'

'Then I shall make the decision and hope that he will accept it.'

'What about the bishop?'

'We know that Pascal de Molesmes has been to see him and asked him to turn it over. The bishop refused. The emperor will now go in person to make his request.'

'When?'

'Within the week. We will ask to meet with the bishop, and I will go to see the emperor. Tomorrow I will give you your instructions. For now, go and rest.'

✝ The sun had not yet risen when the knights completed their first prayers of the day. André de Saint-Rémy was absorbed in a letter he was writing to the emperor, requesting an audience.

The Eastern Orthodox empire was in its death throes. Balduino de Courtenay II was the emperor of Constantinople and the surrounding lands, but little else, and the Templars' relationship with him, the balance of power in the empire, was sometimes difficult, given his frequent demands for credit. The superior had managed the delicate relationship with skill. He was an austere man who had kept himself untainted by the glitter of decadent Constantinople and prevented any concupiscence or comfort from penetrating the walls of the fortress chapter.

Saint-Rémy had not finished putting away his writing

instruments when one of the brother knights, Guy de Beaujeu, rushed into the room.

'My lord, there is a Muslim here asking to speak with you. Three others are with him. . . .'

The Templar superior's expression did not change. He finished putting away his pen and ink and the documents he had written.

'Do we know them?'

'I know not, my lord; his face is covered, and the knights guarding the entrance have preferred not to ask him to reveal himself. He has given them this arrow, made from the branch of a tree, and he says that with these notches you will recognize him.'

Guy de Beaujeu handed the arrow to Saint-Rémy, whose face changed as he examined the rudely cut missile and the five notches in its shaft.

'Have him sent to me.'

A few minutes later a tall, strong-looking man entered the room where Saint-Rémy awaited him. He was dressed simply, but in clothes that denoted nobility.

Saint-Rémy made a gesture to the two Templar knights accompanying the Muslim, and with slight bows they wordlessly left the chamber.

✛ When they were alone, the two men embraced and burst out laughing.

'But Robert, what is this disguise?'

'Would you have recognized me had you not seen the arrow?'

'Of course I would have – do you think me incapable of recognizing my own blood brother?'

'You were to see only a Saracen. My disguise is not as effective as I had hoped.'

'The brothers have not recognized you.'

'Perhaps not. At any rate, I have managed to ride for weeks across the lands of our enemies without anyone suspecting and thought to maintain the mask until I knew your mind. I knew you would remember the arrows we made as children, mine with five notches, yours with three.'

'Have you encountered difficulties, my brother?'

'None that I have not been able to solve with the help of young brother François de Charney.'

'How many men have you journeyed with?'

'Just two Muslim scouts. It is easier for a small party to pass unnoticed.'

'Tell me, what news bring you from the Grand Master?'

'Guillaume de Sonnac is dead.'

'Dead! How?'

'The Temple was fighting alongside the king of France, and the help we gave was both much needed and well received, as you know from the success of the conquest of Damietta. But the king burned to attack Al-Mansurah, although the Grand Master counseled prudence and careful planning unclouded by the taste of triumph. But the king is headstrong and would not pause in pursuit of his vow to recover the Holy Land. He insisted on entering Jerusalem.'

'I sense you bring worse news.'

'I do, I fear. The king's strategy consisted of surrounding the Saracens in Al-Mansurah and attacking them from the rear. But Robert d'Artois, Louis's brother, moved precipitously, wiping out a small encampment before the king's troops were in position and alerting the Ayubis. The battle was bloody.'

Robert de Saint-Rémy wiped his eyes with the back of

his hand, as though to erase the memory of the dead that thronged his mind. He once more saw the crimson-colored earth, wet with the blood of Saracen and Crusader both, and his companions-at-arms fighting furiously, without quarter, their swords like extensions of their arms, piercing the bowels of Saracens on every side. He could still feel the weariness in his bones and the horror in his soul.

'Many of our brothers died. The Grand Master was gravely wounded, but we saved him, at least for a time.'

André remained silent, watching a tempest of emotions sweep across the face of his younger brother.

'The knights Yves de Payens and Beltrán de Aragon and I picked de Sonnac up off the field of battle after a treacherous arrow found him, and we carried him as far as we could. But the effort was in vain; he died in the retreat, of a fever.'

'What about the king?'

'We won the battle. The losses were terrible; thousands of men lay dead or wounded on the ground, but Louis said that God was with him and that he would triumph. With that battle cry he rallied the soldiers, and he was right – we won, but never was a victory so fragile. The Christian troops marched off then toward Damietta, but the king was sick with dysentery and the soldiers were starving, exhausted. I know not how it happened, all I know is that the army capitulated and Louis has been taken prisoner.'

A heavy silence fell over the room, and the two brothers, lost in their own thoughts, hardly moved for long minutes.

Through the window came the echo of knights doing military exercises on the glacis before the fortifications, amid the creaking of wagons and the ringing of the blacksmith's anvil.

At last André broke the silence.

'Who has been elected Grand Master?'

'Our new Grand Master is Renaud de Vichiers, preceptor of France, marichal of the order. You know him.'

'I do. Renaud de Vichiers is a prudent and pious man.'

'He has been sent from Acre in the Holy Land to negotiate with the Saracens for Louis's return. The king's nobles also sent emissaries, with instructions to ask the Saracens to put a price on the king's freedom. Louis is suffering terribly, although he is being attended by the Saracen physicians and receiving good treatment. When I left, the negotiations were making no headway, but the Grand Master trusts he will be able to secure the king's release.'

'What shall the price be?'

'The Saracens are asking that the soldiers of the Crusade return Damietta.'

'And are Louis's nobles willing to withdraw their troops from Damietta?'

'They will do as the king bids them – he alone can capitulate. De Vichiers has sent a message to him, advising him to agree.'

'What orders do you bring me from the Grand Master?'

'I bring you sealed documents and other messages that I have been asked to speak in your ear.'

'Then speak.'

'We must secure the Mandylion for the order. The Grand Master says that the cloth is the only relic whose authenticity is certain. When you have it, I am to take it to him in our fortress of Saint-Jean d'Acre. No one must know that it is in our power. You may buy it or do whatever you believe necessary, but no one must know that the purchase is for the Temple. The Christian kings are capable of killing for the Mandylion. The pope will also demand it for himself. We have lent him many of the relics that you have been buying from Balduino all these years, and others are in the power of Louis of France, sold or given to him by his nephew.

'We know that Louis wants the Mandylion,' Robert continued. 'After the victory at Damietta he sent a delegation with a message for the emperor. The delegation also carried documents with his orders to France.'

'Yes, I know. A few days ago the Comte de Dijon arrived with a letter for the emperor. Louis asked his nephew for the Mandylion in exchange for aid to Constantinople.'

Robert produced several sealed rolls of documents, which André laid on the table.

'Tell me, André, what do you know of our parents?'

His brother's lips tightened and he lowered his eyes to the floor. At last, he replied. 'Our mother is dead. Our sister Casilda likewise. She died during the birth of her fifth child. Our father, though old and ailing with gout, was still alive last winter. He spends his hours sitting in the great hall; he can hardly walk for the terrible swelling in his feet. Our elder brother, Umberto, administers the inheritance – our lands are prosperous and God has given him four healthy children. It has been so long since we left Saint-Rémy. . . .'

'But I still remember the allée of poplars that leads to the castle, and the smell of baking bread, and our mother singing.'

'Robert, we chose to become Templars, and we cannot and must not cling to the things of the past.'

'Oh, my brother! You have always been too severe with yourself!'

'And you, tell me, how is it you have a Saracen squire?'

'I have come to know the Saracens and respect them. There are wise men among them, men of nobility, and chivalry, and honor. They are formidable enemies, whom one must respect. I confess, I have friends among them. It is impossible not to, when we share lands and there is need to have quiet dealings with them. The Grand Master has asked us all to learn their language and has asked some of us, who have an appearance suitable for it, to learn their customs so that we may live in their territory, in their cities, to spy, observe, or carry out missions for the greater glory of the Temple and Christianity. My skin has become yet darker in the sun of the East, and the black of my hair also helps me disguise my true nature. As for their language, I must confess that it has not been hard for me to understand it and write it. I had a good teacher, the squire who accompanies me. Remember, brother, I joined the Temple at an early age, and it was Guillaume de Sonnac who ordered the youngest of us to learn from the Saracens so we might mingle freely with them.

'But you ask about Ali, my squire. He is not the only Muslim who has dealings with the Temple. His town was destroyed by the Crusaders. He and two other children managed to survive. Guillaume de Sonnac found them wandering several days' journey on horseback from Acre. Ali, the youngest of them, was exhausted and delirious from fever. The Grand Master took them to our fortress, where they recovered. And there they remained.'

'And they have been loyal to you?'

'Guillaume de Sonnac would allow them to pray to

Allah and use them as intermediaries. They have never betrayed us.'

'What about Renaud de Vichiers?'

'I do not know, but he made no objection to our traveling here alone with Ali and Said.'

'Well, brother, you must rest, and send me François de Charney, the brother who has come with you.'

'I shall.'

Once André de Saint-Rémy was alone he unrolled the scrolls given him by his brother, and he studied the orders sent by Renaud de Vichiers, the new Grand Master of the Order of the Temple.

✝ The large bedroom resembled a small throne room. The scarlet curtains, the soft cushions, the carved table, the crucifix of pure gold, and other objects of hammered silver spoke eloquently of the wealth in which their occupant lived.

On a small table to one side, several decanters of carved crystal held spiced wine, and on an enormous tray were arranged a colorful variety of sweets from the kitchen of a nearby monastery.

The bishop listened impassively, almost aloofly, to Pascal de Molesmes, who had come again in lieu of Balduino. For an hour the French nobleman had wielded every argument at his command in an attempt to convince the bishop to turn the Mandylion over to the emperor.

The bishop had great love for Balduino; he knew there was kindness in his heart, even though his reign had been marked by a long succession of misadventures. But he was lost in his own thoughts.

Pascal de Molesmes paused in his plea when he realized

that the bishop had stopped listening. The sudden silence broke the bishop's reverie.

'I have listened to you and I understand your reasoning, but the king of France cannot barter the fate of Constantinople for possession of the Mandylion,' he told the nobleman.

'Our most Christian king has promised the emperor aid; if it is not possible to purchase the Mandylion, he wishes, at least, to hold it for some time. Louis is desirous that his Christian mother, Doña Blanca de Castilla, contemplate the true visage of our Lord Jesus Christ. The Church will not lose possession of the Mandylion, and it could profit by this agreement, Your Excellency, in addition to helping relieve Constantinople from the penury that it now suffers. Believe me, your interests and those of the emperor are the same.'

'No, my son, they are not. It is the emperor who needs gold in order to save what remains of the empire.'

'Constantinople is dying; the empire is more fiction than reality – someday Christians will weep over its loss.'

'Seigneur de Molesmes, I know you to be too intelligent to try to convince me that only the Mandylion can save Constantinople. How much has King Louis offered just to hold it – how much to possess it? It would take great amounts of gold to save this kingdom, and the king of France is rich, but he will not ruin his own kingdom financially, no matter how much he loves his nephew or desires the Mandylion.'

De Molesmes's throat was parched. He had not even tasted the glass of no doubt superb Rhodes wine that the bishop had offered him. But such were the sacrifices of diplomacy.

'If the amount was considerable enough, would Your Excellency consent to its sale or lending?'

'No. Tell the emperor that I will not surrender it to him. That is my final word. Pope Innocent would excommunicate me. For many years the pope has desired to possess the Mandylion, and I have always put him off by arguing against exposing the shroud to the perils of such a journey. I would need the Holy Father's permission, and even in the unlikely event he were to consider granting it, you know that he would name a high price – a price that, even should Louis be able to pay, would be for the Church, not for his nephew the emperor.'

Pascal de Molesmes decided to play his last card.

'I remind you, Your Excellency, that the Mandylion does not belong to you. It was the troops of the emperor Romanus Lecapenus who brought it to Constantinople, and the empire has never renounced its ownership of the cloth. The Church is but a repository for the Mandylion. Balduino bids you turn it over voluntarily, and he shall be generous with you and with the Church.'

De Molesmes's words fell like lead on the bishop's spirit.

'Are you threatening me, Seigneur de Molesmes? Is the emperor threatening the Church?'

'Balduino, as you well know, is a most loving and beloved son of the Church, which he would defend with his own life if need be. The Mandylion is part of the empire's legacy, and the emperor is claiming it. I urge you to do your duty.'

'My duty is to defend the image of Christ and preserve it for all Christianity.'

'You did not oppose the sale of the crown of thorns, which was kept in the monastery of Pantocrator, to the king of France.'

'Ah, Seigneur de Molesmes. Do you honestly believe that that was Jesus' crown of thorns?'

'You do not?'

A look of fury came into the bishop's blue eyes. The tension between the two men was rising, and both knew that at any moment the bonds of civility might break.

'Seigneur de Molesmes, nothing you have said has changed my mind. You may tell that to the emperor.'

Pascal de Molesmes bowed his head. The duel had ended for the moment, but both men knew that neither victory nor defeat could be declared on either side.

At the gate of the bishop's palace, de Molesmes's servants were waiting beside his horse, a stallion as black as night, his most trusted companion in turbulent Constantinople.

Would he advise Balduino to go with his soldiers to the bishop's palace and force him to turn over the Mandylion? There was no other choice, it seemed. Innocent would never dare excommunicate Balduino, much less when he knew that the Mandylion would be in the keeping of the most Christian king Louis IX of France. They would lend it to Louis and they would put a high price on it, so that the empire might recover at least part of its lost glory.

The evening breeze was warm and soft, and the emperor's counselor decided to ride down by the shore of the Bosphorus before returning to the imperial palace. From time to time he liked to escape the oppressive walls of the palace, where intrigues, betrayal, and death lay behind every door, at every turning of the stair, and where it was not easy to know who your friends were and who wished you ill, given the refined art of dissembling practiced by the knights and ladies of the court. He trusted only Balduino, for whom, with the passing of the years, he had come to feel true affection, as in earlier days he had felt for good King Louis.

It had been many winters now since the king of France sent him to the court of the emperor to protect the gold the king had sent as payment for the valuable relics Balduino had sold him along with the lands of Namur. Louis had charged de Molesmes with remaining at the court and keeping him informed of all that happened in Constantinople. In a letter that de Molesmes himself had delivered to the emperor, Louis had commended Pascal de Molesmes to his nephew as a good Christian man who, the letter said, looked only to Balduino's good.

Balduino and he had felt a current of sympathy from the first moment, and there he was now, fifteen years later, the emperor's chancellor and friend. De Molesmes greatly admired Balduino's efforts to maintain the dignity of the empire, to preserve Constantinople, to resist the Bulgar pressure on the one side and the encroachments of the Saracens on the other.

If he had not pledged undying loyalty to King Louis and Balduino, he would have asked to join the Order of Templars years ago, so that he might do battle in the Holy Land. But fate had sent him to the heart of the court in Constantinople, where there were as many dangers to negotiate as on the field of battle.

The sun was beginning to drop below the horizon when he realized that he had ridden almost to the gate of the Temple's castle. He had great respect for André de Saint-Rémy, the superior of the order, an austere and upright man who had chosen the cross and sword as his life. Both men were Frenchmen and nobles, and both had found their destiny in Constantinople.

De Molesmes felt a sudden desire to speak with his

compatriot, but the shadows of night were falling and the knights would be at prayer. It would be better to wait until tomorrow to send a message to Saint-Rémy and arrange a meeting, he thought.

✝ Balduino slammed his fist into the wall. Fortunately, a tapestry softened the blow to his knuckles.

Pascal de Molesmes had told him in detail of his conversation with the bishop and the bishop's refusal to hand over the Mandylion.

The emperor had known that it was most unlikely that the bishop would voluntarily agree to his request, but he had prayed for that success most fervently to God, prayed for a miracle to save the empire.

The Frenchman, unable to disguise his irritation at the emperor's display of emotion, looked at him reproachfully.

'Don't look at me like that! I am the most wretched of men!'

'My lord, be calm. The bishop will have no choice but to deliver the Mandylion over to us.'

'And just how will that come about? Do you propose that I go and take it from him by force? Can you imagine the scandal that would cause? My subjects would never forgive me for taking the shroud from them – the shroud they consider to have miraculous properties – and Innocent would excommunicate me. And you tell me to be calm, as though there were a solution to this, when you know there is not.'

'Kings must make difficult decisions, my lord, to save their kingdoms. You are now in that position. You must stop lamenting your fate and act.'

The emperor sat in his regal chair, unable to hide the weariness that was upon him. It was bitter gall that he had tasted as emperor, and now the latest test with which his stewardship of the empire was presenting him was this unthinkable confrontation with the Church.

'Think of another solution.'

'Do you really see another way out?'

'You are my chancellor – think!'

'My lord, the Mandylion belongs to you – claim what is yours, for the good of the empire. That is my counsel.'

'Withdraw.'

De Molesmes left the room and made his way to his study. There, to his surprise, he found Bartolome dos Capelos.

He greeted the Templar warmly, then asked about the superior and the other brothers he knew. After a few minutes of polite conversation, he asked what had brought dos Capelos to the palace.

'My superior, André de Saint-Rémy, desires an audience with the emperor,' the Portuguese Templar said gravely.

'What is happening, my good friend? Is there bad news?'

Dos Capelos had orders not to speak a word more. Clearly the palace had heard nothing of the delicate condition of Louis of France, for when the Comte de Dijon left Damietta, the city was still in the hands of the Franks and the army was advancing victoriously.

'It has been some time since André de Saint-Rémy has met with the emperor, and many things have happened in those months. The audience will be of interest to both men,' dos Capelos replied, sidestepping the question.

De Molesmes realized that the Portuguese would tell him nothing more, but the importance of the audience the Templar superior was requesting was obvious.

'I note your petition, my brother. As soon as the

emperor determines the day and hour for the audience, I will inform André de Saint-Rémy, in person if I may, thereby to enjoy a few minutes' conversation with him.'

'I would beg that the audience be held as soon as possible.'

'I will see to it – you know I am a friend of the Temple. May God be with you.'

'And with you, my lord.'

Pascal de Molesmes was pensive after the meeting with the Templar. The inscrutable expression on dos Capelos's face indicated that the Temple knew something of vital importance that it could tell only the emperor. What would it want in exchange?

The Templars were the only ones in that convulsed world who had money and information always at their disposal. And the two commodities – money and information – gave them a special power, more than that of any king, or even the pope himself.

The relationship between Balduino and Saint-Rémy was one of mutual respect. The superior of the Temple's chapter in Constantinople shared Balduino's anguish at the increasingly grave situation of the impoverished empire. On more than one occasion the Temple had lent him generous amounts of gold – money he had not been able to repay, but in return for which he had put down as deposit certain relics, which had thus become possessions of the Templars. There were other objects, too, which would never return to the empire until the emperor had repaid the debt he had contracted, and that was a most unlikely possibility.

But de Molesmes put those thoughts aside and set about preparing for Balduino's visit to the bishop. He should go in the company of soldiers in armor and bearing weapons, enough to surround the bishop's palace and the Church of St. Mary of Blachernae, where the Mandylion was kept.

No one was to know what the emperor was proposing to do, so as not to alert the people, or the bishop himself, who took Balduino to be a good Christian who would never raise his hand against the Church.

The chancellor sent for the Comte de Dijon, to go over with him the details of the shroud's delivery. The king of France had given the count precise instructions as to what to do when his nephew turned over the shroud and how to arrange payment for it.

Robert de Dijon was around thirty, a powerfully built man of medium height, aquiline nose and blue eyes. The count's beauty had awakened the interest of the ladies at Balduino's court in the short time since his arrival. It was not easy for the servant sent by de Molesmes to find him; he had to bribe several servants in the palace before he discovered him, at last, in the apartment of Doña María, the emperor's recently widowed cousin.

When the Comte de Dijon presented himself in the chancellor's study he still bore traces of the musky perfume the noble lady left always in her wake.

'Tell me, de Molesmes, what the reason is for such great hurry?'

'My lord, I must know the instructions you have been given by good King Louis, so that I may please him.'

'You know that the king wishes the emperor to hand over the Mandylion.'

'Forgive my coming straight to the point: What price is Louis willing to pay for the shroud?'

'Will the emperor accede to his uncle's request, then?'

'My lord, allow me to ask the questions.'

'Before answering them I must know whether Balduino has made a decision.'

In two long strides, de Molesmes planted himself before the count and glared into his eyes, measuring the sort of man he had before him. The Frenchman did not flinch; indeed, he hardly moved a muscle. Unwavering, he held the counselor's gaze.

'The emperor is meditating upon his uncle's offer. But he must know how much the king of France is prepared to pay him for the Mandylion, where it will be taken, and who is to warrant its safety. Without knowing these and other details, the emperor can hardly be expected to make such a weighty decision.'

'My orders are to await the emperor's answer, and if Balduino agrees to deliver the Mandylion to Louis, to take it myself to France and deliver it into the hands of the king's mother, Doña Blanca, who will look after it until the king returns from the Crusade. If the emperor would like to sell the Mandylion, then Louis would give his nephew two sacks of gold, each the weight of a man, and return the lands of Namur to him. He would also make a gift to him of certain lands in France, which he might lease at a good yearly rent. If, on the contrary, the emperor wishes only to lend the shroud for a certain time, the king would likewise give him two sacks of gold, which Balduino would be pledged to repay in order to recover the Mandylion. If by a certain date, to be mutually agreed upon, the emperor did not repay his pledge, then the relic would become the property of the king of France.'

'Louis always wins,' de Molesmes said irritably.

'It is a fair offer.'

'No, it is not. You know as well as I that the Mandylion is the only authentic relic possessed by Christianity.'

'The king's offer is a generous one. Two sacks of gold would allow Balduino to repay his many debts.'

'It is not enough.'

'We are both aware, sir, that two sacks of gold, each the weight of a man, would solve many of the empire's problems. The offer is more than generous if the emperor sells the Mandylion outright, since he would also enjoy the rents of his lands in France for the rest of his days, while if he but pawns it . . . well, I am not certain he would be able to repay such an amount.'

'Yes, you are certain. You know very well he would never be able to recover the shroud. So, tell me, have you journeyed here with two sacks of gold?'

'I have brought a document signed by Louis pledging the payment. I also have a quantity of gold as a guarantee of the king's good faith.'

'And what assurance can you give us that the relic will arrive safely in France?'

'As you know, I journey with a numerous escort, and I am willing to accept in addition as many men as you think necessary to ensure the shroud's safety. My life and my honor are pledged to see the Mandylion safe in France. If the emperor agrees, we will send a message to the king.'

'How much gold do you have with you now?'

'Twenty pounds in weight.'

'I will send for you when the emperor has made his decision.'

'I will be waiting. I confess that I will not mind lingering in Constantinople a few days more.'

✝ François de Charney was practicing his archery with the other Templars, as André de Saint-Rémy watched from the window of the great hall. Young de Charney, like

André's brother Robert, looked much like a Muslim. Both had insisted on the necessity of taking on that appearance in order to cross enemy territory without undue contretemps. They trusted in their Saracen squires, whom they treated as close comrades.

After so many years in the East, the Temple had changed. Its knights had come to appreciate the values of its enemies – the Templars had not been content to engage them only in battle but also in their daily lives, and out of that had grown the mutual respect between the Templar knights and the Saracens.

Guillaume de Sonnac had been a prudent Grand Master, and he had seen something remarkable in Robert and François, qualities that would allow them to be the perfect spies – for thus they were.

The two knights spoke Arabic fluently, and when they were with their squires they comported themselves as true Arabs. With their skin browned by the sun and their vestments of Saracen nobility, it was difficult to see them as the Christian gentlemen they were.

They had told André of their countless adventures in the Holy Land, of the enchantments of the desert where they had learned to live, of writings by the Greek philosophers of antiquity recovered by the wisdom of the Saracens, of the arts of medicine learned from them.

The young men could not conceal their admiration for the enemies they had battled, which would have worried André de Saint-Rémy had he not seen with his own eyes the young men's devotion and commitment to the honor of the Temple.

They would remain in Constantinople until André gave them the Mandylion to take to the Grand Master. He shared with them his hesitation to allow them to journey alone with such a precious relic, but they assured him it was only in that way that the shroud would arrive safe at its destination, the Templar fortress of Saint-Jean d'Acre, where most of the Temple's treasures were held. Of course, Saint-Rémy had to first secure the shroud of Christ, and for that he needed patience and diplomacy, not to mention cunning – all qualities that the superior of the Constantinople chapter of the Temple possessed in no small amount.

32

ADDAIO ENTERED HIS HOUSE QUIETLY, TRYING
not to make any noise. The journey had exhausted him.
Guner would be surprised when he found him in the
morning. Addaio hadn't informed anyone in Urfa he was
coming back so soon.

Bakkalbasi had stayed on in Berlin. From there he
would fly to Zurich to withdraw the money they needed to
pay the two men who were being hired to kill Mendib
before he could be released from prison.

Addaio had known Mendib since he was a child. He was
a fine boy, friendly and intelligent. Obedient. The pastor
remembered how eagerly he had embraced his mission,
their last words before he submitted to the age-old sacrifice
and surrendered his voice forever so that the community
might prevail. But now he was a known link between them
and the cathedral. A link that must be broken.

They had managed to survive the Persians, the
Byzantines, the Crusaders, the Turks. They had been living
their secret lives for century upon century, carrying out the
mission they had inherited.

God's favor should have been with them as the true

Christians they were, but it was not – instead, He sent them terrible trials, and now a faithful young man had to die.

The pastor slowly climbed the stairs and went into his room. The bed was turned down. Guner always did that, even when Addaio was away. He could not have been a more faithful friend, trying always to make Addaio's life comfortable, sensing his wishes before he could make them known.

Guner would never betray him – it had been stupid to think that. If he could not trust Guner, then he would never be able to bear the burden he had carried since he was barely a man.

He heard a soft knock on the door and stepped to open it.

'Did I wake you, Guner?'

'I haven't slept for days. I must know. Is Mendib to die?'

'You got up to ask me about Mendib?'

'Is there anything more important than the life of a man, pastor?'

'Are you determined to torment me?'

'That's the last thing I want. But I can think of nothing else. Addaio, I appeal to your conscience – stop this madness.'

'Guner, go. I need to rest.'

Guner stared at him as if he could see into the depths of his dark soul. Then he abruptly turned and left the room. Addaio pressed his hands to his temples, trying to contain the rage and despair that pounded within him.

33

'HAVE A BAD NIGHT?' GIUSEPPE ASKED ANA, WHO was absentmindedly chewing on a croissant in the hotel's dining room.

'Morning. Yes, I had a terrible night, thanks. Where's Dottoressa Galloni?'

'I'm sure she'll be down any minute. Have you seen my boss?'

'No, I just got here.'

Giuseppe looked around the room. The tables were all occupied. 'Mind if I sit and have coffee with you?' he asked the reporter.

'Of course not! How's the investigation going?'

'Slow. How about you?'

'I've become a history student. I've read dozens of books, spent hours online, but I'll tell you, last night I learned more listening to Sofia than from all of that combined.'

'Yeah, Sofia explains things so well, you can see them. I've had that same experience with her. So, any theories yet?'

'Nothing solid, and today my head feels like jelly. I had nightmares all night.'

'Must have a guilty conscience.'

'What?'

'That's what my mother used to say to me when I woke up from a bad dream. She'd ask me, "Giuseppe, what did you do today that you shouldn't have?" She said that nightmares were a warning from your conscience.'

'Well, I don't remember doing anything yesterday that would bother my conscience. Certainly nothing to merit these nightmares. Are you just a cop, or are you a historian too?'

'Just a cop, which is enough. But I'm lucky to work in Art Crimes – I've learned a lot these years working with Marco.'

'I can tell you all worship him.'

'Yep. Your brother must have told you about him.'

'Santiago has tremendous respect for him, and I like him too. I've been to dinner at his house, and I've seen him a few other times.'

Sofia entered the dining room and spotted them.

'What's wrong, Ana?' she asked as she pulled out a chair.

'I guess I look like hell if you can see it from across the room! Is it so obvious I had a rough night?'

'You look like you've been to war.'

'Ha! I was in the middle of a battle, in fact, and I saw children hacked to pieces, their mothers raped – I even smelled the black smoke from fires burning all over the city. It was awful.'

'I can see that.'

'Sofia, I know I'm probably pushing my luck, but if you have a minute free today and wouldn't mind, could we talk again?'

'I don't know when, but sure, we can talk.'

Marco came in, reading a note, and walked over to the table.

'Good morning, all. Sofia, I have a message here from Padre Charny. Bolard is expecting us ten minutes from now in the cathedral.'

'Who's Padre Charny?' Ana asked.

'You just had dinner with him. The dashing Padre Yves de Charny,' Sofia answered.

'Don't be such a snoop, Ana,' Marco added.

'It's my nature,' the reporter replied with a smile, then winced and pressed her hand to her head.

Marco clearly wasn't interested in lingering. 'All right, let's get going – everybody knows what they're supposed to be doing. Giuseppe, you –'

'Yeah, I'm on it. I'll call you.'

'Let's go, Sofia. If we hurry we can still get there on time. Ana, have a nice day.'

'I'll try.'

On the way to the cathedral Marco asked Sofia about Ana Jiménez.

'What does she know?'

'I don't know. She seems like she's kind of floundering around, but I have a feeling she's got more than she lets on, and she's smart. She asks question after question after question, but she doesn't show her cards, you know? You'd think she didn't have anything, but I'm not so sure.'

'She's young.'

'But sharp.'

'Good for her. I spoke to Europol – they're going to give us a hand. They'll start by securing the borders – airport, customs, train stations – at the right time. No one will get through without careful scrutiny. When we're finished

288

with Bolard this morning, we'll go to carabinieri headquarters; I want you to see the plan that Giuseppe has been organizing. We won't have many men, but I hope there'll be enough. Not that it should be too hard to tail a guy who can't talk.'

'How do you think he'll get in touch with his people when he gets out?'

'I don't know, but if he does in fact belong to some organization, he'll have a contact address, someplace to go to – he'll have to go somewhere. Trojan Horse will get us there, don't you worry. You'll stay at headquarters to coordinate the operation.'

'Me? Oh no, I want to be out in the street.'

'I have no idea what we're going to run into, and you're not a cop. I can't see you racing through the streets of Turin if he takes off.'

'You don't know me – I can work a tail,' Sofia protested, smiling as she lapsed into 'cop talk.'

'Somebody has to stay at headquarters, and you're the best person to anchor us there. We'll all stay in touch with you with walkie-talkies. John Barry has talked his colleagues at the CIA into lending us some micro-cameras and other equipment – unofficially – so we can photograph the mute and track him wherever he goes. You'll pick up the signal at headquarters – it'll be just like you're on the street. Giuseppe has made arrangements with the warden to get us the mute's shoes.'

'You're going to put a tracking chip in them?'

'Yes. Or try to. The problem is that all he has is tennis shoes, and it's hard to get a device in them, but the guys from the CIA will help us out with that.'

'Did the court permission for the operation come through yet?'

'I should have it tomorrow at the latest.'

They arrived at the cathedral. Padre Yves was waiting for them, to take them to the large room in which Bolard and the committee of scientists were examining the shroud. He left Sofia and Marco with them and excused himself, saying he had work that wouldn't wait.

34

Balduino had dressed in his finest robes. De Molesmes had counseled that he alert no one to the visit he was about to make to the bishop. He had also personally chosen the soldiers who would accompany Balduino as well as those who would surround the Church of St. Mary of Blachernae.

The plan was simple. When night fell, the emperor would present himself at the bishop's palace. He would politely request that the bishop turn over the Mandylion; if the bishop did not do so willingly, then the soldiers would enter the Church of St. Mary of Blachernae and take the shroud by force, if need be.

De Molesmes had finally convinced Balduino not to be daunted by the bishop or his power. The giant Vlad, a man from the lands to the north, would also accompany the emperor. His mental faculties were not strong, and he would follow without hesitation any order he was given – qualities that would be useful if it became necessary to bring additional pressure on the churchman.

✚ Darkness had covered the city, and the only sign of life in its houses and palaces was the yellowish light of oil lamps. A pounding was heard on the gate of the bishop's palace. The servant who hurried to open it stepped back in surprise when he found himself face-to-face with the emperor.

The bishop's guards rushed to the gate at the servant's shout. Seigneur de Molesmes ordered them to kneel before the emperor.

The imperial party strode purposefully into the palace despite Balduino's rising terror. The resoluteness of his chancellor was all that prevented him from fleeing in panic from the interview that was to come. The soldiers of the imperial guard took up positions around the lower floors as the emperor and the chancellor ascended the stairs with Vlad.

The bishop had been savoring a glass of Cypriot wine as he reviewed a secret letter that had arrived that day from Pope Innocent. He opened the door of his apartment, alarmed by the noise that reached him from the stairway, and was rendered speechless as Balduino, Pascal de Molesmes, and the giant confronted him.

'What is this! What are you doing here – ' the bishop exclaimed.

'Is this the way you receive the emperor?' de Molesmes interrupted him.

'Calm yourself, Your Excellency,' Balduino said. 'I have come to visit you, as has long been my intention. I regret not having announced my arrival ahead of time, but matters of state prevented me.'

Balduino's smile did not calm the bishop, who remained silent as he backed away from them.

'May we sit down?' the emperor asked.

The bishop finally found his voice. 'Yes, of course, come in, come in,' he stammered. 'Your unexpected visit has surprised me, my lord. I will call my servants to bring us wine. I will have them light more lamps, and –'

'No,' de Molesmes broke in again. 'There is no need for you to do anything. The emperor honors you with his presence. Hear him.' He turned to the servants now clustered anxiously in the hall and dismissed them with reassuring words. Ordering the soldiers to stand by outside the bishop's apartment, he then followed Balduino and the giant inside, closing the heavy doors behind him.

The emperor took a seat in a comfortable armchair and sighed heavily. Constantinople must be saved. Pascal de Molesmes had convinced him that he had no option but to proceed.

Now recovered from his initial alarm, and taking a seat himself, the bishop addressed the emperor in a tone that bordered perilously close to insolence:

'What matter is of such importance that you find it necessary to disturb the peace of this house at this hour? Is it your soul that needs succor, or are you concerned by some matter at court?'

'My good bishop, I have come as a child of the Church to seek your counsel with respect to the empire's problems. Generally, sir, you care for our souls, but those who have souls have bodies, too, and it is regarding earthly problems that I wish to speak to you, for if the kingdom suffers, men suffer.'

Balduino looked toward Pascal de Molesmes for approval of his approach so far. De Molesmes, with a barely perceptible nod, signaled him to continue.

'You know the dire straits of Constantinople as well as I. One need not be privy to the secrets of the court to know that there is no money left in the treasury and that the constant incursions of our neighbors have weakened us terribly. It has been months since our soldiers were paid all they are owed, and that is true also of my courtiers and ambassadors. I am grieved not to be able to contribute to the Church, of which I am, as you know, a loyal and faithful son.'

At this point, Balduino fell silent, fearing that at any moment the bishop would react in anger. But while the tension in the room was palpable, the bishop simply listened – clearly weighing how to respond.

'Although I am not in the confessional,' Balduino went on, 'I wish to share with you my tribulations. I must save the empire, and the only solution is to sell the Mandylion to my uncle the king of France, may God protect him. Louis is willing to give us enough gold to pay the debts that hound us. If I deliver the Mandylion to him I will save Constantinople. And that is why, Your Excellency, as your emperor I am telling you that you must surrender the shroud to me. It will be in good Christian hands, like our own.'

The bishop looked at Balduino fixedly and cleared his throat before speaking.

'My lord, you come as emperor to demand a sacred relic of the Church. You say that in this way you will save Constantinople, but for how long? I cannot give you what does not belong to me; the Mandylion belongs to the Church, and thus to all Christianity. It would be a sacrilege to put such an object in your hands so that you might sell it. The faithful of Constantinople would not countenance it, for they worship the miraculous image of Christ. You have seen the devotion with which they pray to it, Friday after Friday. You must not confuse the things of earth with the things of heaven. Our interests are those of Christianity. My flock would never allow you to sell the relic or to send it to France, however well guarded it may be by good King Louis. Understand that it is not in my power to give you the Holy Shroud of our Savior.'

'I have not come to argue, Your Excellency, and I am not meekly requesting that you give me the Mandylion. I am ordering you to do so.'

Balduino was pleased with having spoken these last words so resoundingly and once again sought the approval of de Molesmes. But the bishop was not to be commanded so easily.

'I must respect you as emperor, my lord, but you owe me obedience as your bishop.'

'Your Excellency, I will not allow what remains of the empire to bleed to death because you insist upon retaining possession of a holy relic. As a Christian I regret having to be separated from the Mandylion, but now my duty is to act as emperor. I ask that you turn over the Mandylion . . . willingly.'

The bishop shot out of his chair and, raising his voice, cried out, 'You dare to threaten me? I warn you, if you rise up against the Church, Innocent will excommunicate you!'

'And will he also excommunicate the king of France for buying the Mandylion?' the emperor asked him, his voice rising.

'I will *not* give you the shroud. It belongs to the Church, and only the pope can dispose of the most sacred of relics –'

'No, it does not belong to the Church, as you well know. It was the emperor Lecapenus who rescued it from Edessa and brought it to Constantinople. It belongs to the empire; it belongs to the emperor. The Church has been but its faithful keeper, and now it shall be the empire that assumes custody.'

'You shall comply with the pope's decision – we shall write to him. You may argue your reasons, and I will bow to his decision.'

Balduino hesitated. He knew that the bishop was trying to buy time, but how was he to refuse what seemed a fair compromise?

Pascal de Molesmes stepped to Balduino's side and glared at the bishop.

'I think, Your Excellency, that you have not understood the emperor.'

'Seigneur de Molesmes, I beg you not to interfere!' shouted the prelate.

'You will not let me speak? On what authority? I, like you, am a subject of Emperor Balduino, and my duty is to protect the interests of the empire. Return the Mandylion to its rightful owner, and we can bring this dispute to a peaceful end.'

'How dare you speak to me in that way! My lord, bid your chancellor be silent!'

'Calm yourselves, both of you,' ordered Balduino, recovered now from his momentary hesitation. 'Your Excellency, Seigneur de Molesmes has spoken rightly – we have come to demand that you return what belongs to me. Delay not a moment longer, or I shall send my soldiers to seize the Mandylion by force.'

With swift steps the bishop strode to the door of his apartments and called out to his guard. When they heard the shouting, a platoon came running.

Emboldened by their presence, the bishop turned back to his inopportune visitors.

'If you dare touch a thread of the Holy Shroud I shall write to the pope and insist that he excommunicate you. Now off with you!' he roared.

Balduino did not move from his chair, but Pascal de Molesmes, equally enraged, leapt to the open doorway.

'Soldiers!' he cried.

In seconds a squad from the imperial guard ran up the stairs and entered the bishop's apartments, while the prelate's own guards stood by in shock.

'You will defy the emperor? I shall have you arrested for treason, and for that, the penalty is death,' exclaimed de Molesmes.

A shiver ran through the bishop's body. He looked in desperation at his soldiers, waiting for them to intervene. But they did not move.

Pascal de Molesmes addressed the frozen Balduino.

'My lord, I beg you give the order for His Excellency to accompany me to St. Mary of Blachernae and turn over to me the Mandylion, which I will carry to the palace for you.'

Balduino rose and, summoning up all his imperial dignity, strode toward the bishop.

'Seigneur de Molesmes represents me. You shall accompany him to the church and hand over the Mandylion. If you do not obey my order, my loyal servant Vlad will personally take you to the palace dungeons, which you will never again leave. I would prefer to see you officiate at the Mass on Sunday, but the decision is yours.'

He said no more. Without another look at the bishop, he swept from the prelate's apartments, surrounded by his soldiers and certain of having comported himself like a true emperor.

✝ Vlad the giant planted himself before the bishop, poised to obey the emperor's order. His Excellency realized that he would gain nothing by resisting. Attempting to snatch from the embers some tatters of his wounded pride, he turned to the chancellor.

'I shall surrender the Mandylion to you, but I shall write the pope.'

Surrounded by soldiers of the imperial guard and under the close watch of Vlad, the bishop made his way with the chancellor to the Church of St. Mary of Blachernae. There, in a silver casket, lay the holy relic.

The bishop opened the casket with a key he wore on a ribbon about his neck, and, unable to contain his tears, he took the shroud and held it out to de Molesmes.

'God will punish you for the sacrilege you are committing!'

The chancellor was unmoved. 'Tell me, what punishment will *you* receive for so many relics sold without the pope's permission and truly belonging to the Church?'

'How dare you accuse me of such a thing!'

'You are the bishop of Constantinople. You should know that nothing that happens is hidden from the eyes of the palace.'

Pascal de Molesmes carefully took the shroud from the hands of the bishop, who fell to his knees, weeping inconsolably.

'I suggest, Your Excellency, that you calm yourself and make use of your intelligence, which I know to be great,' de Molesmes said, as he turned to leave. 'Prevent a conflict between the empire and Rome that will benefit no one. You will not confront Balduino alone; you will confront also the king of France. Think long and well before you act.'

✝ The emperor paced nervously from one end of the room to the other as he awaited the return of de

Molesmes. Balduino veered wildly between heartache and fear at having challenged the Church so dramatically and nervous pride at the successful exercise of his imperial authority.

A red Cypriot wine helped make the wait easier. He had dismissed his wife and servants and given his guards strict orders to allow no one but the chancellor to enter his apartments.

Such was his condition when suddenly he heard rapid footsteps before his door. He threw it open. Escorted by Vlad and carrying the folded shroud, Pascal de Molesmes, looking extremely pleased, entered the emperor's bedchamber.

'Did you have to use force?' Balduino asked fearfully.

'No, my lord. That was not necessary. His Excellency at last saw the light, and he has voluntarily turned over the shroud.'

'Voluntarily? I think not. He will write the pope, and Innocent may well excommunicate me.'

'Your uncle the king of France will not allow it. Do you think Innocent will stand up to Louis? He will not dare challenge Louis for the Mandylion. Do not forget that the shroud has been secured for the king or that for the moment it belongs to you – it has never belonged to the Church. Your conscience can rest.'

De Molesmes held out the shroud to Balduino. The emperor hesitated a moment before taking the cloth in his arms. He looked at it in fear and wonder and then turned quickly to put it into a richly ornamented cask beside his bed. Turning to Vlad, he ordered him not to move from the side of the box and to defend it with his life if necessary.

✝ The entire court had come to Hagia Sophia for Sunday Mass. There was not a noble who had not learned of the dispute between the emperor and the bishop, and even the commoners had heard echoes of the confrontation.

On Friday the faithful had gone, as usual, to St. Mary of Blachernae to pray before the shroud, but they had found the casket empty.

Indignation ran like wildfire through the masses of simple worshippers, but burdened as they were by the precarious state of the empire, no one dared confront the emperor. Nor did the worshippers wish to lose their eyes or ears, and however much they lamented the absence of the shroud, they realized that they would lament even more the loss of those organs.

In Constantinople, gambling was part of the very history of the city. For its inhabitants, anything might be the occasion for a wager – even the confrontation between the emperor and bishop. And so, with the dispute over the Mandylion now common knowledge throughout the city, wagers on the outcome had reached astronomical figures. Some predicted that the bishop would officiate at the Mass, while others wagered that he would not appear, and that with this affront to his authority the emperor would declare war on the papacy.

The Venetian ambassador stroked his beard expectantly, and the envoy from Genoa never took his eyes from the door. It would be good for the interests of both men's republics if the pope excommunicated the emperor, but would Innocent dare defy the king of France?

Balduino entered the basilica with the ostentation worthy of an emperor. Dressed in scarlet, accompanied by his wife, his most loyal nobles, and the chancellor Pascal de Molesmes, he took a seat on the ornate throne that occupied a place of honor in the sanctuary. None of his subjects saw the slightest sign of concern in the emperor's expression as his gaze passed serenely over them.

The seconds seemed like hours, but after only a few minutes His Excellency the bishop of Constantinople appeared. Dressed in his pontifical robes, he strode slowly and ceremoniously toward the altar. The emperor sat impassively on his throne, while a murmur ran through the basilica. De Molesmes had been willing to wait briefly for the bishop, but if he did not appear after that, the chancellor had arranged that the Mass be said by a priest he had generously remunerated for the occasion.

The Mass took place without incident, and the bishop's homily was a call to concord between men and to forgiveness. The emperor took communion from the bishop, and even the chancellor came forward to receive the host and wine. The court understood the message: The Church would not defy the king of France. When the service had concluded, the emperor received his court at a reception abundant with delicacies, accompanied by wine brought from the duchy of Athens, a strong, full-bodied vintage with a lingering taste of pine resin. Balduino was in excellent humor.

The Comte de Dijon approached de Molesmes.

'So, Seigneur de Molesmes, is it possible the emperor has at last made a decision?'

'My dear count, in a very short while the emperor will give you your reply.'

'May I ask what reply I might expect?'

'There are still some details that concern the emperor.'

'What details might those be?'

'Patience, patience. Enjoy the food and wine, and come tomorrow to see me, early.'

'Have you been able to persuade the emperor to grant me an audience?'

'Before the emperor receives you, you and I must talk. I am certain we can arrive at an agreement satisfactory to both your king and mine.'

'I remind you that you are a Frenchman, just as I am, and that you have a duty and obligation to Louis.'

'Ah, my good King Louis! When he sent me to Constantinople he ordered me, with all his heart, to serve his nephew as faithfully as himself.'

The count understood de Molesmes's message. The chancellor's first loyalty was to Balduino.

'Tomorrow, then,' he said, inclining his head.

'I shall be waiting.'

The Comte de Dijon moved away, seeking the eye of María, Balduino's cousin, who was doing all in her power to make the count's stay in Constantinople a pleasant one.

✝ The first light of dawn had not yet broken. André de Saint-Rémy left the chapel, followed by a small group of knights. They made their way to the refectory, where, before going off to their labors, they broke their fast with a round loaf of bread moistened with wine. Their frugal meal done, the Templars Bartolome dos Capelos, Guy de Beaujeu, and Roger Parker directed their steps to Saint-Rémy's study.

Though he had arrived there but minutes earlier, the superior was waiting for them impatiently.

'De Molesmes has still not sent me a message confirming my audience with the emperor. I suppose that the latest events have kept him busy. The Mandylion is being kept by Balduino in a coffer next to his bed, and this very day de Molesmes is to begin negotiations with the Comte de Dijon for the price of its delivery. The court knows nothing of the fate of the king of France, although we must presume that an emissary from Damietta will not be long in coming. We must not wait any longer for the chancellor's call; we will go to the palace now and I will request an audience with the emperor, to tell him that his most august uncle is a prisoner of the Saracens. The three of you will accompany me, and you will speak to no one of what I shall tell the emperor.'

The three knights nodded and, following their superior's rapid steps, they soon came to the glacis before the fortress, where grooms were waiting with horses. Three mounted servants and three mules loaded with heavy sacks were there also and would form part of the Templar delegation.

The sun was just rising when they arrived at the palace in Blachernae. The palace servants were surprised to see the superior of the Templar chapter in person and understood immediately the import of such a visit at that hour.

The chancellor was reading when a servant rushed into his room to tell him of the presence of Saint-Rémy and his knights and of the Templar's desire for an immediate audience with the emperor.

Uneasiness washed over de Molesmes. André de Saint-Rémy would never come to court without a confirmed audience with the emperor unless something grave was afoot.

De Molesmes hurried through the palace to greet the superior.

'My friend, I was not expecting you –'

'It is urgent that I see the emperor,' Saint-Rémy replied brusquely.

'Tell me, what has happened?'

The Templar weighed his answer.

'I bring news of interest to the emperor. We must see him alone.'

The chancellor realized that he would get nothing more from the Templar. He might try to worm the reason for the visit out of him by telling him that Balduino could not receive him on such short notice unless he, de Molesmes, were first apprised of the message, but he saw that this tactic would not work with Saint-Rémy and that, if his wait was prolonged, he might well turn and leave without a word.

'Wait here. I will tell the emperor of your urgency.'

The four Templars stood and waited in silence. They knew they were being watched by those able to read their lips if they spoke to one another. They were still waiting when the Comte de Dijon arrived for his interview with de Molesmes, surprised to see such an imposing delegation from the Temple.

A half hour passed before de Molesmes hurriedly reentered the room. He frowned when he saw the Comte de Dijon, despite the importance of the meeting he and the king's representative had planned.

'The emperor will receive you now in his private apartments,' he announced to the Templars. 'Comte de Dijon, if you will wait for me, the emperor has asked that I stand by his door in case he has need of me.'

Balduino was waiting for them in a small room off the throne room, his eyes revealing concern over this unexpected visit. He sensed that the Templars were bringing unwelcome news.

'Tell me, gentlemen, what is so urgent that it cannot wait for a public audience, as is our wont?'

André de Saint-Rémy went straight to the point.

'My lord, I come to inform you that your uncle, Louis

IX of France, is a prisoner in Al-Mansurah. At this moment, negotiations are being held on the conditions for his freedom. The situation is grave. I thought it prudent that you should know.'

The emperor's face went white, as though the blood had drained from his body. For a few seconds he was unable to speak. He felt his heart beating fast and his lower lip trembling, just as they'd done when he was a boy and had to struggle not to cry, so that his father would not punish him for showing signs of weakness.

The Templar saw the storm of emotions that had taken possession of the emperor, and he continued speaking in order to give him time to recover.

'I know how deep and true is your affection for your uncle. I assure you that all possible efforts are being made to free him.'

Such was the confusion in his mind and heart that Balduino was barely able to stammer a few incoherent words.

'When did you learn this? Who told you?'

Saint-Rémy did not reply, but continued with his message.

'My lord, I know the problems that burden the empire and I have come to offer aid.'

'Aid? Tell me. . . .'

'You are about to sell the Mandylion to Louis. The king sent the Comte de Dijon to negotiate for the shroud's sale or lease. I know that the Holy Shroud is now in your possession and that once the agreement is concluded the count will take it to France, to Doña Blanca de Castilla. You are pressed by the Genovese bankers, and the Venetian ambassador has written to inform the Signoria that within a short time they will be able to buy what remains of the empire at a low price. If you do not pay off part of your debt to the Venetians and the Genovese, you will become an emperor without an empire. Your realm has begun to be a fiction.'

Saint-Rémy's hard words were having their desired effect on the spirit of Balduino, who, despairing, was wringing his hands under the broad sleeves of his scarlet tunic. He had never felt so alone as at this moment. He sought in vain for his chancellor, but the Templars had made it clear that they wished to speak to the emperor in private.

'What do you suggest, gentlemen?' he finally asked.

'The Temple is ready to purchase the Mandylion from you,' Saint-Rémy replied. 'This very day you shall have enough gold to retire your most pressing debts. Genoa and Venice will leave you in peace – unless you incur more debt. Our demand is silence. You must swear upon your honor that you will tell no one – no one, not even your good chancellor – that you have sold the shroud to the Temple. No one must ever know it.'

'Why do you demand my silence?'

'You know that we prefer to act with discretion. If no one knows where the Mandylion is, there will be no disputes or confrontations between Christian and Christian. Silence is part of the price. We trust in you, in your word as a gentleman and emperor, but the bill of sale will state that you will be in the Temple's debt for the full amount we bring you today if you reveal the terms of our agreement. We would also require the immediate repayment of all your other debts to the Temple.'

The emperor could hardly breathe from the intense pain in his chest.

'How do I know that Louis is being held prisoner?' he managed to ask.

'You know, sir, that we are men of honor and would never lie to you about such a matter.'

'When would I have the gold?'

'Now.'

Saint-Rémy knew that the temptation was too great for Balduino, especially with the fate of his chief sponsor, the king of France, in doubt. By simply saying yes, the emperor would eliminate most of his immediate worries; that very morning he could call in the Venetian and Genovese ambassadors and pay his debts to their republics.

'No one in the court will believe that the money has simply fallen from the sky.'

'Tell them the truth – tell them that the Temple has given it to you. You need not tell them why. Let them think it is a loan.'

'And if I do not agree?'

'You are free not to agree, my lord. We have made no threat against this empire, or yourself.'

They stood in silence. Balduino tried frantically to weigh his dwindling options as Saint-Rémy waited calmly.

At last the emperor fixed his gaze on the Templar and in a barely audible voice spoke but four words: 'I accept your offer.'

Bartolome dos Capelos handed his superior a rolled document, and Saint-Rémy in turn extended it toward the emperor.

'This is the agreement. Read it; it contains the terms that I have spoken of. Sign it and our servants will bring the gold we have brought with us and put it where you command.'

'Were you so sure I would agree, then?' moaned Balduino.

Saint-Rémy remained silent, though his eyes never left

the emperor's. Balduino picked up a quill, affixed his mark, and sealed it with the imperial seal.

'Wait here,' he told the Templar, and sighed. 'I will bring the Mandylion.'

The emperor left the room by a door hidden behind a tapestry. A few minutes later he returned with a carefully folded piece of cloth.

The Templars unfolded it enough to ensure that it was the authentic Mandylion. Then they folded it up again.

At a gesture from Saint-Rémy, the Scottish knight Roger Parker and the Portuguese Templar dos Capelos left the room and swiftly made their way to the entrance of the palace, where their servants were waiting.

Pascal de Molesmes, hovering in the antechamber, observed the coming and going of the Templars and their servants loaded down with heavy sacks. He knew it would be futile to ask what they were carrying, and he was bewildered at not having been called by the emperor. Time and again he considered entering the room with the others, but something counseled prudence. He feared provoking Balduino's wrath, and so he waited and watched.

Two hours later, with the sacks of gold deposited in a secret compartment hidden in the tapestry-covered wall, the Templars took their leave of the emperor.

Balduino would keep his promise of silence, not simply because he had given his word as emperor but also because he feared André de Saint-Rémy. The superior of the Templar chapter in Constantinople was a pious man, devoted utterly to the cause of the Lord, but in his eyes shone the man inside, a man whose hand would not tremble if he had to defend that which he believed in or which he had vowed to do.

When de Molesmes entered the royal chamber, he

found Balduino pensive but calm, as though a weight had been lifted from him.

The emperor informed him of the sad fate of his uncle the king of France and how, in view of the circumstances, he had accepted a new loan from the Templars. He would pay off the debt to the Venetians and Genovese and bide his time until good King Louis was once again at liberty.

The chancellor listened with concern, sensing that Balduino was concealing something, but he said nothing.

'Then what will you do with the Mandylion?'

'Nothing. I will keep it in a secret place and wait for Louis to be freed. Then I will decide what to do. This may have been a sign from our Lord to prevent us from sinning by selling his holy image. Call the ambassadors and tell them that we will deliver over to them the gold we owe their cities. And call in the Comte de Dijon – I will tell him of the fate of his king.'

✢ Before the assembled knights of the chapter, André de Saint-Rémy carefully unfolded the shroud, watching the image of the full body of Christ appear. The Templars fell to their knees and, led by their superior, began to pray.

They had never seen the shroud in its entirety. In the casket in which the Mandylion was laid in St. Mary de Blachernae, all that could be seen was the face of Jesus, as though it were a painted portrait. But there before them now was the figure of Christ with the stigmata from the torments he had suffered. Lost in prayer and meditation, the knights were unaware of the hours that passed, but night was falling by the time Saint-Rémy rose and carefully folded the shroud and went with it toward his room. A few minutes later he sent for his brother Robert and the young knight François de Charney.

'Make ready for your departure as soon as possible.'

'If you allow us, sir, we could depart within a few hours, when the shadows of night will protect us,' suggested Robert.

'Will that not be dangerous?' asked the superior.

'No, it is better that we leave the house when no one can see us and the eyes of those who may be watching us are overtaken by sleep. We will tell no one that we are leaving,' de Charney put in.

'I will prepare the Mandylion against the rigors of the journey. Come for it, no matter the hour. You shall also take a letter from me, and other documents, and deliver them to Grand Master Renaud de Vichiers. You must not deviate from the road to Acre for any reason. I suggest that several brothers accompany you – perhaps Guy de Beaujeu, Bartolome dos Capelos –'

'Brother,' interrupted Robert, 'I beg you allow us to go alone. It will be safer. We can lose ourselves in the woods and fields, and we will have our squires with us. If we go alone we will arouse no suspicions, but if we go with a group of brothers, then the spies will know that we are carrying something.'

'You will be carrying the most precious relic of Christianity –'

'– which we will defend with our lives,' interrupted de Charney.

'Then let it be as you say. Now leave me, I must prepare the letter. And pray, pray that God may guide you to your destination. Only He may warrant the success of your journey and your mission.'

✠ There was no moon. Not a single star illuminated the vault of the sky. Robert de Saint-Rémy and François de

Charney crept stealthily from their chambers and made their way to the apartment of André de Saint-Rémy. Silence filled the night, and inside the fortress the other knights were sleeping. On the battlements, a few Templars, with the soldiers in their service, stood guard.

Robert de Saint-Rémy gently pushed open the door of his brother and superior's chamber. They found him on his knees praying before a crucifix on the wall.

When he became aware of the presence of the two knights, he rose and, without a word, handed Robert a cloth sack of no more than middling size.

'Inside, in a wooden coffer, is the Mandylion. And here are the documents you are to take to the Grand Master and gold for the journey. May God be with you.'

The two brothers embraced. They did not know if they would ever see each other again.

Young de Charney and Robert de Saint-Rémy pulled on their Saracen robes and, melting into the blackness of the night, hurried to the stables, where their squires awaited them, calming the impatient horses. They gave the password to the soldiers at the gate and, abandoning the safety of the chapter's fortress, set out on the road to Acre.

35

SLOWLY, MENDIB PACED BACK AND FORTH ACROSS the jail's narrow courtyard, enjoying the sunshine that warmed the morning. He had heard enough to know that he had to remain alert, and the psychologist's and social worker's nervousness had aroused his suspicions further.

He had passed the medical examination, he had been observed at length by the psychologist, and the warden had even sat in on one of those exhausting sessions in which the doctor made him react to those stupid stimuli they baited him with. At last, the parole board had signed the papers for his release, and all that was lacking was the final approval by the judge – ten days at most, and he would be free.

He knew what he was to do. He was to wander through the city until he was certain he wasn't being followed, and then he was to go to the Parco Carrara. He was to go there for several days, observe the community's contact Arslan from a distance, and not drop the note to set a meeting until he was sure that no one was watching.

He feared for his life. That policeman who'd visited him had not seemed to be bluffing – he'd threatened to do everything in his power to see that Mendib spent the rest of his life in prison. Then suddenly, the way was cleared for his release. The carabinieri, he thought, were preparing some trap.

They may think that if I'm released I'll lead them to my contacts. That's it, that's what they want, and I'm just the bait. I have to be careful.

He continued to pace back and forth, back and forth, without realizing that he was being observed. Tall, dark-skinned, their faces blank and stupid from their time in jail, the two Bajerai brothers studied him surreptitiously through one of the windows that opened onto the courtyard as they talked quietly about the murder they would soon commit.

In the warden's office, Marco Valoni was in the midst of an argument.

'I know it's unlikely that anything will happen, but we can't leave that to chance. We have to ensure his safety for the rest of the time he's here,' he insisted to the warden and the head guard.

'Signor Valoni, the mute barely exists for the other inmates – he's of no interest to anyone. He doesn't speak, he has no friends, he communicates with none of them. No one will do him any harm, I assure you,' the guard replied.

'We can't run that risk. Think about it – we don't know who we're dealing with. He may be some poor jerk, or he may not be. We haven't made much noise about releasing him, but it's enough to be heard by those who may be listening. Someone has to answer to me for his safety here.'

'But Marco,' the warden argued, 'we haven't had any

paybacks in this jail or killings among the prisoners – nothing like that – in years. I just don't share your concern here.'

'I don't care. I *am* concerned. I want to talk to the capos here. Signor Genari, as head guard, I'm sure you know who they are.'

Genari shrugged his shoulders. There was no way to convince this guy not to go sticking his nose into jail politics. The cop actually thought that he was going to tell him which prisoners gave the orders inside, as though Genari could do that without risking his own neck.

Marco picked up on Genari's reservations and rephrased his request.

'Look, Genari, there has to be one prisoner inside that the others respect, defer to, you know. Let's talk to him.'

The warden shifted uncomfortably in his chair while Genari maintained a stubborn silence. Finally, he intervened. 'Genari, you know this prison better than anyone – which one of the men fits the bill? Get him in here.'

Genari stood up and walked out of the office. He knew he couldn't stonewall longer without arousing the suspicions of both the warden and this son of a bitch from Rome. His jail ran like a Swiss watch – there were unwritten laws that everyone followed, and now Valoni wanted to know who pulled the strings.

He sent one of the guards for the capo, Frasquello. At that hour he'd be on his cell phone, giving his sons instructions for running the drug-smuggling operation that had sent him to prison – a snitch had paid the price for *that*, but that was another story.

Frasquello swaggered into Genari's little office, looking pissed.

'What do you want? What the fuck is so fucking important?'

'There's a cop who wants to talk to you.'

'I don't talk to cops.'

'Well, you're going to have to talk to this one, because if you don't, he'll turn this prison inside out.'

'There's nothing in it for me – talking to some fucking cop. If he's got a problem, he can solve it himself. Leave me out of it.'

'No! I'm not leaving you out of it!' shouted Genari. 'You're coming with me to see this guy, and you're going to talk to him. The sooner this shit is over the better, so let's go.'

'What's he after? What does he want with me? I don't know any cop, and I don't want to know one. Just leave me the fuck alone.'

The capo made a move to leave the office, but before he could open the door Genari had him against the wall, his arm twisted behind his back.

'Turn me loose, you fuck! Are you crazy? You're a dead man!'

Just then the office door opened. Marco stood there, staring hard at both men.

'Turn him loose!' he ordered Genari.

Genari released his grip on Frasquello, who turned around slowly, measuring the newcomer.

'I decided I'd come down myself. Looks like I got here just in time. Sit down,' he ordered Frasquello.

The capo didn't move. Genari shoved him into a chair.

'I don't know who the fuck you are, but I know my rights, and I don't have to talk to any fucking cop,' the capo spat. 'I'll call my lawyer.'

'You won't call anybody, and you'll listen to me and do

what I tell you, because if you don't you'll be transferred to a place where your good friend Genari won't be looking after you.'

'You can't threaten me.'

'I'm not threatening you.'

For no more than a few seconds, Frasquello considered that.

'Fuck it, what do you want?'

'Well, now that you're being reasonable, I'll tell you: There's a man here in this prison I want protected.'

'Tell Genari – he's the boss. I'm just an inmate.'

'I'm telling you because you're the one who's going to make sure nothing happens to him.'

'Oh, yeah? And how am I supposed to do that?'

'I don't know, and I don't care.'

'Supposing I agree, what's in it for me?'

'Some . . . perks here inside.'

'Ha! That's funny, cop. My friend Genari already takes care of that. Who do you think you're dealing with?'

'All right, I'll look over your file and see if there's some way to reduce your sentence for cooperating.'

'That's not enough – I need a guarantee.'

'I'm not guaranteeing anything. I'll speak with the warden and recommend that the parole board take your behavior into account. But that's it.'

'No deal.'

'If there's no deal, then you're going to start losing some of the accommodations you've gotten used to. Your cell will be turned upside down every other day, and you'll follow the rules. Genari will be transferred, and then we'll move you too. To a place you won't find nearly as comfortable.'

'Who's the man?'

'Will you do it?'

'Tell me who we're talking about.'

'A guy that doesn't talk.'

Frasquello began to laugh. 'You want me to protect that poor jerk? Nobody pays him any attention, cop, nobody cares about him. You know why? Because he's *nobody*.'

'I don't want anything to happen to him in the next week.'

'Who'd be wanting to hurt him?'

'I don't know. But you need to keep it from happening.'

'What do you care about him?'

'That's none of your business. Just do what you need to do and you'll continue to enjoy your little vacation at the state's expense.'

'Okay. I'll babysit the son of a bitch.'

Marco left the office, relieved. The capo was no fool. He'd do it.

Now came the tricky part – getting hold of the tennis shoes the mute wore, the only shoes he owned, and planting the transmitter. The warden had promised he'd send a guard to get the shoes in the next few days. He wasn't sure what excuse he'd make, but he'd get it done. John Barry was sending a colleague to Turin – an expert in microtransmitters who was able, John said, to slip a microphone into a fingernail. Well, Marco would see whether he was as good as he was reported to be.

36

The Duc de Valant had requested an audience with the chancellor. He arrived at the appointed hour in the company of a richly dressed young merchant.

'Tell me, my lord,' the chancellor asked, 'what is this urgent matter that you wish to discuss with the emperor?'

'My dear de Molesmes, I bid you attend this gentleman, who honors me with his friendship. He is a respected merchant in the city of Edessa.'

Pascal de Molesmes, with a bored expression but out of courtesy to the duke, listened to the young merchant, who with no courtly flourishes went directly to the reason for his journey to Constantinople.

'I know of the empire's financial difficulties, and I come with an offer for the emperor.'

'You come with an offer for the emperor?' the chancellor repeated with a mixture of irritation and amusement. 'And what offer might that be?'

'I represent a group of wealthy nobleman merchants in Edessa. As you know, many years ago the armed forces of a certain Byzantine emperor removed from the protection of my city its most treasured relic, the Mandylion. We are men of peace; we live honestly, but we wish to return to our community what once belonged to it but was stolen. I come not to supplicate that you return to us what now belongs to the emperor, for it is known to all that he forced the bishop to deliver it into his keeping and that the king of France swears that his nephew did not sell it to him. If the Mandylion is in the hands of Balduino, we wish to buy it. Whatever the price, we will pay it.'

'What community are you speaking of? Edessa is in Muslim hands, is it not?'

'We are Christians, but we maintain good relations with the governors of Edessa. They have never troubled us. We pay substantial tributes, and in return we carry out our lives in peace. We have nothing to complain of. But the Mandylion belongs to us, and it must return to our city.'

De Molesmes stared intently at the impertinent young man who so brazenly dared to suggest that the Mandylion was for sale.

'And how much are you disposed to pay?'

'Ten sacks of gold of the weight of a man.'

The amount was beyond anything the chancellor had imagined. The empire was once again in debt, and Balduino was desperately seeking sources of loans, even though his uncle the king of France had not abandoned him.

De Molesmes remained impassive. 'I will communicate your offer to the emperor, and I will send for you when there is a reply.'

✚ Balduino listened sorrowfully to his counselor. He knew without doubt that if he broke his vow to the Templars it could cost him his life.

'You must tell this merchant that I reject his offer.'

'But my lord, consider it!'

'No, I cannot. And I forbid you ever again to ask me to sell the Mandylion! Ever!'

Pascal de Molesmes left the throne room crestfallen. He was suspicious of Balduino's discomfort when he spoke to him of the Mandylion. The cloth had been in the possession of the emperor for many months, though no one had seen it, not even he, the emperor's chancellor.

Rumors circulated that the generous amount of gold brought to the palace by the superior of the Templars of Constantinople, André de Saint-Rémy, had been payment for possession of the Mandylion. But Balduino vehemently denied those rumors; he swore that the sacred shroud was in his safekeeping.

When King Louis had been freed and returned to France, he once more sent the Comte de Dijon to Constantinople, with an even more generous offer for the Mandylion. To the surprise of everyone at court, the emperor remained inflexible, and he proclaimed before them all that he would not sell his uncle the relic. Now once more he had rejected a truly substantial offer. Pascal de Molesmes knew the emperor as no other. It was becoming clear to him that Balduino no longer possessed the Mandylion, that he had indeed sold it to the Templars.

That evening he sent for the Duc de Valant and his young protégé to inform them of the emperor's decision. De Molesmes was surprised when the Edessan merchant told him that he was willing to double the offer. But the chancellor would not have the young man harbor false hopes.

'Then it is true what they say at court?' the Duc de Valant asked.

'And what is it they say at court, my friend?'

'That the emperor is no longer the guardian of the Mandylion, that he has delivered it over to the Templars in exchange for the gold the Temple gave him to pay Venice and Genoa. That is the only way one can fathom the emperor's rejection of this very generous offer.'

'I pay no mind to rumors or the other intrigues of the court – and I counsel you not to believe everything you hear. I have brought you the emperor's decision, and there is nothing further to say.'

Pascal de Molesmes had seen men tortured and seen them die. But he would never forget the expression on the young merchant's face when he told him his quest was hopeless. As he saw his visitors out, he knew they had the same suspicions he did: the Templars. The Holy Shroud of the Savior Jesus Christ was now in the hands of the Order of Knights Templar.

✝ The Templar fortress stood on a rocky promontory on the coast. The golden color of the rock it was built upon resembled the sands of the nearby desert, and its height provided it with perspectives over miles of land around it. Saint-Jean d'Acre was one of the last Christian bastions in the Holy Land.

Robert de Saint-Rémy rubbed his eyes as though the vision of the fortress were a mirage. He calculated that in but a few minutes they would be surrounded by knights, who for two or three hours now had been observing them. Both he and François de Charney looked like authentic Saracens; even their horses, purebred Arabians, helped to maintain the illusion.

Ali, his squire, had once more shown himself to be an expert guide and loyal friend. Indeed, Robert owed him his life, for Ali had saved him when the four travelers were attacked by an Ayubi patrol. He fought fiercely by Robert's side, and when a spear was launched straight at Robert's heart, he stepped in front of the Templar and took what could have been a mortal wound to his own flesh. Not one of the Ayubis survived the attack, but Ali lay feverish and on the verge of death for several days. Robert never left his side.

Ali had been returned to life by medicinal compounds made up by Said, de Charney's squire, who had learned special remedies from the Temple's physicians and also from the Muslim physicians whom he had met in his travels. It was Said who pulled the spearhead from Ali's chest and thoroughly cleaned the wound, which he then covered with an unguent he had made from certain herbs he always carried with him. He also had made Ali drink a foul-smelling liquid, which put the young man into a calming sleep.

When asked if Ali would live, Said invariably answered, to the frustration of the two Templars, 'Allah alone knows.' On the seventh day, Ali awoke from the sleep into which he had fallen and which had seemed so much like death. There was a sharp and fiery pain in his lung, and breathing was difficult, but Said at last pronounced that he would live, and at that, the Templars' spirits revived.

It was another seven days before Ali was able to sit up, and seven more before he could ride on his docile steed, to which he lashed himself with leather straps so that should he once more lose consciousness he would not fall off. Over the next days and weeks he recovered, and now here he was, alongside the others, on the last approach to the fortress, when they were suddenly enveloped in a cloud of dust raised by the hooves of a dozen horses. The captain of the patrol shouted at them to halt.

When Saint-Rémy and de Charney revealed who they were, they were escorted to the fortress and taken immediately into the presence of the Grand Master.

Renaud de Vichiers, the Grand Master of the Order of the Temple, received them warmly. Despite their weariness, Saint-Rémy and de Charney sat with de Vichiers for an hour, reporting on the details of their journey and delivering to him the letter and documents that André de Saint-Rémy had given them, as well as the cloth sack that held the Mandylion.

Then the Grand Master sent them off to rest and gave orders that Ali be exempted from any service until he had completely recovered.

When he was alone, with trembling hands Renaud de Vichiers took from the sack the coffer that held the Mandylion. He felt his senses almost overwhelmed by emotion, for he was about to see the face of Jesus, the Christ.

He unfolded the cloth and fell to his knees and prayed, giving thanks to God for having allowed him to contemplate this miracle.

✝ It was dusk on the day after the arrival of Robert de Saint-Rémy and François de Charney when the Grand Master called all the knights of the order into the chapter's grand hall. There on a long table lay the Mandylion, at full length. One by one, they passed before the shroud of Christ, and some of those hardened knights could hardly contain their tears. After prayers, Renaud de Vichiers explained to his brothers that the grave cloth of Jesus would be placed in a cask, hidden from prying eyes. It was the most precious jewel of the order's possessions, and they were to defend it with their lives.

Gathered together, the knights swore a sacred oath: No matter what transpired, until death and after, they would never reveal where the shroud was held. Its very possession would become one of the great secrets of the Order of the Knights Templar.

37

MINERVA, PIETRO, AND ANTONINO HAD ARRIVED in Turin on the first plane that morning, and Marco invited the team to lunch.

They were just finishing when Sofia's cell phone rang. When she recognized the voice on the other end, she blushed and got up and left the room. Pietro's tension was evident when she returned. He had become increasingly nasty. But she knew that as long as she worked in the Art Crimes Department she'd have to deal with him, which just reconfirmed her decision to move on as soon as they'd closed this case.

'Marco, it was D'Alaqua. He invited me to join him tomorrow at some sort of farewell luncheon for Dr. Bolard and the rest of the scientific committee.'

'And you said yes, I hope,' Marco replied.

'No,' Sofia answered. 'Tomorrow is our general run-through with the whole team – I thought I was supposed to coordinate everything.'

'Yeah, but that would have been a golden opportunity to check out the scientists again, especially Bolard.'

'Well, we put it off until the day after tomorrow, although the scientists won't be there.'

Everyone looked at her in surprise, and Marco couldn't suppress a smile.

He called for the check, and the conversation turned to the details of the upcoming operation.

A few kilometers out of Turin, the car D'Alaqua had sent turned down a small road that ended in front of an imposing Renaissance-style palazzo surrounded by woods. Sofia had dressed simply, in jeans and a casual jacket, her hair pulled into a ponytail. She had wanted to underscore the working nature of the lunch but now began to regret not having made more of an effort.

The gate opened automatically as the car approached it. She couldn't spot the security cameras but figured they were everywhere.

Umberto D'Alaqua was waiting for her at the door, wearing an elegant dark gray silk suit. He greeted her warmly and smiled when she complimented him on the loveliness of his home. 'I asked you here because I knew you would enjoy the paintings,' he said as he led her through an imposing entrance hall.

The palazzo was a museum, a museum turned into a house. For more than an hour they wandered through room after room, all boasting impressive works of art hung with intelligence and superb taste. Over a long lunch they talked animatedly about art, politics, literature. The time passed so quickly that Sofia was shocked when D'Alaqua excused himself, saying that he had to get to the airport for a seven o'clock flight to Paris.

'Oh, I'm sorry. I've kept you,' she apologized.

'Not at all, not at all. It's not six yet, and if I didn't have to be in Paris tonight, I'd ask you to stay for dinner. I'll be back in ten days. If you are still in Turin, I'd like to see you again.'

'I'm not sure. . . . By then we may have finished or be close to it.'

'Finished?'

'With the investigation.'

'Oh, yes! How's it going?'

'Fine. We're in the final phase, I think.'

'Have you reached any conclusions?'

'Well. . . .' Sofia paused uncomfortably.

'Don't worry,' D'Alaqua broke in, waving the question away with a smile. 'I understand. When you've finished your work and everything is cleared up, you can tell me about it.'

Sofia was relieved. Marco had absolutely forbidden her to tell him anything, and although she no longer shared her chief's suspicions about D'Alaqua, she would never disobey his direct order.

Two cars were waiting at the door. One would take Sofia back to the Hotel Alexandra and the other would drive D'Alaqua to the airport, where his private plane was waiting. He pressed her hand warmly and held it for a moment as he settled her into her car.

'Why do they want to kill him?' the capo asked his informant.

'I don't know. They've been planning it for days. They're trying to bribe a guard to leave his cell door open, along with theirs. The plan is to go in tomorrow night, slit his throat, and get back to their cell with no one the wiser. Nobody'll know – mutes don't scream.'

'Will the guard take the bribe?'

'Probably. I heard it's fifty thousand euros.'

'Jesus! Who else knows about this?'

'Two other prisoners. Turks, like them.'

'Okay, get out of here.'

'What about my money?'

'You'll get paid.'

Frasquello was thoughtful. Why would the Bajerai brothers want to kill the guy? A murder for hire, sure – but who was hiring?

He sent for his lieutenants, two mafioso serving life sentences for murder. The three met for about half an hour. Then he asked a guard to send for Genari.

The head guard entered the capo's cell after midnight. Frasquello was watching television and didn't move when he heard Genari come in.

'Sit down, and keep quiet. Tell your cop friend he was right. They're going to kill the mute.'

'Who?'

'The Bajerais.'

'But why?' Genari asked in surprise.

'How the fuck should I know! And why should I care? I'm doing my part – tell him he better do his.' The capo spoke in low tones for a few minutes more, filling in the guard on what he had learned.

Genari left the cell and hurried to his office, where he dialed Marco Valoni's cell phone number.

'Signor Valoni, it's Genari.'

Marco looked at the clock – past midnight. He was tired. Yesterday they'd done a run-through of the operation that would swing into action as soon as the mute was released from prison. Today he'd gone back to inspect some of the tunnels under Turin again, and for two hours he'd wandered around, tapping on walls, listening for hollow spots. Comandante Colombaria, making a great show of patience, had come along, continuing to insist there was nothing to find.

'You were right, they're going to try to kill the tongue-less guy.' The guard was clearly agitated.

'Tell me everything.'

'Frasquello's people say that two Turks, the Bajerai brothers, are going to take care of him tomorrow night. They're throwing a lot of money around. We might be able to stop it this time, but we can't protect him for long with that kind of money in play. You need to get him out of here as soon as possible.'

'We can't. He'd suspect there was something going on, and the whole operation would go to shit. Will Frasquello do his job?'

'He already is – he told me to remind you to do yours.'

'I will. Are you at the prison?'

'Yes.'

'All right. I'm going to call the warden. I'll be there in an hour – I want all the information you've got on those two brothers.'

'They're Turks. Good boys, really. They killed a guy in a fight, but they're not murderers – not professionals, anyway.'

'You can tell me about it when I get there. One hour.'

Marco woke up the warden and told him to meet him in his office at the prison. Then he called Minerva.

'Were you asleep?'

'Reading. What's up?'

'Get dressed. I'll be waiting for you downstairs in the lobby in fifteen minutes. I want you to go to carabinieri headquarters, get on their computer, and find whatever you can on a couple of guys we need to know about. I'm going to the prison, and I'll call you from there with everything they've got on them.'

'Wait a minute, wait a minute! What's happening?'

'I'll tell you downstairs. Don't be late.'

When Marco arrived at the prison, the warden was waiting for him in his office, half awake. Genari was there, too, pacing nervously.

'I want everything you've got on these Bajerais,' Marco said without preamble.

'The Bajerai brothers?' the warden sputtered. 'What have they done? You believe Frasquello's story? Listen, Genari, when this is over you've got a lot of explaining to do about your dealings with that thug.'

The warden pulled the files on the Bajerai brothers and handed them to Marco, who plopped down on the sofa and began reading. When he finished, he talked the information through with the warden and Genari and then called Minerva.

'I'm exhausted. I almost fell asleep on the keyboard,' she said.

'Well, wake up. Find everything you can on this family of Turks – they were born here, but their parents were immigrants. I want to know everything about them *and* their families.' He filled her in on what he had. 'Ask Interpol, talk to the Turkish police, let's say three hours for a complete report.'

'Three hours! No way. Give me till morning.'

'Seven o'clock,' Marco snapped.

'Okay, five hours. That's something.'

The hotel dining room opened at seven. Minerva, her eyes red from lack of sleep and hours in front of the

330

computer screen, walked in, confident that she'd find Marco there.

Her boss was reading the newspaper and drinking coffee. Like her, he looked terrible.

Minerva tossed two file folders on the table and dropped into a chair.

'I'm dead!'

'I imagine. Find anything interesting?'

'Depends on what you're interested in.'

'Try me.'

'The Bajerai brothers are the sons of Turkish immigrants, as you know. Their parents went first to Germany and from there came to Turin. They found work in Frankfurt, but the mother didn't like Germany or the Germans, so they decided to try their luck in Italy since they had relatives here. The boys are Italian – they've lived in Turin all their lives. The father worked at the Fiat plant and the mother as a cleaning lady. They were average students in school, no better or worse than most. The older one got into some scraps, seems to have quite a temper, but he's probably the smarter of the two – his grades were better than his brother's. When they finished high school the older one started working for Fiat, like his father. The younger one was hired as a driver for some bigwig in the regional government, guy named Regio, who took him on because the kid's mother had been a cleaning lady at his house. The older one lasted a little while at Fiat, but he didn't like the old eight-to-five, so he rented a stall in the market and started selling fruit and vegetables. Did okay, the both of them, never had any trouble with the cops or anybody else. Nothing. The father is retired, the mother too. They live on a pension from the state and their savings. They've got nothing, really, except their house, which they bought about fifteen years ago, scrimping and saving.

'A couple of years ago, one Saturday night, the brothers were at a discotheque with their girlfriends. A couple of drunks started hitting on the girls – apparently one of them pinched one of the girls' ass. The police report says the brothers pulled out knives and they all went at it. They killed one guy and wounded the other one so bad he can't use his arm anymore. They got twenty years – tantamount to life. Their girlfriends married other people.'

'What do you know about their family in Turkey?'

'Just regular people – poor, struggling. They come from Urfa, near the Iraq border. Through Interpol, the Turkish police e-mailed what they've got on the family there, which is very little – absolutely nothing of interest. The father has a younger brother in Urfa, although younger is relative – he's about to retire. He works in the oil fields. There's also a sister, married to a schoolteacher; they have eight children. They're good, decent people, never gotten into any trouble. The Turks were surprised we were looking at them. The truth is, we may have caused these people some problems – you know how their minds work over there.'

'Anything else?'

'Yeah. Here in Turin, there's a cousin of the mother's – guy named Amin, apparently an exemplary citizen. He's an accountant, been working for years for an advertising agency. He's married to an Italian woman; she works in a high-end clothing store. They have two daughters. The older one is at the university; the younger one is about to graduate from high school. They all go to Mass on Sundays.'

'Mass?'

'Yeah, Mass. Shouldn't be a big surprise – this is Italy.'

'Yeah, but this cousin – he's not Muslim?'

'I don't know – I guess he is, or was, but he's married to an Italian woman, in the Church. He must have converted – although there's nothing in his file about a conversion.'

'Look into him. And try to find out whether the Bajerais belong to a mosque here.'

'Mosque?' Minerva asked skeptically.

'Okay – this is Italy. But somebody must know whether they are – or were – Muslims. And if there are others they associate with. Did you get into their bank records?'

'Yeah – nothing out of the ordinary there. The cousin earns a pretty good salary; so does his wife. They live pretty well, although they've got a mortgage on their apartment. No suspicious deposits. They're a tight-knit family; at least some of them go every visiting day to see the brothers, take them food, sweets, tobacco, books, clothes – they're trying their best for them.'

'Yeah, I know. I've got a copy of the visitors' log. This Amin has visited them twice this month – when he normally visits them once.'

'I wouldn't think visiting them one extra day was anything to get suspicious about.'

'We have to look at everything,' Marco reminded her.

'Yeah, sure – but we shouldn't lose perspective either.'

'You know what strikes me? The fact that this cousin of theirs goes to Mass and was married by the Church. Muslims don't go apostate just like *that*.'

'And you're also going to investigate all the Italians who never set foot in a church? Listen, I've got a girlfriend who converted to Judaism because she fell in love with an Israeli one summer when she was in a kibbutz. The guy's mother was an Orthodox Jew who would never have allowed her darling boy to marry a shiksa, so my friend converted and every Saturday she goes to synagogue. She doesn't believe in anything, but she goes.'

'That's your girlfriend. Here we have two Turks who want to kill somebody.'

'Uh-huh, but they're the killers, not their cousin, and you can't turn him into a suspect because he goes to Mass.'

Pietro came into the dining room and headed over. A minute later, Antonino and Giuseppe joined them. Sofia was the last to arrive.

Minerva brought them up to speed on what had been happening overnight and at Marco's behest handed out copies of the report she'd produced.

'So? What do you think?' Marco asked when they'd all finished reading through the file.

'They aren't pros – if they've been hired for the job it's either because *they've* got some relationship to our guy or because somebody who does trusts the hell out of them,' Pietro observed.

Giuseppe chimed in. 'There are men in that prison who'd cut his throat without thinking twice, but the person who's contracted the hit either doesn't know how to get to those types, which means he doesn't have underworld ties, or, as Pietro says, he trusts these two, who seem to be nothing special. They've never been tied to dirty money, never so much as stolen their neighbor's Vespa for a joyride. A stupid bar fight doesn't put them in the big leagues.'

'Fine, Giuseppe, but tell me something we don't know,' Marco insisted.

'Hold on, Marco, I think Giuseppe and Pietro are saying a lot,' Antonino argued. 'Now we know for sure that our guy *is* a link to something – somebody wants him dead because they know he can lead us to them. That means there's a leak

– they're on to our plans; otherwise they'd have gotten rid of him a long time ago. But no, they want to kill him now, all of a sudden, just as he's about to go free.'

'Who exactly knows about this part the operation?' Sofia asked.

'Too many people,' Marco replied. 'And Antonino is right on target. They know where we're going before we get there. Minerva, Antonino, see what else you can get on the Bajerai family – they're one link. They have to be connected to someone who wants our man dead. Go over everything again, look into even the smallest details. I'm going back to the prison.'

'Why don't we talk to the parents and cousin?' Pietro asked.

'Because we don't want to raise any flags. We can't afford to be more visible than we already are. And we can't pull the mute out of prison, because then it'll be *him* that gets suspicious. We have to keep him alive, out of range of these brothers,' Marco answered.

'How?' asked Sofia.

'A capo in the drug mafia, a guy named Frasquello. I made a deal with him. All right, everybody, let's go,' he said abruptly, brushing aside their questions.

They ran into Ana Jiménez in the lobby. She was leaving the reception desk, carry-on in tow.

'You guys look like you're on to something big,' she joked.

'You're leaving?' Sofia asked.

'I'm on my way to London, and then to France.'

'Work?' Sofia pressed.

'Work. I may call you, dottoressa. I may need your advice.'

The doorman told Ana her taxi was waiting, and she blew them a kiss as she headed out the door.

'That girl makes me nervous,' Marco confessed.

Sofia nodded. 'Yeah, you never much liked her.'

'No, you're wrong, I like her, but I don't like her sticking her nose into our case. What's she going to London for? And France? She either sees something we don't, or she's going to stir things up, chasing after one of her batty theories.'

'I've been impressed by her,' Sofia answered, 'and her theories may not be so batty. Everyone thought Schliemann was a crackpot, and he found Troy.'

'All she needs is you for a defense lawyer! I'd still like to know what she's up to. I'll call Santiago. You and I both know it has something to do with the shroud.'

The prison was silent. The inmates had been locked down for the night two hours earlier. The corridors and passageways were illuminated only by the wan, yellowish light of ten-watt bulbs, and the guards on the night shift were dozing.

The Bajerais pushed at the door to their cell, checking to make sure it was open. Yes, the guard had kept his part of the deal. . . . Keeping close to the wall and crouching until they were almost crawling, the two brothers began to make their way to the other end of the corridor, where the mute's cell was. If everything went as they planned, in less than five minutes they'd be back in their own cell as though they had never left.

They had traveled halfway down the corridor when the smaller one, in back, felt someone's hand grip his neck half a second before a hard blow to the head knocked him unconscious. The older brother turned around just in time to catch a massive fist full in the nose. Blood streaming, he fell to his knees without a sound as a hand of iron fastened on his throat. Struggling for air, finding none, he felt his life slipping away from him.

Light was just beginning to brighten the corridors of the Turin jail when the guard on morning rounds stopped dead in front of the Bajerais' cell. Then he ran to sound the alarm, as the two bloody heaps tangled together on the floor began to stir and moan.

In the infirmary, the doctor ordered the brothers sedated and pumped them full of pain medication. Their faces had been beaten to pulp, their eyes narrow slits within the massive swelling.

When Marco arrived at the warden's office in response to his call, the agitated official relayed what had happened. He had to inform the judicial authorities and the carabinieri.

Marco calmed him down, then asked to see Frasquello.

'I did my part,' the capo spat at him the second he walked into the warden's office.

'Yes, and I'll do mine. What happened?'

'Don't ask questions. It went like you wanted. Your mute is alive and the Turks are too – what more could you ask for, eh? Nobody's been hurt. Those two brothers just got a little bruised, is all.'

'I want you to continue to keep an eye out. They may try again.'

'Who, those two? You're kidding.'

'Them or somebody else, I don't know. Just keep watching.'

'When do you talk to the parole board?'

'When this is over.'

'Which is when?'

'No more than four or five days, I hope.'

'Okay. But you want to do what you said you would, cop, or you'll wish you had.'

'And what *you* want is not to threaten me.'

'Just do it.'

Frasquello slammed the door behind him as he left the office.

38

ADDAIO WAS WORKING IN HIS OFFICE WHEN HIS
cell phone rang. The conversation was brief, but by the
time he hung up, he was red with rage. He shouted for
Guner, who came running.

'What is it, pastor?'

'Find Bakkalbasi at once. I don't care where he is, I have
to see him. And I want *all* the elders here within half an
hour.'

'What has happened?'

'A catastrophe. Now get them.'

When he was alone, he put his hands to his temples and
pressed hard. His head hurt all the time. For days he had
been experiencing terrible, almost unbearable headaches.
He was sleeping badly, and he had no appetite. More and
more, he felt it would be a blessing just to die now. He was
tired of the lifelong trap he was in – the trap of being Addaio.

The news could not have been worse. The Bajerai
brothers had been found out. Someone within the prison
had learned of their plans and blocked them. Perhaps the
two had talked too much, or someone may simply have
been protecting Mendib. It could even be *them,* them again,

339

or that cop, sticking his nose in everywhere. Apparently in the last few days he had been in and out of the warden's office constantly. He was planning something, but what? It had been reported that he met a couple of times with a drug capo, a man named Frasquello. Yes, yes, the pieces fit – no doubt this Valoni had put the mafioso in charge of protecting Mendib. He was their only lead – a lead that could bring them here, to Urfa – and they had to protect him. That was it, yes, that was it.

Pain was eating up his brain. He searched a moment for a key and opened a drawer, took out a bottle of pills, gulped down two, and then sat with his eyes closed to wait for it to pass. With a little luck, by the time the elders arrived it would be better.

Guner knocked softly at the office door. The elders were waiting for Addaio in the large meeting room. When there was no response, Guner entered and found Addaio with his head on the desk, his eyes closed, motionless. Guner approached with trepidation and shook his master gently until he awoke. The servant breathed a soft sigh of relief.

'You were asleep.'

'Yes . . . my head hurt.'

'You should go back to the doctor; this pain is killing you. You need to have a brain scan.'

'I'm fine.' Addaio brushed aside further discussion.

A few minutes later he strode into the meeting room. The eight members of the council made an imposing picture, arrayed around the heavy mahogany table in their black chasubles.

Concern filled their faces as Addaio informed them of the events in the Turin prison.

'Mendib will be released in four or five days and will

attempt to contact us,' Addaio went on. 'We must prevent that; our people cannot fail again. That is why it is imperative that you be there, Bakkalbasi, coordinating the operation, in constant contact with me. We are on the verge of disaster.'

'I have news of Turgut.'

All eyes turned to Talat, their main conduit to the porter in the Turin Cathedral. His piercing blue eyes were fixed on Addaio.

'We should get him out of there. He's becoming more unhinged by the day. He swears he is being followed, that they no longer trust him in the bishop's offices, and that Rome police officers have remained in Turin to arrest him.'

'That is the last thing we can do in the middle of all this, Talat,' Bakkalbasi replied.

'Is Ismet ready to travel?' Addaio asked. 'He was to prepare himself to take his uncle's place at the cathedral. That is our best course for now.'

'His parents have agreed, but the young man seems reluctant. He has a girlfriend here,' Talat explained.

'Girlfriend! And because he has a girlfriend he would endanger the entire community? Call them. He will leave today, with our brother Bakkalbasi. Tell Ismet's parents to call Turgut and tell him they are sending their son to reside with him while he looks for a future in Italy. And do it now.'

Addaio's peremptory tone left no room for hesitation or disagreement. A short while later, the eight left the mansion, each with precise orders to carry out.

39

ANA JIMÉNEZ RANG THE DOORBELL OF A LOVELY Victorian house in one of London's most elegant neighborhoods. An elderly butler opened the door and greeted her politely. The home could have been the residence of a lord. If this was indeed the bastion of the present-day Knights Templar, it was a far cry from the medieval fortresses they had once defended.

Ana introduced herself and asked to see the director of the organization, Anthony McGilles. It had not been easy to secure an appointment with the well-known scholar, but Ana had called friends of friends, trading on connections in diplomatic circles, and the meeting had eventually been arranged.

The butler asked her to wait in a large, handsomely furnished vestibule, its wood parquet floor covered with thick Persian carpet, its walls hung with paintings of religious scenes. A silver-haired gentleman promptly emerged from a nearby office and greeted her cordially.

McGilles directed Ana to the sofa in his office while he took a seat in a leather armchair. They had barely settled themselves when the butler entered with a tea tray.

For several minutes Ana answered McGilles's questions – he was interested in her work as a reporter and in the political situation in Spain. Finally, the professor got to the point of her visit.

'You're interested in the Templars?'

'Yes. I have to say I was surprised to learn that they still exist and even have an Internet address. That's what led me here.'

'This is a center for research and study, that's all. What is it exactly that you want to know?'

'Well, if the Templars really do exist in this day and age, then I'd like to know more about the nature and scope of the organization today, and what it does. And if possible I'd like to ask you about some historical events that the Templars took part in – a very *prominent* part.'

'Well, miss, the Templars as you seem to be imagining them, as they once were, no longer exist.'

'Then the Internet listing isn't authentic?'

'No, it's authentic. You're here speaking with me, aren't you? But don't let your imagination run wild picturing knights in shining armor. This is the twenty-first century.'

'So I've been told.'

'Well, then – we are an organization dedicated to research and study. Our mission is intellectual and social.'

'But you *are* the true heirs of the Temple?'

'When Pope Clement V suspended the order, the Templars became part of other orders. In Aragon, they became part of the Order of Montesa; in Portugal, King Dinis created a new order, the Orden do Cristo; in Germany they became part of the Teutonic Order. Only in Scotland did the order itself never dissolve. The uninterrupted existence of the Order of Scotland embodies how the Templar spirit has come down to our own days. In the fifteenth century the Scottish Templars became part of the French Garde Ecossaise, which protected the king, and they supported the Jacobites in Scotland. Since 1705 the order has been in the open; that year it adopted new statutes, and Louis Philippe of Orleans became its Grand Master. There were Templars who took part in the French Revolution, in Napoleon's empire, in the struggle for Greek independence, and of course they were part of the French resistance during World War Two. . . .'

'But how? Through what organization? I haven't found historical references to the order operating as such. What are they called?'

'Miss Jiménez, through the years the Templars have lived silently, dedicated to reflection and study, taking part as individuals in these events, although always with the knowledge of their brothers. There are various organizations – lodges, if you like – in which groups of knights meet. These lodges are legal; they are scattered through many countries, and they exist under the laws of each one. You should change your focus on the Order of the Temple; as I say, in the twenty-first century you will not find an organization like that of the twelfth or thirteenth – it simply doesn't exist.

'Our institution here is devoted to studying the history of the Temple and the individual and collective events associated with it, from its founding to our own day,' the professor continued. 'We examine archives; as historians we review certain obscure events; we seek out old documents. . . . I believe I detect a look of disappointment on your face.'

'No, it's that. . . .'

'You were expecting a warrior knight? I'm sorry to

disappoint you. I am just a professor retired from the University of Cambridge who, in addition to being a believer, shares with other knights certain principles: a love of truth and justice.'

Ana sensed that behind Anthony McGilles's words there was much more, that everything couldn't be that clear, that simple.

'Professor, I appreciate your kindness in explaining all this. I know I'm taking advantage of your patience, but I wonder if you could help me understand an event that I think the Templars were involved in?'

'I'll try, of course. If I don't know the answer, we'll go to our computerized archive. What's the event?'

'I'd like to know whether the Templars took the Holy Shroud that is now in Turin from Constantinople during the reign of Balduino II. The shroud disappeared at that time and didn't reappear, in France, until almost a century later.'

Had she imagined just the slightest ripple in his urbane demeanor?

'Ah, the shroud. . . . So much controversy! So many legends! My opinion as a historian is that the Temple had nothing to do with its disappearance.'

'Would it be possible for me to explore a bit in your archives? I've come all this way. . . .'

'I think we can arrange that. I'll have Professor McFadden help you.'

'Professor McFadden?'

'I must go to a meeting, but I leave you in good hands. Professor McFadden is our chief archivist, and he'll help you with anything you need.'

McGilles picked up a small silver bell and rang it gently. The butler entered immediately.

'Richard, take Miss Jiménez to the library. Professor McFadden will meet with her there.'

'I appreciate your help, professor.'

'I hope we may be of service to you, Miss Jiménez. Good day.'

40

A.D. 1291

Guillaume de Beaujeu, Grand Master of the Temple, carefully slid the document into the secret drawer in his writing table, his lean face troubled. The missive from the brothers in France was yet more proof that the Temple no longer had as many friends at the court of Philippe IV as they'd had in the time of good King Louis – may God protect him and glorify him, for there had been no more chivalrous and valiant king in all of Christendom.

Philippe owed them gold, a great deal of gold, and the more he owed, the more his resentment against the Temple seemed to grow. In Rome, too, there were religious orders that could not hide their festering envy of the Temple's power.

But in that spring of 1291, Guillaume de Beaujeu had another problem, more urgent than the intrigues within the courts of France and Rome. François de Charney and Said had returned from their incursion into the Mameluke camp with devastating news.

The Mamelukes dominated Egypt and Syria, and they had taken Nazareth, the city in which our Lord Jesus grew from childhood into manhood. Today, their flag flew above the port of Jaffa, scant leagues from the Templar fortress Saint-Jean d'Acre. For a month the knight and his squire had lived among them in their advance military encampment, had listened to the soldiers and shared bread, water, and prayers to Allah the Merciful with them. They had passed themselves off as Egyptian merchants who wished to sell provisions to the army. The information they had gathered led to one inescapable conclusion. In only a few days, fifteen at the most, the Mameluke army would attack Saint-Jean d'Acre. That was what the soldiers were saying, and it had been confirmed by the officers with whom de Charney had fraternized. The Mameluke commanders had boasted that they would be rich when they seized the treasures safeguarded in the fortress at Acre, which they vowed would fall, as so many other fortresses had fallen to their armies.

The soft breeze of March presaged the intense heat of the coming months in a Holy Land watered with Christian blood. Two days ago a select group of Templars had filled chests with the gold and treasures that the Temple kept within the fortress. The Grand Master had ordered them to set sail, as soon as they were ready, on a course for Cyprus and from thence to France. None of the brothers wanted to leave, and they had pleaded with Guillaume de Beaujeu to allow them to stay and defend the city. But the Grand Master would not be swayed: The survival of the order depended in great part on them, for they were charged with saving the Templar treasure. Now all was ready for their departure.

Of all the knights, François de Charney was the most distraught. He had held back bitter tears when de Beaujeu ordered him on a mission far from Acre. The Frenchman begged his superior to let him stay and fight for the Cross, but de Beaujeu forbade further argument. The decision had been made.

The Grand Master descended the stairs into the cool dungeons of the fortress, and there, in a room guarded by knights, he inspected the massive chests that were soon to depart for France.

'We will divide the treasure among three galleys so as not to stake all on one. You each know which ship you will be embarking on. Be prepared to set sail at a moment's notice.'

'I do not yet know my ship,' said de Charney.

Guillaume de Beaujeu's iron gaze fixed upon de Charney. More than sixty years of age but still strong, his face weathered by the sun, he was one of the most veteran of the Templar knights. He had survived a thousand perils, and as a spy he had no equal unless it be his late friend Robert de Saint-Rémy, who had been killed during the defense of Tripoli when a Saracen arrow pierced his heart.

'You, good sir, will accompany me to the chapter meeting hall. We will speak there. But before you depart on your own mission, I must ask you to return to the camp of the Mamelukes. We must know whether they are able to prevent the ships from arriving at their destination, whether some ambush awaits us at sea.'

The Grand Master read in de Charney's eyes the anguish it caused the old knight to leave the land that he now called his own, that life in which most nights he slept on the ground under the stars, most days rode with caravans in search of information, and for weeks at a time lost himself in Saracen camps, from which he had always successfully returned.

For François de Charney, returning to France was a tragedy. The master clasped his shoulder when they were alone together in the meeting hall.

'Know, de Charney, that you are the only man to whom I can entrust this mission. Years ago, when you were little more than a boy and newly initiate in the order, you and Saint-Rémy brought back from Constantinople the only certain relic of our Lord, his grave cloth, upon which was imprinted his face and his figure. It is thanks to that Holy Shroud that we know the face of Jesus, and to it we pray as to the Lord Himself. This has been both our singular privilege and our sacred trust. Knowing the shifting vicissitudes of time and politics, of nations and religious hierarchies and the frailties of the human heart, we have sworn as brothers to hold this precious cloth in secrecy and safety so that it might endure through all the ages of man.

'You are now an old man but serene in your faith, and your strength and valor stand as an example to us all. It is for that reason I am entrusting you with saving the shroud of Christ our Lord. Of all the treasures we possess, this is the most precious, for not only the image but the very blood and holy essence of Jesus are entwined within its threads. You shall save it, de Charney! Once you return from the Mamelukes' camp, you shall leave for Cyprus with whatever men you may choose. You may also choose the route, whether by ship or on horseback. I trust in your good judgment, your devotion, and your strong arm in this mission to bear the Holy Shroud to France. No one must know what you are carrying; you yourself must make all the arrangements for the journey. And now, prepare yourself for your mission.'

✛ De Charney, accompanied by his faithful squire, old Said, once more infiltrated the Mameluke camp. Among the soldiers he could sense the heightened tension that preceded battle, as around the campfires they recalled their families and dreamed of the hazy images of their children, who were now growing into men and women. Soon enough the knight felt sure that no attack was planned against the Templar ships, and he sent Said back to the fortress with the word that they might sail.

For three days more the Templar listened to snatches of conversations between soldiers and among the officers and also to those of the numerous servants to the Saracen leaders, hoping for information that might aid his brothers in defending their redoubt. When he overheard one of the commanders telling his lieutenants that the attack would occur two days later, he hastened back to the fortress.

He entered Saint-Jean d'Acre as the first light of morning was turning the stone walls of the imposing Templar bastion into shimmering gold.

Guillaume de Beaujeu ordered the Templar knights to make their final preparations to resist the attack. Christians raced through the streets frantically, many overcome by hysteria when they could find no means of transport away from the fort, whose fate no one could guarantee. The last ships had sailed, and desperation was spreading among the populace.

De Charney helped his brothers to complete preparations for the defenses, rehearsed a thousand times over, and to calm the disputes among the population – there were men who were capable of killing their neighbor in order to escape.

Night was once more falling when the Grand Master sent for him.

'Dear brother, you must depart. I erred when I sent you to the Mameluke camp – now there is no ship to carry you.'

François de Charney struggled to control his emotions.

'Master, I know. I must beg a favor. I wish to travel alone, in company with only Said.'

'It will be more dangerous.'

'But no one will suspect us – two Mamelukes.'

'Do as you deem best, brother.'

The two men embraced. It was the last time they would see each other on earth; their fates were cast. Both men knew that the Grand Master would die there, defending the fortress of Saint-Jean d'Acre.

✛ De Charney looked for a piece of linen the same size as the Holy Shroud. He did not want the precious cloth exposed to the rigors of the journey, but this time he thought it best not to convey it in a chest. It would be hard to reach Constantinople, from whence he planned to set sail for France, and the less baggage he carried, the better.

Like Said, he was accustomed to sleeping on the ground, eating what they could hunt on the road, whether in the forest or the desert. They needed only two good steeds.

He was overcome with remorse for leaving, for he knew that his brothers-in-arms would surely die. He knew that he was leaving this land forever, that he would never return, and that in sweet France he would remember the dry air of the desert, the happiness of the Saracen camps in which he had forged so many friendships – for in the end, men were men, no matter what god they prayed to. And he had seen honor, justice, grief, happiness, wisdom, and misery in the ranks of his enemies, as he had seen them in his own. They were no different – they but fought under different banners.

He would ask Said to accompany him for a while, but

then he would ride on alone. He could not ask his friend to leave his homeland – Said would never become accustomed to living in France, however much de Charney had told him of the wonders of Lirey, near Troyes, the town of his birth and boyhood. There, de Charney had learned to ride through the green meadows near his family home, to wield the little sword that his father had the ironsmith make for him and his brother so that his sons might grow up to become knights. No – Said had grown old, like him, and it was too late now to learn to live another life.

He carefully finished folding the shroud within the new linen and then he slipped it into the leather shoulder bag he always carried. Then he found Said and told him of the Grand Master's orders. Said simply nodded when de Charney asked him if he would ride with him for a time before they separated to go their own ways. The squire knew that when he returned, there would be no more Christians in Acre. He would return to his own people, to live out what remained to him of his life.

✝ It was raining fire. Hosts of flaming arrows flew over the top of the walls, igniting all they struck. The Mameluke siege of Saint-Jean d'Acre had commenced on April 6 of that year of our Lord 1291. For several days now, after weeks of attacks, the enemy army had been battering the fortress, even as the Templar knights fiercely defended it. How many knights remained? Barely fifty were defending the walls they refused to surrender.

On the day the siege began, Guillaume de Beaujeu had ordered his knights to make their confessions and take communion. He knew that few if any of them would survive, and so he had asked them to make their souls' peace with God.

Now, within the walled city of Acre, in the great Templar fortress, the fighting was body against body as the walls were at last breached. The Templars refused to yield a palm of ground; they defended each inch with their lives, and only when that life was taken from them could the enemy advance.

Guillaume de Beaujeu had been wielding his sword for hours; he did not know how many men he had killed or how many had died around him. He had urged his knights to try to escape before Acre fell, but the petition fell on deaf ears, for they all fought in the knowledge that soon they would be with God.

Even as he fought on, he took comfort in imagining the miles unfolding before François de Charney as he rode ever farther away, bidding farewell to all those places he had called home. He trusted that the knight would save the shroud of Jesus and see it safely to France. His heart had told him to give the cloth over to de Charney, and he knew he had made the right decision. The man who forty years ago had brought the shroud from Constantinople in his youth was now keeping custody of it once more, on the road toward the West.

Two fierce Saracens bore down on the Grand Master, and he felt a new surge of strength, furiously fending off their great scimitars with his sword and shield. But oh! What had he done? Suddenly he felt a terrible pain in his chest. He could see nothing – night had fallen. *Insh'Allah!*

Jean de Perigord pulled the body of Guillaume de Beaujeu over to the wall. The word spread fast: The Grand Master had fallen. Acre was on the verge of being overrun, but God willed that it not be that night.

The Mamelukes returned to their camp, from whence came the smell of spiced lamb and the sound of songs of victory. The knights came together, exhausted, in the chapter meeting hall. They had to elect a new Grand Master, there, now – they could not wait. They were bone tired, and they cared little who became their leader, for tomorrow, or the next day at the latest, they were all to die – what difference could it make? But they prayed and meditated, and they asked God to enlighten them. Thibaut Gaudin was elected successor to the valiant Guillaume de Beaujeu.

On May 28, 1291, it was hot in Acre, and it smelled of death. Before the sun rose, Thibaut Gaudin ordered his remaining knights to Mass. Then they took their positions and once more met the enemy. Swords clashed unceasingly, and arrows blindly found their targets. The fortress resembled a cemetery. Only a handful of knights remained alive.

Before the sun set, the flag of their enemies flew over Acre. *Insh'Allah!*

41

ANA WOKE UP SCREAMING, HER HEART POUND-ing in her chest as though she were in the middle of battle. But she was in the heart of London, in a room in the Dorchester Hotel. Her temples were throbbing, and she felt the sweat running down her back.

Overwhelmed by a sense of grief and anguish, she got out of bed and stumbled to the bathroom. Her hair was stuck to her face and her nightgown was soaked through. She pulled it off and stepped into the shower. This was the second time she'd had a nightmare about a battle. If she believed in the transmigration of souls, she'd swear she'd been there, in the fortress of Saint-Jean d'Acre, watching the Templars die to a man. She could describe the face and behavior of Guillaume de Beaujeu and the color of Thibaut Gaudin's eyes. She had been there; she could feel it. She knew those men.

She stepped out of the shower feeling better, and pulled on a T-shirt. She didn't have another nightgown. The bed was soaked with sweat, so she decided to turn on her laptop and surf the Internet awhile.

Professor McFadden's thoughtful explanations, plus the

documentation he'd provided on the history of the Templars, had affected her deeply. And he had showered her with details on the fall of Saint-Jean d'Acre – according to him, one of the most bitter days in the order's history.

That was surely why she'd dreamed so vividly of the doomed defense of the fortress, as she'd done when Sofia Galloni told her about the Byzantine troops' siege of Edessa.

Tomorrow she was scheduled to see the professor again. This time she was going to try to get something concrete out of him – something other than colorful stories about the slow fall and terrible deaths of the Templars.

42

The smell of the sea lifted his spirit. He did not want to look back. His years were taking their toll, for he had wept without shame when he set sail from Cyprus, the last port of the East, as both he and Said had done when they at last made their farewell. Their parting was akin to one man being cut in two. In all these years it was the first time they had embraced.

For Said, the time had come to return to his own people, while he, François de Charney, was returning to his native land, a land about which he knew almost nothing nor felt to be his own. His homeland was the Temple, and his house, the East. The man who now made his way to France was but a shell. He had left his soul at the foot of the walls of Saint-Jean d'Acre.

Despite the heaviness that had settled into his heart, the presence of a few Templar knights who, like him, were returning to France made the voyage easier, although they were careful to give him his privacy. The crossing was calm, though the Mediterranean was a treacherous sea, as Ulysses himself had learned. But the ship traversed the waves without incident. Guillaume de Beaujeu's orders were clear: De Charney was to deposit the Holy Shroud in the Temple fortress in Marseilles and await new orders there. The master had made him swear that he would never relinquish the relic to those outside the order and that he would defend it with his life.

The port of Marseilles was impressive, with its dozens of boats and countless people milling about, shouting and talking incessantly. When they disembarked, they found waiting for them an escort of knights, who conducted them to the Temple's chapter house in the city. None knew of the relic that de Charney was carrying. De Beaujeu had given him a letter for the precept of the Temple chapter in Marseilles and for the superior. 'They,' he had said, 'will decide what is best.'

Jacques Vazelay, the superior, was a nobleman of curt gestures and few words. But his eyes were kind as he listened to de Charney's story. Then he asked the old knight to show him the holy shroud.

For many years the Templars had known the true face of Christ, for Renaud de Vichiers, the first master to hold the shroud, had had its astounding image copied and sent to every Templar house and chapter. Still, Vichiers had counseled supreme discretion. Each chapter kept its copy of the image in a secret chapel to which only knights went to pray. No others were to see it or even know of its existence.

Thus had the secret of the Temple's possession of the only true relic of Jesus Christ been kept through the years.

De Charney opened his pack and took out the linen-wrapped bundle he had carried so carefully. He unrolled it, and . . . the two men fell to their knees in wonder, such was the miracle that had occurred.

Still on their knees, Jacques Vazelay, superior of the chapter, and François de Charney gave thanks to God for what He had wrought.

43

THE GUARD ENTERED THE CELL AND BEGAN TO
go through Mendib's locker, collecting the few clothes he
found. The mute watched, unmoving.

'Time to look pretty for the outside world, my friend.
Looks like they're going to let you go, and we can't have
prisoners leaving with dirty clothes. I don't know whether
you understand me, but whether you do or not, I'm taking
this stuff to wash it and I'll bring it back clean. Oh! And
those stinking sneakers of yours too – they smell like shit!'

He went to the bed, bent over, and picked up the shoes.
Mendib began to stand up, alarmed, but the guard put a
finger on his chest.

'Now, now, take it easy. I'm just following orders. We'll
bring everything back tomorrow.'

When Mendib was alone again, he closed his eyes. He
didn't want the security cameras to see the turmoil he felt.
He couldn't suppress his excitement at the prospect of
freedom. But something was wrong. He was sure of it.

Marco had been at the prison for hours. He had interrogated the Bajerais, despite the doctor's protests, but he'd

gotten nowhere. He had started with routine questions, those they would expect him to ask. The brothers refused to say where they were going when they were attacked, or who, if anyone, they suspected of beating them. As best as Marco could tell, they weren't aware of Frasquello's involvement.

Then he went on to probe their outside connections, the rumors circulating in the prison about all the money they'd boasted of having. He was trying to walk the tightrope between pushing them to give up the details of the plot and alerting them – and whoever was behind them – that he already knew their target.

But the Bajerais had nothing to say. All they did was moan about their pounding heads and the fact that this cop was torturing them with his questions. They weren't going anywhere, they'd just noticed that the cell door was open, they stuck their heads out, and somebody jumped them. Not a word more. That was their story, and nobody was going to make them change it.

Back in the warden's office, Marco picked up the mute's shoes, freshly laundered, so that the tracking chip could be installed. The warden urged Marco to press the Bajerais explicitly about why they were going after the mute and who had hired them, but Marco continued to resist taking that step. In any prison, hundreds of eyes were watching. Who knew who the link to the outside was? As Marco gathered his papers to return to the hotel, the two agreed to revisit the question in a few days.

Neither of them noticed the cleaning lady leaving the office. She'd been in the warden's private washroom changing the towels, an innocuous part of the prison landscape.

Marco dropped off the shoes at carabinieri headquarters. When he reached the hotel, Antonino, Pietro, and Giuseppe were waiting for him in the bar. Sofia had gone up to bed, and Minerva had promised to come down after she'd called home.

'So – five days to go, and the mute will be on the street. Anything new?' Marco asked.

'Nothing definite,' Antonino replied, 'but it looks like the beautiful city of Turin has special charm for immigrants from Urfa.'

Marco frowned. 'What does that mean?'

'Minerva and I have been working like dogs on this. We put the Bajerai family and everything else we could think of through the computer and did some old-fashioned shoe-leather work, too, and some interesting things came up. You know the old guy in the cathedral, the porter? The one named Turgut? He's from Urfa – I mean *he's* not, but his father is. His story pretty much matches the Bajerai brothers'. His father came to Turin looking for work, found a job with Fiat, married an Italian woman, and Turgut was born here. Other than the similar back-grounds, though, there's no apparent relationship between the families. But you remember Tariq?'

'Tariq?' Marco asked.

'One of the electricians who were working in the cathedral when the fire broke out,' Giuseppe reminded him. 'He's from Urfa too.'

Minerva came into the bar. She was tired, and looked it. Marco felt a twinge of guilt; he'd been piling the work on her and Antonino over the last few days, but she was far and away the best computer person he had, and Antonino's data-gathering and analytical skills were superb. Marco trusted both of them to do the best work it was possible to do.

'Well, Marco!' Minerva exclaimed as she sat down. 'You can't say we don't earn our salary.'

'So I've been hearing,' he replied. 'This Urfa connection is definitely worth pursuing. What else have you turned up?'

'That they're not practicing Muslims – they may not be Muslims at all. They all go to Mass,' Minerva said.

'Let's not forget that Turkey is secular, thanks to Ataturk. The fact that these people aren't practicing Muslims is no big deal. That they go to Mass and by all appearances are devout Christians, though, *is* interesting,' Antonino pointed out.

'Are there many Christians in Urfa?' Marco asked.

'Only a small minority,' replied Minerva.

Antonino jumped back in. 'But in ancient times Urfa was a Christian city – its name then was Edessa, as a matter of fact. And you'll recall that the Byzantines besieged Edessa in 944 in order to capture the Holy Shroud, which was in the hands of a small Christian community there, despite the fact that at the time the city was ruled by Muslims.'

'Get Sofia,' Marco said.

'Why?' Pietro asked.

'Because we're going to brainstorm. We're on to something here. Sofia told me not long ago that the past might be the key to all this. Ana Jiménez thought the same thing.'

Pietro slapped his hand on the bar. 'For God's sake, Marco, let's not go crazy here.'

'What exactly makes you think I'm going crazy?'

'I've seen it coming. These women are running wild with this crap. Give me a break. How many cities are standing on top of older ones? Here in Italy there's a story under every rock, and we don't go chasing through history every time there's a murder or a fire. I know this case is special for you, Marco, but I'm sorry – I think you've gone overboard, bringing us all here, spending all this time, when we've got plenty to do in Rome. There are people here with Turkish backgrounds who can be traced back to a city named Urfa – so what? How many Italians from a single town went off to Frankfurt during the hard times to work in the factories there? I doubt that every time an Italian commits a crime in Germany the German police start digging into the life of Julius Caesar and his legions. All I'm saying is that we can't get carried away by these random coincidences. There's a lot of esoteric shit floating around about the shroud – we need to stick to good police work and not go running after bogeymen, with half-assed historians playing at being cops.'

Minerva and Antonino both began to bluster outraged replies. Marco held up his hand to forestall further debate. He weighed his words carefully. Putting aside the cheap shot at Sofia – for she was the target of *that*, he had no doubt – there was logic in what Pietro said, a lot of logic, so much that Marco realized he might be right. But the Art Crimes chief was an old dog; he'd spent his life sniffing out obscure trails, and his instinct told him that he should stay on this one, however 'esoteric' it might appear to be.

'All right, Pietro. You've said what you have to say. And you may be right. But since we've got nothing to lose, we're going to explore every possibility. Minerva, call Sofia, please. I expect she's still awake. What else do we know about Urfa?'

Antonino gave him a complete file on Urfa, or Edessa. He'd figured his boss would ask for it.

'Pietro, I want you and Giuseppe to go talk to this

porter tomorrow. Tell him that the investigation is still open and that you want to talk to him in case he might have remembered some detail since you last talked.' Marco stared hard at the still-simmering cop.

'He'll get nervous. He was practically in tears when we questioned him the first time,' Giuseppe recalled.

'Right. He's a weak link. That's good. We'll also ask for warrants to tap the phones of any of these nice people from Urfa who have any relation at all to the Bajerais. Those are the only warrants we have a chance of getting. And let's start looking into any churches we can find in Urfa itself.'

Minerva returned with Sofia. The two women glared at Pietro and sat down. When the bar closed at around three, Marco and his team were still talking. Sofia had ranged widely through the history of the shroud, stopping at a number of intriguing intersections. She, Antonino, and Minerva agreed that they had to follow the trail to Urfa, and Giuseppe kept his skepticism in check. Pietro, for his part, made it clear that he thought they were all wasting their time.

But by whatever means they got there, they all went up to bed convinced they were close to a solution.

The old man's eyes fluttered open. His private phone was ringing, rousing him from a deep sleep; he'd gone to bed barely two hours earlier. The duke had been in excellent humor and hadn't let them leave until past midnight. The dinner was splendid and the conversation amusing, as befit gentlemen of their age and position when they found themselves without the company of women.

He got up and, pulling on a soft cashmere robe, went into his study. He locked the door and sat down at his desk, where he pushed a hidden button, activating the scrambler.

The information he received disturbed him: The Art Crimes Department was getting close to the community, to Addaio.

Addaio had failed in his plan to eliminate Mendib, who would soon be free to lead Valoni straight to the pastor and his secrets – and too many of their own secrets.

But it wasn't just that. Now Valoni's team had given free rein to their imaginations, and Dr. Galloni was constructing a hypothesis that was very close to the truth, though she herself couldn't yet suspect that. As for the Spanish reporter, she had a speculative sort of mind and the imagination of a novelist, which in this case were dangerous weapons. Dangerous for *them*.

The sun was coming up by the time he left his study. He returned to his bedroom and began to prepare to leave for the meeting he had just called together in Paris. It was going to be a long day. Everyone would be there, although he was concerned about the suddenness with which they would all be moving. It could draw attention.

44

A.D. 1314

Dusk was fast becoming night as Jacques de Molay, Grand Master of the Order of Knights Templar, sat and read by candlelight the report sent from Vienne by Pierre Berard, informing him of the details of the council meeting.

De Molay's eyes were bloodshot, his noble face creased with lines and shadowed by fatigue. Long sleepless nights had left their mark.

These were evil times for the Temple.

Before Villeneuve du Temple, the immense fortified site of the Templar city, rose the majestic royal palace from which King Philippe IV of France was preparing his great coup against the order. The kingdom's treasury was depleted, and Philippe le Beau owed the Temple a great deal of money – so much money that people said he would have to live ten lives to repay it all.

But Philippe had no intention of paying his debts. His plan, in fact, was quite different: He wished to inherit the order's assets, even if he had to share part of the treasure with the Church. He had approached the Order of Hospitallers for aid, promising them lands and villas if they would support him in his sordid campaign against the Templars. And around Pope Clement were influential clerics whom Philippe paid to conspire against the Temple.

Since he had bought the false testimony of Esquieu de Floryan, Philippe had been inexorably tightening the noose about the Templars' necks, and each day that passed, the moment approached when he would be able to deliver the coup de grâce.

The king secretly envied Jacques de Molay for his courage and integrity, for possessing in full measure the nobility and virtues that he himself lacked. His discomfort in the Grand Master's presence was evident, and he could not bear to stand before the unwavering mirror of the Templar's eyes. He would not stop until he saw him burned at the stake.

Earlier that evening, as on so many others, Jacques de Molay had gone into the chapel to pray for the knights already immolated by order of the king. More were dying each day, denounced as heretics by their sovereign and by their Church. He prayed, too, to be delivered from the tyranny of King Philippe.

For a long while, since Clement had appointed Philippe custodian of the Templars' assets, in Poitiers, he had maintained a tight rein on the order. Now the Grand Master tensely awaited the decision of the Council of Vienne. Philippe had gone in person in order to exert pressure on Clement and the ecclesiastical tribunal. He was not content to administer a treasure that did not belong to him; he wanted it for himself, and the Council of Vienne presented itself as the perfect vehicle by which to deliver the mortal blow to the Temple.

When he had finished reading the report, Jacques de Molay rubbed his eyes and then reached for a sheet of parchment. For the better part of an hour his pen scratched across the paper. The moment he finished he sent for two of his most loyal knights, Beltrán de Santillana and Geoffroy de Charney.

Beltrán de Santillana, born in a sunny house in the mountains of Cantabria in Spain, was a man of silence and meditation. He had entered the order not long after turning eighteen, but even before being initiated as a brother he had already fought in the Holy Land. There he met de Molay and saved his life, covering the Templar with his body as the blade of a Saracen warrior was about to find de Molay's throat. A long scar on Santillana's chest, near his heart, bore witness to that long-ago act of bravery and self-sacrifice.

Geoffroy de Charney, precept of the order in Normandy, was an austere, stern knight whose family had given other sons to the order, renowned knights such as his uncle François de Charney, may he rest in peace, who had died of melancholy years ago on a visit to the family estate.

Jacques de Molay trusted Geoffroy de Charney as he would trust himself. They had fought together in Egypt and before the fortress of Tortosa, and he knew de Charney's courage and piety, as he knew that of Beltrán de Santillana. It was for that reason he had chosen these two knights to carry out the most delicate of missions.

In his report, the Templar knight Pierre Berard had confirmed the worst. Clement was about to accede to Philippe's demands. The order's days were numbered – the death sentence abolishing it was soon to be issued from Vienne. Swift arrangements had to be made for saving the last, most fiercely protected treasures of the Temple.

Distant sounds of revelry from the streets of Paris broke the silence of the night.

De Charney and de Santillana quietly entered the Grand Master's study. Jacques de Molay serenely bade his knights take seats. There were many details to be discussed, and there was no need for preamble as the Grand Master began to outline his instructions. They all knew what they faced.

'Beltrán, you must leave for Portugal at once. Our brother Pierre Berard has informed me that within days the pope will condemn the Temple. It is too soon to know what will happen to our brothers in other countries, but in France our cause is lost. I had thought of sending you to Scotland, for Robert Bruce, the Scottish king, has been excommunicated and is thus beyond Clement's reach. But I trust in good King Dinis of Portugal, from whom I have received assurances of protection for the order. Philippe has taken much from us. But neither gold nor land concern me, only one great treasure, the Temple's crowning jewel – the shroud of Christ. For years, the Christian kings have suspected that it lies in our possession, and they have longed to recover it. The rumors of its magical power to make the man who owns it indestructible have only grown with time. Still, I believe that good King Louis was sincere in his pleas to be allowed to pray before the true image of Christ.

'Events have affirmed the wisdom of our holding the knowledge of our order's policy to maintain our possession of the shroud in strictest secrecy. That secret must now be preserved and defended with more valor and devotion than ever before. Philippe intends, I am certain, to enter the temple and search every nook and corner. He has confided to his advisers that if he finds the Holy Shroud it will redouble his power and extend his supremacy as a Christian king over all the world. He is blinded by ambition, and we have already tasted bitterly of the evil that lies in his soul.

'Now, in our last hours in France, we must save this precious relic as your good uncle de Charney saved it once before. You, Beltrán, will carry the shroud from France to our chapter house in Castro Marim, across the Guadiana. There, you will deliver it to the superior in Portugal, our brother José Sa Beiro. You shall take with you a letter in which I have given instructions for the manner of its protection.

'Only you, Sa Beiro, de Charney, and I will know where the shroud is, and Sa Beiro, at the hour of his death, will pass the secret on to his successor. You will remain in Portugal, Beltrán, to guard the relic. If it becomes necessary, I shall endeavor to send you new instructions. During your journey you will pass through the territories of several Templar chapters in Spain. You shall take a document in which I give instructions to those superiors and priors on how to proceed if death comes, as I fear it will, to the Temple and to its knights. Others already ride across the Christian kingdoms with similar documents for our besieged brothers.'

'When shall I depart, master?' the Spanish knight asked the man for whom he would gladly give his life again.

'As soon as you are ready.'

Geoffroy de Charney could not hide his disappointment when he asked the Grand Master the question that was burning inside him:

'What, sire, is my mission, then?'

'Geoffroy, you shall go to Lirey with the cloth in which your uncle wrapped the holy shroud, and there you shall guard it. I think it best that this cloth remain in France, but in a safe place. For all these years I have wondered about the miracle that occurred on that piece of linen, for miracle it most surely was. Your uncle wept with emotion when he spoke to me of the moment he unfolded the cloth in the presence of the master at Marseilles, and I have come to believe that unto us was delivered the means by which to protect the Holy Shroud of Jesus for all time. Though the first was that in which the body of our Lord was laid, both pieces of cloth are sacred.

'All depends now upon the nobility of the de Charneys, your family, and I know that your brother and your aged father will protect and guard this cloth until the Temple reclaims it.

'Two times François de Charney crossed the desert through infidel lands to bring the shroud to the Temple. We face a desperate juncture once more. And once again the Temple requires the service of your valiant Christian family.'

The three men remained a few seconds in silence, betraying no emotion yet moved to the core of their beings. That same night, the two Templars would each set out bearing precious cargo on journeys that began on separate roads, toward a destination only God could know. For Jacques de Molay was right: God had worked a miracle upon the cloth that had enfolded the Holy Shroud during the long, perilous journey of François de Charney so many years ago – a cloth of soft linen, of the same texture and color as that in which Joseph of Arimathea had laid the body of the Christ to rest.

★   ★   ★

✝ They had ridden for many days, but now, at last, they espied the valley of Bidasoa, in Navarro. Beltrán de Santillana, accompanied by four knights and their squires, spurred his steed. They were anxious to enter Spain, to leave France and the agents of King Philippe behind them.

Knowing they might well be followed by assassins, they had hardly stopped to rest. Philippe had eyes everywhere, and it would not be surprising if someone had whispered to his spies that a group of men had left the fortress Villeneuve du Temple.

Jacques de Molay had asked them not to wear the Templar helmet or mail, so that they might journey unnoticed – at least until they were far from Paris. They were not to change their plain vestments until they were a few leagues past the frontier and safely in Spain. Then they would garb themselves again as what they were – knights, Templar knights, for there was no honor greater than belonging to the Temple and fulfilling its sacred mission – saving its most precious treasure.

Beltrán de Santillana breathed easier as, along the road, he began to recognize the landscape of his near-forgotten homeland, and he savored the sounds of Castilian as he spoke with laborers and with the brothers in the Templar chapters in the lands they passed through.

After riding for days, they came near the town of Jerez, in Extremadura – Jerez de los Caballeros, it was often called, for it was the site of a Templar chapter house. Beltrán announced to the knights and squires accompanying him that they would rest a few days there before beginning the last stage of their journey.

Now that he was in Castile, Beltrán felt a yearning for his past, the days when he had not yet known what the future held for him and dreamed only of being a warrior who would free the Holy Sepulchre from the infidels and return it to Christianity.

It was his father who had encouraged him to enter the Order of Knights Templar and become a warrior for God.

It had been hard for him at first, for although he enjoyed wielding his sword and bow, his exuberant nature was not made for chastity. There were hard years of penitence and sacrifice, until he learned to tame his body, fit it to the motions of his soul, and be worthy of taking the oath of a Templar.

He was now fifty, and old age was upon him, but he felt himself young again on this journey, which had brought him from the north through the south of Castile.

In the distance, profiled against the horizon, rose the Temple's imposing castle. A fertile valley ensured the chapter's food, and generous streams and small rivers quenched its thirst. Laborers working in a field saw them approach and waved. Here, the Templars were yet respected and admired. A squire took their horses and showed them the path to the castle entrance.

Beltrán recounted the recent developments in France to the somber superior and gave him a scroll bearing the seal of Jacques de Molay.

During the days they rested, Beltrán de Santillana took pleasure in the conversation of another Templar born in the mountains of Cantabria, in a town very near his own. They recalled the names of friends they had had in common, servants of the palace in which they had visited, even the names of certain cows that grazed in the fields, indifferent to the shouting and running of the children.

Beltrán never spoke of the mission with which he had been charged. And neither the superior of the chapter nor his Cantabrian brother asked questions of the quiet knight.

But when they said their farewells, they did so with comforted hearts.

✝ A few scattered whitewashed houses caressed by the sun made up the last village before one crossed the river into Portugal. The owner of the barge that ferried passengers and belongings back and forth across the Guadiana each day charged dearly, but the Templars did not dispute his price.

The ferryman took them to the other side of the river and pointed to the road that led to the fortress of Castro Marim, whose massive walls could be seen even from the Castilian side.

✝ From the battlements of the Templar castle, knights could see to the far horizon and the sea. But the fortress was safe against the incursions of any enemy, sitting as it did in a bend in the Guadiana.

José Sa Beiro, master of the chapter house of Castro Marim, was a wise and erudite man who had studied medicine, astronomy, and mathematics, and whose mastery of Arabic had enabled him to read the classics, for the knowledge of Aristotle, Thales of Miletus, Archimedes, and many others, otherwise lost, had been preserved in translations by Arab scholars. He had fought in the Holy Land, known the dry wind of its arid landscape, and still longed for the nights lit by thousands of stars, which in the East looked as though one might clutch them in one's hand.

The superior greeted Beltrán and his accompanying knights warmly and bade them rest and wash from themselves the dust of the road. He would not talk with them until they had eaten and drunk and he was assured they were settled in the austere cells that had been prepared for them.

Beltrán met with Sa Beiro in the master's study, where a large window admitted the breeze from the river.

When the knight finished his story, he reverently unfolded the cloth before the superior. The two men were astounded at the clarity of the image of the Christ figured along its length. There were the marks of the Passion, the suffering the Savior had undergone.

José Sa Beiro gently caressed the cloth, knowing what a monumental privilege it was to do so. Here at his hand was the true image of Jesus, the very image the Templars had worshipped in the privacy of their chapels since Grand Master de Vichiers had sent copies to all the houses of the brotherhood.

The master bade Beltrán sit as he read Jacques de Molay's letter. When he had finished, his eyes burned with the same intensity that had carried him through countless battles in the Holy Land.

'Good knight, we shall defend this cloth with our lives. The Grand Master asks that for the present we tell no one that it is in our possession here. We must wait to find out what happens in France, what effects the decision of the Council of Vienne may have on the order. Jacques de Molay bids me send a knight at once to Paris, as a spy; he must go in disguise, and he must neither go near the Temple nor try to communicate with any Templar, but only look and listen, and when he has discovered the fate that is to be the order's, he is to return immediately. Then shall be the moment to decide whether the shroud is to remain in Castro Marim or be taken to another secure place. This is what the Grand Master instructs, and this is what we shall do.

'I shall send for João de Tomar. He is the man for this mission.'

✛ The town of Troyes was behind him, and it was only a few leagues to the seigneury of Lirey. Geoffroy de Charney had journeyed alone, in the company only of his squire, and he had felt the gaze of Philippe's spies following him all along the road. In his shoulder bag he carried the linen cloth that had protected the shroud, as his uncle François de Charney had done before him.

The laborers in the field were gathering their tools in the fading light. The Templar felt his heart lift, seeing the fields of his youth that had long come to him in dreams, and he spurred his horse, eager to embrace his older brother.

His reunion with his family was filled with emotion. His brother, Paul, pulled him into a fierce embrace, assuring him that he had come home to his own house. His father, closer to death than life, shook with sobs as he gazed upon his younger son. He had never wavered in his admiration for the Temple and had aided the order whenever he had been asked. The renowned service of the family's sons in the Templar ranks had been a source of pride and honor to the de Charneys through the years, and it would stand with the order now.

That night, when the household had retired, Geoffroy revealed to his father and brother the sacred cloth that had been entrusted to their family. He was iron-bound by his vows and by the master's explicit orders from relating the whole of the story to them. But that did not lessen the vital importance of the task before them or the profound devotion with which they undertook this trust.

Knowing the fate that all but certainly awaited Geoffroy,

the older men begged him to remain at Lirey, with them and with the miraculous cloth, to guard it until the end of his days if he might. But he was resolved to rejoin his brothers of the Temple and would not be dissuaded. Nor would he obey his master, for he knew his presence in Lirey would only call attention to the place in which the cloth was to remain hidden. His duty and his destiny lay elsewhere, in Villeneuve du Temple at the side of Jacques de Molay.

For several days, however, Geoffroy allowed himself to bask in the warmth of his family. He played with his nephew, who bore his name and one day would inherit the family home. The brave, bright little fellow followed his uncle about wherever he went, asking him to teach him to fight.

'When I grow up I shall be a Templar,' he would say.

And a lump would come to Geoffroy's throat, for he knew that the doors to the future had been closed to the Temple, probably forever.

On the day of his departure, young Geoffroy bade his uncle farewell with tears in his eyes. He had asked the knight to take him with him to fight in the Holy Land, and he was inconsolable that he could not go. In his innocence he could not know that his uncle was about to enter the worst of battles, against an enemy who knew no nobility in combat and made no claim to honor – an enemy who was no Saracen but rather Philippe of France, their king.

✝ Jacques de Molay was praying in his chamber when a servant announced the return of de Charney. He had the knight brought to him immediately and, on seeing his face and receiving his terse report on his successful mission, wasted no time in chiding him for rejoining his brothers.

All along his journey back to the Templar fortress, de Charney had heard rumors of Philippe's latest movements against the Temple, and the Grand Master now apprised him of the most recent, fatal developments. In no more than a few days, it seemed, they would be tried en masse and burned at the stake. First, though, they would be tortured and calumnies would be heaped upon them, for the king was accusing the Templars of paganism and sodomy, and also of worshipping the devil and of prostrating themselves before an idol they called Baphumet.

And indeed there was a figure to whom the Templars prayed throughout the world in every chapter house, though His name was not Baphumet. Perhaps somewhere, some unfaithful servant had been bribed to reveal the details of life within the Temple's walls and had whispered that the knights often closed themselves up in a chapel that no one else might enter, and there they prayed. And that upon the wall of the secret chapel had been glimpsed a painting, an image of a strange figure, an idol, whom they worshipped.

✝ The fortress Villeneuve du Temple was a sacred and impenetrable sanctuary no more. The king's soldiers had marched in with impunity and seized everything they found. There was little left to take and no sign of where the riches had gone. Months before, Jacques de Molay had divided the remaining gold and distributed it among distant chapter houses and moved the temple's treasures to Scotland, where its secret documents had also been sent. Philippe's fury was terrible. Yet there was one treasure, the greatest of all, that he felt sure must still lie within his grasp.

He sent an emissary to the fortress – the Comte de Champagne, who presented himself at the gate and demanded to see the Grand Master. Jacques de Molay received him with his characteristic tranquillity and grace.

'I come in the name of the king,' the nobleman said grandly when the two men were alone.

'So I imagined. Otherwise I would not have seen you.'

The Grand Master remained standing, and he did not invite the Comte de Champagne to take a seat, a snub that inflamed the count's tender sensibilities and his finely honed mastery of courtly etiquette. He was there representing the full authority of the king of France. Yet he squirmed uncomfortably beneath the knight's steady gaze.

'His Majesty wishes to make you an offer: your life in exchange for the Holy Shroud in which Jesus was buried. The king has not a doubt that the relic is in the Temple's possession – our sainted king Louis believed so too. In the royal archives there are documents concerning this matter, reports from our ambassador to Constantinople, volumes from our spies at the imperial court, confidences from Emperor Balduino himself to his uncle the king of France. We know that the shroud of Christ is in the possession of the Temple. You are hiding it.'

Jacques de Molay listened to the Comte de Champagne's speech in silence, revealing in neither his face nor his posture any reaction, any emotion at all. But mentally he gave thanks to God that he had foreseen the necessity of removing the relic – which by now, he thought, must be safe in Castro Marim, under the protection of good José Sa Beiro.

When the count finished talking, the Grand Master answered coolly, 'My dear count, I assure you that the relic to which you refer is not in my possession. You may be certain, however, that even if it were, I would never make such an exchange. The king should not confuse the values of other men with his own.'

De Champagne's face reddened at the insult to his monarch. Yet he pressed on. Surely this rough knight could be made to see reason.

'De Molay, the king would show you his magnanimity. Think! You wish to die for something that in fact belongs to the Crown, to France and all of Christendom.'

'*Belongs?* Explain to me why it *belongs* to Philippe.'

The count could hardly contain his rage. He would relish the day when this so-called 'master' and his fellows pleaded for the mercy they now spurned so arrogantly.

'You know as well as I how much gold Louis, good King Louis, sent to Byzantium in exchange for holy relics. And you know that the emperor himself agreed that Louis should have the shroud of Christ – until it was stolen away!'

The Templar waved him away.

'I have nothing to do with the trade between kings. My life belongs to God; the king may take it from me, but it *belongs* to God. Go and tell Philippe that I do not have this object he seeks, but that if I did I would never put it in hands such as his for any price whatsoever, including my life. I am a man of honor.'

✝ Scant hours later, Jacques de Molay, Geoffroy de Charney, and the rest of the Templars who remained in Villeneuve du Temple were arrested and taken to the dungeons of the king.

Philippe of France ordered the jailers to torture the Templar knights without mercy. They were to pay special attention to Jacques de Molay, until they secured the answers Philippe sought – namely, where the Grand Master was hiding the holy relic that bore the image of Christ.

✝ The screams of the tortured men echoed within the thick walls of the dungeons. How many days had passed since they were arrested? The Templars had lost count. Broken on the wheel, burned with red-hot iron, their bodies flayed of skin and bathed in vinegar, some confessed crimes they had not committed, praying their agony would end. But their confessions were for naught, for their torturers continued to torment them implacably.

On occasion a man, his face concealed by a hood, watched from the shadows the suffering of the knights, these knights who had once wielded their swords and risked their very lives to defend the cross. Reveling in their torment, sick with avarice and cruelty, Philippe would signal the torturers to go on. . . .

One evening he asked to be taken into the presence of Jacques de Molay. Broken and bloodied, the Grand Master could hardly see, but he sensed who it was beneath the hood. A smile came to his lips when the king demanded that he confess where he had hidden the Holy Shroud of Jesus.

At last, Philippe saw that it was futile to continue. De Molay would not yield. All that was left was public execution, so that the world might know that the Temple had been exterminated for all eternity.

It was March 18 in the year of Our Lord 1314 when the sentence of death was signed for the Grand Master of the Temple and those knights who had survived the interminable tortures that the king had ordered.

On the nineteenth, the city of Paris took on the aspect

of a fair, for the king had ordered that before the majestic spires of Notre Dame a pyre be erected, upon which the proud Jacques de Molay would be publicly burned. Nobles and commoners alike congregated for the event, and there were rumors that the king himself would attend.

By the first light of day, the square was filled with the curious, who shoved and brawled to secure the ideal spot from which to watch the final suffering of the once mighty knights. The people always enjoyed the spectacle of the powerful of the earth humiliated – and the Temple had been powerful, though more good had come of its power than evil.

Jacques de Molay and Geoffroy de Charney were mounted on the same wagon and drawn into the square. They knew that soon their pain would end forever in the flames.

The court had put on its finest clothes, and the king laughed and joked with the ladies. He, Philippe, king of France, had done what no man had ever done before – he had brought the Temple low.

His deed would pass into the history of iniquity.

✝ Fire began to burn the Templars' ravaged flesh. Jacques de Molay's eyes remained fixed on Philippe, and before him and the people of Paris the Grand Master proclaimed his innocence and called down divine justice on the king of France and Pope Clement, summoning them to stand with him before the judgment of God within the year.

A shiver ran down Philippe's spine as de Molay's words rang out. He trembled in fear and had to remind himself that he was king and nothing could harm him, for he had secured the consent of the pope and the highest authorities of the Church before he acted.

No, God could not be on the side of these Templars, these heretics who worshipped a secret idol, who had committed the sin of sodomy, and who were known to be friends of the Saracens. He, Philippe, king of France, was obeying the laws of the Church.

But was he obeying the laws of God?

45

'HAVE YOU FINISHED?'

Ana jumped. 'Professor! You scared me! I was in the middle of reading about the execution of Jacques de Molay. It makes your hair stand on end. What is the judgment of God, anyway?'

Professor McFadden sighed heavily and gave her a bored look. She had been at the institute for two days, poking about in the archives and asking questions that sometimes sounded like pure nonsense.

She was bright but rather ignorant, and he'd had to give her several elementary lessons in history. Her knowledge of the Crusades and the chaotic world of the twelfth, thirteenth, and fourteenth centuries was rudimentary at best. But she was no fool – her academic ignorance seemed to be inversely proportional to her instincts for the pearl within a sea of information, for going straight to the heart of a story. She searched and searched and searched, and she knew where and how to find things. She grasped at a phrase, a single word, an event as she went about her anarchic research. Anything might be a clue.

He had been careful; he'd taken pains to divert her attention from those events that he knew might be dangerous in the hands of a reporter.

He pushed up his glasses and began explaining what the judgment of God was. Ana couldn't contain a shiver when the professor's dramatic rendition repeated the words of Jacques de Molay. Then he came to the payoff.

'Pope Clement died forty days later, and Philip the Fair eight months after that. Their deaths were terrible, as I've told you before. God exacted His justice.'

'I'm glad for Jacques de Molay,' Ana told him.

'I beg your pardon?'

'I like him. He seems to have been a good man, and fair, and Philip the Fair, as you Brits call him, anything but. You have to admit how satisfying it is that, in this case at least, God decided to exact justice, as you put it. It's a shame He doesn't do it more often. But don't you think that the Templars were behind those unpleasant deaths?'

'No, not at all.'

'Why? How can you be so sure?'

'There is detailed documentation on the circumstances of the king's and the pope's deaths, and I assure you that you will find no source that suggests, even as speculation, the possibility that the Templars avenged themselves. Besides, it's not the way the Templars lived or acted. With all you've read, you should realize that.'

'I'd have done it.'

'It?'

'Organize a group of knights to assassinate the pope and Philippe.'

'Perhaps so. But the Knights Templar would never have

allowed themselves such behavior. They killed in pursuit of their duty, as they saw it. But never for revenge.'

'Tell me what this treasure was that the king was after. According to the archives, he'd already taken virtually everything. Yet Philippe insisted that Jacques de Molay hand over a "treasure." What treasure was he talking about? It must have been something concrete, something of great value, right?'

'Philippe was all too aware of the immense wealth the Temple had accumulated. He was obsessed with stripping the order bare and thought that Jacques de Molay had tricked him by concealing most of the order's gold.'

'No . . . I don't think he was looking for more gold.'

'No? How interesting! What do you think he was looking for?'

'Well, something concrete, as I said, something specific. An object of great, great value to the Temple and to the king of France, maybe for Christianity – there are hints of that in these accounts. I've read that the trade in Christian relics was pretty brisk in those days and that those things were considered as valuable as gold – or even more valuable. Why else would it have been such a big deal?'

'Ah. Well, then, tell me what such a thing might be – because I assure you that this is the first time that I've heard such . . . such. . . .'

'If you weren't so polite, you'd say "such nonsense." You might be right – you're a historian and I'm a reporter; you look at known facts, I speculate to get to the facts we don't know.'

'And there we are, Miss Jiménez. We're discussing history, and history, my dear, is not composed of speculation but of proven facts, corroborated by several sources.'

Ana proceeded as though she had not heard a word he'd said.

'According to the archives I've seen so far, in the months prior to his arrest by the king, the Grand Master sent couriers with letters to several chapter houses. Many knights left and none returned. Are there copies of the letters written by de Molay?'

'We have some – copies we've been able to certify as authentic. Others have been lost forever.'

'Could I see the ones you've got?'

'I'll ask whether I can show them to you.'

'I'd really like to see them tomorrow if possible; I'm leaving early the next morning.'

'Oh, you're leaving!'

'Yes, and I can see you're as happy I am.'

'Please, Miss Jiménez!'

'Professor, I know I'm being a pain in the neck and keeping you from your work.'

McFadden allowed himself a smile. 'I'll try to have the documents tomorrow. Are you going back to Spain?'

'No, to Paris.'

'Ah, Paris. Very well, then. Come tomorrow, first thing.'

Ana Jiménez left the mansion early the following evening. She had hoped to talk again to Anthony McGilles, but he seemed to have disappeared into thin air after their first meeting.

She was tired. She'd spent the entire day reading about the Temple's last months. The cold facts, the dates, the anonymous recountings of events – it was mind-numbing.

But she'd been blessed – or cursed, as her brother constantly contended – with a wonderful imagination, so every time she'd read, 'Grand Master Jacques de Molay

389

sent a letter to the chapter house in Maguncia with the knight de Lacey, who departed on the morning of July 15 accompanied by two squires,' she tried to imagine what this de Lacey's face was like, whether he was riding a black horse or a white one, whether it had been hot that day, whether the squires were in a bad mood. But she knew that her imagination could never provide her with the truth about those men and that she would never know anything of importance that Jacques de Molay wrote in his letters to the Templar masters. The copies she had been given dealt with dry administrative matters, nothing more.

There was a detailed list of the knights who had been sent with letters just before the Temple's fall, and contrary to what she had thought, a few of them were said to have returned. One of them, Geoffroy de Charney, precept of Normandy, had burned at the stake alongside his master. All trace of the others had been lost forever, at least so far as she could glean from the archives.

She was leaving for Paris the next morning, for an appointment with a history professor at the Sorbonne. Professor Elianne Marchais, a worthy lady of sixty-something who had written several books of the kind read only by scholars like Marchais herself, was the biggest academic name for the fourteenth century, or so Ana's contacts had told her.

Ana went straight back to her hotel. It was costing her more than she ought to be spending, but she was giving herself the very sweet pleasure of sleeping in the Dorchester like a princess. Plus, she figured she'd be safer in a luxury hotel. She had begun to have the distinct feeling she was being followed. She'd told herself that was stupid – who was going to follow her? And then she'd decided it might be agents from the Art Crimes Department, trying to find out what she knew, and that eased her mind. Or maybe it was just all the double-dealing and death she had been delving into. The fourteenth century was finally getting to her. It had certainly taken over her life otherwise, waking and sleeping. She thought of nothing else.

She called room service for a sandwich and salad, eager to crawl into bed as soon as possible. The people in the Art Crimes Department could think whatever they wanted, but she was more convinced than ever that it was the Templars who'd bought the shroud from poor Balduino. What didn't make sense was that after that, the shroud turned up in Lirey, in France. How had it gotten there? Why, when the Templars seemed to have spirited away everything of value as far from Philippe's clutches as possible, would they have left so valuable a treasure in France?

She hoped that Professor Marchais could explain to her what good Professor McFadden apparently hadn't wanted to. Because every time she approached the subject of whether the Templars had bought the shroud in Constantinople, he snapped at her to stick to the facts. He couldn't, or wouldn't, see past the 'fact' that there was no document, no source, that confirmed her theory – her *mad* theory, as he styled it – and he made it very clear that he found the mysteries people attributed to the Templars tiresome at best.

So Professor McFadden and his institute, an institute purportedly dedicated to the study of the Temple, denied even the possibility that the Templars had ever had possession of the shroud. He had also taken pains to remind her that the relic worshipped in Turin had been dated to the thirteenth or fourteenth century, not the first, so it was a moot point, anyway. He could understand superstition among the common run of people, he told her, but it held no interest for him, nor should it for her.

Ana knew she was missing something. Something right in front of her. The feeling had been driving her crazy all day. She took out her appointment book and began thumbing through it and the notes she'd made, retracing her steps. And suddenly it hit her. There it was. How had she missed it?

Flames shot up before her eyes, climbing to the heavens. Within them writhed the figures of men. Were they screaming? She couldn't tell; she was overcome by the heat and the roar of the conflagration that consumed everything. Then, brighter than the fire, more searing than the tendrils that seemed to scorch her own skin, a pair of eyes stared at her from the depths of the pyre and a voice rose above all else.

'Go, search no more, or upon you will fall the judgment of God.' Once more she bolted awake, terrified, drenched with sweat. She would die if she went on, she was sure of it.

For the rest of the night Ana couldn't sleep. In fact, she rarely got through a night now without being assailed by nightmares. She had tracked grisly stories before, plenty of them, but she had never experienced anything like this. It was as though some external force were dragging her step by step through bloody scenes from the past and making her – a tough twenty-first-century reporter – face true horror, and transcendence.

She knew she'd been there, somehow, that March 19, 1314, in the *parvis* before the Cathedral of Notre Dame, only feet from the pyre on which Jacques de Molay and his knights were executed, and that he had begged – ordered

– her not to go on. Not to search for the truth behind the shroud.

But her fate, she told herself, was cast – she wouldn't stop no matter how much she feared Jacques de Molay, no matter that the truth was forbidden to her. She was not going to turn back. Not now that she saw the link so clearly.

46

BAKKALBASI, THE PASTOR TO ISMET, NEPHEW OF
Francesco Turgut, the cathedral porter, had traveled with
the young man from Istanbul to Turin. Other men of the
community would be arriving via different routes – from
Germany, from other places in Italy, even from Urfa itself.
Each man carried several cell phones, although Addaio's
orders were that they not use them too much and that they
try to communicate with one another over public phones,
to remain as untraceable as possible.

Bakkalbasi suspected that Addaio would be arriving
too. No one would know where he was, but he would be
watching them, controlling their movements, directing the
overall operation. Mendib had to die, and Turgut had to
be brought under control or he, too, would die. There was
no alternative.

The Turkish police had been hanging around their
houses in Urfa, a sure sign that the Art Crimes Department
already knew more than the community would have liked
to admit. Bakkalbasi had been tipped to the surveillance by
a cousin in the Urfa police headquarters, a good member
of the community who had informed them of Interpol's

sudden interest in any Turks who had emigrated from Urfa to Italy. Interpol hadn't told them what they were looking for, but it had asked for complete reports on certain families, all belonging to the community.

All the alarms had sounded then, and Addaio had named a successor, in case anything happened to him. Within the community was another small cell, which lived in even deeper secrecy. It would be they who continued the struggle if the main group were taken down – and they would be taken down; the hollow feeling in the pit of Bakkalbasi's stomach told him so.

As soon as they arrived in Turin, he took Ismet to Turgut's house. When the porter opened the door, he shouted in alarm.

'Calm down, man!' Bakkalbasi gripped the porter's arm and steered him inside. 'Why are you shouting? Do you want to alert the entire cathedral?'

They sat down, and when Turgut recovered his composure, he filled them in on the latest events. He knew he was being watched; he had known it since the day of the fire. And the way Padre Yves looked at him. . . . Oh, yes, he was very friendly toward him, but there was something in his eyes that told Turgut to be careful or he would die – yes, yes, that was exactly the way it felt.

They shared a few more minutes over coffee, and the pastor instructed Ismet not to leave his uncle's side. Turgut would introduce him in the cardinal's offices and announce that his nephew would be living with him. The pastor also urged Turgut to show Ismet the secret door that led into the underground tunnels – some of the men who were coming from Urfa might need to hide there and if they did they would need sustenance that only he could provide.

Then Bakkalbasi left them. He had meetings to attend with other members of the community, in Turin and elsewhere. The time to act was almost upon them.

'What do we do?' Pietro asked. 'Maybe we should follow him.'

He and Giuseppe had rounded the corner of the cathedral, heading for the porter's apartment, just in time to see a man exit and move surreptitiously, it seemed, down the street. Something about him had looked off; he'd glanced back over his shoulder not once but twice.

'We don't know who he is,' Giuseppe answered.

'He's Turkish, you can see that.'

'All right, I'll follow him, then.'

'I don't know – we'll probably get more here. Listen, let's just stick with the plan and talk to the porter; maybe we can get something out of him about his visitor.'

Ismet opened the door, thinking that Bakkalbasi had forgotten something. He frowned when he saw the two men – cops for sure. The cops, he told himself, always look like the cops.

'*Buon giorno,* we'd like to speak with Francesco Turgut,' Pietro said.

The young man shrugged and shook his head as if he wasn't sure what they wanted, and then turned and called back into the room in Turkish. Turgut came to the door, unable to control his trembling.

'*Buon giorno,* Signor Turgut,' Pietro said. 'We're still investigating the fire, and we wanted to see whether you might have remembered anything else, any little detail that was out of the ordinary.'

Turgut broke into a stream of Turkish, waving his arms at them. He seemed to be on the verge of tears. Ismet put a protective arm over his shoulder and answered for him in pidgin Italian mixed with English.

'My uncle is old man, and he have suffered much since the fire. He is fearing that with his years they will think he not as good as before and kick him out, because was not watching enough. Can you not leave him alone now? He has told all what he remembers.'

'And who are you?' Pietro asked.

'I Ismet Turgut, nephew of my uncle here. I arrive today. I come to Turin looking for job.'

'Where have you come from?'

'Urfa. . . . From Urfa.'

'There's no work there?' Giuseppe asked.

'In oil fields, yes, but I, what I want do is get good job, save money, and go home to Urfa to have my own business. I have . . . not wife? Girlfriend?'

The kid seemed likable enough, thought Pietro, even innocent. Maybe he actually was.

'All right, that's fine. Does your uncle keep in touch with other people from Urfa? How about that other guy that just left? Is he from there?' Giuseppe asked.

Turgut felt a shiver. Now he was certain that the police knew everything. Ismet, once again taking charge of the situation, answered quickly, ignoring the question about Bakkalbasi.

'Yes, sure, he does, and I believe I try to be friends with the people from my town too. My uncle, you know, half Italian, but Turks never lose our roots – is it not so, uncle?'

The young man seemed determined not to let Francesco Turgut talk. Pietro asked, 'Signor Turgut, do you know the Bajerai family?'

'Bajerai!' Ismet exclaimed excitedly. 'I went to school with boy named Bajerai! I think here in Turin are cousins or something like that . . . not cousins of boy, you know, but cousins of boy's father.'

'I'd like your uncle to answer my question,' Pietro insisted.

Francesco Turgut swallowed hard and prepared himself to say what he had rehearsed so many times.

'Yes, yes, of course I know them. It is an honorable family that has had a terrible disgrace. Their sons . . . well, their sons made a mistake and they are paying for it. But they are good persons, the parents. Very good. You can ask anyone, they will tell you.'

'Have you visited the Bajerai family recently?'

'No, my health is . . . not good. I do not go out much.'

'Excuse me,' Ismet interrupted with an innocent expression. 'What have done the Bajerai?'

'Why do you think they've done something?' Giuseppe asked.

'Because if you, who are the police, come here and ask about the Bajerai, then they have done something, is it not? You would not ask if they had not, I think.'

The young man smiled, apparently proud of his reasoning. Giuseppe and Pietro looked at him, unable to decide whether he was really as innocent as he looked or was a very good liar.

Giuseppe turned back to Turgut. 'Let's go back to the day of the fire,' he suggested.

'I have told you everything I remember. If I had remembered something more I would have called you,' the old man answered, his voice unsteady.

Pietro pounced again. 'Signor Turgut, who is the man who just left?' he pressed. 'Is he from Urfa?'

The porter shook his head vehemently. 'No, no! A friend, just a friend.' He leaned on his nephew for support. 'I feel unwell,' he said shakily. 'I must rest.'

'I have just arrived,' Ismet broke in pleadingly. 'I have not had time even to ask my uncle where I sleep – can you not return another time?'

Pietro and Giuseppe looked at each other and seemed to reach a decision. 'Give us a call when you're feeling better,' Pietro said. 'I think we have more to talk about.' They said good-bye and left.

'What do you think of the nephew?' Pietro asked his partner as they walked away.

'I don't know, seems like a nice kid.'

'They may have sent him to handle his uncle.'

'Oh, come on!' Giuseppe protested. 'Isn't that a little far-fetched? Listen, I think you're right – Sofia and Marco are blowing this case all out of proportion, although Marco doesn't make mistakes often. . . . But this shroud, it's like an obsession.'

'Well, thanks for leaving me out there swinging in the breeze yesterday when I said that. Why didn't you say something then?'

'What was the point? And what are we arguing about now? We've gotta do what Marco says to do. And that's fine by me. If he's right, great, we've got our case; if not, big deal, at least we tried to find an answer to those fucking fires. Either way, we do what we're told – but we don't have to knock ourselves out, know what I mean?'

'Stiff upper lip and all that, huh? You could be English instead of Italian, my man.'

'It's just that you take everything so seriously, and you're so damn touchy. If I said the sky was blue you'd argue about it.'

'It's that things aren't like they used to be. The team is going to hell.'

'Of course the team is going to hell. You and Sofia tense

up like two spitting cats when you're together, and you'd think you get off fighting with each other. I swear, you both look like you're ready to go for the jugular any second. Marco's right: Work and screwing don't mix. I'm being straight with you, Pietro – it's your own fault things stink right now.'

'Who asked you to be straight with me?'

'Yeah, well, I've been wanting to talk to you about it, so there you go.'

'So let's say it's all Sofia's and my fault. What are we supposed to do?'

'Nothing. It'll pass – and anyway, she's leaving. When the case is over she's outta here, off to greener pastures. She wants to do more than chase down cat burglars.'

'She's really something. . . .' Pietro said, a faraway look in his eyes.

'What's weird is that she'd hook up with you in the first place.'

'Thanks.'

'Come on! People are what they are, and they might as well accept it. You and I are cops. Neither of us is in her league, or Marco's either. He's gotten himself an education, and you can tell it. I mean, I'm happy to be what I am and to have gotten where I've gotten. Working in Art Crimes is good duty, and other cops look up to you.'

'Your dedication moves me.'

'Okay, I'll shut up, but I thought you and I could always be up-front with each other – tell it straight out.'

'Good. You've told me. Let's drop it and get back to headquarters. We'll get Interpol to ask the Turks to send us whatever they've got on this nephew who's landed in Turin.'

47

ELIANNE MARCHAIS WAS A SMALL, ELEGANT woman with that unmistakable French flair. She greeted Ana Jiménez with a mixture of resignation and curiosity.

She didn't like reporters. They simplified everything one told them so much that in the end all they printed were distortions – which was why she didn't give interviews. When people asked her opinion about something, her response was always the same: 'Read my books. Don't ask me to tell you in three words what I've needed three hundred pages to explain.'

But this young woman was a special case. Spain's ambassador to UNESCO had phoned on her behalf, as had two chancellors of prestigious Spanish universities and three colleagues at the Sorbonne. Either the girl was truly important or she was a bulldog who'd stop at nothing until she got what she wanted, in this case that Marchais devote a few minutes of her time to her – because a few minutes was all the professor had patience for.

Ana had decided that with a woman like Elianne Marchais there could be no room for subterfuge. She would tell her the truth straight out, and one of two things would happen: The professor would either throw her out or help her.

It took her no more than a few minutes to explain to Professor Marchais that she wanted to write a history of the Shroud of Turin and that she needed the professor's help in order to separate the fantasy from the truth in the history of the relic.

'And why are you interested in the shroud? Are you Catholic?'

'No . . . I mean . . . I guess I am, in some sense. I was baptized, although I don't go to Mass.'

'You haven't answered my question. Why are you interested in the shroud?'

'Because it's a controversial object that also seems to attract a certain degree of violence – fires, robberies in the cathedral. . . .'

Professor Marchais raised an eyebrow. 'Mademoiselle Jiménez, I'm afraid I can't help you,' she said disdainfully. 'My specialty is not esoteric gobbledygook.'

Ana didn't move from her chair. She looked fixedly at the professor and tried another tack, resolving to proceed carefully.

'I think I may have misspoken, Professor Marchais. I'm not interested in esotericism, and if I've given that impression, I apologize. What I'm trying to do is write a documented history, the furthest thing imaginable from any magical, esoteric interpretations. I'm looking for facts, facts, just facts, not speculation. Which is why I've come to you, so that you can help distinguish what's true in the interpretations of certain more or less recognized authors. You know what happened in France in the thirteenth and fourteenth centuries as though it were yesterday, and it's that knowledge that I need.'

Professor Marchais hesitated. The explanation the young woman had given was at least a serious one.

'I don't have much time, so tell me exactly what you want to know.'

Ana breathed a small sigh of relief. She knew she couldn't make another mistake or she'd be thrown out like yesterday's fish bones.

'Well, specifically, I'd like you to tell me everything you can about the shroud's appearance in France.'

With a bored gesture, the professor began a detailed recitation.

'The best chronicles of the time say that in 1349, Geoffroy de Charny, seigneur of Lirey, announced that he possessed a grave cloth bearing the impression of the body of Jesus, to which his family paid great devotion. Geoffroy sent letters to the pope and the king of France, asking for authorization to build a collegiate church in which to display the shroud so that it might be worshipped by the faithful. A collegiate church – in case your Catholic upbringing didn't clarify that point – is a church very like a cathedral, with an abbot and a "college" of priests, in this case called "canons." It's that college of canons from which the term derives. So, to continue: Neither the pope nor the king replied to his request, which meant the collegiate church couldn't be built. But with the complicity of the clergy of Lirey, who saw an opportunity to increase their influence and importance in the seigneury, the shroud nevertheless began to be an object of public worship.'

'But where had the shroud come from?'

'In the letter de Charny wrote to the king of France, which can be found in the royal archives, he assured the king that he had kept his possession of the shroud a secret so as not to inspire disputes among various communities of Christians, since other shrouds had appeared in places as far-flung as Aix-la-Chapelle and Mainz in Germany, Jaén and Tolosa in Spain, and Rome. It was in Rome, in fact, beginning in 1350, that a shroud, believed of course to be authentic, was displayed in the Vatican basilica. Geoffroy de Charny swore to the king and the pope, on the honor of his family, that the shroud that he possessed was the true one, but what he never told either man was how it had come into his power. Was it a family inheritance? Had he bought it? He never said, and thus we simply do not know.

'He had to wait years for authorization to construct the collegiate church and never lived to see the shroud displayed, since he died in Poitiers saving the life of the French king, whom he shielded with his own body during a battle. His widow donated the shroud to the church in Lirey, which contributed to the wealth of the city's clergy while at the same time inspiring the envy of the prelates of other towns and cities – and that, of course, created tremendous conflict throughout France.

'The bishop of Troyes ordered an exhaustive investigation into the Lirey shroud. An important witness was even brought forward to discredit its authenticity – a painter swore that he had been commissioned by the seigneur of Lirey to paint the image, and with that, the bishop prohibited its further display.

'It was to be another Geoffroy, Geoffroy de Charny II, who years later – in 1389, to be exact – persuaded Pope Clement VII to authorize him once again to display the shroud. And once again, the bishop of Troyes intervened, alarmed by the influx of pilgrims to worship the relic. For a few months he managed to force de Charny to keep the shroud in its coffer and not actually display it, but meanwhile, de Charny reached a further agreement with the pope: He would be allowed to display the shroud on the condition that the clergy in Lirey be required to explain to the faithful that it was a painting done to represent the grave cloth of Christ.'

In the same monotonous tone, Professor Marchais went on down through history, explaining that the daughter of Geoffroy II, Marguerite de Charny, decided to keep the shroud in the castle belonging to her second husband, the Comte de la Roche.

'Why?' asked Ana.

'Because in 1415, during the Hundred Years War, pillaging was rampant. So she thought the relic would be safer in her husband's castle, in Saint-Hippolyte sur le Doubs. She was an inventive woman, and when her second husband died, she added to the small income he had left her by charging a fee of a few pennies to anyone who wanted to see the shroud up close or pray before it. And it was her financial straits that led her several decades later to sell the relic to the House of Savoy, on March 22, 1453, to be precise. The Lirey clergy protested, of course; they considered themselves the owners of the shroud, since the widow of that first Geoffroy de Charny had ceded it to them. But Marguerite ignored that. She lived in Varambom Castle and enjoyed the rents from the seigneury of Miribel, which were granted her by the House of Savoy. There is a contract to that effect, by the way, signed by the Duke of Savoy, Louis I. Since then, the shroud's history is transparent.'

'I wanted to ask you whether it's possible that the shroud came to France through the Templars.'

'Ah! The Templars! So many legends, so unfairly they were treated, and all out of ignorance! It is rubbish, pure rubbish, that pseudoliterature on the Templars. Many organizations – some Masons, for instance – claim to be the heirs of the Temple. Some of them were, to put it in the popular parlance, "on the good side," during the French Revolution, for example, but others. . . .'

'So the Temple has survived?'

'Well, of course there are organizations that, as I say, claim to be its heirs. Remember that in Scotland, the Temple was never dissolved. But in my opinion, the Temple died on March 19, 1314, on the bonfire on which Philippe le Beau ordered the Grand Master Jacques de Molay immolated, along with the other knights who were with him.'

'I've been in London. I found a center for Templar studies.'

'I told you there are lodges and organizations that claim to be heirs of the Temple. I have no interest in them.'

'Why is that?'

'Mademoiselle Jiménez, please. I am a historian.'

'Yes, I know, but –'

'There are no buts. Anything else?'

'Yes, I'd like to know whether the de Charny family has come down to our own day, whether there are any descendants.'

'The grand families intermarry. You should consult an expert in genealogy.'

'Forgive me for pressing, professor, but where do you think this Geoffroy de Charny got the shroud?'

'I do not know. I've explained to you that he never said. Nor did his widow or the descendants who were its possessors until it passed into the hands of the House of Savoy. It could have been bought or received as a gift. Who knows? During those centuries, Europe was full of relics that had been brought back from the Crusades. Most of them were false, of course, which is why there are so many "holy grails," shrouds, saints' bones, pieces of the True Cross. . . .'

'Is there any way to know whether the family of Geoffroy de Charny had any relationship to the Crusades?'

'As I said, you'll have to see a genealogist for that. Of course. . . .'

Professor Marchais became more pensive, tapping the end of her pen on her desk. Ana sat silently, expectantly.

'It is possible, of course, that Geoffroy de Charny, whose name was spelled without the final *e*, may have had something to do with Geoffroy de Charney, with an *e*, the precept of the Temple in Normandy who died at the stake alongside Jacques de Molay and who also fought in the Holy Land. It's a question of the spelling of the name, and –'

'Yes, yes, that's it! They're from the same family!'

'Mademoiselle Jiménez, don't let yourself be led astray by what you *wish* the facts were. I said only that the two names *might* come from the same line, so that the Geoffroy de Charny who possessed the shroud –'

'– had it because years earlier the other Geoffroy brought it back from the Holy Land and kept it in the family home. That's well within the realm of possibility.'

'Actually, it isn't. The precept of Normandy was a Templar. If he had possessed the relic, it would have belonged to the *Temple,* not to him or his family. We have a great deal of documentation on *that* Geoffroy, because he remained faithful to de Molay and the Temple. Let's not let our imagination run away with us.'

'But there may have been some reason he didn't turn the shroud over to the Temple.'

'I doubt it. I'm sorry to have confused you; in my opinion it's not a problem of spelling, it's that the two

Geoffroys belonged to different families. And even if they were related, that would not account for the family's possession of the shroud, as I've just explained to you.'

'I'm going to Lirey.'

'Well, that's fine. Anything else?'

'Professor Marchais, thank you – you may not agree, but I think you've just unveiled part of an enigma.'

By the time Elianne Marchais saw Ana Jiménez to the door she had once again confirmed her opinion of reporters: shallow, for the most part uneducated, and given to the most idiotic fantasies. It was no wonder there was so much rubbish printed in the newspapers.

Ana arrived in Troyes the day after her meeting with Professor Marchais. She rented a car to drive from there to Lirey and was surprised to find just a tiny village, with no more than fifty people living in it.

She wandered through what remained of the old seigneurial manor, her hands stroking the ancient stones, vaguely hoping the contact with them might inspire her. Lately she'd been letting herself be carried along partly by intuition, without planning things beforehand.

She approached a nicely dressed older woman walking her dog along the side of the road.

'*Bonjour.*'

The old lady looked her over from head to toe. '*Bonjour.*'

'This is a lovely place.'

'It is, but the young people don't think so – they prefer the city.'

'Well, there is more work in the city.'

'Work is where one wants to find it. Here in Lirey the land is good. Where are you from?'

'I'm from Spain.'

'Ah! So I thought, from the accent. But you speak French very well.'

'Thank you.'

'And what are you doing here? Are you lost?'

'Oh, no, not at all.' Ana smiled. 'I came specifically to see this place. I'm a reporter, and I'm writing a story on the Shroud of Turin, and since it appeared here, in Lirey –'

'Hmmph! That was hundreds and hundreds of years ago! Now they say the shroud is not authentic, that it is a forgery, that it was painted here.'

'And what do you think?'

'I frankly could not care less – I am an atheist, and I've never been interested in the stories of saints or relics.'

'No, neither have I, but I was sent out to do this story, and work is work.'

'But here you will find nothing. The fortress – what remains of it – well, you see it there.'

'And there are no archives or documents on the de Charny family?'

'In Troyes perhaps, although the descendants of the family live in Paris.'

'Live?'

'Well, there are many branches of the family.'

'How could I find them?'

'I don't know. They don't have much to do with the village now. Once in a while one of them will come around, but not often. Three or four years ago a young man was here. Such a handsome boy! We all came out to see him.'

'Is there anyone here who could tell me more?'

The woman gestured down the way. 'Ask in that house

409

at the end of the valley. Monsieur Didier lives there – he oversees the de Charny lands.'

Ana thanked her and began walking briskly toward the house the woman had indicated, her anticipation mounting with every step. She was certain that in this unassuming little place she would find the nexus between past and present – and concrete evidence to support her suspicions.

Monsieur Didier was a man of about sixty. Tall and strong-looking, with gray hair and a stern face, he looked at Ana mistrustfully.

'Monsieur Didier, I'm a reporter and I'm writing a story on the Holy Shroud,' Ana began. 'I've come to Lirey because it was here that the Shroud of Turin first appeared in Europe. I know this land belonged to the de Charny family, and I'm told you work for them.'

'Your business is of no concern to me, miss,' he said, clearly annoyed. 'What do I care what you're doing? You think I'm going to talk about the de Charnys because you're a reporter?'

'I don't think I'm asking you to do anything wrong, sir. I know you must be proud that the shroud was discovered here in Lirey.'

'We don't give a fig about the shroud, young lady – none of us. If you want to find out about the family, go talk to them in Paris. We're not gossips.'

'Monsieur Didier, you've misunderstood me. I'm not looking for gossip at all, I just want to write a story in which this town and the de Charny family played an important part. They owned the shroud, it was displayed here, and . . . well, I should think you'd all feel proud of that.'

'Some of us are.' Tall and robust, the woman who had

just joined Didier in the doorway looked a bit younger than he, and a good deal friendlier.

'I'm afraid you've awakened my husband from his nap, and that makes him grumpy,' she said to Ana with a warm smile. 'Come in, come in. Would you like some tea, coffee?'

Ana stepped into the house before the invitation could be overruled by the old grump, who finally retreated to the parlor with a parting glare as his wife led the reporter to the kitchen.

There, Ana repeated the purpose of her visit while Madame Didier poured coffee for them both.

'The de Charnys have been the lords of this land for as long as anyone can remember,' Madame Didier told Ana as they sat down. 'You should go to the church – that's where you'll find information on them, and of course in the historical archives in Troyes.'

For a good while she went on to talk about life in Lirey, bemoaning the flight of the younger generation. Her two sons lived in Troyes; one was a doctor, the other worked in a bank. She proceeded to detail the affairs of her entire family while Ana listened patiently, letting her babble on. Finally she managed to steer the conversation back on track.

'What are the de Charnys like?' she asked her hostess. 'It must be exciting when they come to visit.'

'Oh, there are so many different branches now. We don't know many of them, and they don't come around much, but we watch after their land and their interests here. They're a bit stuffy, you know, like all aristocrats. A few years ago a distant relative came – what a handsome young man! And so charming, so kind. Not at all like the others. He came with the superior of the church. He sees more of them than we do – the superior, I mean. We deal with an administrator who lives in Troyes, Monsieur Capell. I'll give you his address so you can call him.'

Two hours later, Ana left the Didiers' house with little more information than she'd come with. She decided to try her luck at the parish church, hoping the superior would see her. The birth records there might tell her what she needed to know.

The parish priest Père Salvaing turned out to be a cheery septuagenarian who seemed more than happy to have a visitor.

'The de Charnys have always been linked to this place,' he told Ana. 'They have continued to own the land, although it's been centuries since they lived here.'

'Do you know the current family?'

'Some of them. One of the branches, the one that's most closely linked to Lirey, has some important people. They live in Paris.'

'Do they come here often?'

'No, really they don't. It's been years since any of them have been here.'

'Madame Didier, in Lirey, told me that three or four years ago a very handsome, nice young man was here, a member of that family.'

'Oh, the priest!'

'Priest?'

'Yes. Does it surprise you that somebody might be a priest?' He laughed.

'No, no, I didn't mean that. It's just that in Lirey all they told me was that he was a very handsome young man – they didn't say anything about his being a priest.'

'They may not have known it; no reason for them to. The

one time he came, he didn't wear a collar and he was dressed like any other young fellow his age. He didn't look like a priest, but he is, and I think he's doing very well. I mean, he didn't look like he'd remain very long as a parish priest. In fact, I understand he's moving up in the Church hierarchy. But he didn't give his name as de Charny, although apparently his ancestors had some relationship with this land. He didn't explain it much. They called me from Paris to say that he'd be coming and asked me to help him if I could.'

Ana was hard-pressed to contain her excitement. After so many weeks chasing ephemeral wisps of information, hints and half-truths buried in a mountain of myth, she at last had the beginning of a solid string of facts almost within her grasp – and confirmation that the link she had seen so clearly in the middle of the night in a London hotel room was very real. And very much alive.

But it was not easy for Ana to persuade Père Salvaing to let her see the baptismal certificates in the collegiate archives, which were locked up like diamonds.

The priest called the canon librarian, who was scandalized when he heard what Ana wanted. 'If you were a scholar, a historian, but you're just a reporter – who knows what you're looking for!' he grumbled.

'I'm trying to write the most complete story possible of the shroud. I want to find out whether a fourteenth-century Templar, Geoffroy de Charney, with an *e*, who died at the stake in 1314, owned the shroud and perhaps hid it here, in the family house, so that Geoffroy de Charny, with no *e*, might appear as its owner thirty-five years later.'

'That is, you want to prove that the shroud belonged to the Templars,' Père Salvaing stated more than asked.

'And if that was not the case, she'll *make* the case,' put in the archivist.

'No, sir, I'm not going to invent anything – if that wasn't the case, then it wasn't the case. I'm just trying to explain why the shroud appeared here, and it seems likely that it was brought by someone from the Holy Land, a Crusader or a Templar knight. Who else might have brought it? If Geoffroy de Charny swore that it was the true shroud, then he must have had some reason.'

'He never proved it,' said the elderly superior.

'Maybe he couldn't. But let me ask you – does either of you believe that the shroud now in the cathedral in Turin is authentic?'

'My dear girl,' said Salvaing after a brief silence, 'the shroud is a relic loved by millions of the faithful. Its authenticity has been questioned by scientists, and yet . . . I must admit I was very moved when I saw it in the Turin Cathedral. There is something supernatural in the cloth, whatever the carbon-fourteen verdict may be.'

For another half hour, Ana earnestly pleaded her case with the two churchmen. Finally, they reluctantly agreed to let her proceed under the supervision of the archivist.

For the better part of the afternoon, they pored through the ancient records. At last, as the sun dipped low on the horizon, she found what she was looking for. In addition to *Charny* in Lirey, there had also been a family that spelled its name *Charney*, with an *e*, and the two families were related. The great Crusader, Geoffroy de Charny, had come home – Ana was sure of it.

Ana had returned to Troyes elated. But although she had established the presence of Geoffroy de Charny's family in Lirey, she had found precious little on the knight himself. She made an appointment to see the administrator of the de Charny properties, Capell, in the morning. After that she would see what she could find in the extensive municipal archives in Troyes.

Monsieur Capell turned out to be a serious man of few words, who very politely made it clear to Ana that he had no intention of giving her any information about his clients. He did, however, confirm that there were dozens of descendants of the de Charny line in France and that his clients were one of those families. She left his office disappointed.

The young man in charge of the town archives in Troyes had piercings in his nose and three studs in each ear. He introduced himself as Jean and confessed he was bored spitless by his job but that all things considered, he'd been lucky to find work at all, since his degree was in library science.

Ana explained what she was looking for and Jean offered to help her.

'So you think that this precept of the Temple in Normandy was an ancestor of our Geoffroy de Charny despite the name difference?'

'I told you – there are traces of both versions of the name in the parish church outside Lirey. Now I'm trying to find more specifics and also more information on Geoffroy de Charny himself – his immediate family and his movements before he burned at the stake with the other Templars in 1314.'

'Well, this isn't going to be easy. I can tell you right now that we're not going to have much, if anything, on the activities of a Templar knight. But if you'll give me a hand we'll see what we can find.'

First they looked in the computerized archives, then

began looking through the old files that hadn't been digitized. Ana was pleasantly surprised at Jean's intelligence and facility with the records. Besides being a librarian he had a degree in French philosophy, so medieval France was familiar territory for him.

They worked steadily and managed to unearth all the available local civil records on the de Charny family tree, but both of them knew the information was incomplete. They still knew nothing of the actual lives of these people who so often married to forge alliances with other noble families and whose traces, and offspring's traces, were almost impossible to follow.

'I think you ought to find a historian with more experience in genealogy,' Jean finally told her over dinner that night.

They had become comfortable, even close, in the course of their work together, and Ana decided to trust the intense young man with the whole story, or at least most of it. She'd known him only briefly, yet they had made one of those rare instant connections that had them feeling they'd been friends for years. Jean was thoughtful, intelligent, and sensible. Behind his half-Gothic facade was a solid man, a man of integrity.

She told him almost everything she knew, not mentioning the Art Crimes Department or her brother, Santiago, and waited for his opinion.

'Maybe the two Geoffroys *were* related, Ana,' Jean began. 'I'll grant you that. But we're attributing possession of the shroud to the first one with no proof whatsoever. There's just no basis for it. If the shroud had been authentic, it would have been in the hands of the Temple. Remember that the knights made a vow of poverty and had no possessions. So it would be almost unthinkable that a Templar would have such an object in his hands or bequeath it to his family.

'Your theory is interesting, but it's a real stretch, and you know it,' he continued. 'You have to be rigorous when you write about this. Otherwise, people will take it as just another fanciful story about the shroud, and you know how many of those there are.'

Ana began to protest, but he held up his hand and went on. 'For a book of esotericism it wouldn't be bad. But the truth is, Ana, all you're talking to me about is "hunches" and "intuitions" and "feelings." What you're telling me, well told, could be an interesting story for a magazine, but nothing you've told me is based on real proof – it's all just obscure family connections. I'm sorry, really, but if I found a story like this in a newspaper, I wouldn't believe it. I'd think it was yarn-spinning by one of those people who write about UFOs and see the image of the Virgin Mary in pepperoni pizzas.'

Ana couldn't hide her disappointment, although deep inside she knew Jean was right. Nevertheless, she raised her chin and responded in a tone as serious as his own.

'I'm not going to give up, Jean. If it turns out I don't find solid proof, I won't publish a word – that's the promise I made at the beginning and I'm making again right now. That way I won't disappoint people like you who've helped me. But I'm going to continue to track this story down if it kills me. I haven't told you, but I know a modern-day de Charny right now, a gallant "knight" of sorts if I've ever seen one.'

'Who is he?'

'A very handsome, very interesting, very mysterious man, who just so happens to have visited the old family home in the past few years. I'm going to Paris; it'll be easier for me to get in touch with his family there, if it is his family.'

Jean put his hand over hers on the table. 'I'd go with you if I could, Ana, but I know there's not a chance they'd give me the vacation time right now. But the second best thing is, I have a friend in Paris who might be able to help. He's originally from here, Troyes. We were at the university together. He moved to Paris and got his doctorate in history at the Sorbonne. He's even taught there. But he fell in love with a Scottish reporter, and in less than three years he turned around and got another degree, in journalism, and now they have a magazine: *Enigmas*. It's not my kind of thing – they publish speculative stuff on history, unsolved mysteries, you know. And they have genealogists, historians, scientists who write for them. We haven't seen each other in years, practically since he got married. His wife had some kind of accident and they haven't been back here. But he's a good friend of mine, and he'll talk to you. I'll call him.'

He blushed as Ana leaned across the table to kiss him on the cheek. 'Jean, you've been wonderful. Thank you,' she said. 'After Paris I think I'll head back to Turin, depending on what else I find. I'll call you and keep you posted. You know, you're the only person I've been able to talk to honestly about this, and I'll count on your good common sense to keep a rein on my wild fantasies.'

48

The Templar knight spurred his horse. In the near distance he could make out the Guadiana River and the battlements of Castro Marim. He had ridden without rest from Paris, where he had powerlessly watched as the Grand Master and his brothers were burned at the stake.

In his ears still echoed the deep voice of Jacques de Molay calling down God's judgment on Philippe le Beau and Pope Clement. He had not the slightest doubt that God would have His revenge for the murder of His faithful servants by the king of France and the pope, that He would not let this abominable crime go unpunished.

They had taken Jacques de Molay's life from him but not his dignity, for there had never been a man as brave and upright in the last moments of his life.

He paid what the boatman asked to ferry him across the river, and once on the Portuguese side he rode quickly to the chapter house that had been his home for the last three years, since he had returned from his battles in Egypt and the defense of Cyprus.

Master José Sa Beiro received João de Tomar immediately. He asked him to be seated and offered him cool water to relieve the thirst of the road. The superior then sat with the knight to listen to the news he had brought from Paris.

For two hours de Tomar gave a vivid account of the last days of the Temple and especially of March 19, that black day on which Jacques de Molay and the last Templars were burned at the stake under the harsh gaze of the commoners and court in Paris. Appalled and horrified by the account, the master had to call upon all the dignity of his position in order to not let his emotion spill over.

Philippe le Beau had sentenced the Temple, if not its knights, to death, and for the next weeks all across Europe the pope's command to suppress the order was relentlessly carried out. The knights were to be tried in ecclesiastical courts in every Christian nation. In some kingdoms they would be absolved, while in others the pope's orders would be interpreted to allow the knights to join other religious orders.

José Sa Beiro knew that King Dinis bore no ill will against the Temple and in fact had good intentions toward it, but would the king of Portugal be able to oppose the dictates of the pope? He needed to know, and to find out he would send a knight who might speak to the king on his behalf and so clarify his position.

'I know you are weary, but I must ask you to take on a new mission,' he said to de Tomar. 'You must go to Lisbon and take a letter to the king. You will tell him all you have seen, leaving out no detail. And you shall await his reply. I will prepare the letter now; meanwhile, go and rest. If possible, you will leave tomorrow.'

The sun had not yet risen when João de Tomar was called again into the presence of the superior.

Sa Beiro handed him the letter and clasped his shoulder. 'To Lisbon now, João. May God be with you.'

*　*　*

✝ Lisbon was lovely in the first light of dawn. De Tomar had been traveling for several days, for he had had to stop awhile for his horse's hoof to recover from a bruise from a stone on the road. The noble steed was his most trusted and loyal friend, and it had saved his life in more than one battle. He himself put a plaster on the hoof and waited for two days while it healed. He would not exchange the horse for another for anything in the world, even at the risk of being reprimanded by his superior for delay.

With King Dinis, Portugal had become a prosperous nation. His genius had given the country a university, and he was overseeing a profound reformation of agriculture, so that for the first time there was an abundance of wheat and olive oil, and good wine to export.

The king took no more than two days to receive João de Tomar, and after presenting Dinis with the letter from José Sa Beiro, the Portuguese Templar once more related what he had lived through in Paris.

The king assured the knight that he would reply soon, that he had already had news of the pope's intentions to dissolve the order.

De Tomar knew of the king's good relations with the clergy, with which he had signed an accord a few years earlier. Would he dare stand up to the pope?

It was another three days before the Templar was called once more into the presence of the king. Dinis had made a decision that was wise, even Solomonic. He would not seek a confrontation with the pope, but he would also not persecute the order. Dinis of Portugal had decided that a new order would be formed, the Order of Christ, and that all the Templars would become members, with their same laws and rules, the only exception being that the new order would be under the power of the king, not the pope.

In this way the prudent king ensured that the Templar riches would remain in Portugal, not pass into the hands of the Church or other orders. He would be able to count on the Templars' gratitude, aid, and, above all, gold, to carry out his plans for his kingdom.

The king's decision was firm, and he would so inform the superiors of all the chapter houses. From that time forward, the Temple in Portugal would be under royal jurisdiction.

When Master José Sa Beiro learned of the king's order, he realized that although the Templars would not be persecuted, hunted down, or burned at the stake as they had been in France, from that moment on, their possessions would be at the disposal of the king. Thus, he had to make a decision of his own, for it was possible that Lisbon might ask him for an inventory of the possessions held in each chapter house.

Castro Marim, therefore, was no longer a safe place to keep the Temple's greatest treasure, and José Sa Beiro determined that he must make arrangements to send it to a place where the hands of neither pope nor king could reach it.

49

THE ODOR OF INCENSE FILLED THE CHURCH.

The Mass had ended just moments earlier. A dark-haired priest, tall and powerfully built, walked quickly toward the confessional farthest from the altar, set in an alcove far from curious eyes. The prayer book he carried looked small in his big-boned hands.

No one knew that Addaio was in Milan, not even Guner. He was there unknown to anyone in the community, to put in motion his own plan to shadow Bakkalbasi's operation to end Mendib's life. The meeting had been set for seven; it was only half past six, but he preferred to be early. He had wandered the neighborhood in his clerical disguise for more than two hours, trying to determine whether he was being followed.

The man he was waiting for was an assassin, a professional who worked alone and had never failed – at least so far.

Addaio had learned about him through a man in Urfa, a member of the community who some years earlier had come to the pastor to ask forgiveness of his sins. The man had emigrated to Germany and then to the United States, but things hadn't worked out for him, he said, and he had taken a dark road, becoming wealthy as a drug dealer, flooding the streets of Europe with heroin. He had sinned, sinned terribly, but he had never betrayed the community. He had returned to Urfa, the home of his youth, when he was diagnosed with terminal cancer, seeking expiation and offering to make a large donation to the community in order to help ensure its survival. The wealthy always think they can buy salvation.

He begged to help with the community's sacred mission, but Addaio rejected his aid. An impious man, even though he was a member of the community, could never be a part of that mission, although Addaio's obligation as a pastor was to counsel him in the last days of his life. And in the course of those conversations-cum-confessions, the penitent had given Addaio contact information for a man he said the pastor should call if he ever needed someone to do a piece of difficult work.

Now Addaio sat in the confessional, lost in thought, awaiting the arrival of the killer.

'*Mi benedica, padre, perché ho peccato.*'

The voice startled him. He hadn't noticed that someone had entered the other side of the confessional and knelt as though to pray. After Addaio hurriedly muttered their prearranged greeting, the man continued. 'You need to be more careful. You weren't paying attention.'

'That's not your concern. But you can be sure it won't happen again,' the pastor snapped, then paused. 'I want you to kill a man,' he finally said.

'That's what I do. You bring a file on him?'

'No, there are no files, no photos. You'll have to find him for yourself.'

'That'll cost you more.'

For the next fifteen minutes, Addaio explained what the assassin was to do. When he had finished, the killer left the confessional and disappeared into the shadows of the church.

Addaio made his way to one of the pews before the altar. There, covering his face with his hands, he broke into tears.

Bakkalbasi sat on the edge of the couch awaiting the others. The house in Berlin was safe; the community had never used it.

He had known these men since his childhood. Three of them were originally from Urfa, members of the community who worked in Germany. The other two, also members of the community, had come directly from Urfa via different routes. All of them were ready to give their lives if necessary, as their brothers and other relatives had done in the past.

When they were assembled, Bakkalbasi explained what they were to do. They received their orders grimly, stricken with sorrow as they contemplated the murder of one of their own. But as Bakkalbasi talked on, it was clear that there was no other way to ensure the ongoing security of the community.

Mendib's great-uncle would be given the opportunity for which he had volunteered – the plan was a mortal wound with a knife – but the five men in the group were to make certain that Mendib died. They were to organize a team to follow the young brother from the moment he stepped outside the prison and to find out what they could about those who were almost definitely using him as a way to the community. Above all, they were not to take any risks or expose themselves to arrest.

They would be aided by two members of the community in Turin. Each man was to travel immediately to the city by his own means, preferably by car. The absence of borders in the European Union would allow them to drive from one country to another without leaving any traces. Then they were to go to the Monumental Cemetery and find tomb 117. A small key hidden in a planter next to the mausoleum door would allow them inside the structure. Once inside, they were to find and trip a hidden lever that would open a door to a secret stairway under the sarcophagi; the stairs led to a tunnel, which led, in turn, to the cathedral – to the house in which Francesco Turgut lived. The community had used the tunnel for centuries and had taken measures to ensure that it remained unknown, unmarked on any map. No one would find them.

They would shelter in a chamber in the tunnel until they accomplished their mission. The cemetery was relatively deserted, although a few curious tourists went there from time to time to see the baroque tombs. The guard was a member of the community – he was an old man, the son of an immigrant from Urfa and an Italian woman, and he was a Christian, as they were, and their best ally in this mission.

Turgut and Ismet had prepared the underground room. If they were able, they were to bring Mendib's body back to the tunnel, to be entombed within the wall for all eternity.

50

WHEN ANA ARRIVED IN PARIS, SHE WENT DIRECTLY to the editorial offices of *Enigmas,* which were located on the second floor of a nineteenth-century building.

Paul Bisol was the exact opposite of Jean. Dressed nattily in a well-cut suit and stylish tie, he looked like an executive with a multinational corporation rather than a journalist. Jean had been as good as his word and had phoned him to enlist his help.

Bisol listened patiently to Ana's story. Not once did he interrupt her, which surprised her.

'Do you know what you're getting into?' he asked when she had finished.

'What do you mean?'

'Mademoiselle Jiménez –'

'Please, call me Ana.'

'All right, then, Ana, first you should know that the Templars *do* still exist. But they are not just those elegant historians that you say you met in London, or other pleasant gentlemen in so-called "secret societies" who style themselves the heirs of the spirit of the Temple. Before he died, Jacques de Molay made certain that the order would continue on. Many knights disappeared without a trace; they slipped into what we might call an underground existence. But all were in contact with the new center, the mother chapter, the Scottish Temple, which is where de Molay had decided that the true and legitimate center of the order would reside. The Templars learned to live out of sight, clandestinely; they infiltrated the courts of Europe, even the papal curia, and they have continued to live that way right down until today. They never "died out." '

Ana was shocked to feel a wave of mistrust and distaste. This man sounded more like one of the illuminati than a historian or serious journalist. She had been chasing around Europe in pursuit of her crazy theories, and she had become inured to the disdain of the 'experts' who urged her not to let herself be carried away by fantasy. Now she found herself with someone who agreed with her, and she didn't like it.

Bisol picked up the telephone and spoke to his secretary, then asked Ana to follow him. He led her to a nearby office, where a woman with dark brown hair and immense green eyes was sitting behind a computer, typing. She smiled as they entered, and Paul introduced her as his wife, Elisabeth.

'Sit down,' she invited Ana. 'So you're a friend of Jean's?'

'Well, actually we met just recently, but we hit it off, I guess, and he's been a huge help to me.'

'That's Jean,' Paul said. 'He's like one of the three musketeers – all for one and one for all – though he's not aware of it, I think. But he's a great judge of character. Now, Ana, I want you to tell Elisabeth everything you've told me.'

The situation began to make Ana nervous. Paul Bisol seemed to be a nice enough person, but there was something about him she didn't like; Elisabeth, too, gave Ana an uneasy feeling, though she couldn't put her finger on why. She just knew she felt like getting out of there as fast as she could. Her years as a reporter had given her a finely honed sense of the dubious and dangerous, and she felt herself sailing into uncharted waters with these two. But she shook off the feeling, at least for the moment, and launched again into her suspicions about the Holy Shroud.

Elisabeth, too, listened without interruption, as her husband had done. When Ana finished, the couple looked at each other, obviously weighing wordlessly how to proceed. Finally Elisabeth broke the tense silence.

'Well, Ana, in my opinion, you're on the right track. We've never made this particular connection, but if you say that you've found links between the Templar de Charney and the shroud family in the Lirey archives, well, then . . . it seems clear that the two Geoffroys were somehow related. So the shroud really did belong to the Templars. I'm not surprised; that fits with indications we've found, too, coming at it from other directions. Why was it in the hands of Geoffroy de Charney? Off the top of my head I'd say that since Philippe le Beau wanted to grab the Temple treasure for himself, the Grand Master may have decided to send it to a safe place. It's so logical – Jacques de Molay ordered Geoffroy de Charney to carry the shroud away to his own lands and secure it there, and years later it turned up in the hands of a relative, the other Geoffroy. There's always been talk of a mysterious treasure associated with the Temple, and the shroud must have been that treasure – after all, they all took it to be authentic.'

'But it isn't,' Ana replied, playing the devil's advocate. 'And they would have known it wasn't. The Holy Shroud dates to the thirteenth or fourteenth century, so. . . .'

'Yes, you're right, but it may have been represented to the Templars as authentic in the Holy Land. Back then it was hard to determine whether a relic was authentic or a fake. What seems clear is that they *believed* it to be real when they sent it off to be safeguarded. You're right about this, Ana, I'm sure of it. But you have to be careful; you don't get near the Templars without risk. We have a good genealogist, one of the best, and he'll help you find out if there are other leads out there. As for your current friend in the family, give me an hour or two and I should be able to tell you a bit more about him.'

As Ana left Elisabeth's office with Paul, she told him she'd be back that afternoon to meet with the genealogist. She'd see then what Elisabeth had found on the man she was sure had visited his family estates in Lirey not so very long ago – Padre Yves de Charny, the secretary to the cardinal of Turin.

She wandered around Paris aimlessly, turning over in her mind everything she knew and had guessed. Around noon she sat in the window alcove of a bistro and had lunch, reading the Spanish newspapers she'd found at a kiosk on the street. It had been days since she'd had any news of what was happening in Spain or Italy. She hadn't even called her newspaper, or Santiago, although she sensed that the Art Crimes investigation must be coming to its end. She was convinced that the Templars had had something to do with the shroud, that as popular suspicions through the centuries suggested, it had been they who had brought it back from Constantinople. She remembered the night in the Dorchester in London, when it had hit her as she looked through her appointment book that the handsome French priest in Turin, the cardinal's secretary, was named de Charny. Until now she'd had no solid lead, just that it appeared that Padre Yves had visited Lirey several years ago – if there was one thing she was sure of, it was that it had been he. There just weren't that many priests so strikingly handsome that everyone who mentioned them said how good-looking they were.

It was possible that Padre Yves was related to the Templars, but was it a relation to the distant past, to long-dead knights, or to something happening now? To people – *Templars* – living now?

But that would mean nothing, she told herself. She could just picture the handsome priest with his innocent smile telling her that, yes, his ancestors fought in the Crusades, and that indeed his family came from the region of Troyes. And what of it? What could that possibly prove? Nothing, it proved *nothing*. She certainly couldn't picture him lighting fires in the cathedral. But her instinct told her that there was a thread that led somewhere – a thread leading from Geoffroy de Charney to Geoffroy de Charny that then wound in twists and circles for generations until it came to Padre Yves.

She hardly ate. She phoned Jean and felt better the minute she heard his voice reassuring her that, even if Paul Bisol was a little strange, he was a good man, and she could trust him.

At three she went back to the *Enigmas* offices. When she arrived, Paul was waiting for her in Elisabeth's office.

'Well, we did turn up something,' Elisabeth said. 'This priest of yours belongs to a very well-connected family. His older brother was a representative to the French National

Assembly and is now in the cabinet, and his sister is a justice of the Supreme Court. They come from the lesser ranks of the nobility, although since the French Revolution the de Charnys, no *e*, live like perfect bourgeois. Yves has protectors high up in the Vatican – Cardinal Visier – in charge of church finances, no less – is a friend of his older brother. But the bombshell is that Edouard, our genealogist, who's been working for three hours on the family tree, is almost certain that this Yves de Charny is indeed a descendant of the de Charneys, with an *e*, who fought in the Crusades and, even more important, is a very close descendant of the Geoffroy de Charney who was precept of the Temple in Normandy and died at the stake alongside Jacques de Molay.'

'Are you sure?' Ana asked, uncertain whether to believe her or not.

'Absolutely,' replied Elisabeth without the slightest hesitation.

Paul Bisol saw the doubt reflected in Ana's eyes.

'Ana, Edouard is a historian, a professor at the university. I know Jean is a little doubtful about our magazine, but I assure you, we've never published anything we can't prove. This is a magazine that investigates enigmas of history and tries to find answers. The answers are always developed and provided by historians, sometimes aided by an investigative team made up of reporters. We have never had to print a retraction or a correction. And we never print anything we aren't absolutely sure of. If somebody has a hypothesis, we print it as a hypothesis, never as a fact.

'You maintain that some of the mishaps in the cathedral of Turin have something to do with events in the past. I don't know – we've never looked into it. You think that the Templars were the owners of the shroud, and there you may be right, just as you're apparently right that this Padre Yves comes from a very ancient family of aristocrats and Templars. You wonder whether the Templars have any relation to the accidents in the cathedral. I can't answer that question – I don't know, but I very much doubt it. I honestly don't think that the Templars have any interest in damaging the shroud, and one thing I can assure you is that if they wanted it for themselves, they'd already have it. They are a very powerful organization, more powerful than you can imagine – right, Elisabeth?'

Paul looked at Elisabeth, who nodded. Ana froze when the chair Elisabeth was sitting in moved from behind her desk and began to advance. She hadn't noticed – it looked like an office chair, but it had been fitted out to serve as a wheelchair as well.

Elisabeth stopped in front of Ana and pulled aside the shawl over her obviously useless legs.

'Ana, I don't think we – or you – have a lot of time. I'm going to give you our part of the story whole, right now. I'm Scottish – I don't know whether Jean told you. My father is Lord McKenny, and he knew Lord McCall. You've probably never heard of him. He's one of the richest men in the world, but you'll never see him in the newspapers or on TV. He lives in a world that allows entry only to the fantastically rich and powerful. Although he spends most of his time in London, he has a castle, an ancient Templar fortress, located on the west coast of Scotland, near the Small Isles. But no one from the general public is ever invited there, and it's staffed by tight-lipped professionals from other places. We Scots are given to legends, and there are quite a few about Lord McCall. Some of the villagers who live near the castle call it Castle Templar, and they say that from time to time men arrive in helicopters to visit, among them members of the English royal family and other noble and well-connected families from around the world.

'One day I was telling Paul about Lord McCall, and it occurred to us that we ought to do a story on the Templar estates and fortresses all across Europe. A kind of inventory, you know: find out which ones are still standing, who owns them, which ones have been destroyed over the course of the centuries. We thought it would be great if Lord McCall would let us visit his castle. We started working and at first we didn't have many problems. There are literally hundreds of Templar fortresses, most of them in ruins. I asked my father to talk to McCall to see if he'd let me visit his castle and photograph it. But my father got nowhere – McCall was always very polite, but he always had some excuse. I was determined not to take no for an answer, so I decided to try to persuade him myself. I called him, but he wouldn't even come to the phone – a very polite secretary informed me that Lord McCall was away, in the United States, so he couldn't receive me, and of course the secretary had no authority to allow me to photograph the fortress. I insisted that he let me at least come to the castle, but the secretary wouldn't budge – without Lord McCall's permission, no one would set foot on the estate.

'But I still wasn't giving up, so I went to the castle, anyway. I was sure that once I was actually there, they'd have to let me at least look around. I don't usually trade on my own family connections, but in this case I thought, stupidly, that they'd provide entrée.

'Before I got to the castle I talked to some of the villagers. All of them have enormous respect for Lord McCall, and they say he's a kind and generous man who makes sure their needs are all seen to. You might say that they more than respect him – they worship him. None of them would ever move a finger to harm him or compromise him in any way. One of them told me that his son was alive thanks to McCall, who had paid all the expenses for open-heart surgery in Houston.

'When I came to the iron gate at the entrance to the estate, I couldn't find any way to get in, and no one responded to the bell. I started walking along the wall, just to see what I might find. Finally I came to a place where the stone had crumbled a bit, just enough to suggest a tenuous handhold or two. You should know that my favorite pastime was rock climbing. I started climbing at ten, and I've climbed a lot of pretty good cliffs. So climbing over that wall didn't look particularly hard to me, despite the fact that I didn't have a rope or anything. Well, I couldn't resist.

'Don't ask me how I did it, but I managed to climb up on the wall and jump inside, onto the grounds of the estate. Off in the distance, in the middle of the woods, I saw an ivy-covered stone chapel and started toward it. I heard a sound, then felt a terrible pain and fell. I don't remember much else. I was crying and writhing in pain. A man was standing there with a rifle, aiming it at me. He called somebody on a walkie-talkie, a four-by-four drove up, they put me in it and drove me to the hospital.

'I was paralyzed. They didn't shoot to kill, but they did aim carefully enough to leave me like this.

'Naturally, everyone said the guards on the estate had been doing their duty. I was a trespasser who'd jumped the wall. And believe me, none of the authorities was interested in pursuing it further.'

Ana had listened to Elisabeth's story in silence. Now,

looking at the vibrant young woman, her heart swelled in sympathy and outrage.

'I'm sorry,' she said. Anything else seemed superfluous.

'Yeah, me too. But the point is, it seems pretty certain that the kindly Lord McCall is anything but. I asked my father to give me a detailed list of everyone he knew of who had any relationship with McCall. He didn't want to do it, but he finally gave in. He hasn't been the same since my accident. He never wanted me to be a reporter, much less devote my career to these things on the fringes. So we kept digging, Paul and I, with more reluctant help from my father, and we did manage to put together a basic picture.

'Lord McCall is a strange person. Never married, a connoisseur of religious art, incredibly wealthy. Every hundred days a group of men arrive at the castle by car or helicopter and stay for three or four days. None of the locals knows who they are, but the sense of the villagers is that they're as important as McCall himself. We've managed to identify some of them, though, and have followed the trail of their businesses, and I can tell you that there is no significant financial event in the world that can't be traced in one way or another to him and his friends.'

'What does that mean?'

'It means they're a group of men who pull the strings, whose financial power is almost as big as governments', which means they influence governments around the world.'

'And what does that have to do with the Templars?'

'Ana, for years now, I've been studying everything written on the order. I have a lot of time, and I've come to some conclusions. In addition to all the organizations that claim to be the heirs of the Temple, there is another, secret organization, made up of men who stay in the shadows, all very important, and who inhabit the very heart of the heart of society. I don't know how many there are or who they all are – or at least I'm not sure that all the ones I suspect of belonging to this group actually do. But I think that the true Templars, the heirs of Jacques de Molay, are *there* and that McCall is one of them. I've learned a lot about his Scottish estate, and it's interesting. Down through the centuries it has passed from hand to hand, always to men who are single – solitary, even – and rich and well connected, and every one of them obsessed with keeping out strangers. I think there's a Templar army, if you will, a silent, well-structured army whose members hold high positions in virtually every country.'

'You seem to be talking about a Masonic organization.'

'No, what I'm referring to is the authentic, core organization, the one nothing is known about, not even that it exists at all. With the list my father gave me and the help of an excellent investigative reporter, I've managed to make a partial organizational chart of this new Temple. But it hasn't been easy, I'll tell you. Michael, the reporter, is dead – a year ago he had a fatal car accident. I suspect they killed him. Nasty things seem to happen to those who get too close. I know – I've followed what has happened to curious people like us.'

'A pretty paranoid vision of things, this worldwide conspiracy, murders, cover-ups.'

'Yes, but still, I think there are two worlds: the one we see, in which the vast majority of us live, and then another, underground world that we know nothing about. That's the place from which these various organizations – financial, Masonic, whatever – pull the strings. And that's where this new Temple can be found, in that underground world.'

'Granting that you're right, which I'm not so sure of, it doesn't explain what relationship the Templars of today have to the shroud.'

'I don't know. I'm sorry. I've told you all this because your Padre Yves could be. . . .'

'Say it.'

'He could be one of them.'

'A Templar in this secret society that you think – *think,* mind you – exists?'

'You think I'm seeing things, that this accident, this wheelchair, has made me paranoid, but I'm a reporter just like you are, Ana, and I can still tell reality from fiction. I've told you what I think. Now you can act as you see fit. If the shroud belonged to the Templars, and Padre Yves comes from the family of Geoffroy de Charney –'

'Even then,' Ana interrupted her. 'Even given all that, the shroud is not the cloth that Christ was buried in. We know it dates from de Charney's time, basically, and I think the Templars would have had to know it was a recent creation, or at least that its provenance was dubious – and I just don't see them staking everything on another half-baked relic, as they seem to have done. . . .'

Listening to Elisabeth, Ana realized how ridiculous she herself must have looked, taking the time of serious scholars to expound on her own theories.

At that moment she didn't like herself much. She felt like a fool that she'd lost her head over a far-fetched story, trying to out-investigate the pros in the Art Crimes Department. It was over, she told herself; she was going back to Barcelona on the next plane. She'd call Santiago. She knew he'd be delighted when she told him she was moving on, that she'd had enough of the shroud to last a lifetime.

Elisabeth and Paul left her to her thoughts. They could see the skepticism – incredulity, really – reflected in her face. They had spoken to only a handful of people about their investigations into the new Temple, because they feared for their lives and the life of anyone who helped them. But this reporter had gotten herself in pretty deep, and they thought she had a right to know what she was up against.

'Elisabeth, are you going to give it to her?'

Paul's words brought Ana out of her reverie.

'Give me what?' asked Ana.

'This file, Ana. It's a summary of my work over the last five years. Michael's and my work, rather. It lists the names and biographies of the men we think are the new masters of the Temple. In my opinion, Lord McCall is the Grand Master. But read it and see what you think. And however ridiculous we seem to you, be careful, for your sake and ours. Only a few people know about this. We're trusting you because we think you're on the verge of an important discovery – we aren't sure exactly what it is, or what direction it'll take you, but you seem to be zeroing in on something, something big, that we've been missing. There are notes and historical details in the file you may want to think about, too, which may be relevant to your shroud, things we've discovered about the fall of the order, where they fled, speculations about what happened to their records and their riches, how they reconstituted themselves. . . .

'If these papers fall into the wrong hands, we'll all die – don't doubt that. So I ask that you confide in no one, absolutely no one. They have ears everywhere – in the judiciary, in the police, in parliaments, in the stock markets – everywhere. I'm sure you're already on their radar. They know you've been with us; what they don't know is what we've told you. We've invested a great deal in security, and we have electronic scanners to find bugs. Even so, it's possible that we haven't found them all.'

'Elisabeth, I'm sorry. This is too far into John le Carré territory, even for me.'

'Think whatever you want, Ana, but you've put yourself into this. Will you do what we ask?'

'Look – you've taken me into your confidence, and I'm grateful. Your secrets are safe with me. Not a word to anyone, I promise. Shall I return this file when I've finished reading it?'

'Destroy it. It's just a summary, but I promise – you'll find it useful, very useful, especially if you decide to go on.'

'What makes you think I'm turning back?'

Elisabeth took a deep breath before replying, then smiled ever so slightly.

'That's what you should do, Ana, believe me. Stop now. But somehow I don't think you will.'

51

IT WAS SEVEN O'CLOCK, AND THE CORE
members of the Art Crimes Department looked like they'd
just gotten out of bed after a sleepless night. Now they
were waiting for their breakfast orders to be brought in.
The hotel dining room had just opened and they'd been
the first guests to enter.

At nine the mute was to be released from the Turin jail.

Marco had planned for the operation to tail him
meticulously. They would be backed up by a group of
carabinieri and by Interpol.

Sofia was nervous, and she thought Minerva looked
uneasy too. Even Antonino showed the tension in the way
he tightened his lips. Marco, Pietro, and Giuseppe;
however, seemed fine – loose and easy. All three were cops,
and for them a tail was routine. They had reviewed their
respective roles and responsibilities until they could
practically recite them in their sleep. There was nothing to
do now but wait.

To fill the time, Sofia began to update Marco and the
team about some of the more intriguing leads – or hints,
really – that she'd come across on her most recent forays

into the shadowy history of the shroud, paging through biblical Apocrypha and books on Edessa and its role as an ancient center of trade. The more she delved into the connection they'd unearthed to Urfa, Edessa's modern incarnation, the more convinced she became that there was indeed a thread stretching from there through the centuries – cryptic allusions to inquiries emanating from powerful forces within the city seeking the whereabouts of a mysterious lost treasure. The probes seemed to reach into every kingdom on the continent and beyond, even as far as England, Scotland, and Ireland. She was certain that the treasure was Edessa's stolen shroud – and that perhaps the effort to recover it hadn't stopped when the historical accounts broke off.

'Jesus, I never heard anything so stupid!' Pietro interrupted her. 'It's too early in the morning for this bullshit, Sofia.'

'This is not bullshit! I mean, it's speculation, I know that, and it's a little "out there," and I'm not saying that it's true, but you can't call everything that doesn't agree with what you think "bullshit."'

'Cool it!' Marco barked. 'Sofia, I don't know . . . it seems a bit fantastic that this could have been going on all these years. But with a little luck, and close attention to the job at hand,' he looked pointedly around the table at them all, 'we'll have some hard answers soon. Now let's run through everything one more time.'

Far from Turin, the animated atmosphere within the opulent penthouse of one of the world's most powerful shipping magnates was in stark contrast to the storm outside now lashing New York City. Guests milled about, chatting happily, laughing, and although it was after midnight, the party seemed to be just beginning. The group of men ensconced comfortably in a discreet corner with champagne and Havana cigars seemed to perfectly reflect the festive mood of the night.

Their conversation, however, belied their relaxed postures.

'Mendib will be leaving the prison about now,' the oldest murmured discreetly to the others. 'Everything is ready.'

'I'm concerned about this situation. Bakkalbasi has seven men in all, Addaio has hired a professional killer, and Marco Valoni has put a whole team of men and equipment in place. Won't we be terribly exposed? Wouldn't it be better to let them resolve this themselves?' the Frenchman asked.

'We have been briefed on all the details of both operations – we can monitor them with little danger of exposure of our people. As for Addaio's man, there is no problem there. He can be easily controlled,' replied the older man.

'Even so, I, too, am inclined to believe that there are too many people in this,' said a gentleman with an indeterminate accent.

'Mendib is a problem for Addaio and for us because Valoni will not let go of this as long as he has a lead,' the older man insisted. 'But I am much more concerned about the reporter, the sister of the Europol representative, and that Dottoressa Galloni. The conclusions those two are reaching bring them perilously close to us. Ana Jiménez has met with Lady Elisabeth McKenny, who gave her a file, or the summary of a file, on the Templars. You know the one. I'm sorry, very sorry, to come to this point, but Lady Elisabeth, Ms. Jiménez, and Dottoressa Galloni are becoming a problem. A threat to our existence, in fact.'

A heavy silence fell over the others, who exchanged surreptitious glances.

'What do you propose to do?' The Italian's tone carried a touch of defiance as he asked the direct question.

'What has to be done. I'm sorry.'

'We mustn't rush into this.'

'And we haven't, which is why they're much further along in their speculations than is comfortable for us. We must act before it is too late. I want your advice, but I also want your consent.'

'Can we not wait awhile longer?' asked the ex-military man.

'No, we can't, not without endangering everything. It would be madness to go on taking risks. I'm sorry, sincerely sorry. The decision is as repugnant to me as it is to you, but I can find no other solution. If you think there is one, tell me.'

The other six men were silent. They all knew deep down that he was right. The enormous amount of money Paul Bisol had spent on security had been for nothing. For years they had intercepted the couple's mail. They had inserted spyware on their computers, a keystroke logger program, and they had tapped *Enigmas'* telephones; they had installed sophisticated bugs in the editorial offices and in their home.

They knew everything about them – as for months they had been learning everything about Sofia Galloni and Ana Jiménez, from the perfume they wore to what they read at night, who they spoke to, their love life . . . everything, absolutely everything.

The other members of the Art Crimes Department had all been under relentless surveillance as well – all their telephone calls, both landline and cellular, had been intercepted, and each of them had been followed around the clock.

'So?' the older man insisted.

'I hesitate to –'

'I understand,' the older man interrupted the Italian, 'I understand. Say no more. You need not take part in the decision.'

'Do you think that lightens my conscience?'

'No, I know it doesn't. But it can help. I think you need that help, spiritual help. We have all passed through moments like this in our lives. It has not been easy, but we have not chosen the easy road – we have chosen the impossible. It is in circumstances such as these that the nobility of our mission becomes the measure of ourselves.'

'After dedicating my entire life . . . do you think that I still have to prove that I am worthy of our mission?'

'Of course not. You need not prove anything,' his master replied. 'But you are suffering. We can all see that. You must look within yourself, and to God, for the strength you have always had. For now, please, trust in our judgment and let us act as we must.'

'No, I cannot agree to that.'

'I can suspend you temporarily, until you are yourself again.'

'You can do that. What else will you do?'

As other guests began to glance toward them, the military man interrupted. 'That's enough. They're looking at us. Let's leave this for another moment.'

'There is no time,' the older man replied. 'I must ask for your consent now.'

'So be it,' said all the men but one, who, lips tight with anger and frustration, turned on his heel and strode away.

*   *   *

Sofia and Minerva were at carabinieri headquarters in Turin. It was two minutes till nine, and through the microphone hidden under the lapel of his jacket, Marco had notified them that the gates of the prison were opening. He watched the mute come out, walking slowly, looking straight ahead, even as the gate closed behind him. His calm was surprising, Marco thought. There was no emotion, no sign that he welcomed freedom after years of confinement.

Mendib told himself that he was being watched. He didn't see them, but he knew they were there, watching. He was going to have to throw them off his trail, lose them, but how? He would try to follow the plan he had made in prison. He would go to the center of the city, wander about, sleep on a bench in some park. He didn't have much money; he could pay for a room in a *pensione* for three or four days at the most and eat only panini. He would also get rid of these clothes and shoes; although he had gone over them carefully and found nothing, he was instinctively uncomfortable about them since they had been in the possession of the guards for laundering.

He knew Turin. Addaio had sent him and his brothers here a year before their attempt to steal the shroud, precisely so that they could become familiar with the city. He had followed the pastor's instructions: walk and walk and walk, all over the city. It was the best way to come to know it. He'd also learned the bus routes.

He was approaching the center of Turin, walking through the Crocetta district. The moment of truth had come – the moment to escape the people who were surely following him.

*   *   *

446

'I think we've got company.'

Marco's voice came over the transmitter in their operations center.

'Who are they?' asked Minerva.

'No idea – but they look like Turks.'

'Turks or Italians,' they heard Giuseppe say. 'Black hair, olive skin.'

'How many are there?' Sofia asked.

'Two, for the moment,' Marco said, 'but there may be more. They're young. The mute seems oblivious. He's wandering around, looking at the windows – as out to lunch as usual.'

They heard Marco give the carabinieri instructions not to lose sight of the two unknown tails.

Neither Marco nor the other police officers focused on a limping old man who was selling lottery tickets. Neither tall nor short, neither heavyset nor thin, dressed anonymously and impersonally, the old man was just part of the landscape of the neighborhood.

But the old man had seen *them*. The killer hired by Addaio missed nothing, and so far he had identified half a dozen cops, plus four of the men sent by Bakkalbasi.

He was irritated – the man who'd hired him hadn't told him that the cops would be swarming all over the place or that there were other killers like him after his target. He'd have to take his time, develop a new plan.

Another man made him suspicious, too, at first, but he'd shaken it off after a while. No, that one was no cop, and he didn't look Turkish either – he didn't have anything to do with this, although the way he moved. . . . Then he was gone, and the killer breathed easy. The guy was nothing.

*   *   *

All day, Mendib wandered through the city. He had rejected the idea of sleeping on a bench; it would be a mistake. If someone wanted to kill him, he would be making it too easy if he slept out in the open in a park. So at dusk he made his way to a homeless shelter that he'd seen that morning, run by the Sisters of Charity. He would be safer there.

Once they established that the mute had eaten and settled himself on a thin mattress near the dormitory entrance, where one of the nuns sat to prevent fights among the inmates, Marco felt confident their subject wouldn't be moving again that night. He decided to go to the hotel and get a little sleep, and he ordered his team to do the same thing, except for Pietro, whom he left in charge with a relief team of three fresh carabinieri – enough to follow the mute if he emerged again unexpectedly.

Ana Jiménez was waiting in the Paris airport for a night flight to Rome. From there she'd continue on to Turin. She was nervous and disturbed by what she'd been reading in Elisabeth's file. If just a fraction of what was in it was true, it would be terrible. There were dimensions to this story she'd never imagined when she began, things that seemed to relate to the shroud – or some great secret – yet had nothing to do with France or Turin. But the reason she'd decided to go back to Turin anyway was that she'd seen one of the names that appeared in the file in another report – the one that Marco Valoni had given her brother to read. And if what Elisabeth said was true, that name belonged to one of the masters of the new Temple and related directly to the shroud.

She had made two decisions: one, to talk to Sofia, and

two, to go to the cathedral and surprise Padre Yves. She'd spent most of the morning and part of the afternoon trying to contact Sofia, but the desk at the Alexandra had informed her that she'd left very early, and Ana had yet to get any reply from the several voice-mail messages she'd left for her. There seemed to be no way to get in touch with the dottoressa at this moment. As for Padre Yves, she'd see him the next day, one way or the other.

Elisabeth was right – she was getting close to something, although to what she wasn't sure.

Bakkalbasi's men had managed to lose the carabinieri. One of them stayed outside the Sisters of Charity shelter, watching to be sure Mendib didn't leave; the others dispersed. By the time they reached the cemetery, it was nightfall and the guard was waiting for them nervously.

'Hurry, hurry, I have to leave,' he hissed as he motioned them inside. 'I will give you a key to the gate, in case you come too late one night and I have had to go.'

The entrance of the mausoleum he led them to was protected by an angel with a sword raised high in one hand. The four men went inside, lighting their way with a flashlight, and disappeared into the bowels of the earth.

Ismet was waiting for them in the underground room. He had brought water for them to wash with, and food. They were hungry and tired, and all they wanted was to sleep.

'Where is Mehmet?'

'He stayed where Mendib is sleeping, in case he decides to leave the shelter tonight. Addaio is right – they want Mendib to lead them to us. They have a big team shadowing him,' said one of the men, who in Urfa was a police officer, as was one of his companions.

449

'Did they see you?' asked Ismet, worried.

'I don't think so,' another of the men answered, 'but we can't be sure – there are a lot of them.'

'You mustn't lead them here. Do you understand? If you think you are being followed, you can't come back here,' Ismet insisted.

'We know, we know,' the police officer reassured him. 'Don't worry. No one followed us.'

By six o'clock Marco was positioned near the Sisters of Charity shelter again. He had called in reinforcements for the carabinieri team, who had lost the two Turkish tails the night before.

'If – when – they show up again, be sure they don't see you,' he snapped. 'I want them alive and squawking when this is over. If they're following the mute, we're going to want them. Meanwhile we need to give them a little more slack.'

His men had nodded. Pietro insisted he was going to keep working, despite the fact that he hadn't slept the night before.

Sofia had heard the rising anxiety in Ana's voice in the voice-mail messages she'd left. At the hotel they'd told her that Ana had also called there five times. She felt a twinge of remorse for not having returned the calls, but this was no time to be distracting herself with the reporter's wild theories. She'd call when they closed the case; until then she was going to concentrate all her energies on following Marco's orders. She and Minerva were about to leave for carabinieri headquarters when a bellman came running toward them.

'Dottoressa Galloni, dottoressa!'

'Yes, what's wrong?'

'You have a telephone call; they say it's urgent.'

'I can't take it now; tell the front desk to take a message and –'

'Front desk told me that Signor D'Alaqua says it's very important.'

'D'Alaqua?'

'Yes. That's who's calling.'

Sofia waved Minerva on, turned, and headed directly to one of the house phones.

'This is Dottoressa Galloni; I think I have a call.'

'Oh, dottoressa, thank goodness! Signor D'Alaqua was very insistent that we find you. One moment, please.'

Umberto D'Alaqua's distinctive voice had a different quality, tense, controlled. 'Sofia. . . .'

'Yes, how are you?'

'I need to see you.'

'I'd love to, but –'

'No buts. My car will be there in ten minutes.'

'I'm sorry – I'm on my way to work. I can't today. Is something wrong?'

'I have a proposal for you. You know that my great passion is archaeology – well, I'm off to Syria. I have permission for a dig there, and my people have found some pieces that I'd like you to look at. I have to leave immediately, but on the way I'd like to talk to you. I'd like to make you a job offer.'

'I appreciate that, really, but right now I can't possibly go. I'm sorry,' she replied, astonished by the entire exchange.

'Sofia, sometimes there are once-in-a-lifetime opportunities.'

'That's true. But there are also responsibilities that one can't abandon. And right now I just can't leave what I'm doing. If you can wait two or three days, then maybe –'

'No, it can't wait three days.'

'Is it so important that you leave for Syria *today*?'

'Yes.'

'Well, I'm sorry. I really am. I might be able to go in a few days. . . .'

'No, I don't think so. I beg you to come with me now.'

Sofia hesitated. Umberto D'Alaqua's proposal was as disconcerting as his peremptory tone.

'What's happening? Tell me.'

'I'm telling you.'

'I'm sorry, truly. Listen, I've got to go, they're waiting for me.'

'Good luck, then, dottoressa,' he said, the life evaporating from his voice. 'Take care of yourself.'

'Yes, of course, thank you.' She heard the line click and placed the phone back in its cradle.

Why was he wishing her good luck? He'd sounded utterly defeated. Good luck with what? Could he possibly know about the operation they were in the midst of?

When she finished the case she'd call him. She was sure that there was something else behind his extraordinary offer and that it was not a love affair he had in mind.

'What did D'Alaqua want?' Minerva had waited for her, and they walked out of the hotel together.

'For me to go with him to Syria.'

'Syria! What for?'

'He's got a permit to do an archaeological excavation there. He wanted me to help him.'

'Some romantic getaway.'

'He was asking me to go away, but it wasn't romantic. He sounded worried.'

*   *   *

By the time they reached carabinieri headquarters, Marco had called twice. He was in a foul mood. The transmitter they'd planted on the mute wasn't working. It was sending out beeps, but the beeps didn't match the direction in which he was walking. They soon realized that their man had changed shoes. The ones he was wearing now were older, more worn-looking. He'd also put on a pair of filthy jeans and an equally filthy jacket. Somebody had made a great deal on the trade.

At the moment they were watching their target walk aimlessly around the Parco Carrara. The two tails from the day before were nowhere to be seen, at least so far.

The mute was carrying a hunk of bread, and as he walked he pinched pieces off it and scattered crumbs for the birds. He crossed paths with a man walking hand-in-hand with two little girls, and Marco thought the man stared into the mute's eyes for a few seconds before he moved on.

The killer came to the same conclusion. That must be the guy's contact. He still couldn't make his move – there was no way; the guy was surrounded by cops. Shooting him would be tantamount to committing suicide. He'd follow him for two more days, and if things didn't change, he'd forget about the contract – he wasn't going to risk his own neck just to kill some miserable tongueless Turk.

Neither Marco nor his men, nor the Turkish tail, nor even, this time, the killer, noticed that they themselves were being watched. After he took his girls home, Arslan, the long-time community contact, called his cousin. Yes, he had seen Mendib; they'd crossed paths in the Parco Carrara. He looked fine. But he hadn't made any sign – nothing. Apparently he didn't feel secure yet – and with good reason.

*　　*　　*

Ana Jiménez asked the taxi driver to take her to the Turin Cathedral. She entered through the door to the cathedral offices and asked to see Padre Yves.

'He is not in, I'm afraid,' said the secretary. 'He is with the cardinal, on a pastoral visit. You do not have an appointment, I think; is that correct?'

'No, you're right, but I know that Padre Yves would be delighted to see me,' Ana said curtly, knowing she was being rude, annoyed by the secretary's smugness.

She'd been doubly unlucky. She'd called Sofia again and missed her. She decided to linger in the neighborhood around the cathedral and wait until Yves de Charny returned.

Listening to the report, Bakkalbasi was in a quandary. Mendib was still wandering around the city – it looked as though it would be very, very difficult, if not impossible, to kill him. There were carabinieri everywhere. If Bakkalbasi's men continued the pursuit, they were going to wind up being spotted themselves.

He didn't know what to tell his team. If the operation failed, Mendib might bring on the fall of the community. Sooner or later he would head to the cemetery, or home. Mendib's great-uncle was waiting. Several days ago he had prepared himself, as so many in the community had done through the centuries. He had had all his teeth pulled, his tongue cut out, and his fingerprints burned off. A doctor had anesthetized him so he would not suffer unduly. Now it was past time to send him in. . . .

Mendib thought he had seen a familiar face, the face of a man from Urfa – was he there to help him or kill him? He knew Addaio, and he knew that he would never allow the community to be discovered. Mendib was aware that if he was careless he could lead unbelievers to the community – and that Addaio would prevent that at all costs. As soon as it got dark, he would go back to the shelter and if possible sneak from there to the cemetery. He would jump the wall and find the tomb. He remembered it perfectly well – and remembered where the key was hidden. He would go through the tunnel to the house of Turgut and ask Turgut to save him. If he could get to Turgut's house without being discovered, Addaio could organize an escape. He did not mind waiting two or three months underground, until the carabinieri tired of looking for him. He had waited for years in a cell.

He walked toward Porta Palazzo, the open-air market, to buy something to eat and try to lose himself among the stalls. The people following him would have a hard time camouflaging themselves in the narrow corridors of the market, and if he could manage to see their faces, it would be easier for him to lose them later.

They had come for him. The old man took the knife from Bakkalbasi without hesitation. His nephew's son had to be killed, and he preferred to do it himself rather than allowing other men to profane themselves.

In the car, Bakkalbasi's cell phone chimed; Mendib was moving toward the Piazza della Republica, probably to Porta Palazzo, the marketplace. Bakkalbasi ordered the driver to head in that direction and stop near the place Mendib had been seen. As they pulled up, he embraced the old man and said good-bye. He prayed that he might complete his mission.

Within minutes, Mendib saw his father's uncle and felt his heart fill with relief. The community, his family, had not forsaken him. He began to make his way carefully toward the old man. Then he saw his great-uncle's anguished expression. It was the look of a desperate man.

Their eyes met. Mendib did not know what to do – flee or approach the old man casually to give him an opportunity to pass a note or whisper instructions.

He decided to trust his great-uncle. The desperation in his eyes no doubt reflected fear, nothing else. Fear of Addaio, fear of the carabinieri.

As their bodies brushed against each other, Mendib felt a deep pain in his side. Then the old man fell to his knees and crumpled facedown on the ground. A knife protruded from his back. People around him began to scream and push away, and Mendib did the same – panicked, he ran. Someone had murdered his father's uncle, but who?

The killer ran along with the crowd, acting as terrified as the rest. He'd stabbed an old man instead of the mute. An old man who was carrying a knife too. That did it; he was not going to make another attempt. The man who'd hired him hadn't told him the whole story by a long shot, and he couldn't work in the dark, not knowing what he'd be facing. The contract was over, and he was keeping the upfront money.

On the edge of the market, Bakkalbasi watched Mendib run away as the old man lay dying on the pavement. Who had killed him? It had not been the carabinieri. Might it have been *them*? But why kill the old man? Distraught, he called Addaio. He didn't know what to do. Everything was coming apart. The pastor listened and gave a brief order. Bakkalbasi nodded, calming himself.

★　　★　　★

With his men right behind him, Marco ran over to the old man lying on the pavement. They were all burned, for anyone who was looking.

'Is he dead?' Pietro asked.

The old man's pulse was fading. He opened his eyes, looked up at Marco as though he wanted to say something, and died.

Sofia and Minerva had followed everything on the police radio; they'd heard Marco's footsteps, running, the orders he was issuing rapid-fire, Pietro's question.

'Marco! Marco! What happened?' Minerva shouted into the mike. 'For God's sake, tell us something!'

'Somebody tried to kill the mute – we don't know who, we didn't see him – but he killed an old man who stepped in front of him. We don't know who he is, he's got no papers. The ambulance is coming. Jesus! Shit, shit, shit!'

'You want us over there?' Sofia asked.

'No, just stay there. Where the hell is the mute?!' they heard him yell.

'We lost him,' said a voice over the walkie-talkies. 'We lost him,' it repeated. 'He got away in the confusion.'

'Son of a bitch! How the hell could you people let him get away? Goddammit!'

'Calm down, Marco, calm down. . . .' Giuseppe was saying.

Minerva and Sofia listened in silence. After so many months of preparation for Trojan Horse, the horse had galloped away.

'Find him! All of you! Find him!'

Well out of the neighborhood by now, Mendib was having trouble breathing. He pressed his hand over the stab wound at his side. The pain was becoming unbearable.

The worst thing was that he was leaving a trail of blood. He stopped and looked for a doorway to step into and rest for a moment. He thought he had managed to throw off his pursuers, but he was not sure. His only chance lay in reaching the cemetery, but it was still far, and he should wait until nightfall. But where?

Willing himself to move onward, he pressed service doors all along the way until one finally gave. It was a little janitor's closet, holding mops and buckets and a large trash container. He sat on the floor behind the trash can, trying not to lose consciousness. He was losing a great deal of blood, and he needed to stanch the wound. He took off the jacket he was wearing and pulled out the lining to make a bandage, which he held tight against the wound. He was exhausted; he did not know how long he would be able to hide there – perhaps until nightfall, if he was lucky.

His old uncle, a man who had loved him since he was a baby, had stabbed him. What was going on? Then Mendib felt himself growing light-headed and lost consciousness.

Ana was sitting on a terrace at the Porta Palatina, waiting to return to Padre Yves's office, when people began to run past, shouting. They were screaming that a man had been killed – the killer was still on the loose. She scanned the crowd and noticed a young man on its fringes running, stumbling. As if he was hurt. He ducked into a doorway and disappeared. She walked in the direction the people had come from, trying to find out what was happening. But except that somebody had been murdered, no one could tell her anything coherent.

She saw two young men, similar in appearance to the one who'd looked hurt, heading in that same direction, and instinctively she followed them.

The two men from Urfa saw the woman lingering behind them, so they began to slow, and then to backtrack. She was probably a cop. They could watch for Mendib to emerge from a distance and keep an eye on her as well. If necessary, they would kill her too.

Yves de Charny had been back in his office for a while. His handsome features were shadowed with worry.

His secretary entered the office. 'Padre, those two friends of yours, the priests Padre Joseph and Padre David, are here. I told them you had just come in and I wasn't sure you could see them.'

'Yes, yes, have them come in. His Eminence doesn't need me anymore, he's going to Rome, and the work for today is almost done. If you want, take the rest of the afternoon off.'

'Have you heard that there was a murder just around the corner, at the Porta Palazzo?'

'Yes, I heard it on the radio. My God, such violence!'

'Heavens, yes, padre. . . . Well, if you don't mind my leaving, I can use the time – I've been wanting to have my hair done; tomorrow I'm having dinner at my daughter's house.'

'Go, go – don't worry.'

Padre Joseph and Padre David looked grim as they entered Padre Yves's office. The three men waited for the sounds of the secretary leaving.

'You heard what's happened,' Padre David finally said, as they heard the outer door closing behind her.

'Yes. Where is he?'

'He's hidden himself near here. Our people are watching him, but it wouldn't be smart to go in after him. The reporter is hanging around too.'

'The reporter! Why?'

'Bad luck. She was sitting on the terrace having a soft drink, probably waiting for you. If she shows up here again, we'll have to do it,' said Padre Joseph.

'Not here – too dangerous.'

'There's nobody here,' Padre Joseph insisted.

'You never know. What about Galloni?'

'Any moment now, as soon as she leaves carabinieri headquarters. Everything is ready,' Padre David reported.

'Sometimes. . . .'

'Sometimes you doubt, as we do, but we are soldiers, and we follow orders,' said Joseph.

'This isn't necessary.' Yves stared hard at him.

'We have no choice but to obey,' David said quietly.

'Yes. But that doesn't mean we can't speak up against our orders, even as we obey them. We have been taught to think for ourselves.'

Finally luck seemed to be turning Marco's way. Giuseppe had just walkie-talkied that he'd spotted one of the Turkish tails near the cathedral, and Marco raced over there. When he arrived in the piazza he slowed his pace to that of the other pedestrians, who were still buzzing about the earlier incident.

'Where is he?' he asked as he joined Giuseppe.

'Over there – they're both there, on the terrace. The same ones as yesterday.'

'Attention all units – stay down. Repeat: Stay down. You're all invisible. Pietro, get over here; the rest of you, surround the piazza, but keep your distance. These tails have already shown us they can lose us. But they're our best bet at this point.'

*   *   *

It was late afternoon, and Ana Jiménez decided to try Padre Yves again. The men who had caught her attention earlier had vanished. No one answered the bell for the cathedral offices, but the door opened when she tried it. Everyone seemed to have gone home for the night, but the porter hadn't yet locked up. She stepped toward Padre Yves's office and was about to knock when she heard voices inside.

She didn't recognize the voice of the man talking, but what he was saying froze her in her tracks.

'Most of them are coming in through the tunnel. They want them off the street with all the carabinieri swarming all over the place. What about the others? . . . All right, we're on our way. If he makes it out, he'll try to hide here; it's the safest place.'

In the office, Padre Joseph closed up his cell phone and turned to the others.

'Two of Addaio's men are waiting out in the piazza, and Mendib is still in his closet. They must not know exactly where he is, but I imagine he'll be on the move again; he's not too secure there.'

'Where's Valoni?' asked Padre David.

'They say he's furious – the operation has gotten away from him,' Padre Joseph answered.

'That's closer to the truth than even *he* thinks,' Padre Yves said wryly.

'No, you're wrong,' said David firmly. 'He doesn't know anything; he just had a good idea – use Mendib to get to the bigger quarry. But he doesn't actually know anything about the community, much less about us.'

'Don't delude yourself,' Padre Yves insisted. 'He's getting dangerously close to Addaio and his people. They've uncovered the Urfa connection with the shroud.

Dottoressa Galloni is pointing them straight in that direction. It's a shame a woman like that has to –'

'All right,' Padre Joseph interrupted. 'They want us in the tunnel. Let's hope Turgut and his nephew are already down there. Our men are at the cemetery.'

Ana crouched behind a filing cabinet in the outer office, trembling, as the three men headed for the door. Was Padre Yves a Templar, or did he belong to another organization? And what about the two with him? Their voices were those of young men.

She held her breath as they hurried across the room and through the main office door. She waited a few moments and then, gathering her courage, glided silently behind them, following the muffled sounds of their progress not far ahead of her.

They reached a small door leading to the cathedral porter's apartment. Padre Yves knocked at the door, but there was no response. A few seconds later, he pulled a key from within his cassock and opened the door. They vanished inside.

Clinging to the wall, Ana crept to the entrance to the porter's apartment and listened. Nothing. She stepped inside, praying that the three men wouldn't surprise her.

52

MENDIB HEARD A NOISE AND HE JUMPED, STAR-
tled. He had regained consciousness not long ago, brought
to by the shooting pain in his side. At least the bleeding had
stopped. His dirty shirt was stiff with a dry, dark stain. He
didn't know whether he could stand up, but he had to try.

He thought about the strange death of his father's
uncle. Could Addaio have sent someone to kill his great-
uncle because he knew he was going to help him? But the
old man had done this to him. He couldn't be wrong
about that.

He trusted no one, much less anyone connected with
Addaio. The pastor was a saintly man but unbending,
capable of doing anything to save the community. Mendib
knew that he himself, without intending to, could reveal
its existence to the authorities and lead them to his
brothers. He wanted to avoid that; he had been trying to
avoid it since he was released. But Addaio no doubt knew
things that he himself did not, and so he could not discard
the possibility that he had been targeted for death by the
pastor. He had known that all along.

The door to the janitor's closet opened. A middle-aged

woman carrying a bag of trash stepped inside before she saw him and gave a little scream. Mendib, making a superhuman effort, shoved himself upright and clamped his hand over her mouth.

Either the woman had to calm down or he would have to beat her unconscious. He had never struck a woman – God forbid! – but now it was a question of saving his own life.

For the first time since his tongue had been cut out, he was filled with anguish at his inability to speak. He pushed the woman against the wall, as she struggled and tried to pull his hand away. He gave her a quick blow on the back of the neck and she crumpled, dazed.

Lying on the floor, she was breathing with difficulty. Mendib fumbled inside her purse and found a pen and a date book, tore out a page, and wrote hurriedly. When she began to recover, he covered her mouth with his hand again and showed her the piece of paper.

Come with me – do what I tell you and nothing will happen to you, but if you scream or try to escape, you will regret it. Do you have a car?

The woman read the odd message and nodded, her eyes wide with fear. Pocketing the paper and pen, Mendib slowly took his hand off her mouth, but he kept a good grip on her arm as they moved outside.

'Marco, can you hear me?'

'I'm here, Sofia.'

'Where are you?'

'Near the cathedral.'

'All right. I've got news from the coroner. The old man who was killed had no tongue or fingerprints. He figures the tongue was cut out not long ago and the fingerprints burned off around the same time. He was carrying no identification of any kind. Oh – he doesn't have any teeth either; his mouth is like an empty cave, nothing.'

'Shit!'

'The coroner hasn't finished the autopsy, but he stepped out to call and let us know we've got another mute.'

A voice interrupted the conversation. It was Pietro.

'Marco, listen up! Our guy is at the corner of the piazza. There's a woman with him – he's got his arm around her. Should we grab him?'

'Just keep on them, unless it looks like he's threatening her. Don't lose him; I'm on my way. Keep on the tails too – if we've seen him, then so have they. And no more fuckups – if any of them loses us again, I'll have your balls.'

The woman took Mendib to her car, a small SUV. He shoved her across the seat and got behind the wheel. His side was on fire and he could hardly breathe, but he managed to start the car and pull out into the chaotic late-afternoon traffic.

He drove aimlessly through the city, thinking furiously. He had to get rid of the woman, but he knew that as soon as he did, she would notify the carabinieri. Even so, he had to take the risk – he could not take her to the cemetery. And if he left the car near the cemetery, the carabinieri would be able to track him down. But he was in no condition to walk far – the blood he had lost and the throbbing wound in his side precluded that. He would pray that the cemetery guard was at his post; the good man was a brother, a member of the community, and he would help him – unless, like the others, he had been ordered by Addaio to kill him.

He decided to risk it: He would chance the cemetery. He had nowhere else to go.

When they were close, but not so close that the woman would realize where he was planning to go, he stopped the car and stared at her, as she looked at him in terror. He took out the pen and paper again and wrote: *I am going to let you go. If you tell the police, you will regret it. Even if they protect you now, there will come a day when they do not, and then I will come. Go, and tell no one what has happened. Remember – if you do, I will come back for you.*

He thrust the note at her, and the terror in her expression redoubled as she read it.

'I swear I won't tell . . . please – let me go. . . .' she pleaded.

Mendib tore the paper into pieces and threw them out the window. Then he got out of the car and straightened up, though not without difficulty. He was afraid of losing consciousness again before he reached the cemetery. As he approached the wall and began to walk along it, he heard the sound of the car pulling away.

He walked for several minutes, sitting down when the pain became unbearable, praying to God that he might live and be saved. He wanted to live – he was no longer willing to give his life for the community, or for anyone. He had given his tongue and two long years of his life locked up in prison.

Marco glimpsed the figure of the mute staggering along. He and his detail stayed well back, as they had while they tailed the SUV. It was clear the man was wounded and could hardly walk. They caught sight of the two Turkish tails again, keeping a good distance away. Marco had kept men on them when the main group split off to follow the mute and his hostage.

'Stay sharp – we have to take them all,' he cautioned

everyone. 'If the tails decide to separate or break off, you know what you have to do – divide up, some of you with them, the others on our man.'

None of them was aware of the others silently monitoring them all, blending seamlessly into the surroundings.

A reddish glow appeared on the horizon as the sun began to set. Mendib tried to walk faster; he wanted to get into the cemetery before the guard closed the gate. Otherwise, he'd have to jump the wall, and he was in no condition to do that. He was bleeding again, and he held a scarf he had taken from the woman against the wound. At least it was clean.

The guard's figure was silhouetted against the cypresses at the cemetery entrance. He looked expectant, as though he was waiting for someone or something.

Mendib could sense the man's fear, and indeed, when the guard saw the mute struggling toward him, he rushed to close the gate. Mendib, marshaling his last strength, reached the entrance and managed to slip inside, shoving the guard aside. He lurched toward tomb 117.

Marco's voice came over the network to all personnel.

'He pushed his way into the cemetery, past the guard. I want you men inside. Where are the Turks?'

A second voice came over the line: 'They're about to come into your view. They're headed for the cemetery too.'

To the surprise of Marco and his watching men, the tails opened the gate with a key, carefully closing it behind them.

When they reached the gate, several of the carabinieri

clambered over the wall to keep the Turks within striking distance, while another worked on the lock. It took him several minutes to open it, as Marco paced impatiently.

'Giuseppe, find the guard,' Marco ordered once inside. 'We haven't seen him leave, so he must be inside somewhere.'

'Right, boss. Then what?'

'Report back to me with what he says, and then we'll decide. Take some backup.'

'Right.'

'You, Pietro, come with me. Where the fuck are they?' Marco asked the carabinieri through the walkie-talkie.

'I think they're heading toward a mausoleum – a big one, with a marble angel above it,' a voice said.

'Good. Where is it? We're on our way.'

No one was in Turgut's apartment – Padre Yves and his friends seemed to have vanished. Ana stood quietly, listening for any sounds, but absolute silence reigned.

She scanned the modest rooms, looking for anything out of the ordinary. Nothing stood out. Tentatively pushing at the door to a bedroom, she peered inside and found it empty too. Back to the living room, the kitchen, even the bathroom. Nothing. But Ana knew they *had* to be here, because the front door was bolted from the inside and that was the only other way out of the house.

She went over the house again. In the kitchen was a door that opened into a pantry. She tapped on the wall, but it seemed solid. Then, down on her knees, she examined the wooden floor, looking for a trapdoor or an opening . . . anything. There had to be some sort of secret passage that led out of the house.

Finally, she found a place where the floor sounded

hollow. And there it was – the faint outlines of a trapdoor. Using a knife, she managed to lift it up enough to get a good grip and then forced it all the way open. A stairway led down into darkness. Not a sound came up out of the dungeon, or whatever it was. They had to have gone this way.

It took her awhile, but finally she found a penlight in a kitchen drawer – it didn't give much light, but it was all she had. She also put a big box of kitchen matches in her purse, just in case. She looked around to see if there was anything else she might need down there, and then, with a little prayer to St. Gemma, patron saint of the impossible – with whose help, she was certain, she had been able to graduate from the university – she started down the narrow stairway that would take her God only knew where.

Mendib groped his way along the tunnel. He remembered every inch of that wet, sticky wall. The old guard had tried to stop him from getting to the tomb, but had finally taken off running when Mendib picked up a thick stick, ready to hit him with it if he had to. When at last he managed to reach the mausoleum, the key was there, hidden under the planter, just as it had been all those years ago. He unlocked the mausoleum entrance, went in, and found the spring behind the sarcophagus that opened the door to the stairway. The narrow steps descended into the tunnel that led ultimately to the cathedral.

It was getting increasingly hard to breathe. The lack of oxygen and the darkness of the tunnel made him woozy, but he knew that his only chance to survive was to reach the house of Turgut. Fighting the pain and summoning the last measure of his dwindling strength, he pushed on.

The light from his old-fashioned cigarette lighter wasn't

enough to illuminate the tunnel, but it was the only light he had. His greatest fear was winding up in the darkness and losing his sense of direction.

Bakkalbasi's men had entered the cemetery a few minutes after Mendib. They ran to the mausoleum, opened it with a key Turgut had provided, and in a few seconds they were underground, on the trail of their dying brother.

'They went in there.' A carabiniere pointed.

Marco looked up at the life-size angel – it was wielding a sword and seemed to be warning them off.

The cop with the pick went to work again. This lock was harder, and while he played with the mechanism, Marco and his men smoked and made their contingency plans, unaware that they, too, were under observation.

Turgut and Ismet paced nervously back and forth in the underground room off the tunnel. Three of the men from Urfa were waiting with them. They had managed to evade the carabinieri and had been in the secret room for several hours, waiting. The rest of Bakkalbasi's men should be coming in at any minute. The pastor had warned them that Mendib might, against all odds, make his way there, too, and that they should calm him down and wait for the other brothers to come back. After that, they knew what they had to do.

None of them ventured far into the shadows that enveloped the tunnel. If they had, they might have seen the three men crouched in a nearby alcove, who had been listening to them for some time. Their collars hidden, their faces grim, Yves, David, and Joseph had abandoned any trappings of the priesthood.

They heard halting footsteps, and Turgut felt a shiver run down his spine. His nephew gave him a pat on the back to try to raise his spirits.

'Calm down. We have our orders, we know what to do.'

'Something terrible is going to happen,' the porter muttered.

'Uncle, stop worrying! It will be okay.'

'No. Something is going to happen. I know it.'

'Quiet, uncle, please!'

Ismet's grip tightened on the old man's shoulder as Mendib staggered into the room. His burning eyes held Turgut's for just a moment, and then he collapsed senseless to the floor. Ismet knelt beside him to take his pulse.

'He's bleeding. He's got a wound near the lung – I don't think it's punctured or he'd be dead by now. Bring me water and something to clean the wound with.'

Old Turgut, his eyes as wide as saucers, scurried over with a bottle of water and a towel. Ismet ripped the filthy shirt off Mendib's body and washed the wound carefully.

'Wasn't there a first-aid kit down here?'

Turgut nodded, unable to speak. He went for the first-aid kit and handed it to his nephew.

Ismet cleaned the wound again with hydrogen peroxide, then swabbed it with gauze soaked in disinfectant. It was all he could do for Mendib, whom he had looked up to as a child in Urfa. None of the others made a move to stop him, although they all knew he was only temporarily fending off fate.

'No need for that.' One of Bakkalbasi's men stepped out of the shadows of the tunnel – one of the policemen from Urfa, who had waited behind to trail the mute from the piazza. Another man followed him. For several minutes, they filled the others in on the pursuit. Their conversation masked subtle new sounds from the dark passageway.

Suddenly Marco, accompanied by Pietro and a clutch of carabinieri, burst into the room, pistols drawn.

'Don't move! *Don't move!* You're all under arrest!' Marco shouted.

53

MARCO HAD NO TIME TO SAY MORE. A BULLET from out of the shadows hissed past his head. Other shots hit two of his men. Bakkalbasi's men seized advantage of the sudden chaos to take cover and open fire themselves.

The carabinieri took cover as best they could. Marco crawled along the floor, attempting to get behind the Turks, but he was cut off when someone shot at him again from the shadows. He twisted around, trying to spot where the shots were coming from. Then, almost immediately, he heard a woman shouting: 'Watch out, Marco, they're up here! Watch out!'

Ana had come out of hiding. For what had seemed like forever, she'd concealed herself, almost unmoving, from the three priests, whom she'd seen – with the grace of God and St. Gemma – before they saw her, after following the tunnel from Turgut's rooms. Padre Yves whirled around, his eyes wide: 'Ana!'

The young woman tried to run, but Padre Joseph caught her. The last thing she saw was a fist aimed at her head. He hit her so hard she lost consciousness.

'What are you doing?!' exclaimed Yves de Charny.

There was no answer. There couldn't be. Shots were coming from every direction, and the priests turned back to their targets, pouring gunfire into the chamber beyond.

It was only minutes before yet more men – those who had pursued the pursuers all along – burst onto the scene. They soon killed old Turgut, his nephew Ismet, and two of Bakkalbasi's men; they did not intend to stop until all their adversaries were dead.

The echoing reports of the gunfire were so loud that pebbles and rubble began to fall from the ceiling and walls, but the firing continued unabated from all sides.

Ana began to regain consciousness. Her head felt as though it had been split open. She staggered up and saw the three priests right in front of her, still shooting. Picking up a good-size rock, she crept forward toward them, and when she was close enough she lifted the rock over her head and brought it down hard on the head of one of Yves's comrades. She had no time to do anything else – the other turned to shoot her. But as he did, stones rained down from the ceiling and knocked him to his knees.

Yves de Charny had rounded on Ana with unconcealed rage, and now he, too, was hit by falling rocks. The reporter started stumbling, running, trying to put distance between herself and the priest and also get out from under the debris falling now in terrifyingly huge clumps and boulders. The blasts of the gunshots and the growing rumble and crash of the collapsing roof disoriented her – she couldn't tell which way she'd come in. She felt panic rising, threatening to engulf her, as she heard Padre Yves right behind her, shouting, and Marco's voice, too, but their words were drowned out by a deafening roar as a whole section of the tunnel came down.

She stumbled and fell. Darkness overtook her.

*   *   *

Ana shrieked as she felt fingers close on her arm.

'Ana?'

'My God!'

She didn't know where she was, but the absence of light was total, all-encompassing. Terrifying. Her head hurt and her body felt bruised all over, as though she'd been beaten. She knew that the hand grasping her arm belonged to Yves de Charny; he offered no resistance as she pulled away. She could no longer hear Marco's voice or the sound of shooting; the silence was absolute. What was happening? Where was she? She screamed, and screamed again, louder, and then sobbed.

'We're lost, Ana, we'll never get out of here.'

Yves de Charny's voice broke, and Ana realized that he was hurt.

'I lost the flashlight following you,' the priest said. 'We're going to die in darkness.'

'Shut up! Shut up!'

'I'm sorry, Ana, truly sorry. You didn't deserve to die, you didn't *have* to die.'

'You people are killing me! You're killing us all! So just shut up!'

De Charny was silent. Ana groped in her purse, miraculously still strapped across her body, and pulled out the penlight and box of matches. She was overjoyed to find them, and then her fingers touched her cell phone. She turned on the small light and saw the handsome face of Padre Yves contorted in pain. He was badly injured.

Ana got up and inspected the cavity they were trapped in. It was not very big, and she could see not the smallest chink in the wall of rock that had buried them. She shouted, and her voice boomed back at her within the small space. Nothing else. It struck her then that indeed she might not get out of there alive.

She propped up the light and sat down beside the priest. Realizing that he had accepted his fate, she decided to play her last card as a reporter. In the shadows that surrounded them, Padre Yves didn't see her take her cell phone out of her purse. The last call she'd made had been to Sofia. God, she hoped she'd answer this time. And she hoped there was a signal that could take their voices out beyond the walls of this otherwise mortal cave they were in. All she had to do was hit the redial button. . . .

With a kitchen towel she'd taken from Turgut's apartment, she pressed hard against a wound she saw just below Yves's rib cage. The priest grimaced and looked up at her with glassy eyes.

'I'm sorry, Ana.'

'Yeah, so you said. Now tell me *why* – what's behind all this insanity?'

'What do you want me to tell you? What difference does it make, if we're both going to die?'

'I want to know *why* I'm going to die. You're a Templar, like those friends of yours.'

'Yes, we are Templars.'

'And who were the others, the ones that looked like Turks, the ones with the porter?'

'Men sent by Addaio.'

'Who's Addaio?'

'The leader, the pastor of the Community of the Shroud. They want it. . . .'

'Want the shroud?'

'Yes.'

'Want to steal it?'

'They think it belongs to them. Jesus sent it to them.'

Ana thought he was delirious. She brought the light to his face and could see the hint of a smile on his lips.

'No, I'm not crazy. In the first century A.D. there was a king in Edessa, King Abgar. He had leprosy, but he was cured by the shroud Jesus had been buried in. That is what the legend says. And that is what the descendants of that first community of Christians believe, the Christian community that came together in Edessa. They believe that someone brought the shroud to Edessa and that when Abgar wrapped himself in it he was cured.'

'But who brought it?'

'One of Jesus' disciples, according to tradition.'

'But the shroud has been through so much since then – it left Edessa hundreds and hundreds of years ago.'

'Yes, but since the shroud was stolen from the Christians in Edessa by the troops of the emperor of Byzantium –'

'Romanus Lecapenus.'

'Yes, Romanus Lecapenus – they swore they would not rest until they'd recovered it. The Christian community in Edessa was – is – one of the oldest in the world, and they have not spared one day in trying to recover their sacred legacy, as they see it, just as we have never stopped trying to prevent them from doing that. The shroud no longer belongs to them, and we are sworn to protect it for all the faithful.'

'And these men without tongues – they're part of this community?'

'Yes, they are Addaio's soldiers, young men who consider it an honor to sacrifice themselves in order to recover the shroud. They have their tongues cut out so they can't talk if they're captured by the police.'

'That's horrible!'

"They believe that was what their ancestors did, to protect the shroud in their time. They've been after it for centuries, and we've been there to stop them. It's funny –

we could wipe them out overnight, but we never have. . . . They're Christians, too, devout in their way, and we ourselves know too well the evils of such persecution . . . and now our fates have become intertwined.' De Charny's head was spinning, and he could barely see Ana's face in the darkness.

He sighed with pain and went on. 'Marco Valoni was right. The fires, the accidents in the cathedral – all staged . . . mostly by the community to cause confusion when they go after the shroud, sometimes by us to attract the authorities before they can succeed. We've always stopped them, but we try to protect them too. They know too much about us now. . . .'

Ana had propped the cell phone next to him. She didn't know whether Sofia had answered, whether someone was hearing their words. She didn't know anything. But she had to try – she couldn't let the truth die with her.

'What do the Templars have to do with the shroud and this community?' she pressed him. 'Why do you care about it so much?'

'We bought it from Emperor Balduino – it's ours. Many of our brothers . . . many . . . died to protect it.'

'But it's a fake! You know that carbon-fourteen dating has proven that the cloth dates only to the thirteenth or fourteenth century.'

'The scientists are right, the cloth is from the late thirteenth century, to be exact. But what about the pollen grains stuck to the cloth – grains exactly like those found in two-thousand-year-old sediment in the area of Lake Genezaret? The blood is authentic too – both venous and arterial. Oh, and the cloth, the cloth is Eastern, and on it scientists have found traces of blood albumin around the outline of the marks where Jesus was scourged.'

'So how do *you* explain that?'

'You know how, or have been about to discover it. You went to France, you were at Lirey.'

'How do you know that?'

'Ana, do you think there is anything you've done that we don't know about? Any of you? We know it all, everything. You're right – I am a descendant of the brother of Geoffroy de Charney, the last precept of the Temple in Normandy. Mine is a family that has given many of its sons to the order.'

Ana was fascinated. Yves de Charny was making a sensational confession – one that might well die with them in their stone tomb. But whether or not she would ever publish it, at that moment she felt a surge of pride, knowing that she had managed to disentangle the mystery.

'Go on.'

'No . . . No, I will not do that.'

Ana felt a rush of power and utter certainty as she clasped the priest's hands, almost as though someone else was speaking to the Templar through her. 'De Charny, you are about to stand before God. Do it with a clear conscience; confess your sins, bring the light to bear on the shadows you have lived behind, the mysteries that have cost so many lives.'

'Confess? To whom?'

'To me. I can help you unburden your conscience and give sense to my own death. If you believe in God, He will be listening.'

'God has no need to listen to know what is in the hearts of men. Do you believe in Him?'

'I'm not sure. I hope He exists.'

Padre Yves said nothing. Then, grimacing, he wiped the pearls of sweat off his forehead and squeezed Ana's hand.

'François de Charney, spelled with an *e* at that time, as you've discovered, was a Templar knight who lived in the East for many years, since the time he was a young man. There is no need for me to tell you all the countless adventures of this ancestor of mine – just that a few days before the fall of Saint-Jean d'Acre in the Holy Land, the Grand Master of the Temple charged him with safeguarding the shroud, which was kept in the fortress along with the rest of the Templar treasures.

'My ancestor wrapped the shroud in a piece of cloth very similar to that of the shroud itself, and he returned with it to France as he had been ordered. To his amazement and the amazement of the master of the Marseilles Temple, when they unwrapped the original shroud, they found that the cloth it had been wrapped in also had the figure of Christ imprinted on it. Maybe there is a, shall we say, "chemical" explanation for this, or we can believe that what happened was a miracle – whatever the case, from that moment on, there were two holy shrouds, with the true image of Christ on both of them.'

'My God!' breathed Ana. 'That explains –'

'That explains that the scientists are right when they say that the cloth in the cathedral in Turin is from the thirteenth or fourteenth century – even if they can't understand the appearance of those pollen grains or blood residue – but it also means that those who believe that the shroud contains the true image of Christ are correct as well. The shroud is sacred; it contains residues, "remains," if you will, of Jesus' calvary and his image – that is what Christ looked like, Ana; that *is* His true image. And that is the miracle with which God honored the House of Charney, although later another branch of the family took our relic – history records this – and sold it to the House of

Savoy. And now you know the secret of the Holy Shroud. Only a handful of the elect in the entire world know the truth. This is the explanation of the inexplicable, of the miracle, Ana, because it *is* a miracle.'

'But you say there are two shrouds: the authentic one, which was bought from Emperor Balduino, and the other one – this one, I mean the one that's in the cathedral – which is something like a photographic negative of the authentic one. Where is that one? Tell me.'

'Where is what?' The Templar's voice was growing weaker, much of his remaining strength expended in relating the remarkable story.

'The authentic shroud, the one the shroud in the cathedral is a copy of.'

'No, it's authentic too.'

'Yes, but where's the *other* one, the first?' cried Ana.

'Even I, a de Charny, do not know that. Jacques de Molay sent it off to be hidden. It is a secret known by only a very few. Only the Grand Master and the six masters know its location now.'

'Could it be in McCall's castle in Scotland?'

'I don't know. I swear it.'

'But you do know that McCall is the Grand Master, and that Umberto D'Alaqua, Paul Bolard, Armando de Quiroz, Geoffrey Mountbatten, Cardinal Visier –'

'Ana, quiet, please . . . the pain is terrible . . . I'm dying.'

But she wouldn't – couldn't – stop. 'They're the masters of the Temple, aren't they, Yves? Which is why they never marry or engage in any of the other activities of men with as much money and power as they have. They stay out of the spotlight, avoid publicity. Elisabeth was right.'

'Lady McKenny is a very intelligent woman, like you, like Dottoressa Galloni.'

'You people are a sect! A dangerous, deadly sect.'

'No, Ana, no. Strong measures are taken, yes . . . but only when absolutely necessary. Measures that we – I – sometimes question. But you should know the good of it too. The Temple survived because the accusations made against it were false. Philippe of France and Pope Clement knew that but they wanted our treasure for themselves. And along with the gold, the king wanted to own the shroud. He thought that if he could get it, he would become the most powerful sovereign in Europe. I swear to you, Ana, that down through the centuries, we Templars have been on the side of good. We have played a role in many fundamental events – the French Revolution, Napoleon's empire, Greece's independence, and the French resistance during the Second World War. We have helped move democratic processes forward around the world –'

Ana shook her head. 'The Temple lives in the shadows, and there is no democracy in the shadows. Its leaders are extremely wealthy men, and no man gets wealthy without paying a moral price.'

'They are wealthy, but theirs is a fortune that does not belong to them – it belongs to the Temple. They administer it, manage it, although it's also true that their own gifts have made them wealthy in their own right – but when they die, everything they own goes to the order.'

'To the order?'

'To a foundation . . . at the heart of the Temple's finances, of everything we are and do. We are everywhere . . . we are everywhere,' Padre Yves repeated, his voice now little more than a whisper.

'Even in the Vatican.'

'May God forgive me.'

Those were the last words that Yves de Charny spoke. Ana cried out in terror when she realized he was dead, his eyes staring sightlessly into infinity. She closed them with the palm of her hand and began to sob, asking herself how long it would take her to die as well. Maybe days, and the worst thing would be not dying but knowing that she was buried alive. She brought the telephone to her lips.

'Sofia? Sofia, help me!'

The telephone was dead. There was no one there.

'Ana, Ana! Hang on! We'll get you out!'

The connection had been broken just seconds earlier. The battery had probably run out on Ana's phone. Sofia had heard the shoot-out in the tunnel over the walkie-talkies, then Marco and the carabinieri shouting that the tunnel was going to come down. She hadn't hesitated a second – she ran for the street. But she hadn't reached the downstairs door when her cell phone began to ring; she thought it was Marco. She froze when she heard the voices of Ana Jiménez and Padre Yves. With the telephone held tight to her ear so as not to miss a word, she stood stock-still, hardly aware of the men rushing past her, racing to save the others trapped in the tunnel.

Minerva found her sobbing, cell phone in hand. She put her arms around her and shook her gently. 'Sofia, please! What's happening? Calm down!'

Sofia was barely coherent, able to blurt out only a small part of what she had heard.

Minerva led her outside. 'Let's go to the cemetery – we can't do anything here.'

There were no official cars in sight. The two women waved down a passing taxi. Tears continued to stream down Sofia's face as Ana's cries rang in her mind.

The taxi stopped at a light. Just as it started up again, the driver shouted. They looked up to see a massive truck headed straight at them. The noise of the crash shattered the silence of the night.

54

ADDAIO WEPT IN SILENCE.

He had locked himself in his office and would allow no one – not even Guner – to enter.

He had been closeted for more than ten hours, sitting, pacing, staring into space, allowing himself to be swept along by a wave of contradictory emotions.

He had failed, and many men had died because of his obstinacy. There was nothing in the newspapers about what had happened, just that a collapse had occurred in the tunnels below Turin and that a number of workers had been killed, among them several Turks.

Mendib, Turgut, Ismet, and other brothers had been buried alive under the rubble – their bodies would never be recovered. He had borne the harsh gaze of Mendib's and Ismet's mothers. They did not forgive him; they would never forgive him. Neither would the mothers of the other young men he had asked to sacrifice themselves on the altar of an impossible mission.

God had turned against him. The community now had to resign itself to never recovering the grave cloth of Christ, for that was God's will. Addaio could not believe that so many failures were simply tests that God put them to in order to confirm their strength.

Perhaps this, the simple acceptance of God's will, was the true legacy of the shroud, a legacy that had always been theirs to embrace. Addaio had learned that too late. He wondered if his old adversaries, those who guarded the shroud so fiercely, might someday embrace it as well.

He finished writing his will. Overriding his previous orders, he was leaving precise instructions about the man to be his successor – a good man of clean heart, with no ambition, and who loved life as he, Addaio, had not. Guner would become their leader, their pastor. He folded the letter and sealed it. It was addressed to the community's eight pastors; it would be they who would see that his last wishes were carried out. He would not be denied, he knew: The pastor of the flock selected the next leader. Thus it had been down through the centuries, and thus it would always be.

He took out a bottle of pills he kept in his desk drawer and took them all. Then he sat in the wingback chair and let himself be overcome by sleep.

Eternity awaited.

55

A.D. 1314

Beltrán de Santillana had carefully folded the Holy
Shroud and placed it in a shoulder bag that was never
out of his sight.

He was waiting for the tide to rise on a boat out in the
river, so that he might reach the sea and the ship that was
to bear him off to Scotland. Of all the nations of
Christendom, Scotland was the only one where news of
the order to dissolve the Temple had not yet reached – or
would ever reach. The king of Scotland, Robert Bruce, had
been excommunicated, and he paid no mind to the
Church, nor the Church to Scotland.

Thus, the Knights Templar had naught to fear from
Robert Bruce, and Scotland had become the only land in
which the Temple might preserve its great power.

José Sa Beiro knew that in order to fulfill the final
instructions of the last Grand Master, the great, murdered
Jacques de Molay, he must send the sacred shroud to
Scotland, to ensure its safety forever. He had made

arrangements for Beltrán de Santillana to travel with the treasure to the Temple house in Arbroath, accompanied by João de Tomar, Wilfred de Payens, and other knights, all of whom were sworn to protect the shroud, to the death if need be.

The master of Castro Marim had given de Santillana a letter for the Scottish master and also the original letter sent by Jacques de Molay, which set forth the reasons for keeping the Temple's possession of the shroud of Jesus a zealously guarded secret. The Scottish master would determine where to hide the relic. It would be his responsibility never to allow the shroud to pass into other than Templar hands, and to preserve the secret of its possession for all time.

The boat doubled the bend in the Guadiana on its way down to the sea, where a ship lay waiting. The knights did not look back; they did not wish to be overcome by emotion as they left Portugal forever.

✝ The knights' ship was about to founder, so great was the tempest that had come upon them in their voyage to Scotland. The wind and rain tossed the boat about like a nutshell, but thus far it had withstood the storm.

At last, the cliffs of the Scottish coast heralded the end of their voyage. They made their way through the wild hills to Arbroath and to sanctuary.

The brothers of the Scottish Temple had heard of and mourned the terror the pope and the king of France had sown among the Templars. Here they and their brothers would be safe, thanks to their good relations with Robert Bruce, alongside whom they fought to defend Scotland from its enemies.

After a time, the master called the entire company into

the chapter meeting hall, together with the brothers who had voyaged from Portugal. There, before the astonished eyes of the assembled knights, he unfolded the full length of the sacred cloth. It bore a great resemblance to the painting they worshipped in the chapter's private chapel – the true face and figure of Christ that had been copied from this holy relic so that the Templars might always have the image of their Savior before them.

The sun was rising over the sea when the knights went forth from the hall where, all through the night, they had prayed together before the singular visage of Christ, imprinted upon the shroud that had held his body within its folds.

Beltrán de Santillana remained behind with the master of the Scottish Templars. The two men talked for a time and then, carefully folding the sacred cloth, they put away the Temple's most precious treasure – a treasure that, with the passing of the centuries and as commanded by the last Grand Master, only a few of the elect would now view.

Here it would lie in a consecrated sanctuary, safe forever from the machinations of those who would seek to corrupt its holy essence for their own ends, or use it to sow discord among the kingdoms of the earth. Those who attempted to disturb it would do so at their peril.

Jacques de Molay could at last rest in peace.

56

IT HAD BEEN ALMOST SEVEN MONTHS SINCE THE accident. She limped. They had operated on her four times, and one leg had been left shorter than the other. Her face no longer glowed as it once had; it was crisscrossed with scars and wrinkles. She'd left the hospital just four days ago. The injuries to her body didn't hurt her, but the grief, as tight about her chest as an iron band, was worse than the pain she'd felt in the accident and its aftermath all those months ago.

Sofia Galloni had just left a meeting in the Minister of the Interior's office. Before that, she'd gone to the cemetery to leave flowers on the graves of Minerva and Pietro. Marco and she had been luckier; they'd survived. Of course Marco would never work again; he was in a wheelchair, and he suffered from periodic panic attacks. He cursed himself for living when so many of his men had died in the rubble of the tunnel, that tunnel he'd always known existed. Well, he'd finally found it.

The Minister of Culture had attended Sofia's meeting with the Minister of the Interior; they continued to share oversight over the Art Crimes Department. They had both asked Sofia to take the director's position, and she had politely refused. She knew she had planted the seed of doubt in the two politicians and that once again her life might be in danger, but she didn't care.

She had sent them a report on the shroud case. It provided a detailed account of everything she knew, including the conversation between Ana Jiménez and Padre Yves. The case had been closed, classified as a state secret never to be disclosed to the public, and Ana was lying dead in a tunnel below Turin next to the last Templar of the House of de Charney.

The ministers told her, very amiably, that the story was unbelievable, that there were no witnesses, nothing – not a single document that corroborated her report. Naturally, they believed her, they said, but wasn't it possible that she was mistaken? They had made inquiries in Paris, but neither Elisabeth McKenny nor her husband, Paul Bisol, were anywhere to be found. They could hardly accuse men like Lord McCall, Umberto D'Alaqua, and Dr. Bolard of criminal association without incontrovertible evidence. These men were pillars of international finance, and their fortunes were essential to the development of their respective nations. How could the minister present himself in the Vatican and tell the pope that Cardinal Visier was a Templar? How could he accuse them of anything – they hadn't done anything, even if everything Sofia told them was true. These men had not conspired against the state, against *any* state; they weren't trying to subvert democratic governance; they weren't connected to the Mafia or any other criminal organization; they'd done nothing even to be *censured* for, let alone accused of. And as for being Templars, well, that was no crime – assuming they *were* Templars.

They tried to convince Sofia to take the job Marco Valoni had left. If she didn't, it would go to Antonino or Giuseppe. What did she think?

But she didn't think – she knew that one of them, either the cop or the historian, was the traitor. One of them had been reporting to the Templars on everything that happened in the Art Crimes Department. Padre Yves had implied as much: They knew everything because they had informers everywhere.

She didn't know what she was going to do with the rest of her life, but she did know she had to face one man, a man with whom she was in love, despite everything. In love with or obsessed by? She had tried to sort that out during her long convalescence and still wasn't sure.

Her leg hurt when she stepped on the accelerator. She hadn't driven in months, not since the crash. She knew it had been no accident, that they had tried to kill her, and that D'Alaqua was trying to save her when he called to beg her to go with him to Syria. *Strong measures,* Padre Yves had said, . . . *only when necessary.*

She arrived at the imposing iron gates that led to the mansion, and she waited. A few seconds later they opened. She drove up to the door and got out of the car.

Umberto D'Alaqua was waiting for her.

'Sofia. . . .'

He led her into his office. He sat behind the desk, maintaining his distance, or perhaps protecting himself from this woman with a limp and a face crisscrossed with scars, a woman whose blue eyes were harder than the last time he'd seen them. Even so, she was still beautiful; now, though, it was a tragic beauty.

'I guess you know that I sent the administration a report on the shroud case,' she said, staring at him. 'A report in which I state that there exists a secret organization made up of powerful men who believe they stand above other men, governments, society itself, and I ask that their identities be revealed and that they be investigated. But you already know that none of that will ever happen, that no one will investigate you, that you will be able to keep doing what you do from the shadows.'

D'Alaqua didn't answer, although he seemed to nod, ever so slightly.

'I know that you are a master of the Temple, that you see your mission as spiritual, and that you have made vows of chastity. Of poverty? No, from what I can see, not poverty. As for the Commandments, I know that you keep the ones that are convenient for you, and those that aren't. . . . It's strange – I've always been impressed by certain men of the Church, and you in some way are one of them. Some of them think they can lie, steal, kill, but that those are all venial sins in comparison with the great mortal sin of . . . fornicating? If I use that word, it doesn't wound your sensibilities, right?'

'I would have come to you in the hospital, but I didn't think you would want to see me,' he broke in. 'I'm sorry for what has happened to you and Signor Valoni and for the loss of your friend Minerva and of your . . . of Pietro. . . .'

'And what about the death of Ana Jiménez, buried alive? Are you sorry about that? Oh, God, I hope those deaths plague your conscience, that you never have another moment of rest. I know I can't do anything about you or your organization. I've just been told that, and they tried to buy me off by offering me the directorship of the Art Crimes Department. How little you people know human beings!'

'What do you want me to do? Tell me. . . .'

'What can you do? Nothing – there's absolutely nothing you can do, because you can't raise the dead, can you? So maybe you can tell me whether I'm still on the list of the people to be disappeared by your organization, whether I'm going to have another of these lamentable traffic accidents, or maybe the elevator in my apartment building will fall. I'd like to know, so I can be sure no one will die with me next time, like Minerva did.'

'Nothing will happen to you, I give my word.'

'And you, what will *you* do? Go on as though what happened was just an accident, a "necessary" accident?'

'If you must know, I am retiring. I am transferring power of attorney over my corporations to others, arranging my affairs so that the businesses can go on functioning without me.'

Sofia felt a shiver. She loved and loathed this man at the same time, in equal parts.

'Does that mean you're leaving the Temple? Impossible – you're a master, one of the seven men who govern the Temple. You know too much, and men like you don't just walk away.'

'I am not walking away. I have nothing and no one to walk away from. I am simply answering your question. I have decided to retire, dedicate myself to study, to helping society in other ways, different from the ways I am helping now.'

'And your celibacy?'

Once more, D'Alaqua said nothing. He knew that she was devastated, wounded deep inside, and that he had nothing to offer her. He didn't know whether he would be able to go any further, finish rooting up what had for so long been the essence of his life.

'Sofia, I have been hurt too. There are wounds, painful wounds, that you can't see, but they are there. I swear that I am sorry for everything that has happened – what you have suffered, the loss of your friends, the disgrace that looms over you now. If it had been in my hands to prevent, I would have, but I am not the master of circumstances, and we human beings have free will. We all decide what we want to do in the play we live in – all of us, including Ana.'

'No, that's not true. She didn't decide to die. She didn't want to die, and neither did Minerva or Pietro or the carabinieri or the men from the community, or even your own men, those friends of Padre Yves, or those others that nothing has been said about but who also died in the shoot-out, while others escaped. Who were your soldiers? The Temple's secret army? No – it's all right, I know you're not going to answer that; you can't, or, rather, you refuse to. You will be a Templar as long as you live, even though you say you're retiring.'

'And what will you do?'

'Are you interested?'

'Yes, you know I'm interested. I want to know what you will be doing, where you will be, where I can find you.'

'I know you *did* come to the hospital and stayed to watch over me a few nights.'

'Answer me. What will you do?'

'Lisa, Mary Stuart's sister, found a place for me at the university. I'll be teaching, starting in September.' She smiled thinly. 'I'm planning to offer a course on the history, provenance, and cultural impact of certain esoteric artistic and religious objects, among other subjects.'

'I'm glad,' he said after a moment.

'Why?'

'Because I know you'll like it and be good at it.'

They looked at each other for a long time, neither saying a word. There was nothing more to say. Sofia rose from her chair, and Umberto D'Alaqua accompanied her to the door. He took her hand in his and kissed it, holding it for a few seconds before he finally let it go.

She limped down the steps without looking back, but she felt D'Alaqua's eyes on her and knew that no one has any power over the past, that the past cannot be changed, that the present is a reflection of what we were, and that there is only a future if you never take a single step back.

ABOUT THE AUTHOR

JULIA NAVARRO is a well-known Madrid-based journalist and political analyst for Agencia OTR/Europa Press, as well as a correspondent for other prominent Spanish radio and television networks and print media. The English translation of her second novel, *The Bible of Clay*, will be published in 2008.

ABOUT THE TRANSLATOR

ANDREW HURLEY is best known for his translation of Jorge Luis Borges's *Collected Fictions* and Reinaldo Arenas's Pentagonia novels, among many other translated works of literature, criticism, history, and memoir. He lives and works in San Juan, Puerto Rico.